THE GLOAMING

HER FIRE.
HIS DARKNESS.
THEIR FATE.

THE GLOAMING

JAMIE DALTON

Copyright © 2025 Jamie Dalton

All rights reserved.

The Gloaming

This is a work of fiction. Names, characters, places, and incidents either are the product of the author's imagination or are used fictitiously. Any resemblance to actual persons, living or dead, events, or locales is entirely coincidental.

No part of this book may be reproduced, stored in a retrieval system, or transmitted in any form or by any means, electronic, mechanical, photocopying, recording, or otherwise, without express written permission from the author.

This work may not be used to train, develop, test or improve artificial intelligence, machine learning algorithms, or similar technologies without explicit written permission from the author.

Cover design by Jamie Dalton

Independently published in the United Kingdom

First Edition: June 2025

ISBN: 9798316351817

www.jamiedalton.co.uk

Content Warning

This novel contains themes and scenes that may be distressing for some readers, including:

Descriptions of violence and gore
References to suicide
Death and murder
Blood drinking
References to historical atrocities (Holocaust)
Intimate sexual content
Strong language
War trauma
Emotional manipulation
Psychological warfare
Descriptions of injuries and torture

For Luke,
Who made fiction a reality.

Near them, near to their precious darkness, their lovely devouring gloom.

Anne Rice, *Queen of the Damned*

Author's Note

Dear Reader,

Welcome to Erin's world of vampire hunting, questionable life choices, and copious amounts of coffee.

If you find yourself wondering how Erin became a hunter or about the true nature of certain enigmatic characters you'll meet along the way… well, me too.

No – in all seriousness, I have the answers. But since this isn't an origin story, I'm not about to tell you everything all at once, am I?

Some mysteries are meant to unfold gradually, and some questions are designed to linger even after the final page.

So pour yourself a strong cup of whatever keeps you sane, and enjoy the hunt. All will be revealed… in due time.

Happy reading,
J

PART ONE

I

THE QUICK AND THE DEAD

AT TWENTY-NINE, I HAD A higher body count than most serial killers. I'd killed for the first time at seventeen years old. The difference was, my targets were already dead.

There's a weird fatigue that comes with hunting vampires – one that sinks into your bones and twists your sense of time. It's not the kind of job you can really switch off from, when an average night has you rolling into bed at 2 A.M., up to your elbows in blood and running on fumes. Your body learns to stay awake whether you want it to or not. Which is how I found myself sprawled on the living room floor at three in the morning, surrounded by half-dried acrylics and an unfinished mural.

It's also why, when a shadow shifted at the edge of my vision, instinct took over. A faint scuffling from behind the fireplace, and I was crouched and alert, every muscle ready for action.

Across the room, Tom appeared in the kitchen doorway, coffee mug halfway to his lips. "What?"

I held up a hand for silence. The shadow moved again, and I whipped my gaze toward it, tracking its trajectory with measured breaths.

Tom's eyes were wide when I glanced his way.

Raising a finger to my lips, I shook my head and inched

forward. My Wonder Woman socks were silent on the bare floorboards as I crept toward the sound, ready to attack. A silhouette in the doorframe, Tom shifted his weight, and the board beneath him let out a long creak. He winced, but it was too late.

A tiny, furry head peeked out from behind the stone fireplace, skittering across the room to hide under the sofa. I dived, hands outstretched, my fingers scrabbling after it. It dashed under the base of the seat, and I wriggled my hand against the velvet, scrambling to get at it.

Behind me, Tom released his breath as he realised what I was doing. "You've got to be kidding me? Erin, it's a bloody mouse. It's the middle of the night. It's what mice do." I heard his exasperation, but it did nothing to stop me from grappling with the sofa.

"Grab a box or something, will you?" I kept my voice low. The scraping sound had stopped.

"What for?"

The cambric was grazing my arm, but I hadn't seen it come out. "To trap it!"

Out of the corner of my eye, I saw him shake his head – but he disappeared into the kitchen. I held my breath, waiting for the mouse to make its move. Tom came back through, not troubling to tiptoe, and handed me a stained plastic box.

A faint scratching sound came from the other side of the sofa. As gently as I could manage, I removed my arm from the tight space underneath and straightened, careful to keep my movements small and silent. Tom watched me with a smirk, and I gestured at him to help me lift it. He shrugged and made his way toward the other end of the substantial three-seater.

I counted to three, mouthing the numbers, and we lifted. The

The Gloaming

floorboards were dusty in the dim light of my table lamp, but the mouse was nowhere to be seen.

Tom let out a bark of laughter and dropped the sofa with a thud.

"It's like a bad documentary," he chuckled, sitting down by the ancient bureau I used as a desk and picking up a deck of cards. "'*The hunter's instincts are sharp and well-honed, allowing her to sense her prey from several miles away.*'"

I gave him the finger and returned to my usual chair, though his Attenborough impression wasn't half bad. "It's a sodding mouse, not a vampire."

Tom continued shuffling the cards. "'*Though the hunter may have been defeated, she must try again, in order to survive in the harsh reality of the jungle.*'"

I settled back into the cushions, resting my feet on the displaced coffee table – pushed aside earlier to make space for my latest mural. "That's basically what Jon's been saying." I ran a hand through my hair, still gazing around for any sign of the mouse. "Then again, it's been quiet lately."

My eyes pricked with tiredness as I surveyed the room, clamping down a yawn. I didn't spend much time at home, so my floorboards were bare, the walls still the same bland ivory they'd been when I moved in almost six years ago. The only hint of personality was the colourful patchwork blanket thrown over the moth-eaten arm of a once-black sofa, and the bureau pushed against the far wall. Acrylic paints in every hue were scattered on the surface and across the floor, but the canvas was still half-finished. I released the yawn and reached for my mug.

"Surely you're not going to drink that. It'll be clock cold by now."

I raised it in Tom's direction, firmly meeting his expression of horror. "Coffee's coffee," I said, downing the cold, sludgy dregs in one delicious mouthful.

"Uh-huh. Is that what you tell the customers?" He plucked the mug from my hand and took it through to the kitchen, and the sound of running water reached my ears a second later.

I rolled my eyes, knowing he couldn't see me. "'Course not. But I hate to waste the caffeine.

The water stopped, and Tom came back through, picking up the cards again. "Have you heard from him, then?" he asked, shuffling them like a pro.

It took me a moment to catch up. "Jon? No. It's been busy at the café. I was planning on calling yesterday, but I've not had time." I paused, glancing at the clock on my phone. "It's probably too late now. But I thought you said he'd messaged?"

"Not a bloody word since he got on the train. Been trying to track his phone but it's either dead or…" He shrugged.

I smirked. "It's only been a couple of weeks. He's probably shacked up with some Scottish girl he met in a bar."

Tom laughed. "Maybe. Or dragging her up a mountain or something."

"Oh, I know all about the 'guy' stuff you get up to when I'm not around, Chowdhury." I waggled a finger at him. "On that much, my instincts are pretty sharp."

He spread the cards across the desk in a fan. "What are we supposed to do while you're off being badass and killing things, eh?"

"I dunno," I mocked. "Tear your hair out with worry? Knit?"

"Come off it," he chuckled along with me. "You're fine on your own."

The Gloaming

I shrugged. "Doesn't hurt to know someone cares."

Tom shook his head and gestured me over. "Play me?"

I glanced at the time again. 3.14 A.M. "Sure. Ready to lose?"

Before he could reply, a beam of blue light fell in through the open curtains of the bay window, flashing around and around in a familiar swirl that caused my stomach to drop. Tom shot me a look of alarm as I stood slowly.

"What did you do?"

"Nothing!" I was already edging into the kitchen, towards the back door.

"Shit. Okay, go. Hide. I'll deal with them."

I hesitated, wracking my brain as I shoved my feet into unlaced Dr Martens. I had no idea what this was about.

"Just hide!"

I RAN. THE ICY WIND BIT INTO MY skin, burning my lungs as I pushed my limbs faster than I'd ever run before. Slowing down wasn't an option.

The skies were clear and starry as I sped toward the city, away from the house. Even now, part of me registered it was a perfect night for hunting. And if killing something would help release the tight, dull ache in my chest, that's what I would do.

My heavy boots battered the ground beneath my feet, never faltering on the icy pavement. It was only November, but the night was deathly cold, and my cheeks grew numb as I forced my body onward. Away. It didn't matter where to. I cast my senses ahead, throwing them before me like a net, seeking the empty patches in my mind that signalled something unnatural. It was after four in the morning, but somewhere, someone might need me. Something would oblige my need for violence.

Pockets of late-night stragglers lingered on the street, huddled close to the light and warmth of the few pubs and bars still open. I sped past, ignoring the bursts of sound from within.

It only took a few minutes of searching before I felt it. An uncomfortable alertness settled over my body like a veil of ice, and I slowed to a walk to catch my breath. Goosebumps crept over my skin, and I shuddered, though my pulse was pounding in my ears and my blood hot. I hadn't seen the cause of the sensation yet, but my instincts were sharp from years of practice. In this, I trusted them absolutely.

I let the feeling take over my mind and body, flooding through me to almost sweep away the unthinkable thoughts the last hour had brought – since I'd first seen those blue lights. There. In the thin white glow from the streetlights, two women turned the corner ahead of me, blending into the shadows of the alley as though they'd never been there at all. My skin prickled, and the hairs raised on the back of my neck. I picked up my pace, keeping close to the wall.

The rich scent of tobacco filled the air as I edged toward the alley where they'd disappeared, and sneaked a glance into the passage. The dark-haired woman had lit a cigarette and handed the lighter to her blonde friend as she leaned against the wall. She inhaled and tilted her head back, closing her eyes as she blew smoke artfully into the frigid night. Both women were attractive, so similar at first sight that you'd assume they were related: high cheekbones, symmetrical features, and large, dark eyes. The blonde was a few inches taller in glossy black heels.

I observed them for a moment, my pulse pounding in my ears. From the sheer, form-fitting dresses and heavy make-up they both wore, they were probably passing as students from one of the local unis. They looked to be about the right age, not that appearances meant much. But the ruse was simple enough to be believable – unless, of course, you happened across someone like me. Keeping an eye on them, I assessed the short, narrow alley. From my position, I should have a slight advantage. Emphasis on *slight*.

I took a deep, silent breath, reigning in the simmering heat in my blood that begged to be released. My body trembled as I held it back, waiting, the taste of fire a metallic tang that filled my mouth.

The blonde was distracted, rifling around in her bag. Now was the moment. I stepped forward, the streetlamp behind throwing my face deeply into shadow. Everything about the alley was dim and filthy, from the sweet stench of refuse to the grotty, spray-painted graffiti across the brickwork. On a normal night, I might have worked harder to draw them out – if only to get away from the smell. But tonight was not a normal night.

"You know, they reckon cigarettes are bad for you. I guess that's not a worry when you're dead?" I frowned. "But second-hand smoke in a public place… that's just rude."

The smoker barely reacted, throwing a lazy glance my way. But her blonde friend's head snapped up at the sound of my voice.

"Excellent," she murmured, scarlet-painted lips curling. "A late-night snack."

I resisted rolling my eyes. Vampires had no imagination.

The brunette straightened as her friend spoke, her head tilting to one side as she looked me over.

"It's you." She tapped the ash from the end of her cigarette with a long, enamelled nail, apparently unconcerned. "I've heard about you."

"I'd bow or curtsy or something, but…" I pushed my hair back from my face. "Manners won't matter much in a few minutes."

The blonde gave a low chuckle as I took a step toward her. I could smell them now – perfume intermingled with something darker.

"Witty." She reached out to push me with both hands, the movement faster than should have been possible.

I stepped back, and her fingertips missed the wool of my coat. "I like to think so." Any minute now…

Anger flooded her pale face, turning her skin an unpleasant mottled pink. But the brunette came between us before I had time to react. I twitched.

"Look," she said, raising her hands. "We get it. But it's late. We haven't done anything."

Something flickered behind her eyes, and I couldn't help but raise an eyebrow.

"So, no one took the bait tonight. What about next time?" My voice hardened. "There's a reason this isn't a negotiation."

"Idiot," the blonde one spat, leaning around her friend. "You'll lose."

They were strong. And fast – I could see as much. Plus, it was two against one. But I'd fought with worse odds, and I was still here.

"Ignore her. We're not looking for a fight," the brunette pressed, edging forward. "Walk away."

I almost laughed. "How considerate of you both. Maybe manners *do* matter after all." Despite their words, bit by bit, they were forcing me against the wall. My mind flashed to the dagger tucked into my boot. "Unfortunately for you," I planted my feet.

The Gloaming

"This is what I do."

"Don't worry—" Blondie took off one of her heels. "You won't be doing it—" and the other, "much longer." Dropping them behind her by the straps, she grew still for a second, a predator's gleam in her eye. I blinked, and with a casual, unnatural swiftness, she attacked.

I dodged the first blow – a punch aimed squarely at my face – and a hunk of brick in the wall behind me shattered under her bare knuckles. Before she had time to step back, I swung my fist up into her abdomen. Molten adrenaline shot through my body as I made contact, and I grinned wildly, revelling in it. This was *exactly* what I needed.

She stumbled away, feet slapping on the damp concrete. I used the pause to wiggle my way out of the corner and shook out my shoulders, the heat spreading through my limbs and finally burning through the haze of grief that had brought me here. The brunette vamp shot a glance between us before starting forward, stubbing out her cigarette on my arm as she tried to grab me. The wool smoked, but I felt nothing.

"That's my favourite bloody coat you've ruined!" I seized the strap of her dress to stop her from getting away. Grabbing her shoulder with my other hand, I dug my fingers into her cold skin and shook her hard before dashing her against the wall. Her skull made an unpleasant crunching sound as it hit the stone, stunning her momentarily.

Taking advantage of the confusion, I spun back to Blondie, who'd recovered her balance.

"You actually are an idiot," she hissed as she advanced, aiming her knee at my gut in a move I almost didn't spot. I backed up, but not fast enough, and flew backwards as her kneecap met flesh, landing on my back with a thud. I groaned inwardly – that was going to leave a hell of a bruise. But I didn't have time to complain.

Twisting up and straightening, I ignored the urge to vomit rocketing up my throat and blocked a couple more punches with my forearms.

"Seriously?" I caught her wrist and wrenched it behind her, grabbing her hair with my other hand. "You're the one calling *me* names?" I smashed her face into the concrete, dropping to a crouch. "You were gonna *eat* me—"

"Oh, fuck off!" she half-yelled, writhing, her mouth full of dirt.

"I don't think I will." I eased my grip for a moment, sure I had her trapped, but she rolled over, ready to bolt. Before she could get far, I shoved the heel of my hand into her shoulder and pinned her other arm to the ground. "If this had gone your way—"

I took a long, ragged breath and shook my head, no longer smelling the rancid stink of the alley. Now was my moment. My favourite dagger was inches from my hand, but I didn't unsheathe it. I felt sick.

I bent nearer, so close I could count her eyelashes. "We both know you're far from innocent," I murmured, mostly to myself. She strained against me, but I tightened my grip, glaring at her. "I'm not the bad guy here."

She hissed, her lips pulling back to expose sharp white canines – but she didn't fight. With a sigh, I let go and she scrambled into a sitting position. Before she could get any further, I drew back my fist and struck out, hitting the sweet spot at the side of her jaw. Her eyes rolled back, and she fell limp. I kicked her away, a quick shiver running through me as I brushed myself off and stood up.

Fuck, I wanted to keep hitting her. For a moment there, she'd helped push away the raw, hollow ache that had settled over my heart earlier tonight. But this wasn't the solution, and some part of me knew it.

Before I could get beyond that thought, something yanked me back by the hood of my coat, and I was thrust against the wall. *Shit.* I'd almost forgotten about the other one, but apparently, she'd found her bearings while I had my tiny breakdown. My cheek scraped the filthy brick and I began to choke as she lifted me by the throat with one hand. My feet dangled uselessly.

"I tried to play nice, hunter. But that little stunt actually hurt. And you're right. I suppose…" Her breath reeked of copper. "I'm the predator. You're the prey."

I kicked out, struggling for oxygen as she tightened her grip. Her lashes lowered as she shifted me higher and bit her lip almost seductively, eyes lingering on my pulse.

I thought fast. My dagger was still in my boot. Bracing one foot against the wall behind me, I jammed my knee into her middle, raising my leg enough to grab the hilt. Before she could work out what I'd done, I forced it between her ribs, straining my wrist to twist the pale steel. Blood spilt over my hand and arm, sticky and almost black in the half-light. As I slid the blade from her chest, she released me, staggering back into the other side of the alley.

The sight of her bleeding left a sour taste in my mouth, and I gulped down oxygen, trying to clear my head. My dagger clattered to the ground, and I stared as blood bubbled and spilled from her lips. She almost seemed surprised as she slid down the wall and went still.

The prickling sensation beneath my skin lessened as her life – or whatever it was – ran out. I pulled my clean hand through my hair, still panting and trying to recover my breath as I took a peek out of the entrance to the alley. There was no one in sight.

Behind me, the blonde stirred. I imagined her waking up – with me, still standing over her. She'd probably run for it when she saw what I'd done to her friend. I wasn't sure how comfortable I was with that.

I should finish her and leave. I knew it – hell, she probably knew it – but I hesitated. The fire in my veins still ran hot, but the blood on my hands felt dirty.

Get your shit together, Erin, for crying out loud.

I swallowed. It felt wrong to kill her while she was semi-conscious. Not even a vamp deserved that. The brunette was thoroughly dead, yeah – I'd got the kill I was craving, in the end – but it hadn't made a blind bit of difference. The knot in my throat was as unbreakable as it had been when it showed up alongside the police.

I sighed. The gold inlay on my blade glinted on the floor, and I scooped it up, shoving it back into my boot without cleaning it. My sleeve and hand were bloody and stained, and I wiped them as best I could on the lining of my coat. It would have to do for now.

Cheery voices floated through the air from the bar four doors down, interrupting my musings. No raised voices, though. No alarm. No one had noticed a thing.

Pulling my hood up over my face, I headed onto the street at a fast walk, leaving the blonde with her hair splayed across the damp ground, the brunette sprawled beside her.

I reined my senses in as I hurried along, shutting down each sensation, desperate for the numbness it would bring. I didn't want to feel any more.

Here and there, stragglers loitered in the doorways, smoking and chatting, most of them still drinking. A few called out as I

The Gloaming

passed, but I ignored them, though the aroma of stale beer followed me.

Violence hadn't helped. I'd been an idiot to think it would – so I guess the vamp had been right about that, at least. The fire in my blood could burn through just about anything, but not this. The truth was, my best friend was dead. Nothing was going to bring Jon back.

My breath condensed into soft white clouds as I picked up the pace. I was so bloody tired. Tired of tonight. Tired of this life. Tired of thinking about death. Twenty-five years of obsessing – I'd been four when I realised I couldn't escape it – and I still hated that it followed me everywhere I went. Sure, I'd done what most people would and pretended it wasn't happening for a while – but when you can sense vampires, they can usually sense you, too.

I crossed the road, leaving the hum of the city behind as the shops and restaurants petered out and turned into houses. Most people were heading home, or already tucked in, but every now and then voices reached my ever-sensitive ears from streets away, squeezing every moment of life from the night.

A shadow across the street caught my attention, almost human as it darted behind a fence. My skin tingled for a second and I froze, before the shape transformed into a small tabby that trotted out and into the road at a run. One by one, I released my taut muscles. *Jumpy much?*

It wasn't like I thought it was a ghost or anything. I'd never seen or talked to spirits. As far as I knew, it wasn't even possible. Vamps were the only thing that went bump in the night, and my talent for spotting them was fairly specific. I sensed them stalking their victims: the quick and the dead. And I took it as a sign that it was my job to stop it.

Obviously it hadn't been enough this time.

Jon was my oldest friend. And let me tell you, when you weird the other schoolkids out for talking about undead people that follow you home, friends are hard to come by. So, for years, he'd been my only friend – the one person who could convince me of the truth when I wanted to pretend I wasn't a hunter. Then we'd met Tom, started the coffee shop… and things had been good. I'd dropped my guard.

The inferno in my veins was receding now, and the cold crept in through the heavy wool of my coat. I shoved my hands more deeply into my pockets, speeding up.

It hadn't even occurred to me to worry when Tom had dropped Jon off at the train station a few weeks ago. He'd announced he was taking a trip to Edinburgh – something about visiting an estranged uncle, he'd said. I don't think I'd even said goodbye.

Then earlier tonight, the police had knocked on the door. Tom answered it, while I panicked and hid. I'd assumed they wanted to speak to me – it wouldn't have been the first time. It was still a blur, trying to get it straight in my head. One minute we were playing cards, the next…

Dragging my mind back to the now, I turned onto my street, a long row of Victorian terraced houses. I lived alone, but Tom would probably still be there, ready to guilt trip me since I'd run off without a word. My fingers were stiff with cold as I tried to fit the key into the lock.

The hallway was dim, the earliest light of dawn behind me. Tom was asleep on the sofa, his long legs and arms dangling under my blanket. The air was tinged with the clean scent of soap and pencil shavings that always seemed to follow him – familiar and quietly grounding. His usually tawny skin looked ashen in the shadow, short black hair sticking up in all directions. He looked at peace, though I knew that wasn't the case.

When he'd opened the door to the police, I'd listened in through the open kitchen window. The officer's tone set my teeth on edge; way too solemn to be anything good. They said they'd found Jon in his hotel room. That his uncle had identified the body. When they called it a suicide, I'd almost burst through and kicked off – it was total bullshit. But as I watched Tom catch hold of the hall table to steady himself, I knew it didn't matter what they called it. The result was the same – Jon was gone. Moments later, I'd run.

I shook off the memory, though it was only an hour or so ago. The air was warm in the living room, perfumed with the comforting scent of coffee and vanilla. Careful not to make too much noise, I laid my coat on the armchair and stretched, my joints popping in protest. Stray strands of my tangled auburn hair caught the dawn light as it filtered softly into the room, and I pushed them aside with my left hand. Crusted brown blood still stained my other hand, so I kicked off my DMs and padded into the kitchen. Tom stirred through the French doors that separated the rooms.

"When did you get back?" He blinked at me as he appeared in the frame, not quite awake.

I shrugged. "A couple of minutes ago. The sun's barely up."

Tom yawned and rubbed his eyes before turning to tidy his blanket away. I turned on the cold tap and washed the blood from my hand, wincing as the water stung my raw knuckles. Without another word, I prepped the coffee machine, grinding beans and pressing them into the portafilter without seeing what I was doing. Behind me, Tom switched on the old radio by the oven.

Slow, melodic piano music floated through the room, and my hands stilled. It was one of Jon's favourites. Tom nudged me aside and took over.

That done, we sat together at my tiny kitchen table, and I picked at the scrubbed, paint-flecked wood. My coffee was too hot to drink, but the bitter aroma and the warmth of the heavy ceramic mug beneath my fingers was soothing.

"Are you going to say something?" He didn't ask where I'd gone, but I was sure he knew.

I shrugged. I should apologise for running out, but I didn't.

Tom raised both eyebrows, waiting.

"Do you…" I swallowed the lump in my throat. "What if he's not really dead?"

I'd been turning it over in the back of my mind since I'd left. If the only explanation was the worst thing I could think of, so be it. It was better than losing him.

Tom's eyes searched my face as he pulled his mug across the table, understanding in an instant. "I don't think so. He wouldn't want that."

The sun blazed in through the leaded glass of the kitchen window, illuminating his face, and I turned away. Of course he'd say that. And it was true. I knew it. But I'd still hoped.

"This whole thing doesn't ring right, though. He wasn't…" He swallowed. "He's not a suicide."

I nodded. The empty chair between us where Jonathan usually sat seemed bigger than usual, and it was a struggle not to stare at it.

"I mean, the body, the way he—" Tom's hands shook, and he dropped his mug to the table with such force that the liquid sloshed over the edges. I stared at the spillage.

The Gloaming

"He must have been released fast," I murmured.

"I guess they didn't think there was anything to investigate." He shook his head. "He wasn't suicidal, and we both know it. But it doesn't seem like anyone else is going to look into it. It has to be us."

I nodded. It sounded morbid, which wasn't exactly out of the ordinary for us – but at least we were on the same page. With Jonathan gone, everything was different. Even if we were wrong – and I didn't believe that was true – we needed to know. Whoever had done this would be held accountable, I'd make bloody well sure of it.

I spent the rest of Sunday in my armchair, turning the pages of a paperback novel without seeing the words. All I could think about was Jon, and how his death had to be my fault, somehow. I hadn't protected him enough, hadn't checked in like I should have… Because the fact of the matter was, anyone connected to me would always be in danger. Of course, I'd thought about it before – but this was the first time the threat had seemed truly real.

While I pondered all this, Tom made what seemed like a hundred phone calls, arranging the things I couldn't bring myself to help with. At barely thirty, Jon already had a will in place and a funeral plan: we just had to set it in motion. I supposed *he'd* understood the threat, at least.

As the afternoon drew on, Tom called a few of our friends. It wasn't a long list these days – people had grown tired of the secrets and excuses, so our circle had grown small. Honestly, I preferred it that way.

"I'm so sorry to—" The person on the other end interrupted Tom. "No. The police told us it was a suicide." He paused, and I admired his tact as he let the other person speak. "No, neither would I. As soon as we know, of course."

I knew I should be doing more than just listening in, but I couldn't talk about Jon in the past tense without my throat closing up. For Tom's sake, I refused to cry – or so I told myself.

Next on his list was the police department; then the hospital that had carried out the post-mortem. I didn't know how he'd found the contact info, but it was Tom, so I wasn't surprised.

"No, Tomal. No, I'm not. He didn't have any—" His tone was polite, but he was getting nowhere. "I understand. Could you let us know if there are any updates?"

My mind wandered, and I wandered. I watched the patch of grass I called a garden through the kitchen window for a while, following the patterns the light made and the shadows that crept up behind. I wanted it to rain or snow or, even better, storm. The mild, sunny day seemed wrong, somehow. *If my eyes must remain dry, then the heavens should at least open.*

Eventually, the house grew silent. Tom dozed off with his notebook still open beside him, the pages full of his tiny, cramped handwriting. The sun slipped below the horizon, the air grew cooler, and our first day without Jonathan was over. I knew he'd been gone for weeks, been dead for days… that I was being silly. But it was different. It was the first day.

2

People Are Either Charming or Tedious

THE MINGLED SCENT OF spearmint and thyme cleared my head as I lathered shampoo into my hair the following morning, the scalding water soothing away the ache in my bones and hammering into the damaged muscles of my back. I breathed the steam deep into my lungs, burning and purifying myself from within – but I didn't feel any cleaner on the inside.

A faint knock interrupted my ritual, and I turned off the water.

"Yeah?"

"I made coffee, when you're done." Tom's voice called through the closed door.

"I'll be out in a few." I climbed out of the shower and wiped the condensation from the mirror over the sink.

My reflection stared back at me, my expression sombre. A faint bruise had started to bloom across my left cheekbone, a souvenir from my most recent fight. Combined with the dark circles under my eyes, I looked washed out and exhausted, my cool grey eyes almost blue despite the sun streaming in from the tiny bathroom window. I ran a hand through my damp hair, lifting it from the back of my neck and stretching. My appearance didn't seem like a priority right now.

I dressed hurriedly in a black shirt and jeans, wrestled my auburn locks into a side braid and arranged a few loose pieces to hide my bruises. Hopefully, it would do the trick.

My back protested despite the heat of the shower as I knelt and reached into the back of my wardrobe and pulled out my preferred Dr Martens. Black, battered, mid-calf – perfect for hiding a knife in.

The dagger I chose today was the most valuable thing I owned, and also happened to be a favourite of mine. The short blade had been made to my requirements after weeks of research, forged of gorgeous Damascus steel and inlaid with gold – the only combination of materials I knew of that could kill a vamp. Add to that a hawthorn handle embellished with a chunk of citrine, and it couldn't be more symbolic of the sun if I tried – and trust me, we'd tried. It was one of several similar weapons that Jon and I had commissioned years ago when we'd realised that a good old-fashioned wooden stake, while effective, was actually pretty difficult to use without some real force behind the blow. And don't even get me started on beheading. So, though my dagger was well-worn, I never left the house without it.

Downstairs, Tom had made himself comfortable at the bureau I used as a desk, sipping at a steaming mug of coffee. Though he was normally on the scruffier side, Tom had taken it to the extreme this morning, and looked more like a disgruntled bear than anything. A flannel-wearing bear that had been disturbed mid-hibernation, maybe.

"Morning," I mumbled, heading toward the kitchen for my own hit.

He didn't reply until I was settled in my armchair, the hot mug warming my hands.

The Gloaming

"You never said where you ran off to." There was no disapproval in his tone, but I still felt guilty. I shouldn't have left him.

I took a quick gulp of the scalding liquid and put my mug down. "I'm sorry."

He continued to watch me. "No need. I'd have done the same thing, if you hadn't done it first."

I raised an eyebrow. "You'd have run off and got in a fight?"

"Well, maybe not the fight part."

I wanted to smile, but my heart wasn't in it.

"It was just a couple of vamps." I picked my mug up again, leaning back into the cushions as I inhaled its life-giving aroma. "Is this the Ethiopian blend?"

Tom ignored me. "You won, I assume?"

I pursed my lips, looking out of the window at the clear sky outside. "I killed one of them. The other…" I paused. "I don't know what happened. I couldn't do it."

He said nothing, but the look he gave me was full of pity.

"I should probably try to find her. The other one."

It wasn't an idea I particularly relished. Tracking blind was a nightmare. To do it, I had to tune into my senses so completely that coming down could take days. My eyes, ears and nose all struggled to shut off afterwards. But the bitchy blonde would be back on the streets soon enough, scouting for another victim. And if she hurt someone, it would be on me.

"Probably," Tom nodded. "Tonight?"

I shrugged. "I guess."

"What about today? Are you going to Jolt?" Jolt was the coffee shop that Tom, Jon, and I owned.

"I wasn't planning on it. Maggie's got it covered."

Tom shifted in his seat, blood flooding his face and turning his nose and ears pink. He'd had a serious crush on the manager we'd hired since the day she started, but he'd yet to do anything about it. "About that. She called twenty minutes ago."

I gulped down the last of my coffee. "Go on."

"The new girl, you know, the one with the teeth?"

"Michelle?"

"Yeah. She's quit. Her boyfriend's apparently the next big thing, and she's gone off touring with him."

"Oh, that'll end well."

Tom's dark eyes gleamed, but he didn't smile. Neither of us were up to it, yet.

"Maggie asked if we would cover. I told her, about…"

"Jon," I finished.

"Yeah. But she can't manage on her own."

I pushed my fingers under my still-damp hair, lifting my braid and massaging my scalp a little. "Right. Looks like I'm going in then. You've got more important things to do."

Tom nodded again and opened his laptop. "I've already started."

"And?"

He shook his head, his face falling. "Bloody coroner wants paperwork from Jon's family before releasing anything. Barely investigated it from what I can tell. I tried the proper way but… I figured sod it, their security is a joke anyway. It was quicker for me to backdoor into their system."

I stood up and stretched, holding back a yawn with difficulty. "Since when can you do that?"

Tom raised his eyebrows across the top of his mug and leaned back into his seat. "Do you even *know* me?"

The Gloaming

"Sorry," I smiled a little at that. "What did you find?"

"There wasn't much, to be honest. I've read better."

I frowned. Whenever there was an incident in the city that looked suspicious, Tom and I poked around in the police records, or the coroner's records, when we could manage it – usually, the authorities were fairly chatty. Most of the time it didn't take much info to write something off as natural causes or human incident. And when we couldn't, we'd start hunting vamps. But since Jon hadn't died here in Sheffield, but two hundred and fifty miles away in Edinburgh, we'd have to work harder than usual. Then again, vampires weren't usually stupid enough to murder my friends unprovoked. So it might not be as difficult as all that.

"Well for a start, someone must have staged it for the police to call it a suicide. The question is, why?"

"To get your attention, I suppose," he paused. "Or mine, but I doubt it."

"I'll hand it to them – it worked."

Tom nodded. "But why the secrecy? By doing it this way, whoever it is hasn't claimed responsibility. If someone wanted us to notice, killing him would have been enough."

I swallowed down the lump in my throat. This was all still a bit too fresh, but I knew we had to talk about it sometime. Unfortunately, all I could think was there must be more to come.

"They're not finished," I said at last, standing up. "Which means Jon's death is only the beginning."

Tom's eyebrows knitted together. "Fuck."

Since I drove at a speed that was technically illegal, I arrived at the coffee shop a few minutes after nine. Maggie was *our* employee – and the most efficient manager we'd ever had – but that meant she had no patience for lateness, and I wasn't about to be the one to annoy her.

The road was empty as I climbed out of the car. Winter's weak morning light filtered between the buildings, creating the distinctive silvery glow Sheffield was known for, catching on the wet pavements where last night's rain still lingered. I winced as I slammed the door shut, momentarily forgetting the bruises across my abdomen until they shot pain through my torso.

Jolt occupied the corner of a long street of mixed medieval, Georgian and Victorian buildings that ran behind the Cathedral, its gothic spires already casting sharp-edged shadows across the tarmac. In the other direction, the street dropped away in one of the city's characteristic steep hills, and its valley position created strange patterns of light and shadow in the early morning air. The property on side one of the café housed a record shop I'd never seen open in all the years we'd been there. To the other stood a second-hand furniture emporium that often spread its wares across the pavement. As for the shopfront itself – that was my design. All dark green and glass, with the name emblazoned across the front door in black and gold. Even in the dead of winter, it felt like home.

Back when we'd first found the building, Jonathan, Tom and I had signed a one-year lease, and Jon had moved into the two-storey flat upstairs. When his parents died a couple of years later, he'd used most of his inheritance to buy the building, including the apartment above. At some point I'd have to go up there and sort through his things – but not today.

The Gloaming

I pushed open the door, and a bell tinkled overhead. The faint scent of old paper and fresh pastries permeated the air beneath the strong, soothing aroma of coffee. Morning light spilled through the large windows, creating pools of gold between the furniture. It was an L-shaped room, lined with bookshelves and filled with mismatched tables and chairs, all ancient but comfy as hell. I always thought of it as our own little library. Coffee, books, music and cake. What more could anyone need?

I flipped the sign on the door and wended my way between the tables toward the back room, where I found Maggie poring over a book of numbers.

"Morning." I forced a smile as I dropped my backpack onto a chair. Before I could take off my coat, she'd crossed the tiny room to hug me tightly. Her wild, gingery hair tickled my nose as I hugged her back, surrounding me with sweet-cinnamon scent of her, and I bit my lip. Crying at work was not an option.

"Tom told me," she said as she pulled away, touching a hand to my bruised face. "I'm sorry I had to call you. It's too soon—"

I took a deep breath and stepped back. "It's fine. I'll keep busy." My eyes were drawn to the sink across the room, where Jon's mug still sat upside down on the drainer. "I don't want to think about it."

She took a long hard look at me, clearly sceptical. "Okay."

It didn't take long before the early rush fulfilled my wish – an endless stream of customers with order after order. I'd never been more grateful for complex, overly specific demands in my life: the brunette with the creepy stare who came in at the crack of dawn every Monday and Thursday for her triple shot, venti, wet caramel macchiato, extra hot, extra foam. Or the cranky old lady who wanted to try six flavours of tea before settling on English Breakfast and a plain scone.

When things calmed down later in the morning, I grabbed a duster and got to work on the bookshelves. They were spotless, but without something for my hands to do, Jon's death intruded on my thoughts like a sore I couldn't stop poking. When that wasn't enough, I unsuccessfully attempted to tune one of the battered guitars we kept in the back corner. Only Maggie's request that I spare her bleeding ears eventually stopped me.

Around lunchtime, Tom called and asked if I would stay after closing to go over his findings. I agreed, mentally rearranging my plans to track the blonde vamp. I assumed he'd got somewhere with his research, but he didn't say more.

The afternoon dragged on. Customers came and went, and I steamed and frothed milk on autopilot, the rich smell of Jon's monthly selection of coffee beans filling the air. The longer I was at the shop, the harder it was to think of anything else – and to push away the guilt that came alongside thoughts of him. I checked the clock every ten minutes, desperate to be done with people. All I wanted was to go home and curl up under the covers. But things didn't quieten down until the light outside had faded from a warm orange to a pale coral.

Maggie and I were in the back when the bell over the door jingled twenty minutes before closing. I made my way through to the counter without looking up.

The watery winter sunlight had almost gone as I went to serve the waiting customer. He was something of a surprise – classically handsome with a shock of tidy, white blonde hair that caught the last pale rays filtering through the windows. He couldn't have been more than thirty, but he was unusually self-assured as he stood, leonine, running his light blue gaze over the bookshelves and furniture like an art connoisseur assessing a new piece.

I cleared my throat, and he broke into an easy, bashful grin. I forced the muscles of my face into a smile. It was probably best not to scare the guy with the glower I'd been hiding all day.

"What can I get you?" I tried not to stare, but there was something unique about him. Every angle of his face was harsh and sharp, though his expression had softened.

He blinked at me. "What would you recommend?"

I held in an exasperated sigh. "It's cold, it's late in the day and I'm feeling indulgent – so something hot, sweet and milky." He continued to stare at me with a blank expression. "Vanilla latte?" I asked.

His face relaxed again. "How could I say no when you justify it so articulately?" he laughed, and half-turned. He had his pick of tables since the shop was almost empty.

He pulled a fine leather wallet from his pocket and placed it on the counter. It probably cost more than everything I was wearing. "Make it two, if you please."

I nodded. "I'll bring them over."

He made his way across the room to the far window, and I watched out of the corner of my eye as he took off his coat and folded it neatly along the arm of our shabbiest sofa, revealing the crisp white shirt and grey trousers he wore beneath. Maggie stuck her head through the door, and I poured milk into a jug as she assessed the new customer.

"He's... striking." Her expression said he was far more than striking.

"Yup," I replied, laying out a saucer and spoon on a tray. "Interested?"

She shook her head and retreated into the back room. "I've got my eye on someone else."

I smirked to myself as I carried the tray across to the stranger and made a mental note to mention her comment to Tom.

As I placed his drinks on the table, the customer put down the novel he'd picked up, leaned back, and spread his arms wide across the back cushions of the sofa. He gestured with one hand to the space beside him. "Would you care to join me?"

Not really. The till needed counting up before we closed – but we weren't busy. "Sure." I took the seat across from him.

"My name is Adam. Adam Locke." He didn't take his eyes off me as he spoke, and I shifted under his steely gaze. The surrounding air smelled fresh, like citrus and cloves.

"Erin."

We sat in silence for a few moments. The couple in the corner had finished up and were getting ready to leave. Adam continued to take in the room, as he had before, watching the others until they left.

"The second coffee is for you, by the way," he said after several long minutes.

"Oh." I picked up the chunky cup and saucer, grateful for something to do with my hands. "Thanks."

What was this? Was he flirting? It didn't seem like it, but I'd been wrong before.

"Are you the owner?" Adam asked as he reached for his latte.

"Yeah," I replied, taking a sip. "Co-owner, with my friends Tom and—" I stopped. I wasn't ready for this conversation.

"Tom and—?" he prompted. His voice was quiet, with a clean-cut, well-spoken accent that stood out in a place like Yorkshire. Jon had been the same.

I realised he was still waiting for an answer. "Tom and I own

The Gloaming

the café," I explained, controlling my expression. "Our friend Jonathan recently died."

Adam looked dismayed, and I almost felt bad for him.

"I am so sorry, Erin," he murmured. "I did not mean to bring up a sensitive topic."

I pinched my lips together and nodded. He couldn't have known what he was asking, and I'd have to get used to saying it eventually.

After a brief pause, he waved a hand at the bookshelves along the wall. "Have you read all of these?"

"Most of them," I replied. "Almost everything in here used to be mine or Jon's or Tom's at some point. A few are second-hand or donated."

Adam beamed, his teeth white and even. "How lovely. One should always pass books on, don't you think? Though I've found the real challenge is getting people to return them."

"Sounds like you've been burned before."

"Several volumes worth, I'm afraid. I'm still waiting on a first edition I lent out in…" he paused. "Well, let's just say I've learned my lesson."

"And yet here you are, in a café full of books to be borrowed," I noted. "Risky."

"What can I say? I live dangerously." His eyes sparkled with amusement.

We chatted easily for a few minutes about our favourites, and he turned out to be a fan of Oscar Wilde – which seemed appropriate.

Maggie came through from the back, and I was half aware of her counting the cash in the till, rattling mugs around and banging cupboard doors. I glanced at the clock, and Adam noticed.

"I fear I'm keeping you from your duties," he said with an apologetic smile. "A young lady such as yourself must have more important things to be doing with your evening than humouring me."

Despite myself, this strange man had broken through the haze I'd carried around all day. Though it felt odd to smile back at him, I did. Maybe it was because he was new, and he hadn't known Jonathan – there were no reminders to worry about.

"No, it's been nice," I said truthfully. "You've taken my mind off things. And I'm always happy to talk about books."

Adam stood and pulled on his dark coat. "Then rest assured, I will be back." He flashed his teeth at me as he opened the door. "It has been a delight, Erin."

"And you," I replied as the door swung closed behind him. The moment he was out of sight, I flipped the closed sign and let out a long sigh. The second day was over. Almost.

Maggie made her way across and began shutting the wooden blinds on the front windows. "Made a friend?" she asked.

"Maybe." I yawned. No amount of coffee had replaced the sleep I'd lost the last two nights. "Nice guy. Bookworm. I reckon he'll be back."

She gave me a thoughtful look. "I'll finish up here if you want – you should get some sleep."

I shook my head. "Can't. Tom's meeting me here to talk about... you know, funeral plans..." I trailed off. I couldn't mention the real reason Tom was coming. Hell, I couldn't tell *anyone*. It hit me that no one would ever know the truth about Jon's death, and I had to steady myself against the wall. *No.*

Oblivious to my train of thought, Maggie's face fell. "I

didn't realise he was coming in." She peered down at her coffee-stained apron. "I'll leave you to it, then. But don't stay too late. Anything you can't do on your own can wait until the morning."

I twisted my mouth into some semblance of a smile and nodded.

3

IS A MISERY SHARED A MISERY HALVED?

TOM TURNED UP JUST AS Maggie was leaving, and I rested my elbows on the counter and watched their awkward exchange through the glass door. Tom said something that Maggie laughed at, and his cheeks flushed pink. I couldn't help but think about how good they'd be for each other. And he deserved someone in his life that didn't drag him down with death and violence. Namely, anyone but me.

Maggie went to leave, and I dashed over to hold the door open as Tom pushed through with his arms full of cables and his laptop bag.

I tried and failed to keep back a chuckle. "You know, she's absolutely bloody smitten. You should have seen the guy she dismissed today because she '*had her eye on someone,*' apparently."

Tom averted his eyes and bustled through to the back room, but he was fooling no one. There was a little happiness playing around his mouth.

"I asked her out. We have a date next Friday."

I froze. "What? Just now? Wow."

"And?" As usual, Tom had layered up multiple t-shirts and checked flannel shirts with a scarf and fingerless gloves rather than do the sensible thing and buy a warm winter coat. One by one, he peeled off the layers, not meeting my eye – but the tip of his nose had turned red. A dead giveaway.

I thought about it as I sat down. "I dunno. You normally dawdle more, I guess."

He didn't meet my eye as I watched him. "It seemed like the right thing to do. Seize the day, and all that."

Of course. I sighed. *Must be nice.*

I'd always known my days were numbered. Eventually, I'd pick a fight I couldn't win – it was the way things were for hunters, or so I assumed. But Jon's death had made that final fight seem closer than ever before, and my pride in Tom's courage was heavily coloured by my own worry that I wasn't making the most of my life. Then again, the fire was addictive. There was something dark in me, and I knew it. How was I supposed to share a life with someone, knowing that? First dates are awkward enough without having to explain why you keep a sword in your car.

I tucked a strand of hair behind my ear and settled into the chair beside Tom. "Go on then, what's so important it couldn't wait til I got back?"

He cleared his throat and spun the laptop around, his dark eyes dancing. "Oh, you know. Only the most notorious vampire I've ever come across."

I rolled my eyes. Sometimes he really didn't get it. "Why do you seem excited about that?"

"Because this woman is… old, Erin. She's legendary."

I huffed, but I humoured him. "Well I hope by legendary you mean fictional. Because legendary doesn't sound like a fight I want to have." Before he could respond, I held up a hand. "Start at the beginning."

The Gloaming

"Alright." With a few taps on the trackpad, Tom brought up an image. "So this is her—"

It was a classic Renaissance portrait: a beautiful young woman, around twenty, with ebony curls wired into an elaborate hairstyle and an intense gaze that looked right through the screen at me. The text at the bottom of the page dated the image as sixteenth century.

"A Tudor portrait? Really? What's next, Dracula?"

"Don't be ridiculous," Tom said, but he couldn't hide his grin. "Dracula could never be this interesting. Though now you mention it—"

"Focus, Chowdhury."

"So, Jon's post-mortem report was useless, but I got hold of the crime scene notes, and there were a few things that seemed way off. I wasn't sure if I was wasting my time to start with—"

"Can we skip your entire train of thought, Tom?" I interrupted.

"Sorry. Anyway, the forensic specialist noted that there were flowers on the bedside table. A posy." He dug out a printed photograph of a bundle of indigo blossoms bound with thread. "I'd read about something similar before."

"He could have picked them up on a hike?"

"Maybe," he conceded. "But there were two silver coins, too."

"Silver coins?"

"Plain silver discs. No stamp or date, but pure silver."

I frowned. "Okay. What for?"

"Payment for the kill?" Tom shrugged.

"Or the ferryman," I added darkly.

"Either way, it's not the first death like that. And the coins led me to *her*."

I sensed Tom might finally get to his point. "Who is she?"

"Isabel Wyatt. She sometimes goes by Elizabeth, but the records are sketchy as to whether she's the same person. Most often she's recorded as Izzie Misery."

The name wasn't familiar, but my stomach stirred uncomfortably. It wasn't often vamps built up enough of a reputation to gain a moniker like that.

"Was she a noblewoman?" I asked, taking the laptop from him and scrolling through the image search results. "I've never heard of her."

"No, but the painter—" he gestured at the screen. "I think it's a Holbein. And there are rumours online about his other work. You know the Anne Boleyn one, with the pearl necklace? It's supposedly based on—" He cut himself off.

"Are we arriving close to your point any time soon? Because I haven't got all day."

He glared at me. "The point is, she's *old*. She must have been around since the early fifteen-hundreds at least. I mean, that's back with bloody Henry the Eighth for crying out loud. This is big."

I raised an eyebrow. "Vampires never live that long. It's part of the myth, remember?"

"I think we were wrong." He shook his head, and I wondered what it was about this woman that he found so fascinating. "Her history is... well, the usual vague stuff to start with – nothing solid. But it doesn't seem like she's ever been out of action for longer than thirty, maybe forty years. She's a survivor."

It was odd, there was no doubt about it. The oldest vamps we'd ever met had spent time underground, sleeping to escape the mobs when the death count got too high. But even the most resilient of them had been human before 1900.

The Gloaming

"She'd be what, five hundred?" It was hard to get my head around. Sure, vampires were immortal. But half a millennium was a bloody long time. "Fuck."

"Yeah," Tom was wide-eyed. "And it all seems to fit."

I indicated he should go on, but part of me hoped he'd put two and two together and made five. It was plausible that this woman existed. But he was as desperate for answers as I was.

"So far you haven't said anything that connects her though."

"You know how I usually need six coffees before I'll consider a conspiracy theory?"

I nodded warily.

"Well, I'm undercaffeinated and still convinced. But… I don't know if you really want to hear the rest." He looked as unsure as I felt. "I managed to get the details, and it's… it's not good."

"Just get it over with." I needed to know.

"He was in the hotel for four days." Tom's voice was carefully neutral. "Barely ate or slept. Just paced and stood by the window for hours, unresponsive." He trailed off, staring into his coffee. "The coroner ruled it suicide, but…"

I tried to reconcile this with the Jon I knew – so steady, so grounded. It was like someone had been determined to break him first or something.

"They linked Wyatt to similar deaths in the 1720s," Tom continued. "They were pretty distinctive." He hesitated. "He was hanged, Erin. With wire, not rope."

I blanched and closed my eyes, massaging my temples with my fingers as it played out behind my eyelids. The wire would have cut deep into his neck from the force of the drop. Jon was a huge guy. Tall. Muscled. His body weight alone would have been enough. *Fuck. Fuck, fuck, fuck.*

Tom was still talking. They'd found him in his hotel room, suspended from an old Victorian roof beam. He'd probably have been conscious as he bled out.

I felt sick. It was so much worse than I'd imagined.

"Keep going," I mumbled, opening my eyes.

Tom nodded. "There was a witness to the Wyatt deaths – there's almost no doubt it was her, even though they were considered suicides at first. And at every scene, there were flowers and two silver coins."

I didn't want to be convinced, but I could see why Tom thought he'd made a breakthrough. "Why now? Where's her motive?"

He pinched the bridge of his nose. "I know she's here," he said, gathering the papers he'd spread across the table. "She has a huge following online—"

"She's not a fucking influencer, Tom."

"Look, it's not a perfect answer. But there are these groups of believers who try to track her – I've never seen anything like it." He pushed a printout of an old newspaper at me, jabbing a finger at the headline. "Cologne after the war. Then Frankfurt. Then sodding Nuremberg for crying out loud."

I scanned the articles. Most of them were published in the years following the Second World War. "These are from almost a century ago. And they're pretty damn far from Yorkshire."

It didn't faze him. "If she's survived this long, I don't think it's beyond the realm of possibility." Tom shrugged and spun the laptop back to face him, clicking away. "She has accomplices. Companions. There could be someone we've – well, *you've* – dealt with, linked to her."

I sighed. I could feel a headache coming on. "But what's her

The Gloaming

connection to Jon?" I asked. "Is there a link to Edinburgh?"

"Since you mention it, yeah. There was one guy… a vamp she was with in the 1800s, for almost a century. The forums don't have much on him, but he was Scottish, I think. Nicholas something – there wasn't a picture…" He was scrolling through the page again.

"Alright," I stood up, pulled the tie from the end of my plait and ran my fingers through the waves. It was getting late, and I didn't want to argue. "There's enough to dig a bit deeper, I guess."

Tom nodded, but I suspected I'd irritated him with my lack of enthusiasm.

"You okay?" I asked.

He shrugged. "You need to read this stuff. I get why it seems like a stretch, but the more I see, the more it fits—"

"I know. I trust you. I just… need a bit more. If she killed him in Edinburgh, she must have known he was travelling. Maybe even waited until he was." I hesitated, but our next move seemed obvious to me. "I'll have to find Solace. She'll know something."

Sheffield was a big city. But there was always one person I could rely on to know who came in and out – and who died here. Unfortunately, it wasn't someone I wanted to owe a favour to. And if they could get me the information I needed on this Izzie Misery, I'd owe more than a favour.

Tom stopped to level a look over the top of his laptop screen. "You want to go back, after last time?"

"You know I don't. But if anyone would know…" I let the thought trail off. I was still wearing my apron and quickly unknotted it, hanging it up.

He pulled the screen half-closed, and I knew what he was planning to say before he said it.

"I'm not going to the morgue," I cut across him before he even

41

opened his mouth. "I can't. Not this time." That wasn't the way I wanted to remember Jon. I swallowed, blinking away the tears that threatened.

"We might have to," Tom said, voice low. "But you don't have to, you know, *look*. Just go through his stuff. There could be something there that the police missed."

I swallowed again, gazing at the sky-blue walls of the tiny room. *Suck it up, Erin.*

"Maybe."

Our options were fairly limited at this stage. Dodgy dealers or the morgue. When had my life started to look like a TV drama?

Tom broke the silence. "Jon's uncle is coming over for dinner tomorrow evening, so it'll have to wait, anyway. He wants to discuss the funeral plans." His eyes fixed avidly on the screen once more.

"Oh."

"We spoke this afternoon; he called your house. I meant to mention it." He hesitated. "He sort of… took care of everything."

I froze, glancing sharply at Tom. "What do you mean? I thought—"

"I know. He wasn't supposed to, but he did. Honestly, from what he said I don't think we'd have done much differently. Jon might even like it." He pulled a face. "You know, if it wasn't his funeral."

I shook my head, but if I was honest, I was grateful we could avoid going over it all. It was too much, way too soon.

"I gave him Jon's requests: the envelope. I checked it first, obviously, in case he'd said something weird." He leaned back. "I told him we'd choose the music, though. You know how he was about his tunes."

The Gloaming

I ran another hand through my hair. It must have been sticking up on end. "Are you okay to do that?"

A look of surprise flitted across his face. "If you want me to."

I did and I didn't. Music was everything to Jon. You name it, he knew it. Play a track from the last seventy-odd years, and he could probably share at least a titbit about it. The three of us had spent many a night in my living room, listening to records while he analysed every note and lyric in a song like it was some undiscovered new Shakespeare.

I nodded at Tom and wandered into the shop to get my coat. No, I couldn't help with the music. It was too final. Tom would have to do it.

I knew he was grieving as much as I was. It could be that he was dealing with it better than me, but so far, I hated every fucking minute. We'd just gone along with our lives like Jon hadn't been basically decapitated a few days ago. I should've been crippled, struggling to function. Unable to eat or breathe or brush my damn hair. Instead, things had carried on as normal.

Jon would have told me to keep fighting. He'd have been right, as he often was. But the weight in my chest felt right, too. I would hold on to it for as long as possible. It was all I had left of my best friend.

JON'S UNCLE WAS A SHOCK. TOM answered the door in a frilly novelty apron – he'd been concocting something in the kitchen for over an hour, though I had no idea what – and he stood there, staring. I came downstairs to see a silhouette in the doorway, and my heart leapt. But it wasn't Jon, despite the resemblance.

Jim, as he insisted we call him, was an easygoing sort, much like his estranged nephew. Though I started out on edge in my tea dress and tights, I soon relaxed as he chattered away. Tom's fresh pasta went down a treat, and I was proud that my mask never faltered. But it was hard not to wonder, seeing this man in his sixties – he was almost an older version of my friend. One I'd never get to meet.

"I'll admit, it surprised me to hear Jonathan planned to visit Edinburgh," Jim said, as Tom cleared our plates away. His Edinburgh accent was almost non-existent, clearly educated out of him.

"Oh?" I took a sip from my glass of wine to avoid answering and quickly regretted it. I'd never been a fan of red wine.

"Yes. Did he tell you much of our family history?" he asked.

I swallowed with difficulty before I replied. "He said you'd moved to Scotland when he was a kid. That you'd had a falling out with his dad."

Tom poured himself another drink as he sat back down. He shot me a glare that told me to keep my mouth shut. Jim, however, didn't seem to mind.

"Family can be complicated," he said.

"Too right," Tom muttered, more to his wineglass than to either of us. "Sometimes the distance is better for everyone."

Jim gave him a piercing look. "You sound like you speak from experience."

Tom shrugged, suddenly fascinated by a bit of pasta sauce on the table. "Let's just say my parents had very specific expectations for their only son. History and literature weren't on the list. Neither was opening a coffee shop." He gave a short, humourless laugh. "The last proper conversation we had, my dad told me I was throwing away generations of tradition for, and I quote, '*serving*

The Gloaming

fancy drinks to hipsters.'"

I'd heard this story before, though Tom didn't bring his family up much these days. It was a definite sore spot.

"Hmm," Jim said quietly. "Following your own path takes courage. If only I'd understood that sooner." He sighed. "There was a row over something with Jonathan's father – unimportant now, of course. I regret to say I missed out on knowing my nephew because of it."

"Jon was excited to meet you, though," I interrupted his reverie, trying to lighten the mood. "He wouldn't shut up about your research into the family tree."

Jim nodded. "I've devoted my life to the pursuit of history, though what good it will do now there's no one to carry on the line, I can't say."

"You don't have kids?" Tom asked.

"No. I never considered settling down to be an option until it was too late, really. The time for romance has been and gone." He smiled, but it didn't reach his eyes. "I have my work, though – and my greenhouse and such. I get along."

"Jon wanted kids," I said through the veil of fuzziness settling over my mind. "Three or four. He said the world would stay a horrid place until we put nicer people in it."

Tom and Jim stared at me in silence, Tom with sadness and Jim with something like calculation. I blinked, and it was gone.

"I can't understand it. Why would a young man with such ambition want to take his own life? It's a terrible thing," Jim said finally, smoothing the napkin on his lap.

Tom and I shared a look. This was the moment I'd been dreading, but I couldn't lie. It wasn't fair.

"Anyone for dessert?" Tom asked, standing up. I nodded, and

Jim relaxed, confirming dessert would be lovely.

I tried to change the subject at every opportunity after that. Thankfully, no one seemed to notice, and before I knew it, the evening was over, and Jim was pulling on his coat. I stayed at the kitchen table, massaging my temples while Tom hovered in the hallway with him, talking in undertones.

The door clicked shut, and Tom came back through. "The funeral is next Thursday."

I nodded and stood to clear the plates. With Tom helping, the washing up didn't take long – despite him having used every bloody dish in the house. While we worked, he filled me in on his chosen music. They all seemed like obvious choices, but if I was honest with myself, Jon would have understood that his funeral wasn't really for him. It was for those of us left behind – and most of the guests would probably be opposed to some of his heavier favourites.

As he was pulling on his coat to leave, Tom turned. "You hunting tonight?"

He hadn't mentioned the morgue again, and I'd followed his lead.

"I'll do a quick sweep, but I've had too much wine for much else." I rubbed my arms, already cold at the idea of coming back to an empty house.

Tom barked a quick laugh. "Fair enough. Just be careful, yeah?"

Closing the door behind him, I bounded up the stairs. I couldn't get out of my uncomfortable dress fast enough, the fitted black jumper and combat jeans I pulled on were far more my style. Folding the roll neck down and loosening my hair, I glimpsed my reflection in the mirror as I left the room – a cold-weather assassin. That was the plan, anyway.

4
TALL, DARK AND SCOTTISH

Standing on the front doorstep, every surface glistened with a fragile frost in the moonlight. I took a slow breath and looked upward, past the stark white of the streetlights and the city, stamping my feet to get the blood flowing. A scattering of stars winked in and out of existence, barely visible despite the clear night. The air held the sharp, clean scent of ice, and I wondered whether we'd see snow soon as I set off along the shimmering pavement. Before I reached the end of the street, the fog of wine had begun to recede, replaced instead by a bone-deep cold.

Without much thought for where I was going, I headed toward a nearby park, casting my senses out into the night before me. It was a strange sensation, to pick up on points of light and warmth in some unknown part of my mind, but I'd long grown used to it. It was easy to tune the humdrum out – at least, at times like now, when there was no sign of anything more sinister. Other times I'd get a vibe about something kinky the neighbours were up to, and nothing on earth could help me shut that shit down, no matter how hard I tried.

I scanned the shadows as I strolled around the park's fenced perimeter, my thoughts tugged back to a conversation I'd once had with Jon about dying. That same night, we'd written down our last wishes, sealing them into three envelopes for safekeeping. I'd never really believed we'd have to open them. At least, Jon's or Tom's.

I pulled my sleeves down over my fingers, tucking them into the wool. My breath condensed in a cloud of vapour before me, blurring my vision. The envelopes had been a precaution. I'd known the chances of my slip of paper seeing the light of day grew higher every night, but I'd thought my friends were safe. What could possibly happen from the safety of home, researching and training, never really fighting? I wouldn't have gotten this far without them.

Tom resented it, I knew. He wanted to be out every night, with me – and I got it. To him, clearing out the vamps was a question of moral responsibility and goodness. He didn't know I enjoyed it far too much for it to be *good*. The thrill of the fight, the rush of a kill. What was moral about that?

The park entrance was already locked when I reached it, but I vaulted the iron gate with ease. A lock had never kept me out of anywhere as a kid, and it wouldn't keep out the determined ones now, either. Maybe moody teens were all I'd find tonight – but a newbie vamp or two would make a better dessert than Tom's tiramisu had.

The sweeping lawns and gentle hills of the park stretched toward the horizon, their colour leeched away by the artificial light. In the day, the trees would be glorious: fireworks of orange and yellow leaves clinging to the last vestiges of autumn. Now, the dim lamps only illuminated the paths, forcing the life and colour of the day to retreat into shadow.

As I made my way between the odd, abandoned stone buildings that were placed at key locations around the park, I

The Gloaming

wondered what the original owners would think of the place now. I'd read it had once been the grounds of a mansion home until the aristocracy that lived there had gone bankrupt and were forced to auction off the land and property. The house itself had fallen into disrepair and been demolished decades ago, but the grounds had been bought by the local government and now belonged to the public. Which included my favourite place, and all that remained of the former stately home: overgrown walled gardens behind the old lodge.

My legs took me in that direction without much thought, and I pushed through the curtain of winter jasmine that hid the rotting wooden gate, breathing in its heady fragrance. A small pond ahead was green and overrun with lilies, the paths cracked and uneven underfoot, and ivy had overtaken a good portion of the place, crawling up every tree and pergola. But it was undeniably beautiful. There was something about walking under the trellises that felt like you were in on an ancient secret, and a peaceful silence lay over everything.

The old lodge loomed ahead, its stone walls weathered by decades of neglect. Empty windows gaped like a hollowed-out pumpkin in the moonlight, the shattered glazing long gone.

There was no light or sound from within, even when I turned my senses up to eleven. But once in a while, the lodge's occupants would spot me coming from the upper storey and hide. I sighed, but I'd come this far. It was always worth double-checking.

Pushing aside the heavy door, I stepped into the room I thought of as the kitchen, a cracked porcelain sink in one corner the only piece of furniture. I cast my senses outward and upward, shuddering with effort, but no warmth or light echoed back.

The stone steps were worn smooth from centuries of footfall, but the gritstone held firm beneath my boots. Moonlight filtered through the empty windows, casting strange shadows across the stairwell. I'd been here enough times to know where it was safe to put my feet, but if I was honest, I knew they should tear the place down – for the sake of the local teens' safety, if nothing else. The problem was, if that happened, people would realise the garden was here, and they would overrun my little place.

The first landing was as empty as I'd suspected, the internal walls and floor now almost entirely gone. Taking care with each step, I proceeded across the main beam that ran through the house. The joists on either side were heavy with rot, but I'd crossed this one plenty of times with no problem – and it was the only way to get to the attic stairs at the other side of the building. I paused at the edge of the room and listened once more. Nothing looked out of place – the usual debris littered the remaining areas of floorboards, along with a fair number of discarded drinks cans and crisp packets. I shivered at a creak in the room above me. As silently as possible, I made my way up.

Teenagers didn't normally make it this far in – it was fairly precarious without the added benefit of supernatural balance and speed. It had happened once or twice, but chances were, if there was something up here besides a pigeon or two, I'd have a fight on my hands.

At the top of the stairs, a gust of wind swept through the hollow building with an eerie howl, almost knocking me back a step. A small, furry creature scurried away into a dark shadowy corner across the room, but otherwise, everything seemed as abandoned as ever.

I waited, freezing in the cold wind. My usual approach of throwing out my senses said the place was empty, but deeper down, something didn't feel… right. Maybe my aim was off, or the wine was still working its way out of my system. I had to be sure.

There were plenty of floorboards remaining up here, but none of them looked particularly safe. I scanned them, searching for the supporting joists beneath decades of dust and rubbish. The central beam seemed least damaged – but was farthest from the support of the walls. Typical.

Steeling myself, I took small steps onto the beam. Each movement sent tiny vibrations through the timber, my excellent balance the only thing between me and the shadows below. A few more steps and I was halfway. One more step… An ominous creak shuddered beneath my boots as my senses jangled, screaming at me to stop. I spun into a crouch without thinking.

If I hadn't been so hyped up, the resounding crack as wood splintered beneath me would probably have happened in slow motion. But my senses were sharp, and instead, I was momentarily weightless as the beam split and the floor collapsed around me. With a cry, I threw out my arms, smashing into the next beam on the floor below. The fall forced the air from my lungs, and I gasped, winded, and tried to gather myself to crawl to the edge of the room. Before I could turn, the wood beneath me groaned and splintered, the sound echoing through the hollow building. I scrabbled for a handhold, my fingers slipping through the dirt and debris, but everything around me was falling too.

My muscles reacted faster than my mind, and I twisted in on myself to avoid cracking my head as I landed, throwing out my left arm to cushion my skull. My ankle, hip and ribs jarred on impact with the bare stone, the shock reverberating through my body. Icy, stagnant water saturated my clothes as my eyes drifted closed.

When I became aware of the room again, the dust from above

was still settling around me like powdery snow. Winded as I was, I struggled to breathe through it – but adrenaline pounded through my system, forcing me to keep pulling in air. Bit by bit, my heart rate slowed, and my panic subsided as oxygen flooded back into my lungs. I let out a low groan. *What the actual fuck was that?*

Pain pulsed down one side of my body, where I'd taken the force of the fall. My head told me to get up and out of the unstable building, but it was all I could do to close my eyes against the ringing that vibrated through my skull. I breathed deeply, willing it to stop.

It's the middle of the bloody night, Erin. Nobody knows you're here. Move your arse.

With an effort, I pulled myself into a sitting position. "Fuckfuckfuckfuckfuck!" I swore through my teeth.

My left elbow throbbed – the most noticeable of my injuries – and I struggled to focus on much else until a voice spoke behind me.

"Easy there, lass. Best stay still a moment while we make sure you're in one piece." The words had a soft cadence, but I still jumped at the sound. It wasn't often anyone sneaked up on me.

In the moonlight that fell through the fractured ceiling, my heart caught in my throat. The voice belonged to a figure in the doorway – an all too familiar ghost. As he stepped into the light, I found myself staring at his finely drawn features.

A wariness entered his expression as his eyes travelled across my filthy, soaked form. "Are you okay?"

I knew he'd asked a question, but I couldn't answer. Green, almond-shaped eyes flecked with gold peered at me in utter confusion, and that nagging sense of familiarity tugged at me again – though Jon's eyes had been hazel, and he *definitely* wasn't Jon.

The Gloaming

This stranger was striking in his own right – high, wide cheekbones, a firm jaw and a full mouth currently pulled into an expression of worry. His long coat and loose scarf gave him an air of easy elegance, even as he crouched in the rubble beside me, arms resting on his knees.

I shook my head, instantly regretting it when the night spun around me. "My elbow's hurt. And my ankle and hip. And, you know, my pride."

Fuck, he looks like him. But it isn't. Look. Listen. He's gone.

"Ah." One side of his mouth twitched up into a half-smile. "Well, tis to be expected, I should think." His chuckle was warm and smooth, like caramel. "The bleeding seems to have stopped already, though—" He reached out toward my face and hesitated, withdrawing his hand as he straightened and stood.

I touched my fingers to my forehead, and they came away black and sticky in the darkness. Passing an assessing hand over the rest of my features, I caught several splinters embedded in my cheek and hissed at the sting. At least it was nothing Tom couldn't fix with a couple of butterfly stitches.

Wiping the blood onto my already filthy jeans, and attempting to brush some of the dust from my shoulders and hair, I peeked at the stranger, who was looking back at me with equal curiosity.

"May I—?" His touch was light as he stepped behind me and assessed my injuries, his fingers trailing along my spine with a practised precision that was both clinical and intimate. I held my breath, hyperaware of every point of contact even through the heavy knit of my jumper, but nothing seemed to be damaged.

"Where did you come from?" I asked, pushing myself up on my uninjured arm. He held out a hand to help, stepping back as soon as I was upright.

"I saw you disappear into the gardens, afore. I didnae ken they were here and found myself intrigued," he shrugged. "I'm sorry I wisnae following more closely. I could've helped."

His story was believable enough, but I forced myself to look away. The light from above put the kitchen of the old lodge on full display, highlighting the disrepair. What had I been thinking, going out on that beam?

"It's alright," I told him. "Unless you were planning on catching me, it wouldn't have made a difference." I tried a few steps and found my ankle didn't want to bear my weight. The stranger held out an arm for me to lean on. "Thanks," I said, taking it without thinking.

"Still…" He cast a brief look at my hand where it rested on his arm, and to my face. "I'm Cole. And despite the circumstances, pleased to make your acquaintance." He gave me a rueful smile and tilted his head to assess me, his eyes lingering on my mouth. "I must admit, I'm fair amazed you're *conscious*. Is that an impolite thing to say?" I placed his Scottish brogue now, much stronger than Jim's had been.

I laughed and winced when the pain from my ankle pulsed up my leg. "Oh, I blacked out for a moment there. Don't doubt it."

With Cole's hold firm on my arm, he guided me out of the lodge, positioning himself between me and the unstable structure. The paths, with their cracks and overgrown foliage, were now more dangerous than before. Usually, having a stranger so close would make me uneasy, but without him, getting home seemed nigh on impossible.

"Are you a doctor?" I asked, remembering his quick, competent analysis as he adjusted his stride to match my shorter steps, creating a shield against the bitter wind.

The Gloaming

He gave me a roguish grin. "That depends on who's asking, lass."

We'd reached the garden's edge, and as I gazed up at him under the pale glow of the streetlamps, I noticed the smile lines around his eyes and mouth as he looked at me, bemused. I'd guess late twenties, early thirties, maybe a little older than me, and remarkably pleasant to look at. Dark waves of hair fell in a careless tumble past his ears, constantly threatening to obscure those striking eyes. A lock fell across his forehead as I watched, and he absently pushed it back, only for it to escape again moments later. The warm mahogany tones complemented his refined features well, and *fuck*, was that rakish little move distracting. I shook my head, as I realised he'd been scrutinising me just as closely.

"I can probably manage from here," I said, pulling my eyes away. It was true, but my ankle was as good an excuse as any to prolong the conversation. I was leaning into him despite myself, though my clothes were still drenched and icy. Maybe I was concussed.

"Ah, but what kind of gentleman would I be, leaving a lady to brave these treacherous paths alone? Another ruin might fall on ye. Or mayhap a tree." He grinned down at me, eyes crinkling. "I dinnae need the worry of a strange, pretty lass on my conscience. Bold as the moon you may be, climbing in the rafters – but soft as stardust and prone to breaking."

I blushed hard, but I was pleased. "Are you always this poetic about potential concussions?"

"Only the bonnie ones," he smiled.

As we walked, I couldn't help but notice how his height and frame carried an effortless kind of strength. At least six foot four, maybe six five, his height gave him an agile grace that made my stumbling seem more awkward than ever. The thick navy jumper he wore beneath his coat pulled taut across his chest and shoulders, and there was something quietly devastating about the artistry of his face and the firm steadiness of his hands as he supported me. The cut of his coat had hidden it at first, but this close, I was intensely aware of the solid strength of his body against mine.

I wanted to keep him close, and it was more than the need for physical support. It was hard to explain, but Cole felt… safe.

"Do you mind if I ask what you were doing in the lodge?" He asked. "Seems a wee bit dreich to be out so late."

"I needed to clear my head," I lied. "Exploring sometimes helps."

Cole nodded. "Aye, I ken the feeling. When your head's so full…" he paused. "How *is* your head?"

"Fuzzy, but not too bad." I touched my temple again, conscious of the streaks of dirt and blood on my face. "My arm took the brunt of it."

He came to a stop and seemed to be appraising my outfit. "Are you cold? You must be soaked through."

I grimaced, comparing my dirty jumper to his smart coat, which hung around him in perfect, tailored lines.

"I'll be fine," I clenched my teeth together to hide my shivering, but he wasn't fooled. Barely letting go of my arm, he removed his coat in a singular smooth motion and draped it over my shoulders. I felt warmer immediately, but had to resist the urge to bury my nose in the collar, surrounded by his woodsy, pine-like scent.

For a few minutes, we made silent, steady progress along tidier paths. My ankle throbbed with each step, but it wasn't enough to distract from my curiosity about Cole now that my teeth had stopped chattering. I tried not to steal glances at him as we walked, but several times I caught him looking back at me. Each time our eyes met, my stomach did a little flip. His half-smiles were doing dangerous things to my ability to focus on walking straight, injured ankle or not. *Play it cool, Erin.*

We stopped as we reached the edge of the park, and I gawked up at the fence I'd leapt so confidently before. Cole's mouth quirked up into a grin – clearly, I wasn't great at hiding my emotions from this guy.

"It was open when I arrived, I swear." He held up a hand in mock solemnity. "We'll find another way out. You cannae climb over a fence like that in this state."

I had to agree with him. "I think there's a wall nearby where the fence is lower. I might be able to make it there," I suggested.

"A true midnight wanderer," he replied, tightening his grip on my arm. "You must spend a lot of time here."

I didn't answer. It was safer not to.

We soon found the right place, where the railings had been cut down and their metal taken for munitions during the Second World War. The stumps left in the stone were rusted over, but Cole helped to hoist me onto the top without difficulty. His hold never faltered as I clambered one leg at a time through the narrow gap. His hands were steady at my waist, and I tried not to focus on how easily he lifted me, or how my skin tingled where we touched.

"Not exactly my most graceful display," I commented.

Amusement played around his lips in a crooked smile as he climbed after me, but the look in his eyes said something else entirely. "Words couldnae describe it."

As we walked along the empty streets, the wind began to pick up, whipping my hair around my face. I tried to place the odd expression I'd seen, but the pain in my elbow and ankle was growing distracting, and I struggled to think straight.

"This is me," I said as we reached the steps leading up to my front door. I pulled away from the comfort and support of his arm to rest on the wall.

Cole looked up at the house. The lamp I'd left on in the living room window cast a warm glow into the dark street, highlighting those remarkable cheekbones and the way his too-long hair fell across his forehead.

"How's your head, now?" he asked, his voice somewhere between concern and amusement. "You mightn't want to fall asleep yet, in case of concussion and such."

I bit back a laugh – he seemed genuinely worried. And of course, he was right.

"Honestly, I've had worse," I said, hauling myself up the three steps to the door. I fumbled through my keys at the top, my fingers numb with cold.

"Worse falls or worse head injuries?" He raised an eyebrow, a challenge dancing in his eyes. Before I could protest, he'd swiftly taken my keys and straightened them out with the same calm efficiency he'd shown while examining my back. I gaped at him, and the already familiar expression returned, the corner of his mouth twitching up.

"Thanks," I mumbled. Remembering his coat, I shrugged it off and handed it over. He took it with a nod, and in a slow deliberate gesture, reached for the uninjured side of my face, drawing his hand down my cheekbone with an impossible gentleness that made me shiver. I closed my eyes for a second, wondering, and when I opened them, he was at the bottom of the steps.

"I'd usually prefer dinner and dancing to moonlit adventures in ruins. But I have to admit, this has been far more…

memorable," he pushed his hands deeply into his pockets as he spoke. "Still, if ye'd promise no to go exploring another derelict building any time soon, I'd sleep easier, lass. For my peace of mind, eh?" He dipped his head, reminding me of an actor from an old black-and-white film. And without waiting for an answer, walked away.

I admired his retreating silhouette for a few seconds, marvelling at the strangeness of a stranger and already missing his presence – but it was too cold to dawdle, and I hurried into the warmth of the house. Resting on the table in the hallway, I closed my eyes and breathed deeply, dropping into a quick, semi-meditative state to assess the damage. The pain of every injury seemed poignant and sharp, but I had to take stock of how bad it was.

The brunt of the fall had messed up most of my left side, and besides my sprained ankle, my elbow had begun to swell. *Fan-fucking-tastic*. It didn't feel like a proper break, but it was probably fractured. My ribs were sore, too, and I reckoned a couple were cracked, but that was par for the course. I'd heal in a week or so.

I looked blankly at the dark hallway and considered a hot bath before bed. A glance at my phone – mercifully undamaged – told me it was later than I'd planned to be home, but a long soak seemed like a good idea. Cole had been right about staying awake.

The trip upstairs was a Herculean task, and some idle part of my brain contemplated what might have happened if I'd invited Cole in to help a little longer. Still, I couldn't get around the weird expression I'd seen on his face before, when I'd climbed the fence. It was familiar, but I wasn't sure why.

As the bath ran, I rummaged around in the cabinet under the

sink for the strongest painkillers I had, mulling it over. It wasn't until I sank into the hot water and the scent of spearmint cleared my mind that I worked it out. But it made no sense.

Disbelief, I thought. *Utter disbelief.*

5
The Dead We Cannot Save

No matter the day of the week, I never found enough time for sleep. It felt like minutes had passed since I'd closed my eyes when a pounding on the bedroom door brought me back to consciousness. I groaned and rolled over, pulling the duvet up to muffle the sound.

The banging stopped for a moment, before resuming twice as loud.

"Unless the house is on fire or you've discovered time travel, this better be bloody good," I called, dragging myself upright. Pain shot through my elbow as I put weight on it, and I swore loudly.

"Are you decent?" Tom stuck his head around the door. "Shit, Erin. What happened?" As was his custom, he immediately spotted the now livid bruising along my left arm. I flexed it experimentally. It probably looked worse than it was.

"I fell," I answered, swinging my legs out of bed and wincing as I stumbled.

He hurried across the room and pulled my uninjured arm around his shoulder. "I'll help you downstairs, and you can tell me over breakfast."

"Thanks," I grinned. "Does that mean you're cooking?"

He ignored me.

In the chilly kitchen, I hopped between cupboards, looking for more painkillers as Tom fiddled with the thermostat. When he noticed what I was doing, he slid a bottle of cocodamol across the worktop.

"So, you fell?" He watched me struggle with the child-safe container as I sat at the table across from him.

"Honestly," I replied, grasping the lid in my teeth while tugging a lumpy cushion out from beneath me with the other hand. "No vamp involvement whatsoever." It popped open and spilled sugary pills over the counter.

"Right. You just… fell. Nothing to do with the fact you vanished for hours after—"

"Through the floor of the old lodge, actually."

He stared at me, shoving two pieces of bread into the toaster without looking at them. "You're kidding. The same floor I specifically told you would collapse if you kept—"

"If you say 'I told you so,' I will throw this cushion at your head."

"Wouldn't dream of it," he said, holding up both hands. "Though I did. Tell you so, I mean." He dodged the cushion with ease. "How are you not—?"

"Dead or smashed to bits? Smart question, Chowdhury." I heaved my injured ankle onto the chair between us, throwing back the pills.

The toaster pinged, and Tom's dark eyes followed me thoughtfully as he crossed the room to grab a plate and put more bread in. "You know, you're oddly durable. Have you noticed? I mean, most people don't treat falling through floors like it's a minor inconvenience. You're like a human rubber ball."

Of course I'd noticed. Most people didn't heal cracked ribs and broken bones in a fortnight. But saying that sort of thing out loud made me feel… well, insane.

"Pass the first aid box?" I asked instead.

"I've given it a lot of thought," he continued, ignoring me. But he reached under the sink and tossed the box over anyway.

"Hmm?"

"Yeah. Because when you break it down, what would be the point of your heightened senses, and the vamp stuff, if you didn't have the strength to do something about it?"

I pursed my lips, concentrating on the tub of antiseptic cream and tweezers I'd dug from the jam-packed box. A little more rummaging, and I produced a mirror and cotton swabs.

"I mean, Jon was great at martial arts, but he couldn't take you in a fight."

I cleared my throat. "I'm not planning on testing this theory if that's what you're after."

"Fine by me," he smiled tightly. "But you still need time to heal. Rest. Call Maggie and ask her to cover."

I tugged down the skin beneath my left eye, and swabbed antiseptic across the shallow cuts there. "And your motives are honourable, right? Nothing to do with wanting to spend more time with her?"

"We work together, that's a good enough reason." His smile was smug as he grabbed the tweezers from my hand and took over, removing the remaining splinters. "But she's got family visiting at the weekend, so we moved our date to tomorrow."

I wiggled my eyebrows at him. "Nervous?"

"I thought I would be." The tip of his nose turned red. "But I really like her, and she's already heard my stupid jokes and knows my bad habits. That's got to be a good start."

I smiled and nodded. He deserved someone in his life after everything that had happened lately. Though I hated to admit it, I was sort of jealous – but that wasn't my path, and I'd accepted that. I danced too close to the darkness to bring anyone over the edge with me.

"So long as I get the juicy details afterwards." I winked at him. "That is if you're not too busy."

The smell of burnt toast filled the room, and I stood to remove it before it got worse, laughing with Tom. Maggie would be perfect for him.

Despite his transparent motives, Tom had a fair point about taking time to heal. I made my way through four mugs of coffee before I noticed the caffeine wasn't waking me up in the slightest, so after he left for Jolt, I climbed back into bed and slept the day away. Cocooned in the warmth of my duvet, it was a relief to forget the world for a while. Even to forget the heavy feeling in my chest that hadn't lifted since we'd heard about Jon's death.

Everything was still stiff and sore the next morning, but at least I could move more easily. An ultra-hot shower helped loosen up my limbs, and I made a vague plan of how my day could go as I ran conditioner through my hair, dried myself off and headed upstairs.

Technically, my work room was a loft space my landlord had glorified in the hopes of adding another bedroom to the house and bumping up the rent. He'd installed windows at either end of the steep, angled roof, and fitted some plasterboard with access into the eaves for insulation – but that was about as far as he'd gotten. I could only get in using the pull-down ladder from the hatch in my bedroom ceiling, which took more effort than usual with a dodgy ankle. Still, I managed it.

A battered yellow couch stood in one corner by a set of drawers that contained my paints, paper, pencils and charcoals. At the opposite end, a paint-spattered easel sat by a three-legged stool. Early morning sun flooded the room, and dust motes danced on the air currents around me, swirling in patterns my paintbrush could never capture. I sighed. Okay, I'd made it up here. Now what?

The light was too beautiful to ignore, so I dragged the sofa from the corner into the middle of the room and grabbed a sketchbook from my desk. The urge to draw had been growing fainter for years – my time was pretty much eaten up by life-or-death situations instead – but right now, something was tugging at the edges of my consciousness, and I wanted to get it down before I lost the feeling.

Splaying my fingers across the heavy paper, I let my pencil make its own decisions, its lead a familiar weight in my hand. The shapes and lines were meaningless at first, without context on an expanse of white. Little by little, features took form, and soon the face became familiar. I shivered, pulling my cardigan more closely around me as I held the result at arm's length.

A strong jaw swept up toward a dark hairline; heavy waves of hair fell across a forehead – too long for the shape of his face. High, wide cheekbones melted into a smooth brow, the hunter eyes beneath shadowed and crinkled with the ghost of laughter. A straight nose and sculpted lips completed the image, pulled into a half-smile. Apparently my subconscious had been dwelling on my stranger. Cole.

Before I stopped to consider it, I'd crossed the room for my pastels. In short, quick movements, I highlighted the warm chocolate tones of his hair and the freckles across the bridge of his nose. His eyes were more difficult. None of the colours in my box were quite right, and despite my blending of greens, browns and even blues, I couldn't find the right combination to create the golden flecks that were so unusual and, well, gorgeous. Apparently 'genuinely stunning' wasn't a standard colour in my pastel set.

I stared hard at the drawing. The resemblance to Jon was still there – I hadn't imagined it. But now I had a name for him and had heard his voice, the differences were clear. I shook my head, rolled up the sketch and snapped an elastic band over it. Now wasn't the time for my musings, but I still wanted to finish it. I shoved it in my satchel to think about later, and my stomach gave a loud growl.

As always, time had flown while I was drawing. I made my way slowly downstairs, bringing the satchel with me, though I couldn't have said why. Cooking was more of a Tom thing, really, but I could hunt in the kitchen, too, and soon tracked down a tin of soup. A glance at the kitchen clock said it was almost one.

I stirred the pan, pondering the drawing. No. Thinking about Cole. It wasn't only his face that had been familiar – his voice, his mannerisms, even his laugh made me feel like I'd met him before. But I knew I hadn't. I'd remember. So why couldn't I get him out of my head?

I wondered what Maggie would make of him. She'd probably tease me mercilessly about meeting a mysterious Scot in the dark, but her eyes would light up at the romance of it all. Fuck knows, I had no other female friends to share this sort of thing with – even if I did have to fudge half of the story.

I grabbed a bowl from the nearest cupboard and served up.

The Gloaming

There was no harm in heading into the shop early tomorrow, before the morning rush. Maggie could fill me in on her date with Tom too, since I knew he'd just roll his eyes about Cole and be oh-so-evasive about dinner.

The soup was hot, tangy and warming in the cold of the old house, and I savoured it slowly in the chair by the bay window, watching the odd passerby hurry past. November had turned cold fast, and I didn't envy those stuck outside in the chill. Somewhere deep in the house, the thermostat clicked on. Warm air from the radiator by my feet washed over me, and sleep followed.

I woke with a gasp to a shrill, piercing sound that jolted me out of my seat. Grabbing my phone, I saw it was Tom.

"What's up?"

"Erin?" His voice was unexpectedly ragged.

"Aren't you supposed to be out with Maggie?" I asked, glancing out of the window at the fading daylight.

"I'm at her flat. I need you to get here. Now." Something was wrong. My heart plummeted. It never occurred to me to stop and think whether my ankle was fit for driving – I'd have to manage.

"I'm on my way."

Twenty minutes later, I pulled up behind an ambulance and two police cars. I spotted Tom, perched on the low wall in front of a stone building that looked to have once been a school. The streaky pink light of the violet hour contrasted with his dark hair and jacket, and as I watched he lowered his face into his hands.

I made my way over and sat beside him, glancing around for some clue as to what was going on. A pair of police officers nearby shot me a look, speaking amongst themselves. "What happened?" I asked, already dreading the answer.

He moved stiffly, indicating an open window with ugly floral glass behind us – probably a bathroom. Dried tear tracks marked his cheeks, making him appear much younger than he was.

"I got here for our date and tried knocking, but she didn't answer. I called, and I could hear her phone ringing…"

I still wasn't sure what he was getting at. *Or you don't want to get it.*

"Is she… hurt?"

Tom shook his head and glared at the two officers who were still standing by the door, speaking in undertones to a paramedic. A small group had gathered by the barriers that had been placed a few metres down the street. "They think she killed herself."

A shiver of horror made its way down my spine. This couldn't be happening.

"She can't have," he continued. "I saw her an hour ago at the shop, and she was fine. We booked a table for tonight, so she can't have, right?"

He stared at me, but I didn't have the answers he needed.

"It's like—" He cut himself off.

Jonathan. I didn't say it, but there wasn't a single part of me that believed this was a coincidence. It hadn't even been a week, but Maggie's death was one more piece in the puzzle, and the message was clearer than ever: this was personal.

I swallowed, chewing it over. "Was it the same? With the… you know, the wire?" A police officer moved towards us. "I know it's not—"

Tom shook his head again, staring at the ground this time. I couldn't tell him it would be alright – I'd be lying to him. I'd pulled him into this shitty little dark corner of reality, and now I had to get us out of it. I just didn't see how the hell I would manage it.

"Excuse me? Sir?" The young officer standing by the curb was

The Gloaming

barely more than a teenager, and I suspected he'd swapped his acne cream for a badge about fifteen minutes ago. "We've got a few more questions for you about Miss Everett, if you wouldn't mind?" He shifted from foot to foot. The reek of his nervous sweat was pungent, even from a few feet away. It was probably the first death he'd dealt with.

I turned aside from the scene, allowing Tom some privacy as my thoughts raced. Something glinted behind the ambulance, the light bouncing from Maggie's flat windows and momentarily blinding me. Squinting, I stood up to see beyond the rows of cars parked on the cramped road and spotted a familiar pale, golden head.

What the hell was Adam Locke doing climbing out of a sleek black Maserati at a crime scene? Who was he?

As I watched, a dark head joined him from the passenger side, and dread twisted in my stomach. Even in profile, she was unmistakable, but the pixilated image on Tom's laptop had barely captured her. Austere and commanding despite her small stature, raw power radiated from her, and my senses recoiled despite the distance. Though Adam seemed tense and unhappy in the last of the indigo evening light, they made a striking pair – bright and dark. I swallowed.

What have you gotten yourself into now?

It took everything in me to turn my back to them and act as though I was engaged in conversation with Tom and the police officer. My skin crawled with goosebumps, and I shuddered. But Tom hadn't seen a thing.

I kept my face turned away, my teeth on edge and my heart pounding. Eventually, after expressing his sympathy for our loss, the officer told Tom he was free to go. Releasing the breath I'd been holding, I risked a glance behind, but Adam and Wyatt had gone.

6
How Much More Morbid Could You Be?

THE DAYS BLURRED TOGETHER, A cycle of frenzied thoughts, panic, worry and if I was honest, a fair amount of fear. To top it off, I felt like a complete idiot – Tom had been right about Wyatt, and I hadn't taken him seriously. This was my fault, and the guilt was piling up.

I wanted to talk to him about it, but when we'd returned that night he was having none of it. While my mind raced, worrying about what all this meant and how the hell I was supposed to deal with it all, he was detached and distracted, passing his days in the chair by the window and staring into nothingness. I couldn't tell him what I'd seen – not while he was in this state – and I'd never known him like this. He'd been friends with Jon for over a decade and worked with Maggie for less than a year, but his grief seemed more raw when it came to her.

The problem was, I needed to get my thoughts out. That was my process, and if I could talk things through with someone, I knew I'd feel calmer. But Tom was all I had, and one look at him was enough to tell me he needed more time. Unfortunately, I'd never been known for my patience, and on the second day of silence, I cracked.

"Tom?" I approached him with caution, but he didn't look up or even react. "Look, I don't mean to be harsh, but you've gotta get out of that bloody chair."

I ran a hand through my hair, watching his reflection and mine in the glass. "Chowdhury. Fucking *wake up*." I knelt in front of him, grabbing the arms of the chair. "I need to talk to you."

It wasn't the first time I'd tried since we'd returned from Maggie's flat. And I was upset about her too – Maggie had been one of the sweetest, funniest people I'd ever known. But being a hunter meant keeping my grief at arm's length, especially now I knew that Wyatt was involved. So I needed to know what Tom knew – before I buggered up again.

"Okay," I stood and leaned against the windowsill, blocking his view of the drizzly street outside. "If you won't talk, I will. Isabel Wyatt was at Maggie's."

Tom's grip on the arms of the chair tightened. "What?"

"When you were talking to the police officer. She pulled up in a car down the street with a guy I met in the shop last week." My words were almost a whisper as I confessed.

"Did they see you?"

I shook my head. "I don't think so."

Tom shifted in his chair. "Good. You'd get yourself killed."

His words hurt, though he was right. The strength I'd felt from Wyatt had been unlike anything I'd ever known, even at a distance. My skin crawled in memory, and for the first time in a long time, I was scared. I fought a lot of vampires, and I was damn good at it, but she was something different.

I should have taken Tom more seriously. I should have been protecting Maggie, but I hadn't even considered it. I searched for the words to apologise – this was well and truly my fault. But a tiny part of me couldn't help but think that if I'd protected her, we wouldn't know for certain about Wyatt right now. We'd have nothing more to go on than we had before. It was a horrid, traitorous thought – but it was true.

AFTER OUR BRIEF CHAT, TOM WENT right back to his creepy silence. I brought him sandwiches, mugs of tea… I even went out and fetched his favourite pastries, but he barely touched them. I wasn't sure if he was grieving or just pissed at me, but I suspected it might be a bit of both. Still, he hadn't left. He stayed, and there was some comfort in that.

The morning of Jon's funeral came around fast, the dawn dark and cold. I'd planned to stay away from Jolt and its distractions for the day, but standing by my bedroom window and cradling a hot mug of coffee, I changed my mind.

I stared at my bed. I'd laid out a smart black dress and tights for later that day, but they looked pathetic and rumpled against the dark red sheets. Jon would've found the idea of me in a dress hilarious – I was more the chunky Doc Martens and jeans type – and I wondered if we should have tried harder to get involved in the funeral plans. Would Jon be mad that everyone was in formalwear? *Duh, Erin.*

Branches from the tree outside my window scratched against the glass as a blast of wind rolled down the street. The sky was only now beginning to grow light, but I'd been awake for well over an hour already. Despite my utter exhaustion from the long, solo days in the shop, sleeping well had become a thing of the past. Tom needed time before coming back. Hell, I'd needed time. I was drowning on my own.

Pulling my cardigan more closely around me, I turned back to stare at the dress on the bed. I hated this. I couldn't sit and wait all morning to say goodbye, when he was already long gone. Gulping down the last of my coffee, I headed for the shower. I'd go and collect the post. It was a mundane way to find some normalcy in a day that shouldn't even be happening, but it was what I had.

Once I'd scraped the ice off my car windscreen, it didn't take long to get to Jolt. The sun had only just breached the horizon in my rearview mirror, and by the time I pulled up its pale glow was beginning to reflect off the gold lettering on the glass front door. The shop was warmer than I'd expected inside as I scooped up the pile of junk mail and bills that must have been delivered the previous afternoon.

Sorting through the bits and pieces, one envelope in particular stood out. Palest blue. Heavy textured paper. Expensive. I sliced open the top with a knife and a single sheet fluttered to the ground. The sloping cursive was unfamiliar, but the name and phone number at the bottom were clear enough.

It is not as it may have appeared. Please call at your earliest convenience.
Adam Locke

Shit. It hadn't even occurred to me that Adam might have seen me at Maggie's. He'd seemed almost as on edge as I was, but that was all I could really remember, what with Wyatt showing up. I couldn't think of anything else he could be referring to, though. Maybe my observational skills were on the fritz.

The Gloaming

The bell over the door jingled merrily and I glanced at the clock on my phone. It was only just seven – well before opening time, even if we were open today. But the person walking through the door wasn't exactly a regular.

"Well, if it isnae my midnight wanderer."

Standing near the door with his face in shadow, the smile in his already familiar voice was clear. Even in the dim light, there was something easy about the way he moved as he stepped inside, all quiet confidence. His presence made the shop feel smaller.

"Cole, right?" He knew I knew his name. But what else was I supposed to say?

"The verra one." Walking toward the counter, he took in the shop with apparent interest. "So, this is where you spend your days, eh?"

I shoved the blue paper deep into my satchel and pulled the leather flap down, suddenly over-conscious of the drawing still inside. "Mostly the ones that end in 'y', yeah. We're not actually open—"

"I didnae think so at this hour," he interrupted. "But I spotted ye through the glass and had to say hello." As he spoke, he leaned against the worn wood of the counter, the movement drawing my eyes to the way his shirt pulled taut across his broad shoulders. His green and gold eyes danced with amusement as he watched me right back. I found myself noticing details I'd missed in the dark – how his mahogany hair caught the golden shades of the light, curling a little at the back of his neck, and the strong forearms revealed beneath his rolled-up sleeves when he removed his coat. "Seems you're on my route home. Night shift."

"Just happened to be passing, did you?" I tried not to sound as flustered as I felt.

"I doubt anything 'just' happens around you, lass." The corner of his mouth twitched.

I resisted a small smile, unsure what to say. Today was supposed to be about Jonathan, and yet here I was, tongue-tied over a stranger who happened to remind me of him. *Get a grip, Erin.*

Cole studied me over the top of the till, his quiet assessment accompanied by a faint crooked smile. I thought back to the odd look he'd given me before, the one I'd interpreted as disbelief. I still didn't understand it.

"How're ye farin'? After your fall, and all?"

I raised both eyebrows and shrugged. "I'm walking and talking. My ankle's still dodgy, but I'll live."

He nodded, still studying me. "Aye, you seem well enough."

"Do you want a coffee?" I asked, turning away from him to busy myself washing the cups. "This is a coffee shop, after all."

"I'm fine, thanks," he replied. "No sure the caffeine'll do me much good at this point." I watched his reflection in the shiny chrome of the espresso machine as he straightened and rubbed a hand across the back of his neck. "Need any help?"

I shot him a quick grin. "Chivalrous as ever, eh?"

His eyes twinkled, and he made his way around the counter. "If you say so, lass."

I pointed him to an apron, and once he'd tied it on, we got to work in amiable silence. It was bizarre, having him here like this. I didn't really know anything about him, except that he was pretty good under pressure and smelled *great* – like the forest after a storm, or something. But he was also infinitely better company than I'd had of late.

As I scrubbed at a particularly stubborn coffee stain on a mug, I glanced over at him carefully stacking plates.

The Gloaming

"So… night shift. And handy in a crisis. But you said you're not a doctor?" I asked, unable to contain my curiosity.

Cole's mouth twitched into that half-smile that was becoming dangerously familiar. "I think you'll find I said nothing o' the sort."

"Evasive too. Intriguing." I raised an eyebrow at him, resting against the counter.

"Aye, well that seems to be fair common these days." He threw me a thoughtful look, his eyes bright even in the dim morning light. "Out for a walk in the middle o' the night, and all that."

Okay, fair point. I turned back to the sink, returning to the impossible-to-shift stain.

"So what do you do besides rescue concussed women in parks? And wash dirty coffee cups?" I asked over my shoulder.

He considered the question for a moment, folding a dishtowel into precise thirds. "A wee bit of this and that."

I spun around, my hands dripping with soapy water. "Evasive again? Really?" I placed the last clean mug on the draining board, balancing it precariously. "Who *are* you, Cole? There must be more to you than a half-smile and a sexy accent?"

Cole's eyes crinkled as he smirked, catching the mug before it could topple over. "Sexy, is it? Good to know." His voice dropped slightly. "But I ken your meanin'. Only I dinnae ken *you*, lass. Do I no deserve to learn about my interrogator?"

I sighed and dried my hands. "Sure. Ask away."

"You own this place?" He picked up another mug.

"I do. Co-owner with a friend of mine, Tom." I watched his long fingers work the cloth over the ceramic with hypnotic precision.

"And when you're no falling through ceilings and serving coffee? You read?" He indicated the bookshelves with a nod of his head, a dark lock of hair falling into his eyes before he shook it away.

I reached up to tuck a strand of my own hair behind my ear, abruptly aware of how dishevelled I must look. His eyes followed my hand. "When I have the time for it, yeah. Time seems to be in short supply though."

"Aye, I can imagine so." He nodded. "You draw?"

I froze. "How did you know?"

"Your name's below the sketch on the wall back there." He gestured toward the door with the tea towel. "Seemed too much to assume there was more than one Erin workin' here."

He was observant, I'd give him that much. Hopefully not so observant that he'd force me to lie to him. I busied myself with re-organising the clean cups, avoiding his gaze.

"No, no other Erins. Reading, painting, music, coffee. That about sums me up."

His face lit up, eyebrows raised. "Music?"

I couldn't help but smile at his sudden enthusiasm. "You're into your music, huh?"

"Aye, ye might say that." He leaned back on the counter, animated in a way I hadn't yet seen him.

Well at least Jon would approve of this guy.

"Listening or playing?" I asked.

He ran a hand through his hair, leaving it slightly mussed in a way that was unfairly attractive. "Both. I havnae played an instrument for many a year, but that doesnae mean I'm done doin' so."

"What sort of music?" I folded my arms across my chest and watched him as he thought it through.

"Ach, what a question." He stretched an arm up to rub the back of his neck. "A wee bit o' everythin', mostly. Anything with a melody. Wi' a *heart*."

"Favourite song?" I pressed.

"I couldnae say. Tis different every day."

I unfolded my arms and stepped a little closer, feigning nonchalance as I glanced up at him. He was so bloody tall. "And today?"

He met my eyes, his own gold-flecked ones intense. "'*Lover, You Should've Come Over.*'"

I swallowed. I knew it. I loved it. And I couldn't help but feel a slow warmth spreading in my lower belly at the way he looked at me as said it. Something in his expression made me feel like I was missing something important.

He raised a quick eyebrow and threw me that crooked smile again. I cleared my throat and turned back to the glasses on the counter, putting some distance between us.

"It's a good song." I managed eventually.

"Aye." He paused for a moment, tapping his long fingers on the counter. "This Tom you mentioned… he's just a friend?"

I laughed. "Yes, just a friend."

He took a minute to process this. "And you dinnae have any other… friends?"

The question caught me off-guard. I placed the last cup in the cabinet with extra care. "No, not really."

He didn't reply, and I didn't break the silence. It hadn't occurred to me to think about it that way. My circle had been small for so long… and now it was just me and Tom.

After a few minutes, he paused, dish towel in mid-air. "Is everything alright? I didnae mean to upset ye, lass. Only, ye seem… sad, now. Not that I'd assume my presence would light up a room of course, but…" A wolfish grin crossed his face. "It usually does."

"Oh yeah?" I shook my head, shaking off the feeling and holding back a laugh. "No, I get that a lot. Resting bitch face and all that."

He didn't seem convinced. "You're sure?"

I wanted to tell him my secrets. I wanted to get to know him, and for him to know me. Maybe it was because he was a stranger, or maybe I was tired of holding it all in. Either way, it didn't matter. My secrets were secrets for a reason.

"I'm going to a funeral this afternoon," I said. "So yeah, I suppose you could say I'm sad."

"Ah. Someone you were close to?"

I swallowed. "My best friend. And the whole place will be full of people who think he killed himself." *Stop it, Erin.*

"Did he?" His tone was innocent enough, but there was real curiosity there. Suicide seemed to bring that out in people.

"No. He wasn't capable of it." Why was I telling him the truth? "There was too much life in Jon for that."

Cole didn't respond, slowly drying the inside of a cup and placing it on the counter beside the others.

"I don't mean to bare my soul or anything. I'm just pissed about the whole thing." I pulled the plug from the sink with more force than was necessary, splashing water all down my front. "And I miss him," I added quietly.

When I went to grab a towel, Cole was standing close behind me. My fingertips barely brushed the sleeve of his shirt, but it was enough to set my skin alight. I was suddenly very aware of how his height made me feel small, how his presence seemed to fill the narrow space between the counters, the cool air between us charged with something I didn't want to name yet.

"Aye," he said, voice low. "I can tell."

The Gloaming

I tried to shrug it off and faced the sink again. "I'm not sure what I'm supposed to do without him. This place—" I gestured to the huge espresso machine, the mismatched tables and the bookshelves pressed against the walls. "It was *ours*, all of us, and now he's gone and I'm supposed to do it on my own. It's too much, and all I can think about is the stupid bloody dress…" I knew I was rambling, but the words held back my threatening tears.

"A dress?" The corner of his mouth twitched as I glanced up.

I shook my head. "I got a dress out to wear, and I feel like Jon would laugh at me for wearing it, but I don't know what else to do."

Cole's chuckle reverberated in the small space between us, and I fell into its contagious rumble, laughing with him and marvelling as it filled my heart with something beyond heaviness and grief.

"Aye, well that's one thing to focus on," he said when we finally quieted down. "But think o' it this way: your friend, Jon, you said? Would he truly mock you?"

I snorted. "Honestly, he wouldn't give a shit what I wore."

"Then there you have it, love," Cole tilted his head, a mischievous glint in his eye. "Wear the damn dress." He paused, then added, "Sometimes the best tribute is showin' the world you're still here, dress and all."

THE WAKE WAS UNBEARABLE FROM start to finish.

"Such a waste…" I had no idea who said it first, but it was on everyone's lips as we walked from the graveside, the cloying perfume of coffin lilies lingering in the cold air. I searched for Tom, hoping to find his hand and some comfort, but he was already at the gates, making polite conversation with Jim. I caught the end of their conversation as I got closer.

"… young. I can't imagine what he must have been feeling. So lost and alone and with no other way out."

I grimaced, and for a second, I thought Tom was trying to catch my eye – I'd been surprised to find him already dressed and ready to leave when I returned from the shop, but even now he was still keeping his distance. I mean, I wanted to grieve in peace and everything, but that peace included Tom. Instead, we were ignoring each other while we made idle chit-chat with strangers, all the time perpetuating the lie.

As the wake drew to a close, I peered around to see where Tom had gotten to, knowing what had to come next would be easier to deal with if he was there with me. Almost everyone was gone – just a few staff clearing away trays of leftover food and rearranging chairs remained. *On your own again then, Erin.*

Maggie's funeral was the following day, which meant it was my last chance to find out more about her death. Grabbing my coat from the cloakroom, I gave the room one last glance before heading to my car. Turning up the music and singing along loudly, I tried to distract myself. *Not exactly a day I want to remember*, I thought. Nothing about it reflected my grief, or how I'd felt about my friend.

I pulled up outside the Medico-Legal Centre as the sun was going down – though it had barely gotten light anyway. The city's public mortuary was inside, but though I dealt with death regularly, I'd never had much occasion to visit in person before. Unfortunately, it was time to get hands-on. Now that I'd seen Wyatt here in the city with my own two eyes, I knew the only way to get what I needed was in the square, red brick building in front of me. I got out of the car and closed the door quietly, wishing I'd changed out of my funeral dress.

The whole drive I'd gone over scenarios and backstories, trying to come up with a viable reason a coffee shop owner might need to see her friend's corpse. Pushing through the double doors at the entrance, it quickly became apparent that there wasn't all that much in the way of security in a place like this – in fact, there might be cover enough for me to quickly sneak my way into the back. There was a reception desk in the lobby, but while the computer was humming quietly, there was no one manning it. As calmly as I could, I hurried past and through the door behind, the overpowering scent of air freshener stinging my nose – not quite strong enough to cover the stench of death.

The long corridor beyond had several doors dotted along it. They appeared to lead to offices, but that wasn't what I was after. Tom and I had been exploring the coroner's computer servers for years, so it had been no problem to discover there was never any intent to open a formal inquest into Maggie's death. However, I also knew it was standard procedure to carry out a post-mortem examination on suicide cases. The only snag was that this particular coroner was pretty old school – which meant if I wanted to learn anything useful, I needed the hard copies of his notes.

I finally spotted the door I wanted at the end of the hall and was almost through it when someone called out behind me. I swore under my breath.

Mind racing, I breathed a sigh of relief at the face that greeted me.

"Bradley!" I smiled, "Holy fuck, you scared the shit out of me!"

"Erin?" he whispered, clearly annoyed. "What the hell are you doing here?"

"You know, the usual." I jerked my head towards the door behind me. "I won't be a minute, I promise."

Bradley pulled a face, his rich, dark skin puckering around his mouth as he thought it through.

"I wouldn't be here if I didn't have to be," I insisted. "Especially this time."

"I know," he sighed. "But Carl's got it in for me at the minute, reckons I've been stealing his lunch or some rubbish. I know full well it's Brenda on reception that takes those stupid mini cheeses he eats, but—"

"Your workplace drama is remarkably normal for someone who cuts up dead people for a living."

"Says the woman who hunts vampires," he muttered. "At least my clients don't fight back."

I held back the threatening eye roll and went with it. "You can handle Carl, Brad. You always do. And I'll owe you one – I just need to see something." I gave him my best pleading look. I'd known the pathologist a few years now, having bumped into him repeatedly at suspicious crime scenes – and I couldn't forget the childish rivalry between him and his elderly co-worker.

"You owe me about six already, and I don't know what you think you've got to offer to pay me back." He huffed as he said it, but was already leading me back along the corridor, fumbling with a keychain before unlocking the final door. "I don't get why you're so interested in what's in there anyway, it's only a suicide. Not your remit, right?"

"You'd be amazed at what's become my remit," I murmured, following him through.

"I don't want to know." He shook his head. "Just get done what you've got to and go. She's due to be picked up in the next hour, anyway."

I nodded, swallowing as I took in the wall of steel. Most of the deaths on this side of the city came through here eventually. One day, so would I. Hopefully not any time soon.

Bradley didn't seem to notice my apprehension and crossed over to the nearest drawer, pulling it out without a word. I turned my face away. I knew I had to look, but now the moment was here, I felt woefully under prepared.

"Margaret Elizabeth Everett," he read aloud from the hastily scrawled label on the drawer.

"Do you have the full file for her?" I asked, still staring at the white tiled floor. I'd never known Maggie and I shared a middle name. I shook myself as a wave of nausea rolled over me, suddenly eternally grateful for the awful aftershave Brad wore, that was apparently potent enough to block out any additional odours in the room.

"Give me a moment, I'll be back," he replied, closing the door behind him and leaving me alone with her.

I raised my eyes to the steel drawer. There was a crisp white sheet over her body, but her head had been left uncovered. Her unruly curls of ginger hair looked different somehow – too bright against her stark, waxy skin. She didn't look like my friend at all.

Maggie had been the first person we'd recruited at Jolt. Despite our best intentions, it hadn't taken long before Jonathan, Tom and I had realised we weren't up to organising a business ourselves. Jon had recruited her, though it occurred to me now he'd never said how – we'd just accepted she'd had an amazing trial day, and even better: she understood the accounts. Maybe Tom would have talked to her about how she'd got the job if they'd ever managed to go on that date. She and Tom might have talked about a lot of things. We'd never know.

Swallowing back the tears I'd contained earlier, I hardened myself. I hadn't had the opportunity to examine Jon's body for clues – and given the circumstances, I was happier not to have to see what the killer had left of him – but I *needed* to find something on Maggie to point me in the right direction. The tang of copper filled my mouth, my heightened senses confirming that her body had come into contact with a vampire recently – but it wasn't enough.

Walking around to the other side of the drawer, I examined her face and hair again. Nothing seemed amiss, but I hadn't expected it to. There was no way Wyatt had survived this long and been sloppy to boot. I pulled back the sheet, silently apologising.

The colour was bleached from her skin, no longer the creamy smoothness I'd once envied. Vertical cuts at her wrists had been stitched neatly together along the veins, but I could see they were deep. Probably deeper than I'd expect the average person to be able to make unaided, but I wasn't a professional. It was the method I'd been expecting, given that she'd been found in a bathroom. But a glance showed me nothing else was unusual – there wasn't even a puncture wound. I pulled the sheet carefully back over her and sighed. *Now what?*

I might not have believed Tom about Wyatt initially, but that didn't mean I hadn't done the reading – there had been killings like this before. And I couldn't help but notice how it echoed one of the many myths about the origins of the vampire species; women who would bathe in the blood of the young to preserve their youth and live forever, never ageing. It was sick.

Bradley snuck back in as I was closing the drawer up. He handed me a thin paper file in a brown wallet, glancing back into

The Gloaming

the hall behind.

"Did anyone see you?"

"Of course they did, but I work here – I'm not the one behaving suspiciously," he snapped back.

I ignored him, opening the file. As well as photos of Maggie's injuries and details from the post-mortem scribbled in an almost illegible hand, there were images from the crime scene. I pulled them out and spread them across the small, immaculately tidy desk in the corner.

"Do you normally keep this kind of thing?" I asked. If I was honest, I hadn't been expecting anything this useful.

Bradley shuffled his feet. "It's not typical, no. But since… well, some of the things you've told me about the stuff going on – I figured there was no harm in being a bit more thorough. It's another reason Carl's pissed off with me, actually; he thinks I'm being unnecessarily morbid," he explained.

"You're a pathologist," I pointed out. "How much more morbid could you be?"

He gave me a small smile and a shrug. "You'd think it would be part of the job description, but apparently there's a sweet spot."

I worked my way from one end of the table to the other, examining each picture. Most of them had been taken after Maggie had been removed from the scene, and I recognised the patterned glass of her bathroom window in the background. The bathtub was full of deep pink water, but it wasn't the crimson you'd normally expect – unless vampires were involved, of course. I pointed this out to Bradley.

"Yeah, I wondered about that," he agreed. "Some of the other details don't add up either – I mean, even the water temperature must have been perfectly regulated, kept exactly above the point where blood stops clotting. You wouldn't normally see that kind of precision in a suicide." He shifted uncomfortably. "Reminds me of some case studies I read about Nazi medical experiments, actually. But Carl's written up plenty of explanations, and I left him to it. I keep noticing details that don't quite fit, and he hates it when I do that." He paused. "You don't think she killed herself, then?"

"I know she didn't. I even think the person who killed her showed up at the crime scene. I've just got to prove it before anyone else gets hurt." I selected a wide-angled photo taken from the doorway that showed the full room. "Somehow," I added quietly.

It wasn't a large bathroom. The sink was on top of a small, white unit right by the side of the tub. And by the sink was a tiny spray of flowers. I didn't recognise the blooms, but alarm bells rang in my head.

"Do you know what kind of plant that is?" I asked Bradley, pulling out my phone to take a close-up of the image with the sink.

He examined the photograph and shook his head. "Why?"

"Didn't anyone think it was weird, that they were just lying there?" I spoke more to myself than to him.

"It's not that strange. People seem to romanticise death in cases like this – we'll arrive on the scene to rose petals, candles burning, music playing, the lot."

Tom had said Wyatt left coins or flowers at her scenes – and Maggie was severely allergic to all kinds of pollen.

"She had seriously bad hay fever. She suffered from it year-round." I told him. It wasn't much, but it was something.

"You think it's a calling card?" I could tell he wasn't happy with the idea.

"I do," I replied, pulling myself out of my thoughts. "Yeah. I think I've got what I needed." I hurriedly gathered the photographs and rammed them back into the folder, passing it back to Bradley.

"Are you sure?" he asked. "There are more somewhere, I kept as much as I could—"

"No, you're fine Brad," I answered. "You've already done more than I was expecting. Unless – you didn't happen to notice if there were coins anywhere in the bathroom? Like, I dunno, coins that you'd have noticed?" It was a long shot, but still.

He waited before answering. "I don't think so. I mean, people leave money lying around. I don't think I'd have given it a second thought." He sounded apologetic as we closed the door behind us, lowering his voice as we made our way down the corridor as quietly as possible.

"That's okay," I reassured him. "It was worth asking."

The reception was still empty as he followed me out. I wondered where the receptionist could be.

"So – you don't think this woman killed herself? It was one of your guys?" Bradley asked as I went to leave.

I looked up at him, gangly in his lab coat. I sometimes forgot how young he was. "I thought you didn't want to know?" I sighed. "Yeah, I'm pretty certain. But there's nothing you can do other than keep an eye out," I added, quashing his protests. "We couldn't prove it if we tried. And you need to keep your head down and stay safe."

He nodded, his mouth downturned. "Let me know if there's anything else you need," he said instead of a goodbye. I made my way out to the car without responding. He was another person to keep out of it. Wyatt was my problem to fix.

7
More Than Mortality Allows

When I got home, Tom was asleep in my favourite armchair. Part of me wondered why he kept coming back here if he wasn't going to speak to me – his breathing was a little too heavy for real sleep – but then I didn't want to be on my own, either. But I wasn't in the mood to convince him to talk, even if it meant keeping what I'd learned about Maggie's death to myself. Her funeral was tomorrow, and it could wait a little longer.

As it turned out, Tom had no intention of going.

"I can't."

"It's just a few hours. People will miss you if you don't go," I begged.

But no amount of cajoling would get him to move. I went alone, still limping slightly as I wove my way through the heavy autumn rain to the graveside. There were more people than the previous day – probably more people than I'd ever met. But Maggie had a full life, complete with friends, family and people who genuinely loved her. Jonathan hadn't had the chance for anything like that. He'd been pulled into my darkness early on, at the expense of everything else. It was no wonder the two events were so vastly different.

A grey-haired man in a suit spoke words over Maggie's coffin, repeatedly calling her Margaret, which she'd never been a fan of. I barely heard him. I was on edge, unable to shake the feeling of being watched by eyes hidden beneath the many umbrellas around the graveside. The wind picked up, and I didn't stay for the wake. There were too many questions I couldn't answer truthfully, and my guilt was inescapable – chilling me far more than the English winter.

On the way home I cranked up my car's sound system as loud as it would go and made a deal with myself. No matter what happened this afternoon, I would go to work the next morning. This limbo could only go on for so long, and as much as working alone was weird, the distraction would be welcome. Maybe I'd force Tom to come with me – I reckoned I could dress him myself and drag him by his hair if push came to shove.

The house was filled with an unexpected warmth and spice when I stepped through the front door, shrugging off my coat. I breathed it in, shaking out my damp curls. Ginger, maybe? And something deeper, earthier – cardamom? The scent wrapped around me like a blanket, and I followed it into the kitchen.

Tom was standing over the stove, his back to me as he stirred a small pot. Several tiny bowls were arranged in a precise row on the counter beside him. A stick of cinnamon, star-shaped pods, and what looked like black peppercorns – all waiting their turn.

"You're cooking?" I asked, my voice still rough from trying to keep my shit together.

He glanced over his shoulder and nodded. "Proper chai. Not that powdered crap we serve." He gestured with his wooden spoon to a chair. "Sit."

I sank down into it, grateful that he was at least animated

again. Scrawl-filled notepads and empty coffee mugs were scattered across the table, so he'd clearly been researching before this odd new behaviour began.

"I didn't know you could make it from scratch," I said, watching him crush something between his fingers before adding it to the pot.

Tom's shoulders tensed slightly. "Yeah. It's my grandmother's recipe, actually. She'd make it whenever someone…" He trailed off, focusing intently on the pot. "I was going to teach Maggie how to make it. Maybe put it on the menu."

He tapped the spoon against the side of the pot a little too forcefully.

I didn't say anything. The last thing I needed was to send him back into a zombie state with a careless word or look.

"She said she'd never had real chai before," he said quietly. "It seemed like an important thing to fix."

The liquid in the pot reached a simmer, releasing another wave of fragrance. He added what looked like loose black tea and a splash of milk.

"Shit," he muttered after a moment, setting down the spoon. "I'm out of star anise." He rubbed a hand across his face. "I'll pop out. I can grab some sandwiches too, while I'm at it – I dunno about you, but I'm starving."

I nodded, my stomach grumbling in confirmation. "It smells amazing, Tom."

A ghost of a smile touched his lips. "It's medicinal." He paused, halfway to the door. "We should still add it to the menu. The real thing. Maggie would have…" He swallowed hard. "She'd have liked that."

Before I could respond, he grabbed his keys and slipped out, leaving me alone with the comforting aroma of spices and a grief that even his grandmother's recipe couldn't quite resolve.

Padding back into the living room, my tights slipping on the bare floorboards, I noticed his laptop was still switched on at the bureau. I sat down to read the article he'd left open while I waited for him to come back, unsure if I should interfere with his pan or not. The name Nicholas Murray was highlighted across the page, and I skim-read it at speed, frowning. There were some disturbing and familiar patterns to this guy's MO. Red-headed women, ritual murder – I had to assume this was the Wyatt accomplice that Tom had mentioned.

I sat back and took a deep breath. This wasn't what we did. Sheffield had its share of vamps, like any major city. There was a dark history here, sure – but serial killings that lasted for decades? That sounded more like a murder documentary than my life. It was well beyond anything we had experience with.

A quiet knock on the door shook me from my trance, and I slammed the laptop closed.

"Did you—?" I stopped with the door half open as I recognised the person in the doorway.

"Hello, Erin." Adam's smile was friendly as he stepped past me into the hall. "Could we talk?"

I closed the front door without a word and followed him into the living room. He stood by the fireplace, running a hand along the mantelpiece and gazing up at the ceiling.

So much for your self-preservation instincts, Erin.

"What a lovely home. Quite typical of the period, of course, but a well-preserved example." He seemed perfectly at ease, despite his lack of invitation.

I didn't know how to react. I cast my senses out toward him, but they hit a wall. There was absolutely nothing there. As far as my confusing and weird sixth sense was concerned, I was alone – and I might have convinced myself that was actually the case, if not for the exotic aroma of what I assumed to be his expensive cologne.

"What are you—" I started, but he cut across me.

"Let me correct myself – I do not require you to talk. In fact, all I require from you is a ready ear. Please, listen."

I slumped onto the sofa. This couldn't be happening. I should be afraid of Adam. I'd already seen for myself who he associated with – though he'd seemed like a decent enough guy when we'd met at Jolt. But as I looked up at him standing by the fireplace, the milky afternoon light highlighting the silvery shades of his blonde hair, I realised why I wasn't panicking. It wasn't dark yet.

"You're not a vampire?" The words were out of my mouth before I could stop them.

"Of course not," he pulled a face. "But that was an effective segue into why I'm here."

With those few words, I understood he'd never been who I thought he was. There was no way he'd been at the coffee shop by coincidence. *There's always more to it, Erin.*

Adam took a seat on the other, less comfortable sofa across from me, smoothed the creases from his shirt, and entwined his fingers together before him – watching me all the while.

"So Wyatt is a friend of yours," I stated dully, throwing out all pretences.

"Aren't *we* friends?" he asked, his eyes penetrating. I'd forgotten how attractively, intimidatingly blonde he was.

"I barely know you, Adam. I've met you once – which I'm guessing was no accident – and now, somehow, here you are." My tone was as neutral as I could manage, but my frustration seeped through.

"Yes. If you recall, I did try to contact you in a less invasive manner. But since you failed to respond, my hand was forced." He leaned forward, his voice urgent. "Izzie is here. I have no doubt you're already aware of who she is and so on… but unfortunately, I am here to tell you she is not involved in this particular… spree."

"Of course you'd say that," I retorted. "You seemed pretty chummy, last time I saw you both."

"I am no friend of Isabel Wyatt. She and I may have known each other a long time, but I would insist that *barely tolerated acquaintance* is a more apt description." A sneer marred his mouth for a moment before he expertly hid it.

I shook my head. "Then why have you come to defend her? I was ready to believe she wasn't even in the city until I saw the two of you at Maggie's."

"The woman from the coffee shop?" He paused in thought, and an odd look passed over his face. "Yes, that would make sense…" he spoke to himself. "But loath as I am to admit it, Izzie has nothing to do with this."

"Who then?"

Adam sighed and crossed his legs. "Nick. Murray, or whatever he's going by these days."

Surprised, I was certain Adam read my expression before I could hide it. "Keep talking."

"You see, Nick *is* a good friend of mine. And reformed, one might say. On a mission of redemption, if you want to be dramatic about it. But Izzie is convinced that these deaths… first your friend, and now I suppose, the waitress too—"

"Jonathan and Maggie," I corrected.

The Gloaming

"Yes, yes." He dismissed my words with an impatient gesture. "Izzie believes Nick is behind it all. The style of it, you see. She's seen it all before. And I'm inclined to agree that he may have… relapsed."

"Right. So, I'm supposed to accept she's identified another murderer that conveniently puts her in the clear?" I stood up, shaking my head. "I don't know you that well, Adam, but I can tell you're not an idiot. You must know how that sounds."

"I understand—" he began, but before he could finish the front door swung open, wind gusting through the hallway. Seconds later, Tom stepped in, a soggy paper bag in one hand and a bent umbrella in the other.

"Hi?" he said blankly, looking between us. "Am I, erm… interrupting something?"

I glared at Adam, and he stood apologetically. "Adam was just leaving."

He sighed loudly but didn't protest. "Very well."

He straightened his coat out with a little flourish. Tom stepped aside as he strode out of the still-open door, paling visibly as he watched him leave.

I unpacked the sandwiches in silence, and we ate together without speaking. I'd been avoiding difficult conversations with Tom for days, so now was the perfect time to break that and explain what was going on. But how do you start something like that? *Hey, Tom – that guy who was here just now? Yeah, he's friends with that mass-murdering vamp you were telling me about. You know, the one I didn't believe was even here?*

I chewed slowly, barely tasting the food. I was already getting the details tangled up. First, there'd been Wyatt. Now this Murray character had been thrown into the mix. And technically, I'd met

Adam before everything – even Maggie's murder. But that didn't mean he wasn't involved. Fuck, this was so much more than I'd signed up for – and the scariest thing? The common element in these deaths could well be *me*.

So how could I explain myself to Tom? The one friend I'd got left, who hadn't been driven away yet even though the last murder had been his would-be-girlfriend. The more I dwelled on it, the more it felt like *my* choice to get involved in what went on in the city, way back when, might be the reason we were a target now.

I piled up the lunch plates and took them through to the kitchen. Tom cleared his throat behind me, and I jumped. I hadn't even realised he'd followed me. *Keen observation skills.*

He moved to the stove, lifting the lid on his abandoned chai. The rich aroma filled the kitchen again, momentarily masking the tension in the air.

"Ruined," he muttered, turning off the heat. "That's the second batch this week."

I watched him dump the contents into the sink, the spiced liquid disappearing down the drain. His movements were precise despite his obvious frustration, the way they always were when he was trying to maintain control.

"I got the star anise," he said quietly, placing a small paper bag on the counter. He stared at it for a moment before turning to face me.

"I'll make you a deal, Erin."

I leaned on the worktop, facing him.

"I'll tell you everything I know about what happened with Maggie." His voice broke on her name. "If you explain to me why a guy who might be an accomplice in her murder was calmly sitting in your living room."

The Gloaming

I shook my head in disbelief. "Are you accusing me of something, Tom?"

"He seemed pretty damn comfortable," he continued. "So, I think maybe I am, yeah."

I ignored the urge to defend myself and tried to answer calmly. "Adam was here to talk about Wyatt," I said. "According to *him*, she's not behind all this. But Wyatt thinks she knows who might be."

His brow furrowed. "It *was* her, then? I was right. And she didn't tell you this herself, she sent her errand boy…" he said humourlessly. "Who's she accusing?"

"Nicholas Murray."

Astonishment flickered across his face. He'd obviously not believed his own theories on that one. "No. That can't be right. All the clues point back to her, not him. His only link was the Edinburgh thing."

"Look, I don't know any more about it than you do! You came back, and I didn't let him stay to explain," I pointed out.

Tom sank into a chair, picking at a thread in the torn knee of his jeans. Minutes passed without a word.

"Maggie was in the bath when they found her," he said finally. "She… bled to death, or so the coroner claims. They cut her wrists straight along the femoral artery. There was a kitchen knife on the floor," he paused. "I doubt the ratio of blood to water was all that high."

I sighed. "It wasn't. I wanted to tell you before, but you were so…" I didn't want to sound accusatory, so I shrugged. "I went to the mortuary yesterday before they moved her. Brad was there. He got me the file from the crime scene—"

"You could have told me," Tom cut in.

"I wanted to. You've hardly been easy to talk to lately."

He didn't meet my eye as I continued.

"It sounds like you've already got most of it, anyway. But I did spot one thing. I'm guessing you haven't seen the photos?"

He shook his head. "They wouldn't let me up."

"There were flowers, Tom. Like you said."

He shot me an inscrutable look. "What kind of flowers?" On his feet, he rummaged amongst the papers on the desk, bringing back a badly scanned image of hand-drawn flowers, with an illegible scribble underneath. "Were they like this?"

I squinted at the black-and-white image, trying to bring it into focus. The blossoms might have been similar to the ones I'd seen in the photograph, but I couldn't say for certain given the resolution. I reached over to the coffee table for my phone to compare the two.

"I'd say so, yeah. I mean, it's not a great drawing…"

Tom nodded, looking as though I'd confirmed something for him.

"Does it fit in with anything we know about this Murray guy?" I asked.

"No," Tom blurted. "Well, there's the red hair, but not really. I've been digging through the archives all morning while you were… gone. Their filing system's bloody medieval, but I managed to piece some stuff together."

I eyed him sharply, but he carried on.

"When Wyatt was setting up these fake suicides, it was around the same time she was with Murray, right? I mean, it's difficult to say for certain because the stories are so sketchy, and the police reports haven't been digitised very well, if at all. Their scanners suck – as you can see." He waved the paper at me. "Their filing is worse if you can believe it."

My face twitched into a smile, and the tense atmosphere broke all at once. I sat down beside him, and he shuffled through the papers again.

"So they were together. And she's definitely here, in town."

Tom nodded. "And this Adam guy believes her? He trusts her?"

"He doesn't seem to like her very much. He said Murray was the one he was friends with, actually…." I trailed off. We finally had some solid information, despite what Tom said about the old police files. But there were a few parts that didn't quite add up.

As far as I could tell, either the infamous Izzie Misery was killing locals and trying to cover it up by pointing the finger at her old boyfriend, or she was telling the truth and this Murray person *was* behind it. There was a third option, of course, but that was even more ridiculous: that it was someone else altogether. But I'd already seen Wyatt with my own eyes, and it seemed unlikely she just happened to be here when people started to turn up dead. And there was also the matter of Adam – what the hell would drive him to deliver messages for a vampire he supposedly hated? I didn't know *what* he was, if anything, but I was sure it couldn't be anything good if Murray was his bestie.

I sighed. I knew there was only one option left if I wanted some answers.

"I need to seek Solace," I said.

Tom's head snapped up. "Is that a good idea, right now?"

"I don't see another way. You've more than exhausted the limited police data, and I'm sick of relying on shady forums for information online. She owes me one, if I remember correctly. I should be okay."

"You really want to call that favour in, for this?"

"I'm not saving it for a rainy day," I protested. "And there's no way someone as perceptive and well-connected as her didn't hear about it the moment Wyatt crossed the city limits."

"But who's to say she'll have more information than that? She can't be trusted; she's as shady as the bloody forums are." He pushed the heels of his hands into his eyes for a moment, and I waited until he could see me again before replying.

"Have I ever said I trusted a vamp? Give me a break, Tom."

He regarded me for a long minute. "Alright. 'Find Solace.' Just remember her motives aren't the same as ours."

"I know. But if she wants to keep her precious balance, she'll tell me the truth," I threatened, standing up. I stretched, admiring the yellow bruising still blotted along my arm. Tom was looking at it too.

"You'd do well to wear long sleeves, later. No sign of weakness and all that."

"That's the plan," I agreed.

8
SOLACE DOESN'T ALWAYS MEAN COMFORT

WITH NOTHING BETTER to do as I waited for the sun to set, I caught up on the rest of the notes Tom had made about Wyatt and Murray. There wasn't much. Plenty of reports of violence, but nothing I didn't already know about. And as for Adam – well, he was absent from history altogether it seemed. At least, the history we could dredge up on the internet. But there was nothing Tom couldn't uncover – he'd find something, given time.

Flipping through pages of handwritten scribble, I realised that when Tom had described Isabel Wyatt as notorious, I'd assumed he was indulging his flare for drama. But even if she'd killed a few people a year, given the time she'd been alive, her body count was astronomical. And, of course, feeding once or twice a year wouldn't be practical.

By the time four o'clock came around, my impatience was making me twitchy. The more I read, the more I couldn't stand the inactivity. My ankle had healed enough to handle my chunkiest DMs, and I laced them up methodically as I watched the last of the daylight fade from the sky. Heavy purple clouds invaded the horizon as the sunlight faded away, and I could sense a huge storm gathering to the south.

The rain was just beginning to dance against the windscreen, and I was congratulating myself on my perfect timing – I'd be safely inside Solace's before the real downpour hit – when my engine made a sickening grinding noise.

"Fuck," I muttered, glancing at the dashboard. Nothing looked amiss, no warning lights to be seen, but the sound persisted. And my car wasn't exactly a spring chicken.

I pulled over onto a quiet side street. I was only about halfway to my destination, and other than knowing where I had to *get* to, I was basically clueless. This wasn't a neighbourhood I knew well – just a route that kept me on main roads while avoiding the dodgier parts of town. I thought there might be a hospital nearby, but my mental map wasn't all that precise without the aid of Google.

I turned off the ignition, hoping that the old IT solution might work on cars too. *Have you tried turning it off and on again?* When I tried to restart, the engine made the same grinding noise, louder this time. I thumped the steering wheel.

At least I wasn't actually at Solace's yet. But I was too far from home to walk back – at least not in the pissing-it-down rain with no coat – and even further from the industrial district I was headed toward. My options were fairly limited: call Tom to come pick me up and deal with his lecture about my crappy vehicle; abandon the trip to Solace's entirely; or try and fix it myself. None of them seemed particularly appealing.

I popped the bonnet and climbed out, wincing as the first drops of rain hit my face. I was only wearing a chunky green jumper, and it was far from weather-proof. The wind cut straight through the wool.

Staring down at the engine, it may as well have been a space rocket. My knowledge of cars was about as extensive as understanding where the oil went and how to top up my wiper fluid. Everything looked filthy, decrepit and as far as I could tell, normal.

"Car trouble, eh?"

I straightened so quickly I whacked my head on the bonnet. The lilt was unmistakable. Cole stood a few paces away, an ancient black leather jacket buttoned against the crappy weather, and his hair already damp from the increasing rain.

"It's making a weird grinding noise when I try to start it," I nodded. "What are you doing here?"

He tilted his head at me with a crooked smile. "Can I see?"

I stepped aside. "You can't know any less than I do."

Approaching, he ducked his head under the bonnet, unfastening his jacket and shrugging it off as he did so. The rain was falling more steadily now, soaking through my jumper. He held the jacket out to me, already taking in the engine with what seemed like a practised eye.

"Here, lass. Ye'll catch your death in this weather."

I hesitated, but another gust of wind made my decision for me. "Thanks."

The jacket was far too big as I slipped it on, the sleeves falling past my fingers, but it was gloriously warm and buttery-soft against my skin. It smelled of him, too – the same earthy scent I'd noticed before, like the forest after a rainfall.

Cole bent over the engine, fiddling with something, now wearing only a long-sleeved white t-shirt that was rapidly becoming as soaked as my jumper. The rain plastered the fabric to his back, outlining the lean muscles beneath. As he leaned deeper in, I caught a glimpse of ink showing through the wet cotton – a tattoo of some kind curving around his ribs.

"Can ye try and start it again?" He called over his shoulder.

I slid back into the driver's seat and turned the key. The grinding was even worse.

He listened intently, then gestured for me to turn it off. "Could be your drive belt," he said, reaching further into the engine. "Sounds like it's come loose. Might be worn too."

I joined him at the front of the car, curious and sheltering my head under the bonnet. He didn't look particularly worried. "Don't tell me you can actually fix it?"

He chuckled. "Aye, I reckon I can." He pushed up his sleeves, revealing strong forearms dusted with dark hair. "Tis only a temporary solution, mind. Ye'll want to take it to a garage."

I watched as he worked, struck by the confidence in his movements. His hands were large, but his long fingers were dexterous, navigating bits and pieces that meant nothing to me with complete ease. Water streamed down his face and back, but he didn't seem to mind. The rain hitting the metal of the bonnet created a rhythmic pitter-patter, and mixed with the scent of engine oil and his distinctive smell, it all combined to make a surprisingly cosy environment. Standing in a downpour watching a near-stranger fix my car should have been weird, but something about his presence made it almost… comfortable.

"I didnae expect to see you again so soon," he said quietly, without looking up from his work. "Though I cannae say I'm disappointed."

I leaned against the car, tucking my hands into the oversized sleeves of his jacket. "You're the one making a habit of turning up in unexpected places."

A smile quirked his lips. "I work nearby. I heard your engine complainin' and… well, when I saw you climb out I couldnae resist." He glanced up, green-gold eyes sparkling with amusement despite the rain soaking his face. "And your wee car here has character. I felt sorry for it."

"Is 'character' a polite way of saying 'temperamental piece of crap?'"

He laughed warmly. "Aye, mayhap it is. But there's somethin' honest about mechanical things. The new ones, electric and the like… they're too damn quiet with their computers runnin' everything – they dinnae have a *soul* in them, like this one does." He patted what I thought was the engine with something like affection. "She might be temperamental, but she winnae shy away from tellin' ye what's wrong, either."

"You know a lot about cars." It wasn't really a question.

"I ken what I need to. I've had to learn my share." He reached for something deep within the engine compartment. "Do you have a spanner?"

"I think so, in the boot." I headed around to the back of the car and was careful to manoeuvre the toolbox out without too much noise – the last thing I needed was this hot, almost-stranger noticing that I kept a sword and a duffel bag full of weapons in my car. And I was too bloody damp to come up with an explanation for that on the fly, right now.

Bringing the toolbox around to him, I dug out the spanner and passed it over, our fingers brushing. Despite the chill, his touch sent warmth radiating up my arm. A tiny spark of something flared inside me, and my thoughts turned, unbidden, to the drawing of him, still in my satchel on the passenger seat. Why hadn't I gotten rid of it? What if he saw it, somehow?

Almost bent in half, absorbed in his task, I barely heard him as he asked: "Did you wear the dress?"

It took me a moment to register what he meant. "Yeah, I did in the end."

"And? Was it as terrible as ye thought?"

"No. And yes." I pulled his jacket closer around me. "People commented about the suicide – and I couldn't say anything, didn't feel like I could—"

He glanced up, pausing what he was doing to assess me with that unusual emerald-gold gaze of his. "Would it have helped? If they'd known? It winnae ha' brought him back, now, would it?"

I shook my head, and a small laugh escaped despite myself. "No, but it would have shut them up."

Cole's mouth quirked up into a half-smile. "Aye," he murmured, returning to his work. "And well I ken that can be enough, sometimes."

Nothing you could do would have been enough, Erin. Forget it.

I took a deep breath and huddled closer under the shelter of the bonnet. "So… engines. Have you always been interested in cars?" He might have been a relative stranger, but he didn't *have* to be. I didn't exactly have time for a relationship, but… something about him made me want to push for more.

He considered this, adjusting something I couldn't see. "I like to ken how things work, so aye, I suppose you could say that. No just cars, mind. Technology's come a long way, and I like to keep up. But I'll admit, there's more satisfaction in a-fixin' a car." He straightened, wiping his hands on his now completely transparent t-shirt. "You cannae fix a computer with just your hands and wit."

Water streamed down his face, droplets catching in his eyelashes and the stubble along his jaw as he stepped back from the engine. "Can you pop round and try it again?" he asked.

The Gloaming

I got back into the driver's seat and turned the key. This time the car started smoothly – probably better than it had in months.

Relief washed over me. Climbing back out to thank him, I found him rubbing his hands together, as if to warm them. Despite his earlier nonchalance, he seemed to be shivering now.

"Thank you," I said, trying to put my extreme gratitude into the two small words. "There was no way I could have fixed that, and Tom would have taken the piss if I'd called him…" I trailed off. "I'd basically have been stranded."

"Twas my pleasure, lass." His voice was rougher than before, either from the cold or… something else. "Though I warn ye, she needs to see a proper garage soon. That belt winnae last long."

I started to remove his jacket. "Here – you should take this back – or do you need a lift?" I still needed to get to Solace's, but a slight detour wouldn't kill me. Probably.

He shook his head, dark rain-soaked waves of hair falling into his face before he pushed them back, smearing dirt across his temple as he did. "I'll be fine, lass. You keep it for now." His eyes held mine. "That way I have an excuse to see ye again, eh?"

There was something in the way he said it – a certainty that made my pulse quicken. Standing there in the rain, rivulets of water tracing the strong, sharp lines of his face, he was absolutely breathtaking. I should have been suspicious of how he'd just happened to be nearby – it hadn't escaped my notice that he'd never answered my question – but instead of keeping my guard up, I was letting it down, instead. *Get your shit together, Erin.*

"But you're soaked," I said, stepping closer without quite meaning to. "Honestly, I'll be in the car…"

"I've weathered worse." The corner of his mouth lifted in a half-smile that made my chest ache. "Though I dinnae quite remember ever enjoying being caught in a storm quite so well."

A bolt of lightning illuminated the darkening sky, followed by a rumble of thunder that seemed to shake the ground beneath us. Neither of us moved.

"You didnae say where you were headed," he said softly.

"Just… meeting a friend." The lie came easily, but his eyes narrowed slightly. I could already read him well enough to see he saw straight through it.

"Aye, well. I suppose we all have our secrets." He reached out, almost absently, and tucked a strand of damp hair behind my ear. The gesture caught me off-guard, and I swallowed.

I stared at the smudge of engine oil by his hairline, dark against his pale skin. "You've got—" I gestured to my own face.

"Ah." He tried to wipe it away but only managed to spread it further.

"Here." I stepped closer, standing on my tiptoes to reach him and using my thumb to gently wipe away the streak. His skin was cool beneath the rainwater, and my fingertips lingered a moment too long without my consent, my entire body hyperaware of his every move. His eyes darkened almost imperceptibly, and for a second, I thought he might lean down toward me.

Thunder rumbled again, closer this time. I stepped back.

"I should get going," I said. My voice wasn't anywhere close to steady. What was it about this guy?

"Aye, the storm's near upon us." He closed the bonnet with a decisive thud. "Best no linger."

As I moved to get back in the car, he caught my arm gently. "Be careful tonight," he said, his voice low and serious. "There are things in the darkness on nights like this ye'd do well to avoid."

I raised an eyebrow at him, but he didn't elaborate. Was that a warning? Did he know something? Before I could decide, he released me with a slight bow of his head.

"Until next time, lass," he said, already backing away.

I watched in the rearview mirror as he strolled away, tall and graceful despite his sodden clothes, until the darkness and rain swallowed him.

It wasn't until I was nearly at Solace's that I realised I was still wearing his jacket, the scent of him surrounding me like a cocoon. The worn leather had already absorbed some of my body heat, creating a strange intimacy, as if I were wrapped in his arms rather than just his clothing. I should have felt uncomfortable with the intrusion into my life, but instead, I found myself hoping he was right – that our paths would cross again, and soon.

Shaking my head, I forced myself to focus. There were more important things going on. I tightened my grip on the steering wheel, ignoring the lingering heat where his fingers had touched my skin.

Solace was waiting, and I had questions that needed answers.

SOLACE'S PLACE WAS ON THE OTHER side of the city, in a mostly disused industrial neighbourhood riddled with condemned buildings and overgrown, empty lots. Some of the better-kept warehouses at one end had been converted into offices and storage facilities, but the far end of the district was almost abandoned.

It was so cold out, and I was still so soaked, that I sat idling in the car for a long minute, warming my hands against the tiny car heater. Seven – Warehouse Seven – was about as unobtrusive as it got. Bordered on either side by other, larger warehouses, the only thing that marked it as unusual was the lack of windows. To the casual observer, it was just another neglected oblong of brick and the heavy, corrugated steel that Sheffield was known for. In reality, it was the ideal den: one roll-down security shutter that never opened, bricked-up windows and a single, small, *heavily* reinforced side door. Luckily, I wasn't trying to break in.

I parked my car some distance away and stood for a moment, watching my breath cloud up in front of me. Seven had a strict no-weapons policy that I wasn't a fan of, but I'd long since accepted. Still, it made me uneasy as I made my way across the lot.

At the door, I knocked three times and waited unsheltered as heavy drops of rain fell from the overhanging roof above, narrowly missing rolling right down the inside of Cole's jacket. A male voice answered almost immediately.

"Yes?"

"I come seeking Solace," I replied. The call and response was an unspoken declaration that I didn't mean any harm. I hated it.

"And Solace you shall find."

I cringed at the screeching sound of several bolts being drawn back, and the door opened inward. Stepping into the warehouse, I scanned the room as the male locked the door behind me – one more reason I could never relax in here, no matter how often I was driven to visit. Our truce was an uneasy one, and my mouth filled with the taste of copper.

Inside, the once-white brickwork was now peeling and flaking off through neglect, but large floodlights stood in each corner, bringing some semblance of life to the open space and ensuring the central area was brightly lit. At the far end of the room was a raised platform built from old wooden pallets, criss-crossed by shadows from the truss system high above. A collection of mismatched chairs stood around it in a mockery of a royal court, and I clocked that several of the seats were already occupied. I counted the vamp who'd answered the door, six sitting in two groups and talking amongst themselves, and an eighth. She was lying on the floor to one side of the platform, unmoving, her mousy hair splayed across the pale concrete. On the dais was a moth-eaten, wing-backed velvet armchair, the once red fabric almost entirely faded to brown – guess she'd been redecorating. The vampire seated there was lounging with one foot resting on her knee, the mobile phone in her hand and the smell of dampness in the air somewhat tempering her attempt at grandeur.

"Solace," I called across the length of the room. Her eyes glistened darkly as she shot me a cool smile that didn't reach her eyes.

"Erin Alexandra Elizabeth Conrad. To what do I owe the pleasure?" She put down her phone and leaned back into the depths of her seat, as obnoxious as ever. "Did we get caught in the rain?"

I made my way down the makeshift aisle created by the chairs and raised my eyes to her – the arrangement of the room was no accident, and she smirked a little at my obvious irritation.

Solace could have been no more than sixteen when she'd been sired, but she was at least four times that by now. Her glossy black hair hung loose down to the middle of her back, swinging as she stood at my approach. She wore close-fitting jeans and a sheer black shirt that accentuated every feminine curve of her body, as striking as the many other vampires I'd met – yet Solace had a little more edge than most. As always, her dark eyes were unreadable through their heavy ringing of kohl.

"I need information," I kept my tone flat and ignored her comment. Her setup was designed to humiliate me and anyone else who needed her help, and I refused to give her any more satisfaction than I already had.

"If it were anyone other than you, I'd expect better manners, Erin." She tilted her head, examining me. "What information could I have for you that you couldn't get for yourself, hmm? I thought *you* were the local power?" Her innocent tone infuriated me, as I'm sure she knew it would.

"Well, since you seem to have acquired a frickin' throne since I last saw you, seems like you might be the one with delusions of grandeur…" I shrugged. "But I'll get to the point. Isabel Wyatt, Nicholas Murray and Adam Locke. What do you know?"

She stared long and hard at me before finally speaking. "The last one, I've got no clue," she waved a hand dismissively in a gesture reminiscent of Adam's that same morning. "I might have something on the others."

"So they're in the city?" I didn't need her confirmation on Wyatt, but I wanted what she knew about Murray.

"Do you have something to bargain with?" She lifted a dark eyebrow.

"You owe me," I reminded her.

She made a tutting noise behind her teeth. "No, Erin. I don't think I do. That last little trick of yours cost me two guys. Useless they may have been, but they were *mine*."

I tried not to smile at the memory, but I didn't have time to argue over the details of who was responsible for what.

I glanced to either side of the aisle, mentally scrambling for something to bargain with. The nearness of so many vamps put me on edge, but I did my best to ignore it. Most of them were watching Solace, waiting to see what would happen – which made the conspicuously ducked blonde head by the unconscious girl all that more noticeable. I should have spotted her straight off – it was the one I'd let go in town, after Jonathan's death. I jerked my head towards her, looking back toward Solace.

"Her," I said. "She's here, alive. I let her go."

Solace laughed coldly. "It doesn't work like that, Erin," she paused, watching me. "That was weeks ago. I want future favours, something I can *use*. If I share what I know, then you, hunter, owe me one. In fact, you'll owe me two, since I can tell you two things." She held up two fingers, her nails filed to a point.

"Right. Because one piece of information would be far too straightforward for your little court here."

"Mm-hmm. And where would be the fun in that?" Her dark eyes glittered.

My fingers twitched, itching for a weapon that wasn't there. "Fair enough. I'll play. Tell me what you know."

"First, why are you asking?" A look of calculation crept into her face, bizarrely mature on her youthful features.

I rolled my eyes. "None of your business."

She held up her hands in mock offence. "Alright, if that's how you want to be."

"Tell me what you know, and you've earned two favours," I repeated her terms.

Solace stood and assessed the vampires below her, obviously weighing up whether the information was worth keeping from them. Finally, she came forward and crouched in front of me, so she was almost at my eye level, bringing the aroma of sandalwood incense with her.

"Wyatt's in town, but you already knew that. What I can tell you is, she's wicked mad and she's stirring things up." She gave me a shrewd look. "According to my guys, she's looking for Murray –

she calls him Baird Murray – but I've given orders not to comply or approach. I can't have someone like her drawing too much attention in the city, and she's not one of mine. I don't do handouts, no matter who you are." Her voice was quiet, all humour gone.

"She's already drawn too much attention. I'm looking for her, aren't I?" I kept my voice low, too, but I knew the others would hear me.

"Yes, but so far only those in the know have noticed what she's up to. And the deaths… well, they're not enough to worry about yet, but there's more than the usual number of bodies to clean up – vampires and humans. Definitely more than I'd attribute to *you*, anyway." For a moment, she looked worried. "It's gone beyond the normal territorial stuff at this point, and it has to be her. Since you might be able to put a stop to the entitled old bat, I'll tell you what I wouldn't tell *her*." She glanced around the room, apparently checking to see who was still listening.

"He's here. Murray. He's damn good at hiding, I'll give him that much, but the cards don't lie. I can sense more energy than I'd pick up from only *one* of the Old Ones," her voice quickened. "The city is crackling with power. I can practically taste him in the air."

"No one's seen him, though?" I asked. I needed something more before my favour ran out. Solace's ability to pick up on vampire energy was unrivalled, and I needed to know everything she did.

"No," she said. "Like I said, he's good at hiding. He could be anyone."

"I'm working on a picture. That'd be a start," I confided.

Solace shook her head. "It's a waste of time. I've made it my business to know about the Old Ones, you know that – even the eyewitness accounts don't add up."

I nodded. I didn't like it, but she was probably right. Solace straightened, and our bubble of confidence broke, all business again.

It wasn't much, but it would have to be enough. I knew Solace wouldn't have mentioned Murray if she wasn't certain, whether she said so or not. I could never truly trust a vampire, but her reputation relied on her honesty, and I could trust her reputation was everything to her. If she was backing up Wyatt's story, that was something I could use.

"I'll let you know when I need to call in those favours, Erin," Solace called over her shoulder as she returned to her seat, picking up a deck of tarot cards and shuffling them deftly.

It was clear she was dismissing me, but I didn't move. As we'd talked, I'd tried to ignore the vamps in my peripheral vision. Now that we were done, I couldn't help but notice that the blonde and the unconscious girl had vanished. I weighed it up. One exit, not much of a lead: I figured they couldn't have gone far. And the neutrality agreement of Solace's place only extended as far as the exit. After that, it was happy hunting. I'd worry about what favours I might owe later.

I thanked Solace without looking at her, and left in a hurry, not waiting for her lackeys to open the door.

Outside the storm had well and truly set in. I dashed toward my car, but Cole's ancient leather jacket didn't come with the convenience of a hood, and my hair plastered darkly to my face. I sighed. At least my feet were dry.

Pulling open the boot of my car offered a temporary reprieve, but I didn't have time to linger if I wanted to catch up. I unzipped the black duffel bag tucked into the far corner and pulled out my favourite weapon: a neat, narrow sword. Old-fashioned? Maybe. Conspicuous? Definitely. But oh, so *very* pretty.

The shining blade had a gorgeous, distinctive wavy pattern to the steel that almost glowed in the stormy grey night, with thin lines of gold tracing down its length. I'd had it made at the same local workshop as my dagger, but in this larger form, the metal seemed to hold more magic, somehow. It wasn't ideal for everyday use, but I had a certain fondness for its sturdy practicality. Beyond the chunk of raw citrine in the hilt and the gold inlays, there wasn't much to it, but the thin blade was so highly polished I could see my face in it – and I kept my sword *sharp*.

Grasping the leather-wrapped handle and sheathing it, I strapped the scabbard over my jacket. Tom had tried to talk me into wearing it on my hip at first, but have you ever tried running with a blade banging against your leg? No thanks. On my back was safer – even if it had taken me weeks to figure out how to draw it without losing an ear. And who doesn't look cool pulling a sword from their back?

Turning back to the rain, I closed my eyes against the downpour for a moment and attempted to centre myself. Rain hammered against the steel buildings around me, almost drowning out the noise from the busy dual carriageway beyond my sightline. I breathed deeply and let myself open up, tuning out every distraction. Intuition or instinct, it was hard to say how I could possibly know where the blonde had gone – but when I opened my eyes seconds later, I knew. Her presence pulsed in my mind like an icy blot, and I turned toward the feeling.

Across the lot, several smaller buildings were clumped together untidily in what I assumed was once some sort of admin area. I guessed the pissing-it-down rain had discouraged her from going too far, and I made my way over, keeping low out of habit. The first three buildings were empty and dark through the cracked and broken windows, but the fourth may as well have had a flashing neon sign above the door. Swathes of heavy, dark fabric had been hung haphazardly against the remaining glass, keeping the light in and the sun out.

Vampires. Masters of subtlety since… well, never.

I allowed myself a moment when I reached the door, and leaned back against the cold, wet metal of the wall. All the time I'd been speaking to Solace I'd worked hard to suppress the familiar goosebumps that announced the presence of nearby vampires. Now, I let the sensation flood through me – I could sense at least two of them – and I wasn't willing to let anyone go this time. The sour tang of metal flooded my mouth, and I swallowed, turning to slide open the door.

It was much darker inside, and I blinked to let my eyes adjust. The sole source of light in the warehouse was a small fire in the far-right corner that filled the air with smoke – almost but not quite hiding the smell of damp and mildew in the air. The blonde was slouched on a decrepit old sofa that hid most of the fire from view, but its light cast shadows across the corrugated walls, and I could make out enough to form a vague plan.

The young girl I'd seen before was slumped unconscious in a broken deckchair by the sofa, her chin on her chest and her breathing shallow. Her arm was outstretched, and her hand rested palm up on the arm of the sofa beside her, where the blonde's long fingernails stroked it, almost caressing. Bite marks and long shallow cuts marred the girl's arm, and I wondered how long the blonde had been keeping her around.

I drew my sword, and the sound of the metal on leather finally got the blonde's attention. She dropped the girl's hand, jumped up and spun to face me.

"You!" she spat. "You can't be here, not with that," she nodded toward the blade, but her gaze darted to the door. "Solace's place is a sanctuary."

I had to laugh. "Is that what you think? A sanctuary?" The stuff vamps convinced themselves of never ceased to amaze me. "It's a neutral zone for passing information, you idiot. She'd no more hide you in there than she'd hide me – not if it put her neck on the line." I took a few slow steps toward her, keeping my sword steady. "Besides, this doesn't look like her place to me."

Frustration flashed across her face as I closed the space between us, and she snuck a glance at the girl. Apparently, it hadn't occurred to her that setting up in the far corner meant she had further to go to get to the door.

"Who is she?" I asked.

"She's here by choice. You can't kill me for that." Something like incredulity made its way into her voice.

"Right," I replied flatly. "Because I need a reason."

She took a step back, away from both me and the girl. Strange. She seemed more than ready to bolt despite her arrogance the last time we'd met. But on second look, I had to admit – something was off. Her hair was dirty and bedraggled, her previously immaculate manicure now chipped. In stretched-out tracksuit bottoms and a torn baby tee, she was barely recognisable as the polished vamp I'd fought before. Maybe she was just having a crappy day, but my intuition disagreed – bad hair days didn't normally come with a healthy dose of fear, and I couldn't help but think there might be something more sinister behind the change in her.

The Gloaming

It was a fairly small space, and a few steps toward her closed the gap between us. I raised the point of my sword up and under her chin in a single smooth movement, but she never shifted. The tip rested at her throat. I could kill her in moments – and still, she made no move to escape.

"What happened to you?" I asked, genuinely curious despite myself. "You look like shit." Her answer wouldn't make the slightest bit of difference to how dead she was going to be – but she hadn't even attempted to come at me. And by now, my heightened senses were singing. I wanted her to fight. I needed it.

Her eyes flicked to the girl again, returning to stare at something behind me. A peculiar look of glazed contentment came across her face, but I didn't buy it.

"It's my night off," she answered finally. Dreamily. "I've still got to eat, you know?"

Urgh. "She's a kid. Not a bloody Happy Meal."

A snort of laughter came from the shadows somewhere to my left, a movement where before there had only been darkness. A figure dragged himself upright from the floor, and into the flickering light from the fire. I'd guess he was maybe mid-thirties – or he had been when he was turned – and not exactly in his prime. From the smears of what was probably blood down the front of his faded blue hoodie to the oversized jeans and wallet chain, he was the embodiment of a total waster.

"This Happy Meal was delivered to the door. Can't go turning these things down." He smirked, unsteady on his feet. If I didn't know better I'd say he was stoned out of his nut, but I wasn't sure vamps could even get high. Tom might know, though.

"This is the hunter girl you were on about?"

"Shut up, Will," she snapped, apparently feeling a little more herself again.

"Doesn't look like much," he shrugged, moving closer and planting his feet. "Not sure how she got the drop on Michelle." He crossed his arms across his chest, eyelids half lowered.

"I've never heard *that* before." I rolled my eyes. "Can I kill one of you at a time, please? Is that too much to ask?" I kept talking, but I was annoyed at my stupidity. I should have finished her quickly, but as usual, I was too damn nosy.

"Give it a shot." He uncrossed his arms and dropped his body slightly, his knees bent in some semblance of a predator. "I mean, you already lost to our April once…"

"I showed mercy," I flicked my sword downward to hover over the blonde's heart, the blade poised. "But I was having a pretty shitty day."

I thrust it forward, and her soft flesh broke all at once. As the tip hit muscle, I paused. It wasn't enough to kill her yet, but it would seriously hurt. She gasped, choking as blood bubbled up between her lips.

"I'll be taking the girl," I nodded towards the deck chair.

"You can't. We need her—" he started, his eyes on the sword as he backed away a little.

"Funny thing. I don't really care what you need, *Will*." I put as much of my revulsion into his name as I could muster. "Or who told you it was *safe*. Solace's so-called protection doesn't extend to scum like you feeding on children. In fact, there's no way I'd let you get away with that even in Seven."

"None of us are safe anyway," he muttered, looking around again. "Not with what's out there—" He broke off abruptly, like he'd said too much.

I'd seen some truly disgusting, vile behaviour from vampires over the years – and while Will and April's type weren't the worst of it, they were pretty close to the bottom in my opinion. I'd truly never understand how anyone who used to be human could do what they were doing.

From my position, in the light of the fire, I could see bruises and bite marks on every exposed inch of the girl's skin; some half-healed, some still oozing. She was nothing but a living, breathing food source – permanently on the brink between unconsciousness and waking, and too weak to fight or argue.

The blonde made a faint gurgling noise as she tried to speak. "You have to let her—"

My eyes still on the girl, I thrust the sword deeper into her chest, puncturing her heart and twisting the blade as I tugged the weapon back out. She collapsed to the ground, already behind me as I strode towards the teen, who had slid from her chair to the filthy floor, her breathing shallow. I felt the precise moment the blonde's life flickered out in the back of my mind – a sense of relief; like a weight had been lifted. I shivered, and stood taller.

Will was quicker than I'd anticipated. Already closer to the girl than I was, he had no trouble grabbing her while I was still paces away. He yanked her roughly to her feet, carrying most of her weight with ease, and began to pull her towards the exit.

Before he got far, I seized the girl's other arm, wrenching the pair of them around to swing my bloodied sword up between his legs. He baulked.

"I don't care how she got here, but she's not staying." I hissed the words through gritted teeth, trying to keep a firm grip on the girl with my left hand. My elbow protested at the strain, still not fully healed.

Will didn't say a word, so I nudged the blade upward. All at once, he released the girl, who crumpled to the floor with a thud.

He raised his hands in surrender. "I didn't bring her here – I swear. She was a gift."

I laughed humourlessly. "Oh, so that makes it okay?" I paused, unable to resist. "A gift from who?"

"I can't—" He stopped in a panic as I twitched the sword again and glanced around. "I can't tell you that."

I glared at him. Less than five minutes ago he'd been another cocky vamp. Now there was genuine fear in his eyes – and I had the uncomfortable feeling it had nothing to do with me. Neither he nor April had tried to defend themselves. It was almost like they thought someone would protect them.

In the seconds it took to come to this conclusion, he seemed unable to stop looking between the weapon in my hand and the rest of the room. I couldn't sense anyone else with us, but I could have sworn he thought he was being watched – and I was beginning to think he might be right.

"Murray?" I whispered.

His gaze whipped to my face, his eyes widening in a warning. Without thinking, I pulled back the sword and sank it into his chest, deep into his heart and straight through. His face went slack. As I retrieved the blade from his rib cage, he fell to the ground, a puddle of dark blood spreading beneath him. I took a step back to avoid dirtying my boots and caught the girl's arm to pull her away, too.

Shit. Why the fuck did I do that?

The tingling beneath my skin eased off, but it wasn't gone. I cast my senses out into the night, throwing them as far as I could – nothing. Yet somehow, I *knew* there was someone else in the warehouse. There were still eyes on me, but I saw and felt no one.

The Gloaming

And I'd just – stupidly – killed my best lead. What was wrong with me?

I shivered. If there was something in here protecting vamps, or even just scaring them into obedience, I needed to get out *now*. The undead I could handle, but something that evaded my senses... Now wasn't the time to start something I couldn't win. Trying to appear as though I didn't suspect anything, I heaved the girl across the room and gently rested her against the wall by the exit while I finished up. She wasn't conscious enough to see what that entailed, thankfully.

Staring down at the female vampire, I had to remind myself for the thousandth time that despite how she might look now, she wasn't human. It was much harder to tell when they were dead. And I wanted to be certain she was – which meant her head needed to come off.

I could still feel the goosebumps under my jacket. My heart was pounding, adrenaline pumping through me like icy water. Trying to seem nonchalant, I removed the heads of the two vamps as fast as I could manage, throwing them into the bonfire by their hair and cleaning my sword on Will's filthy hoodie.

I didn't stay to watch them burn. Grabbing the girl, I fled.

AT THE PRECISE MOMENT THE fiery-haired girl slammed the door behind her, the vampire straightened and dropped to the ground from the topmost metal strut of the warehouse roof. It had followed the hunter on foot and had no trouble getting into the building unseen.

It moved to stand in the doorway, the building's steel frame shaking in the storm's wind. The vampire's gaze followed the girl closely as she half-carried the younger one to her vehicle, strapped her into the passenger seat and drove away. It breathed deeply of her bouquet, still lingering in the warmed air. It wasn't time yet to taste her. But soon.

9

MISERY LOVES COMPANY

B̲Y THE TIME I'D DROPPED the still-unconscious teen at the A&E and driven back across the city, I'd almost managed to convince myself I'd imagined the strange presence at the Warehouse Seven lot. But that feeling – like there were eyes on me – was difficult to shake. As I got home and trudged upstairs, still in my soggy boots, I already knew I had no intention of telling Tom about it. I was sure the old him would have had some quippy remark about my paranoia, or maybe a doom-and-gloom reality check to cheer me up with, but that wouldn't be enough this time. And with the way he'd been lately… why worry him unnecessarily?

The next few days fell back into a predictable routine. I'd wake up, shower, and drive to Jolt. Tom showed up on time each day, and even made an effort to put out an ad for new staff – but it was clear he was running on autopilot, and barely functioning beyond that. His easy laugh and smart-arse commentary were gone.

Days after I'd been to see Solace, Tom was still questioning her information. "She definitely said she sensed more than one? You didn't mishear?"

"For crying out loud, *yes*," I replied, wiping the counter down for the hundredth time that morning. It was too early to go over this again. "But she's obsessed with the Old Ones – she'd love to think she could sense them. She could still be exaggerating for effect."

Tom stopped in the middle of stacking the cups by the coffee machine and gave me a look. "I don't like her. You don't like her." He shrugged. "But we both know she's reliable."

I sighed. "It doesn't mean anything, even if it's true. If Wyatt *and* Murray are in town, we still can't take Adam's word that she's not behind all this, and Murray *is*."

Tom didn't reply – I got the feeling he was still pissed off about Adam turning up at the house – and that was the last we said about it. Instead, each night, I hunted. Tom was still trying to find something about Wyatt, Murray or even Adam online, but beyond a couple of disturbing fan forums, he wasn't getting anywhere. I couldn't go back to Solace with favours hanging over my head, even if she had more to share. So I chose the old-fashioned way – punching vamps until they talked. But for some reason, it didn't seem to be as effective as usual.

There was no shortage of vamps to question – one of the perks of living in a big, northern city – but most of the ones I came across had no clue who Izzie Misery was, much less Nicholas Murray. Whether they were being truthful was another thing altogether – especially after the weird way April and Will had been acting before they popped it.

The third night, I thought my luck was in. I tracked a vamp to an abandoned warehouse near the canal – the constant hum of distant traffic was perfect for masking any sounds of a struggle. I'd spotted him earlier in the night, outside a nightclub and chatting up a girl that must have been half his age – or his apparent age, anyway. There was an overconfident swagger about him that told me he was newly sired and convinced he was invincible. He'd looked right at me across the crowd, a smirk playing across his lips before he vanished.

"Evening," I called, my voice carrying across the cavernous space. He turned slowly, unsurprised.

"The famous hunter," he replied, voice soft but loud enough to carry. "I was wondering when you'd catch up."

I took a few steps toward him, twirling my dagger between my fingers. "Never knew I had a fan."

"Oh, you're quite the legend in some circles," he said, tugging on the sleeves of his leather jacket. It was nice – he had good taste, I'd give him that. "The fiery redhead with the golden blade. Some say you can smell us a mile away."

I laughed. "And yet here you are, making my job easy." I stopped a few paces from him. "Unless you've got something to trade, that is?"

His smile faltered for just a moment before returning, colder. "I know what you're after. I can't help you." He began circling me with measured steps. "Though I will say, your reputation doesn't do you justice. You're much more… captivating in person."

I mirrored his movements, maintaining the distance between us. "Maybe you're not a fan after all – otherwise you'd know flattery won't get you far."

He laughed, the sound bouncing between the concrete ground and the metal walls of the warehouse. "I'm just saying it like it is."

In a blur of movement, he lunged. I pivoted, feeling the air rush past as his fist missed my face by inches, the driving heat in my blood rising up to meet him. I countered with a strike to his kidney, but he twisted away, impossibly fast.

"Good reflexes," he noted, straightening his shirt. "But I'm not like the rest of them, little hunter."

"No?" I smiled sweetly. "Funny how you all say that, and yet you all burn just the same."

His next attack came from the side – a sweeping kick that would have taken my legs out if I hadn't jumped over it. I used the momentum to drive my elbow into his temple, sending him staggering. Molten fire surged through me in a glorious rush as I followed with a flurry of strikes – knee to stomach, fist to throat, boot to chest. He crashed into a stack of old pallets that splintered under the impact.

"I've been at this for days. My patience is pretty fucking thin right now, so last chance," I said, advancing on him. "Wyatt. Murray. Talk."

"I don't know what you're on about," he growled, though his eyes darted around, searching the shadows.

"Mm-hmm." I flipped the dagger over, again and again, closing the short distance between us. "You're full of shit."

He charged again, feinting left before diving right. I read the move too late and caught a glancing blow to my ribs that knocked the wind out of me. Before I could recover, he grabbed my jacket and hurled me into the door of the nearest warehouse, the sharp, rusting hinge of a door slicing deep into my left shoulder blade, straight through my jacket.

With a quick roll, I was back up in an instant, ignoring the fresh throb in my shoulder. The pain only stoked the inferno burning through me, turning it white-hot and fuelling our pure, savage dance.

"Okay, that wasn't half bad," I conceded, adjusting my grip on my dagger. "But I've killed stronger."

"You hunt us like animals," he spat. "We're just trying to survive."

The Gloaming

I tried to resist rolling my eyes. I failed.

Pretending to retreat, my hands up in surrender, he predictably pressed his advantage, and I dropped to the ground, sweeping his legs out from under him. He went down hard, and I was on him in a second, my knee on his chest, dagger pressed against his throat.

"Names. Wyatt. Murray. What do you know?"

Fear flashed across his face, genuine this time. His eyes skimmed past me, to the rafters, the doorways, and the broken windows. My scalp prickled, and goosebumps spread across the skin of my forearms. There was someone else here.

"I can't," he whispered. "They'll kill me."

"I'll kill you if you don't," I countered, pressing my blade deeper until a bead of blood welled up.

His face hardened "Just fucking do it. It'll be faster."

I studied him. He was serious. A newly turned vamp, absolutely bloody shitting himself and ready to die rather than… what?

"Who's 'they'?" I demanded.

Instead of answering, he bucked wildly, catching me off-guard. His fist connected with my jaw, and I swore as lights danced behind my eyes. I rolled with the blow, using the motion to flip backwards and regain my footing.

He was already running for the exit, moving with the desperate speed of true terror – it wasn't quite the flitting I knew vampires were capable of, but there was no way I'd keep pace with him. I could have thrown my dagger – I might have even caught him – but something held me back as the heat in my blood cooled.

"Coward," I muttered to myself. That was the fourth one tonight to waste my time – though I hadn't let the others run, so the ache of unfulfilment in my veins wasn't quite as hollow as it might have been.

As I turned to leave, running a hand through my hair, the familiar prickling sensation edged its way up my spine, stronger than ever. I whirled, casting my senses out across the darkened warehouse and into the night. But there was nothing. Just the wind, whispering through broken windows, and the far-off rumble of the city. Still, the feeling persisted – that oh-so-creepy awareness of being… stalked.

"Enjoying the show?" I called to the empty air, forcing the shake out of my voice.

Only silence answered, but the prickling feeling followed me all the way back to my car.

That was just one night in a series of dead ends. Every single vampire I interrogated either knew nothing or was too scared to speak. Some attacked the moment I mentioned Wyatt or Murray, but I couldn't shake the thought that they were the least of my problems.

More and more, it seemed like Solace was the one vampire powerful enough to have sensed anything unusual going off. And eventually, after six nights of the same pointless routine, a whole lot more bruises and a torn suede jacket, I gave up asking. It was all very well taking out my frustrations on any unwitting vamp that crossed my path, but it was killing my autumn wardrobe options.

By the time the calendar showed a week after Maggie's funeral, hope had started to creep in. My nightly routine and Tom's research might have gone absolutely nowhere, but there was one lonely ray of sunshine – there'd been no more murders. Wyatt, Murray, someone else entirely… it didn't matter. Whoever was behind it was either bored and done or waiting for something. I couldn't begin to think what, but I was desperate to believe they'd tired of their gruesome game.

It was hard to hold on to that positivity, though, when the feeling of being watched never quite went away. At Jolt, I had a bit of a mad moment and ripped through every cupboard and corner looking for something – anything – to prove there were eyes on me. I didn't achieve anything other than creating a massive clean-up job for myself, but I *knew*. Someone was following me. Yet each time I became aware of the presence, it disappeared. It was peculiar, to say the least. Until, of course, it wasn't.

I WAS LOCKING UP THE CAFÉ AFTER hours when the familiar sensation of vampire eyes on me made me pause, key still in the door. Feigning ignorance, I went through the motions, keeping my eyes on the play of the sun's last rays on the window as I made a show of zipping up my backpack – and slipped my favourite dagger up my sleeve. In the violet-tinged reflection of the glass, there was movement under the trees across the road. I turned slowly, knowing who I would see before she came into focus.

She stood in the gloaming with no outward appearance of distress, at ease in the half-light that was not quite the day but not quite the night. I'd read about older vamps with a stronger tolerance for sunlight, but I'd fiercely hoped it was a rumour. Unfortunately, it seemed Isabel Wyatt was determined to dampen that optimism and presumably impress upon me exactly how strong she was.

Though dressed from head to toe in black, she was still less dramatic in appearance than I'd expected. At Maggie's, my main impression had been the icy terror she'd evoked, and I'd begun to think of her as I'd seen her in her portrait – posed, formal, dressed in the clothes of a different era. I had to admit, the dark cigarette trousers and smart jacket ensemble she wore now were classy as hell, but it was the way she held herself that marked her as a woman of another time. She was much thinner than in the images I'd seen though, almost hauntingly so – some time must have passed between the painting and her siring.

We assessed each other for a long minute, neither of us moving in the empty street. Without any visible prompt, she gestured imperiously with one leather-gloved hand for me to cross the road. Without thinking, I obeyed, careful to remain in the last of the sunlight.

"Good evening, Erin." She didn't smile as I'd expected. She didn't seem to be trying to intimidate me at all, actually. I breathed deeply, controlling each breath and feeling slightly better prepared for her this time – but she didn't need to try to terrify me. I was ready to run. Though lovely in every visible way, a raw animalistic strength rolled from her in waves.

"Izzie Misery."

"Please, do not call me that," she sighed. "It was never a particularly inventive name to begin with." Her accent had an odd flair to it. Definitely southern, definitely well-spoken. But odd. Old.

"You can't deny it's apt." My voice was much calmer than I'd expected. "Misery's a mild word for the things you've done."

She raised her chin a little. "True."

I took another deep breath. "What do you want?"

"Adam informs me you dismissed him from your home. I wanted to make my stance as clear as possible, since you did not allow him to. I assumed you might feel safer if I approached you here, in the open." A breeze blew her hair softly around her face, carrying her scent with it. Lilacs and ice.

I adjusted my feet, my fingertips caressing the blade in my sleeve. "You've made yourself clear enough," I replied. "You deny killing my friends. But I've seen no proof."

"What cause would I have to lie to you, Erin? And I would have no qualms about ensuring you knew the truth if I *were* responsible." She gazed at me, her dark eyes large – open in every sense of the word. "However, I believe these cases are the handiwork of my old friend, Nicholas."

"Murray?" I resisted rolling my eyes. "That's what Adam said, yeah."

"Murray. Yes." She smirked at some unknown joke. "He and I spent time together, some years ago. We… collaborated, for lack of a better word, and eventually became friends. But I had hoped we'd both grown since."

I wasn't certain, but she seemed unsure.

"The recent deaths are similar to those he committed to draw my initial attention, once upon a time," she continued. "Many of those deaths were falsely attributed to me, though the more recent killings here and in Edinburgh have been somewhat more erratic, I'll admit."

I swallowed. How could anyone set up something so depraved just to impress someone? Shit, what sort of person would be impressed?

"We've barely spoken since the war," Wyatt continued, oblivious to disgust and anger raging through me, mere feet away. "I know he resents me for being so distant – which is why I've come to suspect that this—" she gestured vaguely, "might be his attempt to get my attention once more."

I didn't respond. I didn't want to piss her off and provoke a fight, so I couldn't say what was really on my mind. But at least she'd confirmed that the conclusions Tom and I had drawn about the link between Wyatt and Murray were spot on. The problem was the reality of those conclusions – how could anyone stand there so boldly, and admit to working with another vamp to help them become a more efficient, vicious killer? I mean, what the actual fuck?

"So he's trying to get you to talk to him again," I said, finally. "Are you going to? Has he impressed you, killing my friends?" The words were clipped, my temper rising above my fear. You'd think a text would have done the trick.

She shrugged, the movement elegant on her. "I am not the vampire I once was, Erin. I am not so angry as I was in my youth. And this revisiting of the past that Nicholas seems intent upon… it holds little appeal."

I didn't want to believe her. But she was right – she had no reason to lie. I wasn't anywhere close to being a threat to her. The waves of power rolling from her told me as much. Despite my pounding heart and the hot, metallic taste in my mouth that had my body prepping for war… I knew my reaction was based on *what* she was, not who she was. So yes, I believed her – and there was only one thing to do about it.

"How do I find him?"

Her blank expression wavered. "I don't know," she admitted. "I haven't been able to sense him, and the vampires of this city are proving to be stubbornly uncooperative." A frown crossed her face for a moment before it was gone. I couldn't help but wonder if she was used to people doing as she asked, and what was different now that she was here.

Wyatt tugged at the gloved fingertips of her right hand,

removing one finely made leather glove, and then the other. On the third finger of her left hand, she wore a simple, pale golden band.

Noticing my attention, she smiled a little and continued. "Be assured, had I knowledge of his whereabouts I would have put an end to this already. We live in a new world. Discretion is no longer simply good manners, but a requirement for survival." She pursed her lips in irritation. "It is not as easy to hide from modern technology as it was to hide from a poorly organised police force."

So there *was* something she was afraid of – or at least worried about. The thought gave me a vindictive moment of pleasure.

"What do you expect me to do about it? I don't see how I'd be more likely to find him than you."

"You are the target, Erin." I wasn't a fan of the humour in her voice. "Nicholas might be after my attention, but I am certain the only reason he chose this city, this world… is you. The girl who died – your friend – she looked a little like you, did she not?"

I nodded, my mouth suddenly dry. "Why are you trying to help me? You said you were friends."

When she sighed, I almost believed she was genuinely sad. "I also told you I am not the same vampire you have read so much about. Nicholas and I have a great deal of history, it's true. But if it was *your* friend risking the exposure of your species, would you allow it?

"When you have lived as long as I, loss is inevitable. But murder is not. I will kill when killing is necessary, but even the thrill of holding a life in one's hands loses its appeal after a while. For him, it seems the appeal of the game remains."

The way she said it sounded so reasonable, I didn't know what to make of it.

"Oh."

Her face broke into a smile that lit up her face, though it also emphasised the stark sharpness of her teeth. For a second she almost seemed youthful. Even carefree.

"It is difficult to believe, I know. But the boy who helps you, he will be able to confirm the truth. I challenge him, here and now, to find a death linked to my name in the last century." She paused and blinked. "An innocent death, anyway."

The sun was almost gone now. While we'd been speaking, my nerves had settled. My dagger was still a reassuring weight against my arm as I considered her words, but I wasn't as afraid anymore. She was powerful, but in this at least, she wanted my help.

"Okay. You've got me. But if you want us to look for this Murray guy, surely you've got an idea where we can start?"

Wyatt sighed. "Unfortunately, I believe he will find you before you find him. You're—" Her gaze travelled up and down my body and I tried not to flush, "Very much Cole's type."

I looked away, and ran a hand through my tangled hair, watching the last few rays of light ebb away as the sun fell below the horizon. Was that what made her think I was a target? My red hair? Had Maggie been killed over something so petty?

"Wait, what do you mean, Cole?" I turned back to ask, but she was gone.

10

WINGED CUPID, PAINTED BLIND

THAT EVENING, I SAT CROSS-LEGGED in the icy chill of the attic, staring blankly at my incomplete mural and rubbing my hands together over the electric heater. The painting was pretty much a lost cause at this point. When I'd planned it, I'd hoped for a warm, fresh nature piece – something in autumnal shades to bring some colour to Jolt. But that was before Jon had died. I hadn't touched it since, and now, with my mood soured, the whole scene came off as... well, menacing.

I'd messaged Tom the moment I'd arrived home, hoping he might come over so I could recount my still somewhat surreal conversation with Wyatt – but he hadn't read any of my messages. Given the way things had been going lately, I couldn't help but worry.

The canvas felt like it was pulling me into its dark corners as I gazed at it, and I had to tear my eyes away to focus. Wyatt's last words still lingered in my mind, and though I didn't much like it, it hit me that she might have given me just enough to lure Murray into the open. I turned over the idea. Any sane person would say it was too risky – but I was already downstairs, pulling on my favourite DMs. I'd have preferred to have talked it through with Tom first, but I wasn't sure how long the current reprieve from deaths would last, and it didn't feel like I had the luxury of time.

As I unlocked the front door, I caught sight of the leather jacket Cole had lent me when he'd helped fix my car. It seemed like forever ago, and for a moment I contemplated pulling it on – wrapping myself in its warmth and inhaling the scent that I was sure still lingered in the fabric... *No, wrong move, Erin.*

It took a few minutes for the mist to clear from my car windows once the engine was on. I waited, trying to keep my breathing under control. I had to relax to make this work. If I seemed even a little unnatural or tense, the whole plan was doomed. I pulled out onto the empty street.

Sheffield was a city of contrasts, industrial to the end but filled with lush trees and greenery that bled into the glorious rolling countryside and hills of the Peak District. No matter where you were in the city, you could look up and see hills and trees, with wide open spaces a quick car ride away – which was why I could never leave this place for long. A blend of opposites, literally anyone could find an escape here. Unless you were looking to escape the rain, in which case you were out of luck.

I set off along the already slushy roads, the engine warming the inside of my car until I was uncomfortably hot in my scarf. For a moment, I convinced myself that the headlights behind me were following me, but I shook it off. I didn't come this way in the dark all that often – I knew better than most what could hide beyond the city lights. As the thought crossed my mind, I reached the edge of the last row of houses, and like a candle sputtering out, the streetlights simply stopped.

My brights came on automatically, cutting a pale, narrow path through the darkness ahead. Mile by mile, my isolation grew until finally the weight of solitude settled around me and I pulled over into a barely visible lay-by. As the hum of the engine died away, I climbed out of the car and crossed over to the old wooden bench that was a favourite spot of mine: surrounded by endless hills and valleys on one side and a panoramic city view on the other.

The snow had subsided to a few odd flakes here and there, but the air was bitingly crisp and clear. Even knowing why I'd come, it was peaceful. It felt like a lifetime since I'd last made it to my spot – though looking at the city from above had a way of soothing me. I should have made more effort to come up here in the last few weeks. I'd have felt better for it.

The city was bathed in a shimmering aura of light – like a glowing bubble of protection around its occupants, who slept on, unaware of the undead that prowled their streets while they dreamed. Up here, though, there was nothing but the sound of the wind and my breath to distract me as I waited. I inhaled slowly and deliberately – the last thing I needed was to seem on edge right now. Around me, the snow on the ground sparkled, muffling sound from the road behind. But it was late, and I didn't expect to be disturbed. As I watched, one by one, the stars winked into existence.

My eyes were still on the sky when I felt it. A gentle brush against my mind. Far from the familiar skin pricking sensation I'd been expecting. I hadn't heard an engine, but a dark silhouette walked softly along the centre of the road, blacker than the surrounding night. His solid physique was impossible to ignore at this distance – all lean muscle and lethal grace. A wave of anticipation surged through me, and my body thrummed with the energy of it.

"Hullo, Erin." His voice was the same smooth, velvet brogue I remembered. Tall and imposing in the half-light, his tumble of dark hair was swept back from sharp cheekbones. He was the same striking figure who'd helped me before, but his easy elegance seemed more dangerous now than it had then. He wasn't trying to hide it, this time. Without a word, he crossed and sat beside me on the bench.

"I never actually told you my name, *Nicholas*." My voice broke on the last word, but the shiver that ran through my body as he spoke didn't feel like fear. It was true though – I hadn't even noticed, but he'd known all along who *I* was.

He chuckled. "No, I suppose you didnae." He drew a deep breath and took in the panorama of the city. "Though tis something of a speciality of mine to ken the things I shouldnae. Particularly when it comes to beautiful women." His eyes met mine, a glint of mischief in their green-gold depths. He gestured to the scenery. "I'd say forgive the intrusion, but ye have to admit… it's quite the view. I'm no sure you can lay claim to it."

"You'd never know what's been going on down there," I agreed. I fought back the urge to look at him.

"Aye," he drew out the word. "I hear Isabel's been telling all sorts of tall tales. You'd think she'd know better." The disappointment in his tone was clear.

"You disagree with her?" I asked – it was harder than I'd thought to keep control of the conversation. This could well be my only opportunity to learn about them both, and I knew that. But his low, lilting voice made it hard to focus on much else.

I sensed rather than saw him smile. "Isabel and I have long been friends. She kens better than most what sort of man I am. Before we met, I'd spent a century in solitude – I hadnae realised how lonely eternity could be, til I found her friendship."

Don't start feeling sorry for this… monster, *Erin. Don't you*

The Gloaming

friggin' dare.

"You'd call it friendship? Even after her accusations?" I asked, shivering as the wind made its way beneath my scarf. His knee brushed against mine, sending a jolt of heat through me, and I pulled away, closing my eyes to the lingering sensation.

"Truly, I would. She'd tease I was her apprentice, sometimes, but our relationship wisnae that simple." He leaned forward, broad shoulders tense as he gripped the cold, smooth wood of the bench. The movement emphasised the width of his chest, the lean strength in his arms that I remembered all too well.

"We left a wake of carnage, Isabel and I... we built our reputations on fear. Tis why twas so hard to admit the kind of life we led wisnae really what either of us wanted." Flakes of snow drifted between us as he waited for my response, his expression unreadable.

And I wanted to keep going. His words, like brushstrokes, painted a vivid image; a deadly, beautiful couple tearing apart lives for the thrill of it. The contrast between that picture and the man sitting next to me was startling, and it made it that much easier to keep talking.

"So... is that why you went your separate ways?"

He shrugged, sitting back and adjusting the scarf knotted loosely around his neck. "Twas one reason, aye. But there were others. Her decisions frustrated me – and in turn, my ideas frustrated her. Our kinship was – *is* – built on our shared affinities, but that didnae mean we agreed on everything. I—" he paused and glanced at me. "Well, I spent many a year searching for somethin' I hoped would change everything. Meanwhile, she didnae believe that thing existed." Another smile crossed his face, though there was sadness in it. "And o' course, Izzie winnae leave her bonnie

England behind. No back then. So I was forced to continue my search alone."

My curiosity was beginning to get the better of me. "Why? What were you looking for?"

His eyes burned into mine, and I leaned into it, heart pounding. As quickly as it had begun, the moment passed. He turned back to the city, and continued as though I hadn't asked.

"Years later, in London again, she found the verra thing she needed to finally understand my search. Did your research tell you that?" He hesitated, his expression unsure.

I shook my head. He seemed torn about how much to share – I couldn't help but think he wanted to tell me everything.

"She wed a soldier from the north – no too far from here, actually. Nineteen-fourteen, nae, fifteen, I think it was."

"Wyatt's *married*?" I remembered the ring on her left hand. "To a human?"

His laugh was as familiar and musical as I remembered. "Aye, though I ne'er had the pleasure of meeting the man as could steal Miss Isabel Wyatt's heart."

"Wait." I did the mental arithmetic. "Did he… die?" There were more important questions to ask, but there was still time. He'd said he was searching for something. I had to know what.

"He did, aye. I would have been there, but I was in Europe, preoccupied wi' troubles of my own," he murmured, shaking his head. "Gods… I hadnae stopped to think on it, but I suppose Paris – before the war – was the last time any of us kent a bit o' peace. After that… well, twas a tough time for us."

So we'd all lost someone, it seemed. That Wyatt still wore her ring told me enough to know it was a weakness I could exploit – but I didn't exactly relish the thought. I put it out of my mind for now, instead wondering about the dates he'd mentioned.

"Were you involved in the war, then?" I could imagine him in a military uniform – something about his bearing said there was a soldier in him.

"*Involved*, eh? Truth be told, I've fought in more battles than I can rightly recall. But then… twas a war like no other." His mouth twisted into a grimace. "Have you e'er heard of Sachsenhausen?"

I shook my head, already apprehensive about his next words. It sounded German, even with his accent.

"Twas a camp, north of Berlin. A dark place, by any account. I'm no surprised you dinnae know it. But there are those of us who remember it well enough. Those who learned about human cruelty the hard way." He fell silent, his words hanging in the air. I waited, but he didn't continue, lost in the past.

I swallowed, but I had to ask. "Were you a… a prisoner?"

Even knowing who he was and the things he'd done, the nod he gave in response horrified me. Though I had no clue how a vampire could get caught in the first place – the idea seemed absurd. "And you made it out? How?"

He exhaled sharply, a plume of white breath escaping into the cold air. "With nae help from Isabel, I'll tell you that. It wisnae easy, but I managed to get a few letters out of the camp, begging for her aid. I'd thought it worth the risk, that my friend would come and we'd… Well, it isnae worth dwelling on. It was a long time ago."

"I don't understand," I pushed. "Surely for… someone like you – it'd be easy to escape a place like that?" Not to mention, I didn't see how he could have kept his true nature a secret in such close quarters. He'd have to have fed somehow.

"For a vampire, you mean?" He dug his right thumb into the

palm of his left hand, grinding it into the flesh and edging forward to rest his elbows on his knees. "Mayhap you're right, love. A three-metre wall isnae so difficult to scale," he said, his voice doubtful, "but there were others. And I was all they had.

"Those who dared to run rarely made it far – and believe me, plenty tried. The camp was well-equipped for shooting runaways, and making an example of them." He shook his head, and a lock of unruly hair fell into his eyes. "It winnae ha' been the first time I'd been shot, either – that wisnae the issue. After the battles I've seen, t'would be a miracle if I hadnae had my fair share of wounds, from gun and from blade. But back then, the unknown was the thing I was most afeart of. Their automatic machines were new. The world was changed, and I had no way but the hard way to ken how their weapons might affect me." He paused. "The camp was liberated no long after, but still… I lost good friends to that place."

He shifted in his seat, his eyes fixed on the moon as the last wisp of cloud drifted across its surface, leaving a clear indigo-black expanse. I watched his clasped hands, his long fingers moving restlessly. I didn't know what to say.

"While I stayed, I could help. Without Isabel, twas all I dared do." His accent became more pronounced as he grew more restless. "I lost count o' the times my true self was almost exposed. I believed, foolishly, she'd at least wish to keep our secret." He shook his head. "At least my… *special diet* reduced the Nazi ranks a bit."

Considering all Wyatt had said, it seemed senseless for her to abandon him like that. "Why didn't she help?"

"Grief," he said plainly, turning to face me. This time I didn't look away. "Love, you might say. She was mournin' her husband."

I blinked a few stray snowflakes from my eyelashes and met his eye – his emerald gaze was bright and clear. Caught up in his stare,

The Gloaming

I had to remind myself – again – that I was talking to a murderer. A vampire, despite everything he'd been through. A tremor ran through me, and I pulled my scarf more tightly around myself.

"Is that why you've come here? For revenge? Or reconciliation?" I fought to keep my voice steady as I took back control of the conversation, with little success.

"I'm hurt ye'd trust her word, Erin," he said, rubbing one hand across the faint line of stubble at his jaw.

I bristled. "So I'm supposed to trust you, instead?" I took a deep breath, trying to reign in my emotions. "What am I supposed to think, Cole? Nicholas – whatever your name really is. As far as I can tell, you're both accusing each other – and you're doing it right to my face, with no thought for the fact that my friends are *dying*."

"I havnae accused anybody," he shot back. "Though I've given it a deal o' thought," he admitted. "And despite everything, I ken Izzie. She values family above all else, and she winnae go so far as to harm mine." He ran his fingers through his already windswept hair, the dark waves falling across his forehead as he dislodged a few snowflakes.

"Family?" I echoed. Several things slipped into place in my mind like the pieces of a jigsaw. I could almost see it—

"Jonathan Weston."

"Jonathan wasn't a vamp—" I began.

"Aye," he cut across me. "But as you know, he didnae have to be. He was visiting his uncle in Edinburgh, was he no?" He smiled, looking out across the dam below. "My home, if I can still call it that."

This was it. Finally. The full picture.

"I left at fifteen. Abandoned my responsibilities at home to follow the Earl of Tullibardine into battle, though my pa disagreed with supporting the Covenanters," he explained, sitting up straighter as he spoke of his father. "I was too young to fight, but I was already tall. And no one paid much mind. The Earl needed soldiers, I supposed, and I didnae even really care which side I fought on. I only wanted to fight."

It was easy to forget he'd been human once – though he didn't exactly seem like the usual vampires I came across even now. He'd had a father and a mother. Which meant he could still have living relatives – and the possibility of Jon being one of them was suddenly very real.

"I first fought at Tippermuir. I dinnae ken what I thought I'd find on the battlefield, but I didnae find it. Gods, I barely understood the politics enough to ken if Scotland had won or lost." He almost smiled, but these weren't stories I'd heard of. I had no idea how to respond.

"I read about it, after. They called it a bloodbath. But history books cannae tell you what twas really like. It's hard to imagine, the things we'll do to one another in times of war."

He started to rise, before apparently thinking better of it and clasping his hands together once more.

"I wondered more than once if I was in hell. I'd left my home to be a soldier, and part of me wanted to stay and do my duty, but… in the end, I deserted. Dinnae ken quite how I managed it, but I fled. Ran til I couldnae hear the sounds of battle." He paused again; his voice rougher. "I couldnae go back to my family. I knew my pa winnae forgive cowardice, even if he'd approved o' the cause. So it wisnae til years later that I finally learned I had a brother."

"Jonathan's ancestor," I murmured, staring at him in awe. It wasn't a question.

"Aye. The latest and last of my descendants, if you dinnae

count James – though I've long doubted he'll have children o' his own. With Jonathan gone, my bloodline will be lost to time."

A passing cloud momentarily obscured the moon, shrouding his green eyes in shadow and turning them black. My gaze was locked on his and I barely noticed the clouds rolling in, the soft hush of snow swirling softly around us.

There it was. Jonathan Weston shared blood with Nicholas Murray… it explained why I'd felt such familiarity with Cole when we'd first met – like some part of me had known him forever. But even that didn't make sense, did it?

I sighed, breaking free of the moment. "So you were always the soldier… Why, if you hated it so much?"

His smile was rueful as he answered. "I was naïve, Erin. I wanted glory. To be remembered in history as a warrior – after all, those were the stories I'd heard as a child.

"I suppose I found a wee bit o' notoriety, after all. As a vampire, my deeds grew more vicious… and my reputation grew, too. Twas a long time before I kent I wanted more. I was no hero of legend – and there was no honour left in me." His face grew dark again, and he broke his gaze away.

The wind howled a mournful tune around us, buffeting the dry snow up from the ground – but around us was a pocket of calm and stillness. He spoke of atrocities committed by and against him with unnerving ease, but I couldn't find the fear or the fire to fight him. I'd come here to lure him out – and now I had, I was more confused than ever.

As I reached to slip a loose curl of hair back into my hat, his fingertips brushed mine, and for a moment I forgot how to breathe. He gently brought my hand back to my lap, and I was struck by how artfully he moved, even in such a simple gesture.

His breath was almost warm on my skin as he leaned in close, tucking another strand of hair from my face.

"I was told you liked red hair, once upon a time," I said, the words tumbling out before I could stop them. Pain flashed across his face.

"Izzie told ye?"

"Not in so many words," I admitted.

His expression grew serious – almost imploring. "I've been searchin' for you for a verra long time, Erin. So long, I almost believed you didnae exist after all." The corner of his mouth lifted in a devastating half-smile. "When I saw you in the park that night, there was nae doubt about it. Even covered in dust and swearin' like a sailor, you were unmistakable."

His body was still close, near enough I should be able to feel the heat of him, if he'd been anyone else. His touch rough, he traced his fingers along the back of my bare hand. So close, I could smell his skin – like the outdoors. Soft earth and pine.

"The women that looked like me—" I whispered. I couldn't forget what he'd done, but I didn't pull away.

"Were no you," he replied simply.

Nicholas's face drew closer to mine, and I found myself leaning in despite myself. His cool breath caressed my cheek as we lingered there, suspended in the moment. A shiver of pleasure ran through me, our eyes locked as I imagined reaching up to touch the soft hair at the back of his neck. Letting this – whatever *this* was – happen.

I caught myself. *No.*

His arm moved as if to circle my waist, but instead his fingers brushed the fabric of my coat. Even that small whisper of contact was enough to make me feel far more than I wanted to, and I pressed my eyes closed, trying to dispel the feeling.

In that fleeting moment of darkness, his lips brushed mine – the barest ghost of a kiss – and I felt rather than heard him exhale sharply. I pressed a hand against his chest, placing my palm on the heavy wool between his heart and mine, though whether I planned to push him away or pull him closer, I wasn't sure.

To my surprise, there was a faint thump beneath my hand as his heart beat once beneath my fingers. He stilled and drew back, sooty lashes lowered, searching my face with an intensity that made heat pool low in my belly.

"Nicholas—" I breathed, my head swimming, but he pulled away further, shaking his head as he stood with the casual swiftness of a vampire.

I turned to see what had distracted him, but a breeze caught my hair, whipping it across my face. When my vision cleared, I was alone again in the snow. A single set of footprints led from the road, and he was gone.

11

SURPRISE, REGRET & SOMETHING STRONGER

UNSURPRISINGLY, IT HAD escaped my notice that the snow was falling in earnest again, cloaking my view of the city and the dam. Thick wet flakes settled on my coat and in my hair, creating a haze in the sky that left me cold and isolated. My fingers were growing more numb by the second, but I was still too dumbstruck to move.

What the hell was that, *Erin? Did that actually happen?*

I stared across the valley without seeing it, replaying the last few minutes over and over again. It didn't really matter how I looked at it, I still didn't know what to feel. My emotions slipped and shifted, alternating between horror at what had almost happened, and confusion about why. And if I was entirely honest, part of me was a little bit thrilled and felt wholly guilty about that.

Why hadn't I stopped it? Was I being a complete fool or had my connection with him been… well, real? I mean, fuck. It had felt real. My skin was still tingling with electricity. And there'd been a definite, blazing spark before – I just hadn't known who I was dealing with.

I tugged off my hat and ran both hands through my hair, pulling the damp strands away from my scalp. What was wrong with me? *Nicholas Murray* had been right there – within reach – and I'd done nothing. Okay, not nothing. But what was the point in my plan to lure him out, if I couldn't follow through with the kill? And yeah, hindsight had a lot to say. He was older and stronger, I'd needed to get the full story from him… blah blah blah. Every reason I came up with was another excuse.

The fact was, deep down I'd forgotten, temporarily, that he was one of *them*. And my entire life, that had been enough to go in swinging. Just not this time.

I rose and began pacing back and forth. My feet were still warm and dry in my Doc Martens, and I kicked up the snow as I marched, my tracks quickly filling behind me.

What the fuck, Erin. What the actual fuck.

He was a vampire. Three or four centuries older than me at least. And I'd let that happen, there was no denying it. I had pulled right into his body, held myself against him, breathed in that ridiculously alluring scent… I shivered, but I knew it wasn't from the cold.

I mean, he didn't seem to want to hurt me. There was no threat there at all, actually – in anything he'd said or done. And no fear either – I wasn't afraid of him in the slightest, beyond the theoretical idea of his past. So yes, my head didn't trust him. But my heart inexplicably did. The thing was, without that fear behind the steering wheel, I had no idea how I was supposed to do what had to be done. The idea brought me to a standstill.

I let out a long groan, and watched as my breath condensed in the frigid air, disappearing as quickly as it appeared. The soft hush of the snow only amplified the feeling that the answers I needed weren't here. I just wasn't sure where I'd find them.

I made my way back to the car and clambered in, my limbs

stiff and aching from the nasty combination of my recent injuries and the biting cold. I drove home in a stupor, only breaking out of it as the temperature gauge on the dashboard plummeted and the snow hardened into ice, forcing me to pay attention to the road.

My first instinct was to speak to Jon – obviously that was off the cards. Next was Tom, but I knew I'd be judged the second I told him about the kiss – because lips had damn well touched, and what else was I supposed to call… *that?* Tom already thought I was keeping things from him, and after Adam's surprise visit, I couldn't afford to push him any further away. Shit, he hadn't even heard about Wyatt showing up at the shop yet – though if he'd pick up his damn phone occasionally, it might be less of an issue.

I shook my head, dismissing the idea of confiding in Tom. If I casually dropped into a conversation that I'd kissed the man who *might have* murdered his date, he'd snap. He was already on the edge.

The problem was, I didn't do well with secrets. I had to talk things out with someone and justify myself or I'd go mad with overthinking it all.

Damn it, Jonathan. I missed him with an almost physical ache. He would have listened without judging. And considering what I'd learned about who he was, maybe he'd understand where I was coming from.

As I neared home, the golden light of the city brightening my vision, I knew I had one friend left, if I could call him that. And he might be too close to the situation.

THE HOUSE WAS DARK AND UNWELCOMING when I opened the front door. Despite myself, I'd been hoping to find Tom draped across the living room sofa with a hot drink and a battered paperback – but no such luck. Instead, I wandered through the rooms, shivering in my coat, and switched on the lamps while I waited for the thermostat to kick back in.

I needed hard caffeine, but instant coffee would have to do. While the kettle boiled, I grabbed my satchel from the table and dug out the pale blue envelope and my mobile phone. I swiped away a few notifications telling me my inbox storage was full, and without stopping to consider what to say, dialled the number.

"Yes?" His cut-glass voice answered on the third ring. I almost hung up.

"Adam?" I asked tentatively.

"Erin?" I thought I heard the surprise in his voice. "Are you alright?"

In a rush, I remembered the last time we'd spoken. How rude I'd been. He probably thought I hated him. But right now, I needed the friendly guy I'd met at the café. I had to give him a chance.

"Yeah, it's me. I'm – I'm fine. I just… I wanted to speak to you again, if it's not… you know, inconvenient? Could I—" I hesitated. "Would that be okay?"

He paused, the line crackling. "Yes, of course. You should come over. I'll give you my address."

Relieved, I put him on speaker while I scribbled down the postcode on the back of the blue envelope. I recognised the street name – it was a fancy neighbourhood; somewhere I'd had little reason to visit before now. Not for the first time, I wondered who Adam Locke really was.

The Gloaming

"Thank you, Adam," I said sincerely as I hung up. I'd have to swallow my pride to go over there. But glancing at the three empty chairs around the table, I knew it wouldn't take too long.

I PULLED UP ON THE DARK STREET less than an hour later and quadruple-checked the address. I'd been expecting something nice, but this? *Holy shit.*

It was a manor. Not a house – not even a really big house. An actual, Georgian manor. Imposing symmetrical façade and all. The building itself was set back from the road, and a winding drive led up the slight incline toward it. Most of the surrounding grounds were hidden by tall hedges, broken only by huge wrought-iron gates right across from where I was parked. There was a small, ultra-modern-looking security intercom on the gate that Adam had told me to use. I knew with one glance at it – and the intimidating spikes on top of the gates – that I'd have no chance of getting into this place without help, should the need ever arise. Hopefully, it never would. But I couldn't help but wonder… Who the hell *was* this guy?

The last of the engine's warmth was beginning to fade away inside my car, and I took a deep breath, savouring it. Places like this made me nervous anyway, but I also barely knew Adam – and I had mixed feelings about the things I *did* know.

I took my rare moment of apprehension and worked with it, allowing myself to speculate. Exactly *what* was Adam? He wasn't a vamp; I knew that much. But he ran in the same circles, and had close friends who were. The way they all talked, it sounded like they'd known each other a long time – maybe more than a human lifetime. I'd have said he was in his early to mid-thirties to look at, but in my experience, that didn't mean much. And even amongst the supernatural, it was still rude to ask.

I got out of the car and closed the door as quietly as possible, very aware that it was well into the night at this point. Crossing the road, I couldn't help but gawk, staring through the gate and up the driveway. A few of the windows on the second floor were lit up.

A movement by the left side of the gate threw my body into instant high alert and I froze, casting my senses out instinctively. A moment later, Adam stepped into view, surprisingly casual in torn grey jeans and an immaculate white t-shirt. I didn't want to contemplate just how cold he must have been, with the snow still falling.

"I saw you pull up," he explained as he opened a smaller gate set into the larger one, the iron gliding open silently. "I should have given you the entry code before, but I wasn't sure you would come."

I bobbed my head in response but didn't speak as we walked up the crunchy gravel path to the manor. Inside, through one of a pair of colossal oak doors, Adam pointed me in the direction of a coat rack. I left my boots beside it before following him across the gorgeous, open entrance hall.

It was fair to say someone had restored this place with love, and it was clear that whoever it was knew what they were doing. I didn't know much about architecture – I'd only ever seen homes like this that were museums – but the artist in me could tell that this restoration had been done to perfection. I'd guess the gleaming, chequerboard tiles were the original Georgian ones laid down when the place was built – though I had to admit they were more than a little treacherous to navigate in my socks.

The Gloaming

Along the wide hallway, several tall doorways stood, mostly closed, beneath lofty ceilings and stunning plasterwork roses that I could only assume had been painstakingly restored. Other than that, it appeared to have been completely modernised. Throughout, the décor was light and warm, which gave it a homely feel despite the vastness of just about everything I could see. The faint aroma of warm vanilla scented the air, and while I'd expected to be chilly in a house of this size – especially at this time of year – I was comfortable in my jeans and t-shirt.

"Follow me," Adam said as I stood transfixed in the middle of the hall. I nodded, barely paying attention.

I couldn't help but wonder if Adam was the one behind the work that had been done here. Just based on his appearance alone, he seemed like he might be the type. I glanced at the designer watch on his left wrist, and the careful styling of his white blonde locks. Both told me attention to detail was important to him. And honestly, it was impressive. I'd be perfectly content if more people gave a shit about art like this – because it *was* art. I was jealous as hell of his home, and my own little rented terraced couldn't hold a candle to it.

At the end of the hall was a wide, carpeted staircase that curved gently up and around to the left, but we didn't take it, passing beyond and through the final set of doors in the hall instead. Through a tall window beneath the stairs, I caught a fleeting glance at the back of the house – the garden must have been twice the size of the building, its winter flowerbeds perfectly maintained and as symmetrical as the façade.

The kitchen was enormous, but cosier than I'd been expecting. I gaped, resting my hands on the doorframe as I took in the chunky wooden worktops, dark cabinets and artful underlighting. Beneath my feet the clay tiles were warm, and I grinned – but Adam paid me no mind as I turned on the spot. Huge, high windows took up most of the back wall, and I could tell that come morning, this room would be stunning. And filled with sunlight. No wonder it felt safe here.

Adam was contemplating the contents of the huge, brushed steel fridge that stood by another, smaller door, and said something I didn't catch.

I shuffled my way toward a stool at the breakfast bar, running a hand through my still-damp hair to air it. "Hmm?"

"Would you like something to drink?" he repeated, half closing the fridge door to look at me.

My body was desperate for caffeine, but I couldn't seem to find my voice. Instead, I nodded, and stared at my hands on the counter. I could practically feel Adam's gaze boring into me, and I knew his pale blue eyes were assessing my bedraggled appearance. He closed the fridge with a small sigh.

"Perhaps this calls for something stronger," he mused before raising his voice a shade and resting his hand on my shoulder. "Come with me."

We didn't speak as I followed him out of the kitchen, across the hallway and through another door that stood ajar near the bottom of the staircase. Adam paused on the threshold.

"This used to be the smoking room. Of course, I haven't indulged in the habit in years, so I had it converted…"

"It's a music room?" I guessed. One wall showcased a sleek, expensive-looking sound system, its polished chrome gleaming against the rich, dark wood-panelled walls.

Everything was set for ultimate comfort – presumably so Adam could enjoy the music better. Soft throws, deep armchairs, all centred around a majestic stone fireplace complete with roaring log fire. It could have been a set from a catalogue... or something Jon cooked up.

"Yes. I thought you might like it," he gestured to the sofa, and obediently I sank into it, grateful to be closer to the flames. I tucked my feet under myself as Adam fiddled with several dials, and a quiet acoustic track began to play, filling the room from every direction with the female vocalist's lament. Taking a deep breath of the balmy applewood smoke and vanilla scent that seemed to fill the room, the tension finally began to leave my body.

"No bookshelves." I gestured at the walls. It was true – the room was panelled from floor to ceiling, but there wasn't a book in sight. "I thought you were a lover of literature?"

His returning look was solemn as he took two cut crystal tumblers from a cabinet built into the wall, but I could tell he was holding back a smile. "The library is on the first floor."

"You're not serious?" I asked, though, on second thought, I had no doubt it was true. "Can I see?"

Adam laughed, his eyes crinkling at the corners, making him momentarily look older. "I imagine I will show it to you, but I don't think now is the time..." He trailed off as the laughter left his face. "I dare say, I was surprised to hear from you tonight."

I remained silent as he poured two drinks from a crystal decanter of golden-amber liquid. He handed one to me without a word, and I took a sip. There was a honeyed sweetness to it that I hadn't been expecting, smooth and smoky and strong.

"What is this?" I examined my glass and took another sip.

He added a dash of water to his own glass. "Whisky. They call it the Golden Dram."

I nodded, waiting. "I met your friend."

A crease appeared between Adam's eyebrows, smoothed away quickly. "I see. Well, that explains quite a lot."

"I met Isabel Wyatt too, although it seems like days ago already."

He nodded, apparently already aware of this. "She mentioned she might try to speak with you. She believes I did not make enough of an effort, though I explained the situation."

My earlier guilt returned immediately. "I'm sorry about that, Adam. Honestly. I... I'd just got back from a funeral, and Tom was being weird, and – well, the last time I saw you, you were with Wyatt, outside Maggie's flat!" I sipped. "What was I supposed to think?"

Adam held his glass delicately to his lips and took a drink, glancing at me sideways. "I quite understand. Had I been in your position, I would imagine I'd have had thrown me out too. It was all very suspicious."

"I didn't throw you out—" I protested.

"I was joking." He put the glass down beside a vase of purple-lipped irises, and faced me, pulling one knee up onto the sofa. "But the point remains – I don't think Izzie is committing these crimes, and I can't bear to think it could be Nick."

I sighed and took another taste. It was warming me far more effectively than the fire. "I need more than your word on it, Adam."

He took a deep breath, reaching for his glass again. "I have little more than that. All I can tell you is I've known both of them for a great many years, and in that time, I have never known either of them to do anything like this. But Izzie seems quite certain, and no doubt she has her reasons."

"Right," I scoffed. "They're fluffy little bunnies, the pair of them."

"I mean it." He gazed at me intently, and I pursed my lips. He seemed to think his word was enough. "I know what you're thinking, but… you are wrong."

I remembered what Nicholas had said on the hilltop, and Wyatt's words before that. Everyone was denying responsibility, but *someone* was to blame. Jonathan was dead. Maggie was dead. I needed a better answer than outright denial. Yet, I was here with Adam, socialising… and maybe even trusting him.

"Truly, I didn't know he was here. Not for certain." Adam quietly interrupted my musings. "What did he say to you?"

"Wyatt told me she couldn't sense him, either. But I knew – somehow. Don't ask me how, but I knew I could lure him out." I was avoiding his question, as stupid as that was. It was the whole reason I'd come here, wasn't it?

"What did Nick say to you, Erin?" he repeated.

I peeked sideways at him before answering. "He told me it wasn't him, but he didn't think Wyatt had killed Maggie or Jonathan either."

Adam barked out a short laugh. "After Paris and the war… I had thought Izzie would have been the first person he would accuse." He swirled his remaining whisky. "I know I would. Did he provide any justification?"

I nodded, emptying my glass and placing it on the table. "He said Isabel wouldn't hurt his family."

Adam paled visibly and put a hand to his mouth in an almost laughable gesture of shock.

"I should have known!" he muttered to himself. "*That* Jonathan? I'd lost track, but…" he trailed off before raising his voice so I could hear him. "I mean, he couldn't have meant the woman; what was her name?"

"Maggie." I supplied, resisting the urge to tell him he was being disrespectful to the dead. "Nicholas said Jonathan was a descendant of… his brother?"

Adam nodded. "There have been many, over the years. Occasionally Nick has been known to get involved in their lives. It is not something he does often."

It made sense. But it shouldn't – everyone seemed to be telling the truth, and no one knew what had really happened to Jon. Or Maggie. I was back at square one. Tom would be fuming that all his research had come to nothing.

Adam poured another measure into my empty glass, and topped up his own, resting back on the sofa cushions – every inch the aristocrat.

"How well do you know them?" I asked eventually.

"Nick and Izzie?" he clarified. "Nick has been a friend from the very first time I encountered him in London, years ago. My, I was young," he closed his eyes and shook his head, remembering. "Izzie has been… more of an unavoidable side effect of that friendship. The two of them were joined at the hip, once."

"Why don't you like her?" I asked. "Aside from the obvious." I noticed he hadn't said specifically *when* they'd met.

Adam laughed, the firelight glinting golden in his hair as he shook his head. "I have never understood why *anyone* likes Izzie Misery if I am quite honest. The woman is arrogant and demanding to the point of utter exasperation. It's a consequence of her upbringing, unfortunately."

"Her upbringing?" I leaned forward. "Who is she, exactly?"

"That isn't my story to tell," Adam raised an eyebrow at me expertly. "As much as it's a good one."

I didn't think he'd give up the information so easily, but it had been worth a try.

"All I'll say is she's lived a most different life to you or I. But how about you, dearest Erin? What's your story, I wonder?"

I rolled my eyes at him but found myself explaining what it had been like to grow up seeing things other people couldn't, and how I'd come to do something about it with Jon's help. I told him about feeling, always, like something was missing; how empty and dark I felt inside. The drink seemed to be loosening my tongue, but it was a relief to get it out.

Adam listened without interruption. Really listened, the way Jonathan once had. It was an effortless thing to open up to him, which I absolutely should have been on my guard about, but… I'd come here to talk. I needed a friend.

As easily as the conversation flowed, eventually, I had to hold myself back. I couldn't bring myself to tell him what I'd really done, up on the hilltop. But between being furious at myself and my reluctance to analyse my feelings about everything, I just wasn't ready for the inevitable questioning. It wasn't that I didn't have the answers yet – but admitting to them was a whole different thing.

It had been late when I'd arrived at the manor, and my eyes grew heavy as we talked. Chatting and drinking in the music room, I relaxed for the first time since those blue lights had shone through my living room window. It wasn't surprising then, when the warmth of the fire, the delicious honey whisky and several nights of restless nightmares caught up with me. I dozed off when the conversation lulled, vaguely aware of Adam dimming the lights and covering me with a blanket.

I awoke with a start, disorientated. Scrambling up off the sofa, I checked the time on my phone – it was after seven in the morning, not quite sunrise. I groaned inwardly, my head pounding. There was a loud crashing sound from down the hallway, and I realised belatedly it must have been what woke me.

Adam was nowhere to be seen, and I needed to get the coffee shop ready for opening before the customers started showing up demanding their morning lattes. Narrowly avoiding slipping, I crept across the chilly hallway in my socks and was almost to the front door when the sound of voices reached me – presumably from the kitchen since it was the only open doorway I could see. One voice was unmistakably Adam, but the other…

"I was certain he was in the city. It confirms everything." Isabel Wyatt's melodic voice carried through the doorway, more clipped than it had been the last time we'd spoken.

"From what I gather, it's not that simple." Adam's voice was low, and I shifted closer, pressing my body against the wall to hear. They could only be talking about Murray.

"How much simpler could it be?" Wyatt sneered, "The *vânător* confirmed it, did she not?"

I frowned, not recognising the term – the way she pronounced it, with a strange accent, it almost sounded like 'hunter'.

"Izzie, I need you to listen – Nick is not that man anymore. We both know it's true, regardless of whatever grudge you've been holding against him for the better part of the century. Erin said—"

"I shall not suffer the excuses he gave her, Adam. Truly, I am surprised Erin did not kill him where he stood." It sounded like she was pacing the kitchen. "But you know it couldn't be anyone else. The deaths… they were identical. Far too exacting for another to have imitated."

The Gloaming

"It isn't beyond the realm of possibility he's told someone the details, Izzie. Be reasonable. You yourself said the flowers might not be—" Adam sounded exasperated, and cut himself off, but I was glad he was talking sense. "What do you propose to do? Kill him? You are supposed to be his friend."

Wyatt sighed loudly, and her footsteps grew louder. "I may have to. The *vânător* does not seem capable, particularly if she has already succumbed – and I can't continue to allow him to draw such attention to himself."

"Your kind has never been subtle," he pointed out.

"Then they must learn to be," she snapped back.

I backed away from the door hastily as her footsteps grew closer, sprinting and sliding down the hallway. *So much for keeping quiet.*

My mind was racing through the implications of what I'd heard, but mostly I was pissed that I'd let myself fall asleep in a bloody vampire's house. I was lucky to be alive.

I'd almost finished lacing up my boots when Adam spoke quietly over my shoulder, his aroma of orange and cloves announcing his arrival before he said a word. I took a deep breath.

"Can I assume you caught some of that?"

"You can," I said, trying and failing to keep my voice neutral. "Fuck, Adam, I can't believe you let me stay here, in her house!"

"Actually, Locke Manor is mine." He extended his hand, examining his fingernails without looking at me. "I have allowed Izzie to stay here temporarily because I believe it is better to keep an eye on her."

I let out a short laugh, opening the front door. "She's not

under anyone's control, Adam. Don't fool yourself. She's still a murderer."

I walked away without looking back, but Adam's parting words carried across the crisp morning air without difficulty.

"Aren't we all, these days?"

12

CAN THE DEVIL SPEAK TRUE?

THE ENTIRE DRIVE BACK I was on edge – partly due to what I'd overheard, but also because it hadn't been that long ago I'd been drunk enough to fall asleep in a stranger's house. The last thing I needed was to be pulled for drunk driving.

A weak winter dawn struggled through lingering clouds, the streetlamps still reflecting off the dirty slush. Morning mist rose from where the snow was already melting against the warm stone buildings. Jolt's windows were dark against the grudging daylight when I pulled up just down the street. Once inside, a quick glance at the calendar confirmed what I already knew – Tom wasn't scheduled to work, so I wouldn't have to explain the state I was in.

In the back room, I took a moment to tidy myself up. The tiny porcelain sink was barely functional, but the cold ceramic beneath my hands and the icy water I splashed on my face helped bring me back to reality a little.

I wasn't particularly hungover, but I still felt like hell, and a glance in the mirror told me I looked like it, too. The bruising under my eye had almost faded, the faint dusting of freckles across my cheekbones visible once more – but the dark circles under my eyes hadn't improved much. If anything, they were worse. With a sigh, I pulled my t-shirt over my head and grabbed a spare from my satchel – the perks of being used to finding blood on my clothes – and wriggled into it. My make-up bag fell out as I did so, and I caught it before my limited supplies shattered all over the tiled floor. I didn't wear much, day-to-day, but if any time ever called for a good concealer and a bit of blush, today was it.

The once simple and now kind of harried job of prepping for opening went smoothly enough, even doing it alone. I absentmindedly switched on machines, opened bags, and retrieved the pastry delivery from the back doorstep.

Adam's parting words were still ringing in my ears as I artfully arranged croissants and brownies behind the glass display, and honestly, it was making me uncomfortable. For the first time since I'd confessed what I was to Jonathan all those years ago, my mind was actually stalling on the subject of what I did. At what being a hunter really was.

'*Aren't we all, these days?*' That was what he'd said. All murderers. And maybe he wasn't talking about me, but the thought was stuck in my head anyway.

Until recently, I'd always had this unshakeable conviction that there was no such thing as a good, honest vamp – that it just wasn't possible. Solace was probably the closest to amenable I'd come across, and she was still a total pain in my arse.

I splashed a little milk into a steel jug and shoved the steaming wand in with far more aggression than was necessary, waiting for my double espresso shot. There was no way I was going to sit here until opening contemplating morality without a good half pint of caffeine pumping through me.

I tapped my foot against the unit below the sink, worsening the scuffs that were already there. How was I supposed to focus on such a convoluted concept when my instincts sent such a clear message? When I came across one, it repulsed me. My body reacted on a visceral level, and it wasn't pleasant – so excuse me if I didn't sit around assessing what the right thing to do was. Yes, I just *reacted*.

If I wanted to be effective at my job, that was the only way. I mean, it's not like there were hunters popping up all over to help me out – I'd never met anyone else who had my capabilities or did what I did. Though to be fair, most places I'd spent time in over the years didn't have a vampire population as large as Sheffield did, either. I figured it was the hills that did it – drawing out the nights and shortening the days, since the sun took longer to rise in parts of the city.

But now, here I was, learning that I'd been acting like a close-minded little shit for the best part of a decade. With Murray and Wyatt around, it was my responsibility to question my beliefs more deeply. I still wasn't sure what I believed, but it was time to get my head on straight.

I pulled out a chair at a table by the front window and wrapped my hands around my coffee, breathing in the steamy sweet scent. A stale croissant gave my hands something to do while I thought. While I mulled it over, I followed the pale winter sun as it caught patches of melting snow, the morning light diffused by a layer of mist and cloud.

Fact one: they'd killed Jonathan first – and it turned out he was Murray's descendant. Nicholas had claimed he wouldn't kill his family, and Wyatt wouldn't do that to him, either. But I'd seen vampires kill their own before. That was the start of a disturbing lack of proper facts.

Then there was Adam. He'd seemed initially concerned about

Murray being off the wagon, but was now insisting neither he nor Wyatt had hurt a fly in years. *Slight exaggeration, Erin.*

So what remained? I swallowed down a bite of dry croissant in an attempt to bypass the lump in my throat. A third, unknown party. That was the only other option.

A new player, who knew everything about Murray and Wyatt's M.O – which might really only be Murray's M.O, come to think of it. I mean, what were the chances?

I took a deep breath, and a shiver ran through me. *Huh.* I cast my senses out quickly, but there was nothing unusual nearby. Still, I couldn't shake the feeling of being watched – again.

A glance at my phone told me it was time to get the shop open anyway, and the busy café mercifully distracted me from any further pondering or worrying. As my exhaustion finally set in, my focus shifted to more practical concerns: I needed to hire staff. I couldn't manage alone much longer, and Tom's erratic behaviour made him unreliable.

The sun went down just before four in the afternoon, and it was long after dark by the time I drove home, my headache finally fading after copious amounts of espresso and a greasy lunch. Once again, the house was dark when I pulled up outside. Unreliable Tom may be, but I missed him. The old Tom, anyway. My friend from before all of this. I wasn't sure if it was possible to get him back.

Hunger and that gross feeling you get when you sleep in your clothes only *slightly* overpowered my need for sleep. I showered, put on pyjamas, and made pasta from a packet on the stove. It wasn't exactly a complete pyramid of needs, but it would do for now.

I took my time over my meal, staring at the window from my

usual seat at the kitchen table, but I saw only myself reflected in the black glass. I hadn't been out on a hunt for days, what with so many other things to think about, and the guilt was beginning to eat at me. There were other vamps in the world, I reminded myself – not just my own little drama. Jonathan would have said as much. I'd just have to put my moral quandary to one side for now.

Abruptly decisive, I dropped my unwashed dish in the sink, pounded upstairs, and changed into jeans and a heavy green knit that I reserved for only the coldest winter nights. I could go over to Adam's, tell him what had really happened the night before, then do a quick round through the parks afterwards, to appease that part of my conscience. Tomorrow, I'd get hold of Tom, and we'd decide what to do next, *together*. There was still justice to be had for Jon and Maggie, after all. Only I wasn't sure who I'd have to kill to get it.

I SPED TOWARD LOCKE MANOR THROUGH empty streets, the stark white streetlamps casting pools of light across the empty, slushy pavements. It seemed like the chill in the air had forced the usual pedestrians to stay home.

My fingers drummed against the steering wheel as I rehearsed what I'd say to Adam. Down the street from the main gate, I pulled over and was about to climb out when a movement in my peripheral vision made me pause.

Adam and Nicholas emerged from a concealed side door, the moonlight betraying their presence as it caught Adam's pale hair. They drifted along at a casual pace, speaking occasionally, clearly unconcerned about being seen or followed. I scowled at the dashboard clock. Adam had seemed genuinely surprised by

Nicholas's arrival in town, yet here they were. Maybe I'd read him wrong, but I was usually pretty good at that sort of thing.

My heart pounded at the unexpected sight of Nicholas – seeing him again made my skin tingle in a way I barely understood, and the way he wore the *shit* out of yet another leather jacket wasn't helping matters. But right now, I was unwilling to fight the sensation. I tried to push it down and ignore it instead. The rational part of my brain knew I should be more concerned about what this late-night excursion meant, but my body had other ideas about where to focus its attention.

Waiting until they'd disappeared around the corner, I followed on foot, easing the car door shut. I walked in the road, and stuck close to the curb, avoiding the untouched snow on the pavement. Out here, away from the city centre's warmth, it hadn't yet melted, and it filled my nose with the cold, clean tang of winter.

I had to move fast to keep up. Trailing them, almost half an hour passed before I lost them on an empty road of boutique shops, their windows dark and shuttered for the night. I despaired for a moment as I peered around at the tall brick buildings. Then I heard it – jazz music floating from a fire door at the end of a side street, quiet but unmistakable.

I hesitated at the doorway, my hand outstretched. I wasn't sure what I would find on the other side, be it a strip club or a vamp den. The music filtered through faintly, but my heightened senses remained oddly quiet. There was no telltale prickling to indicate vampires. Still, I cursed at myself under my breath for leaving my weapons in the car. *Amateur move, Erin.*

The empty street stretched dark and silent in both directions. I could at least peek inside and see if following them was worth the risk. My breath gathered in a cloud before dissipating into the

The Gloaming

winter night as I reached for the handle.

Pushing my way in, stale air hit me in the face, filled with the uniquely human fragrance of warm bodies, expensive liquor and overpriced perfume. It was one of those places where everyone was pretending to like jazz, but mostly the clientele just thought it made them look sophisticated. I shivered as I took in the busy room with a practised eye: noting the exits, how many people there were and where. A highly polished bar dominated the right side of the club, alongside a row of plush booths.

Small round tables filled the other side of the room, all occupied. On a raised stage at one end, three musicians played over the chatter of the crowd – human, as far as I could tell. It was so dark inside that I struggled to see: the only light came from the small, fringed lamps decorating each table, and the backlight of the bottle-filled shelves behind the bar. I waited for my eyes to adjust, mentally comparing the place to something from a Fitzgerald novel as I breathed in the stuffy atmosphere, sweltering in my jumper.

Closing the door behind me, I tried to make myself as invisible as possible as I made my way over to a recently vacated booth. It was a trick I'd had plenty of practice at, keeping my head down and consciously closing myself off from onlookers. As I'd hoped, the few customers who noticed me quickly lost interest.

From my new and improved position, I spotted Nicholas and Adam seated on tall stools at the furthest end of the bar, chatting with two brunette women in their early twenties. Adam appeared to be more interested in the musicians than the women, who were both flirting heavily – that much was obvious even from this distance. Leaning in close to talk over the noise of the room, the taller of the two was clearly about to make a move.

I scowled, watching Nicholas's reaction to her as she gazed up at him through her eyelashes. He smiled and whispered something in her ear – the same measured, charming smile he'd given me so many times. But this time it seemed mechanical, like he was going through motions he'd practiced a thousand times. He seemed distracted, though maybe I was just hoping that was the case. Unsure what to make of it, I directed my attention to the barman just to look away. He, too, was watching the group, a scowl marring his otherwise friendly face.

After a few uneventful minutes, Adam stood abruptly and led the second woman over to a table that had cleared. Once there, he glared resolutely at the stage, apparently uninterested in anything she had to say. Visibly offended by his inattentiveness, she got up to leave – but she didn't return to her friend. The friend Nicholas was now angling his body toward, head tilted in that attentive way that I knew made her feel like she was the only person in the room. Maybe it was wishful thinking, but his eyes seemed to be looking through her rather than at her.

I retreated more deeply into the shadowy corner of my booth to see how the scene played out, though I wasn't sure what role Adam played in this whole charade – since I now realised that was what this was. This was Nicholas hunting, which made sense; but surely Adam had no part in it? I watched him, watching his vampire friend with barely hidden indifference.

Without warning, Nicholas got up and wove his way towards the front entrance with the brunette in tow, her hand resting awkwardly in the crook of his elbow as he picked up the pace, practically marching her to the door. Mirroring him, Adam followed at some distance. He never took his eyes from the woman who clung to his friend's arm, even as she stumbled, unsteady on her feet and still talking animatedly.

The Gloaming

I got up to follow too, but Adam paused in the doorway, his profile frozen in the light from outside. Slowly, he turned and stared across the room at me, his gaze cutting through the crowd. With no change in his blank expression, he nodded in my direction and left.

I grimaced. *How did he know I was here?* Determined to catch up, and feeling rushed, I still couldn't help but stop to get the barman's attention.

Dark-haired and short, he appeared to be as tired as I was. "What can I get you?"

I shook my head. More alcohol was the opposite of what I needed after last night. "Those guys that just left—" I glanced at the door. "Do they come in here a lot?"

"Pretty boys?" He paused in wiping down a glass, his lip curling. "First time I've seen the blonde dude." The glass clinked against the counter as he set it down harder than necessary. "The other guy's been in here maybe three, four times in the last week or so. Takes a different girl home every time, love, if that's what you're thinking." He leaned closer across the bar, voice dropping to an undertone as he resumed polishing glasses. "One time he left with another guy."

I nodded, his words confirming what I'd already suspected – this was a feeding ground. I threw a fiver onto the bar in thanks and hurried out after them.

On the main road, I finally recognised where I was. Icy patches of snow glittered on the pavement as I headed away from the busier street, thrusting my hands deep into my pockets. There was an icy wind blowing, getting into all the gaps in my clothing. It was bloody freezing.

I gave a cursory glance to each side street out of habit, checking for signs of activity as I cast out my senses, determined to find them. My feet were going numb in my boots when, at last, a familiar shivery sensation came over me. Without thinking, I shifted closer to the wall, pulling my body against the brickwork, and leaned around to look down into the alley I'd been about to walk past.

The streetlamp above was broken – recently, judging by the smashed glass littering the ground beneath it – leaving the path in utter darkness. I blinked a few times, trying to get my eyes to adjust.

I could make out Adam's blonde head and leonine shape leaning against the wall, arms folded and watching a recessed area further along. He wasn't fidgeting, but I got the impression he was resisting tapping his foot. In the alcove, nearly impossible to make out, were Murray and the woman from the bar. I took a few silent steps closer, my mouth filling with the metallic flavour of vampire presence that I'd never experienced with this particular vamp before. Adam didn't react, but he must have sensed my movement from his position.

Nicholas's fingers dug into the woman's upper arms, deep enough to leave bruises that would bloom by morning. She looked up at him with a vacant, blank gaze as he bent his face toward her throat, his body trembling with what I could only assume was barely contained hunger. From this distance, it might be possible to mistake what I was seeing for intimacy, but I flinched along with her as his teeth broke the skin at her neck like tissue paper. His throat worked as he swallowed deeply, maintaining just enough control to keep from draining her completely. Throughout it all, her face never changed, eyes focused dead ahead under his thrall. I was unsure if her mind was even present as he fed, and I held my breath, unable to move.

You knew what he was. Nicholas was a killer, and this was the way he sustained his life. But on some level, I felt disappointed in him. Which was perhaps why, though I had to turn away from the scene before me – I didn't stop him. My heart had been wrong to trust him.

As I walked away, some small semblance of the clarity I'd been hoping the evening would bring finally settled over me. He was one of them, after all. Whether he was behind Jon and Maggie's murders was inconsequential – and things were as black-and-white as they had always been. It didn't matter how I felt about it: Nicholas Murray must die.

PART TWO

13

Bloody, Bruised and Kinda Biased

After collapsing into bed well after two in the morning, I slept straight through my alarm and awoke just before ten. A glance at my phone told me I had several messages from Tom. Without bothering to read them or get out of bed, I called him.

"About time!" Tom's voice carried over the café's background clatter.

I dragged myself upright, head pounding. "Sorry. Late night again."

"I figured after the tenth missed call. Were you, you know – hunting?" He asked, lowering his voice. He was probably serving a customer while we spoke. One of his – and my – least favourite things to do at work, besides taking fiddly drink orders and negotiating with the bakery.

"I literally just woke up. Let me get dressed and I'll be there in maybe half an hour? I'll explain everything then."

"Alright," he replied, pausing. "But I hate this. I need to know what's going on, what you're thinking. That's how we're supposed to work, remember? As a team."

I sighed as I hung up, padding into the bathroom to jump in the shower. I didn't want to keep things from him, but he wasn't exactly being fair. It wasn't like I hadn't *tried* to talk to him, but he still didn't seem in a good headspace, and I could only be patient for so long before it got someone else killed. Not to mention, when and if he heard the whole truth, there'd be some questions that I wasn't sure I was ready to answer – if I had the answers at all.

Jolt was absolutely rammed when I arrived, and I was surprised to see Tom had hung festive holiday lights in the windows and even put a little Yule log display out on the counter. The last traces of the Diwali lanterns had finally been packed away, replaced by winter greenery along the shelves. Not that we didn't decorate usually, but I hadn't realised we were almost mid-way through December already. I wasn't sure how I'd managed to miss so much.

It took until after the lunch rush before we could grab hasty sandwiches in the back room, and it was clear Tom was still tense from a morning of explaining to disappointed students that we'd run out of orange brownies.

His laptop sat on the table between us, surrounded by research notes. At the sight of it, I fled back into the café, pissed at my own cowardice. But time has a funny way of speeding up when you're dreading something, and closing time came around with uncanny swiftness.

"That was a day." Tom slumped in his chair, the warm brown of his skin ashen with exhaustion as he pinched the bridge of his nose.

He wasn't wrong. "If I have to make one more extra hot triple shot half oat caramel whatever, I might fucking scream."

"Better than the guy last week who wanted his coffee '*as black as his soul*,'" Tom replied. "I gave him the usual roast. I doubt his soul was that dark."

I half laughed, but I remembered the guy. He was

becoming a regular.

"Fancy a drink?"

Don't, Tom. I swallowed. "You don't need to get me drunk to talk to you, you know."

Something dark flickered behind his eyes. "I just miss it. The three of us, staying late, just… hanging out." The empty chair between us seemed to mock us both.

I nodded. "I'll admit, this place feels weird without him," I said. The silence was a stark contrast to the old days: staying late after closing, Jonathan trying to get Tom to listen to something other than classic rock music, and the three of us playing cards until I could barely count.

"I've been worried about you," he half-mumbled, retrieving a bottle of knock-off Jägermeister and three green shot glasses from under the sink. His hand lingered on the third glass, fingers tracing its rim before carefully placing it back on the shelf. "You're being…" He searched for a word as he poured two shots. "Sneaky? Secretive?"

I took the glass he handed me but didn't drink it. "It's not intentional. I'm trying to figure things out," I said eventually. "There's a lot to consider, and you're hardly the picture of togetherness lately."

Tom clenched his jaw as he took the shot in one go and sat back down across from me. His almost black hair needed a trim, and the shadows it cast over his face hid his expression.

"This is all still about Maggie and Jonathan?"

"Of course." My answer came a moment too late, and I knew he didn't believe me. I kept my eyes on him as he thought it through.

"I'm sorry. I've been a tit," he said, eyes fixed on his glass.

"We've both lost people, and I know you wouldn't keep things from me. But when I saw that Locke guy…" He trailed off, leaving the rest unsaid.

I nodded, keeping my face carefully blank. Yes, he had been a tit. But I *was* keeping things from him. That needed to stop.

"So… no more weirdness?" he asked, dark eyes worried.

I wondered what it was he was really asking and weighed my words before replying.

"No more weirdness," I confirmed. "I still want to know what happened to Jon and Maggs, I do. But we've got two big bad vamps in town, and no matter what they say, they're still vampires." I stared into my glass, voice dropping. "And I can't let them live for that reason."

I took the shot, shuddering at the taste but relishing the warmth of it as it spread through my body. Tom just watched me.

"Okay," he said finally. "I'll forget the idea that you ever considered *not* doing something about them, because I think we've both been… you know, out of sorts." He grabbed the bottle and looked as though he might pour another shot, but didn't. "What I won't forget is how much older and stronger they are – this is going to take some thinking through."

I bit my lip to stop myself from replying and topped up my glass. I knocked it back in one, but waited before answering.

No time like the present. Just get on with it.

I sighed and began. Tom sat in silence as I recounted leaving the café to find Isabel Wyatt on the doorstep, everything she'd told me and the casual ease with which she'd stood there before night had even fallen. But when I got to the part about luring out Murray – just as I'd predicted – he was pissed.

"Are you fucking *insane*? Erin, he could have killed you

without breaking a sweat. And you went out into the middle of nowhere with him – have you got a death wish or something?"

"No," I swallowed. "I know. I'm sorry. But I knew he wouldn't hurt me."

Tom snorted. "You rely way too much on your instincts. Just because you're usually on the mark doesn't mean you *always* are."

I nodded, taking a deep breath, and continued. I explained who Murray really was, some – but not all – of his history. Overall, Tom reacted better than expected. I could tell he was still trying to hold in his temper, though. The rich brown of his complexion darkened along his cheekbones – a telltale sign he was angry with me.

"So… do you believe them?" he asked when I eventually paused long enough to let him speak.

I put my head in my hands. The truth was, I did – but it wasn't enough.

"I don't think it matters. Or it shouldn't matter. Whether or not they killed Jon and Maggie, they've both been getting away with murder for fuck knows how long." I hadn't mentioned those last few moments, where we'd almost—

Well, thankfully he didn't question my motivations for ignoring their avowals of innocence.

"And you said Adam isn't a vampire," he pointed out. "What about him?"

I loved Tom like a brother, but he had a particularly annoying knack for finding the weak spots in my arguments. Honestly, I had no clue how Adam would react when his friends were dead by my hand – and I didn't want to think about it.

"He's biased," I answered with a shrug, trying to convince myself. "Intuition tells me he's a decent person, fundamentally. But he's too involved with both of them to be objective."

Tom said nothing, but raised an eyebrow and poured another measure into my glass and his own. I stared at the table, fixating on the dust motes caught within the white paint.

Eventually, I looked up. He was still scrutinising me.

"I've wondered before you know, what you'd do when you have time to stop and think about morality. About killing vamps, and if they're all as bad as each other." Tom hesitated. "I don't want to tell you what to do either way, but you've had genuine conversations with these people – and I suppose that's it, isn't it?" He waited for me to acknowledge his words, but I kept quiet. "They've become people to you, not just monsters. It's going to make it a lot harder to do what has to be done."

"I know," I mumbled, my words blending together. Wow, my head was fuzzy. "I wish I'd just killed them in the first place, before I bothered to think about it."

Tom snorted quietly. "It's not like you had the opportunity to, Erin," he pointed out. "Besides, it's about justice as well. I dunno about you, but I want to be sure. I mean, I want to look them in the eye and *know*." He glowered and tugged at a tuft of black hair sticking out at the back of his neck.

"Unless this whole thing turns out to be an elaborate plot by someone else, we'll never know. I could kill them – or die trying – and there might be someone else already lined up for a faux-suicide next week anyway," I laughed bitterly.

"Don't say stuff like that. We won't let it happen again. We can't." I noticed his glass was still full. "We'll sort it like we always do."

Tom took the bottle from the table and put it back in the cupboard where he'd found it, shooting me a regretful look.

The Gloaming

"I have to get going, Erin. I've got the landlord coming at six for an inspection." He pulled his khaki jacket from the rack and fished his car keys out of the pocket. "Are you going to be alright getting home? I didn't drink much. I can give you a lift."

"I knew you were just trying to get me to talk," I laughed. He was right though, the Jäger had gone straight to my head. "I'm fine, I'll get a taxi or walk or something." Finishing the glass, I put it back down with a clatter and stood. To my surprise, I was quite steady. "I have a few things to do around here first."

For a moment, he gave me such a knowing look I thought I'd said something I shouldn't have. The booze probably didn't help my paranoia.

"Fine," he said finally. "I'll see you later tonight, maybe? I'll let you know."

I didn't watch him leave, but sat back down and closed my eyes, resting my head on the table. I rarely drank anymore, but this was twice in a matter of days and my body wasn't as young and sprightly as it used to be. That didn't mean I could wallow, though.

I stood up and stared blankly at the blue wall for a moment – the exact colour of a summer sky. That was it, then. I'd said the words out loud to Tom, and it may as well have been a commitment signed in blood – I had to follow through. Last night in the bar had been a brutal reminder of what I'd forgotten lately – it was my job to kill vampires. The thing was, I'd never hated the idea before.

Tom was right. Murray and Wyatt were people to me now, and I wasn't sure I could kill real people. Stab the broken soldier I was so irrationally drawn to? Even Isabel – I could have sworn she'd shown genuine remorse. And now I had to, what, cut her head off? Set her on fire?

I unlocked my phone, dismissed more pointless notifications about my overflowing email inbox, and opened up my taxi app. Some bits of spam were meant to be ignored, especially with a pounding headache.

Jonathan and Maggie were still dead, and who knew how many others? So I'd fight them, like a good little hunter. And if I survived – and that was a big if – I'd spend the rest of my life knowing I'd killed the only man I'd ever truly cared for.

THAT NIGHT, I DREAMED I WAS PAINTING. My canvas loomed bright white in the dark attic, but each stroke I made was smeared with startling crimson, far too vivid in the shadows. The sticky substance coated my hands to the elbows, and as it ran down my arms and dripped into my lap, I knew it wasn't paint.

I fell back onto the floor. The ceiling dissolved above me, revealing stars of impossible clarity. A thousand pinpricks of light watched me, their white radiance shifting to glorious emerald before they fell like rain. They sizzled against my fiery skin as a voice whispered, and I jerked awake, shivering despite the phantom burn.

The window was open, letting in a freezing draft. I stumbled over to close it, my dream already fading – leaving only impressions of green light and golden fire. As I burrowed back under my duvet, I realised the shiver that had woken me wasn't from the cold or the dream. I shot up, searching the darkness for the source.

Izzie Misery was standing calmly under the attic hatch.

"What the—?" I sputtered.

"Forgive the intrusion, Erin." She crossed the short distance to the bed and perched lightly on the end. The mattress barely shifted.

"I had thought a gradual revelation would prove most delicate. Evidently, I was incorrect."

"How did you get in?" I scrambled to pull on some pyjamas over the pants I slept in.

Moron, Erin. Of course, vampires don't need an invitation. Maggie was at home, remember?

Isabel tilted her head toward the window, which I'd thought was painted shut.

"What do you want?" The resigned understanding in her eyes shouldn't have given me pause, but it did. I glanced at my weapons chest across the room, and she caught me looking. "You know it's the middle of the night for us mere mortals, right?"

She nodded. "I spoke to Adam this evening. He informs me he met with Cole." Her mouth turned down delicately. "Sorry, Nicholas."

"Oh."

Something about her phrasing made me wonder what she was holding back, but then everything with her so far had been a game of cat and mouse. I didn't want her to know I already knew about Adam and Murray either, but as I watched, something came over her eerily lovely face. It was clear she was upset – which meant she wasn't really here to listen to anything I had to say.

Damn her. I didn't like to think of her as being capable of actual emotion, especially now I'd come to my own conclusions about what I had to do to her. Which made her showing up in my room… well, awkward.

She seemed to notice I was watching her and smiled gently at me. "I confess, a part of me harboured hope that he mightn't be involved. I know you've spoken with him about this matter, too."

Fuck. Fuck. Fuck.

She continued, "I am here to inform you that you have my support. Though I wish to remain indirectly involved unless necessary."

My chest tightened at the thought of it. Apparently, my heart still had some hope, too – no matter what my brain had agreed to.

"How can you be sure, Isabel?" I knew it was desperate, but I didn't care. "Don't you want to talk to him before you give a hunter the go-ahead?"

She gave me a shrewd look. "You do not know him as I do, Erin. Nick can be very persuasive – it has always been so. Were I to speak to him, I might lose all conviction." She paused. "We must stop him to keep the secret, before—" She didn't finish, as there was a crash from downstairs.

"What the—?" I jumped up, already out of the room and halfway down the stairs. Isabel was ahead of me – I barely saw her move.

"I've searched the house. There is no one else here," she breathed. As she spoke, she jerked her head towards the front door, taking a slow, silent step closer before wrenching the handle open.

Bruised and bloody, Tom fell through the doorway onto the carpet with a heavy thud, barely conscious. Bloodstains darkened his khaki jacket around the shoulder and throat. What was visible of his face beneath the blood was swollen and already purpling on one side, the colour stark against his brown skin.

I crossed the hall in three strides, kneeling to support his head. Blood bubbled out of the corner of his mouth, and his eyelids fluttered. The metallic tang of copper grew stronger with each ragged breath he took, filling the small room until I could taste it. Isabel seemed to still completely, her nostrils flaring – the only sign that the scent affected her at all.

The Gloaming

"He's not dead," Isabel stated flatly. She moved with uncanny grace as she reached for him, too smooth to be human. When she lifted him, there was none of the usual awkward shuffling or strain – she raised him as though he weighed nothing at all, her spine straight and steps measured.

"The sofa—" I stood to let her by as she carried him into the living room. To her credit, it seemed like she was trying not to jostle him as she laid him down and backed away. I tried to ignore her thoughtfulness.

"Erin…" Tom moaned, his voice almost inaudible.

"What – what happened?" My hands were shaking as I tugged his jacket away from his throat and exposed the wound there. It almost seemed like his flesh had been gnawed at by a wild animal, the skin torn and bleeding heavily. The tang of blood hit my nose again, and I looked away.

"Murray." The word came out as barely a breath as Isabel came to stand beside him. Her face paled visibly at his words, despite her already chalky complexion.

I peeked up at Isabel from beneath my hair, knowing it made no sense. She shrugged at me, failing to appear indifferent as she handed me antiseptic and cotton wool pads I recognised from under the kitchen sink.

As carefully as I could, I tried to clean the shredded flesh of his throat to see the damage better. Blood had already congealed around the edges of the wound, thick and dark. But each time I dabbed at it, fresh crimson welled up from beneath. The sweet-metallic smell grew stronger, mixing sickeningly with the antiseptic.

"No major arteries appear to have been ruptured," Isabel murmured, watching over my shoulder. "There would be more blood than this."

She reached for the cotton in my hand and rapidly cleared away most of the mess, but it was still flowing sluggishly. "But this was no feed; it was intended to cause suffering." Her voice was as tight as her expression.

"And his face?" I asked.

"It's hard to say. I imagine the attacker tried to knock him unconscious, though I can't see why. Younger vampires may find it is simpler to feed if they can subdue humans in such a way, but Nicholas has more than enough control over himself."

"It was him," Tom said faintly. His eyes were closed, and I was grateful he hadn't noticed who I was talking with.

"You're sure?" I kept my tone light, but it didn't make much sense to me. As far as I knew, Tom still only had a vague description of Nicholas to go on. He didn't answer my question, drifting back into semi-consciousness.

I straightened, looking absently around the room. Isabel continued to disinfect the wound at Tom's throat, followed by his face. After her initial reaction, his blood didn't seem to affect her at all – and somehow, I wasn't worried about her hurting him. It was like watching a nurse dealing with a patient – utterly detached as she examined the wound, pressing gauze onto it delicately.

Everything I knew about Nicholas screamed this wasn't him – he had no reason to hurt Tom except to hurt me. Tom had seen his attacker, yes, but he didn't know Nicholas the way I did. Despite the evidence, that magnetic pull toward my Scottish vampire wouldn't let me believe it. My heart had found its answer, even if my head disagreed. But Isabel and Tom didn't believe that, and I had nothing to persuade them with.

I perched on the edge of the desk chair and observed as Isabel worked on Tom, my head spinning. Each gentle motion she made contradicted years of certainty. For a second, I was transported back to Jon's apartment, late one night after a hunt.

"What if we're wrong sometimes?" he'd mused, a few too many beers slurring his voice "Not about hunting, but about – I don't know – them all being the same?" I'd dismissed it as drunken philosophising. Tom had figured Jon had a crush on some vamp.

Now, watching Isabel clean Tom's wounds with a healer's precision, I wondered if Jon had been onto something I'd been too stubborn to consider. That maybe a monster could show mercy.

Eventually, the vampire stood, and I followed her into the kitchen. She closed the doors behind us, and the room filled with a fragrance I was beginning to associate with Isabel; like fresh lilacs and cold winter nights.

"He likely lost a considerable amount of blood before he made it here," she stated. Her hands were stained red, and she wiped them carelessly on her black jeans. "He may require a transfusion, but I ask that you don't take him to the hospital yet – provided we watch him closely, and he gets the correct nutrition, he should recover without further medical care."

I gave her a questioning look.

"Hospitalising him would lead to awkward questions about his injuries," she explained. "I would recommend painkillers, anti-inflammatories, plenty of fluids, and to keep the wound clean and dry. I cannot smell any infection, but I will return tomorrow to confirm, once he has had time to rest. If so, he may require antibiotics."

Where the hell was she getting all this from? Who was this woman?

My thoughts must have shown on my face, because she gave a

small laugh that was more empathetic than cruel.

"Necessity has made me quite well versed in human medicine," she said, her tone warming slightly as if this were a normal conversation. "I like to help where I can."

I nodded, momentarily speechless. The absolute insanity of the situation wasn't lost on me – standing in my kitchen, taking medical advice from a damn vampire. Someone who, according to everything I'd ever known, shouldn't give the slightest shit about human life. And yet here she was, bloodstained hands and all, speaking with the confidence of a doctor about how to help Tom. Part of me wanted to laugh at the absurdity of it. The other part was just plain grateful.

"Thank you, Isabel." I glanced at Tom's sleeping form. "Nicholas—"

"You must deal with him, Erin," she said, shaking her head. "What has transpired tonight is just another example of why. This was meant to convey intent, leaving your friend on the doorstep in such a state. We cannot turn a blind eye to such deeds." Her voice returned to its previous formal tone as she spoke.

"I don't know if I could deal with him if I tried," I edged. "You're the oldest of your kind I've ever come across, and…" I chuckled quietly, not wanting to admit the truth. "I didn't see you move back there; you were so fast. I never knew vamps could be as strong as you."

Isabel leaned back on the kitchen counter. "We tend to strengthen the longer we live," she agreed. "But you surely know this? You are a *vânător*." She said it as though that settled the matter, the strange term she'd used once before.

"How could I have known?" I asked. "Tom and Jonathan and I… we've done a lot, but finding out the truth when the world loves its fiction? No chance."

She considered my words. "There are things I can share that may help – with Nicholas," she added.

I gaped at her. It couldn't have escaped her notice that I could use any information she gave me against her, too.

"You have a pulse," I stated, thinking of Nicholas. My fingers unconsciously found my throat.

"Yes," she said, looking at me curiously. "I recall the shock of learning I still lived. The elder who changed me had failed to share that detail." She paused, collecting herself. "Of course, biologically speaking, we can pass as dead – but our hearts pump blood in the same way that yours does. Only much more slowly."

I took a moment to absorb this, watching as she absently traced the veins in her wrist. "What about healing?"

"We will always heal faster with fresh blood in our system. It functions a little like adrenaline, for us. Speeding our heart rates and almost every other process. Though I've yet to see evidence that we age."

"Sunlight?"

A blush crept high onto her cheekbones, only enhancing her beauty. "One I have been unwilling to fully test. For a youngling, it would be instantly fatal, but as I'm sure you remember, I can work within the shade when necessary."

"And you came in here without an invitation?"

"I would have hoped you were not taken in by that particular myth," Isabel smiled, but it faded as she considered it. "Nicholas could come here; do you understand?" she asked quietly.

A thrill went through me at the idea. I tamped it down furiously. I needed time to think about the conclusions I'd reached tonight – that became more certain each time I went over them.

Isabel had as much as said she wanted me to kill Nicholas, and for reasons I didn't yet understand, she wasn't able or willing to herself. I was grateful for that, but until I had enough information to persuade her she was wrong, I needed her to think I was willing to work with her.

How can so much change in an hour, eh?

"I do," I said finally. "Once Tom's up to being moved, we'll leave. I'll find somewhere safer for us."

Isabel nodded, clearly already miles ahead of me. "Would you be able to come to the manor tomorrow evening – or I should say, tonight?" She checked a tiny, expensive-looking wristwatch. "Tom should be safe for a few hours, and it would allow us to discuss Nicholas's weaknesses further. I would like to do what I can to help, but I know I am asking a lot of you."

"Okay." I was uncertain how else to respond.

Isabel scrutinised me, a crease appearing between her brows. "Can I trust you, Erin?"

I glanced at Tom in the other room, at the blood under Isabel's fingernails. The weight of centuries hung in the air between us – her long memory of Nicholas, my fresh loss. Trust felt like a currency neither of us could afford.

"We'll see."

14

THE DOPPELGÄNGER

AFTER ISABEL LEFT, I SANK into the old chair by the window and settled in for my vigil, watching the street outside. The sun crept across the sky beneath a veil of clouds, and occasional snow flurries danced past the glass. Tom barely stirred when I checked on him. The rich brown of his complexion had faded to a grey undertone that scared me more than the wounds themselves, his face slack in a drugged sleep. But he was getting some rest, which had to be helping.

Around noon, a flicker of movement caught my eye – across the road, a shadow seemed to shift behind a parked car. I blinked, focusing on the spot, but there was nothing that might have drawn my attention. *That's just what you need, paranoia in the mix with everything else.* I rubbed my tired eyes, chalking it up to exhaustion, but I couldn't shake the uneasy feeling.

In the few moments Tom was semi-awake, I tried to make him sip some water and nibble something. He seemed to be hallucinating. He kept mumbling about Nicholas and Isabel, and it was all I could do to reassure him he was safe.

The hours stretched, each tick of the clock taking me back to that moment on the hilltop with Nicholas, when he'd all but admitted to the murders of countless red-headed women. Yet here

I was, alive and unharmed. So, what made me different? Was it the same thing that made me feel the way I did toward him? More importantly – was it connected to why my friends were dying? Because the key link between Jon, Maggie, and now Tom seemed all the more obvious: me.

Isabel and Adam were a whole different puzzle. Isabel seemed more concerned with keeping secrets than killing me, which sort of made sense. Adam's motives were a little clearer – I trusted him, even after seeing him with Nicholas at the jazz club. That had been the first time I'd sensed Nicholas with my hunter abilities, my first glimpse of his more… animalistic side. I could only figure he and Isabel usually kept that part of themselves well hidden.

And there it was. The only answer that made sense. There must be a third player.

By the time the sun went down around four, Tom's sleep had become less fitful, and I was sure of two things. First, Tom would live – Isabel had saved him, and for that alone, I owed her the benefit of the doubt. And second, more importantly… Nicholas and Isabel were being set up.

WHEN I'D AGREED TO MEET ISABEL at the manor, I hadn't quite thought my plans through. Tom was unconscious, and wouldn't be handing out lifts any time soon, and my car was still at Jolt.

Locke Manor was miles away. If the weather had been warmer, I might have considered the walk – but in freezing temperatures, it seemed better to get the tram into town and just pick up my car. No way could I afford another taxi fare.

I'd left my favourite yellow hat and scarf in my car – of course – so I wrapped up in an old, long wool coat that I rarely wore.

The Gloaming

Though admittedly there was something to be said for how satisfyingly swishy it was. I tugged on my boots, strapped my dagger onto my belt and headed out to take a shortcut through the park to the tram stop. It didn't take long to get my blood pumping after a day of sitting on my arse, and with my headphones over my ears and my hands deep in my pockets, I soon warmed up.

Cranking up the volume, it struck me that I hadn't listened to any of Jon's favourite bands since he'd died. Actually, I'd barely listened to any music at all. But now, pacing it up the icy paths, it didn't make me as sad as I'd expected. I lost myself in the melody for a few minutes as Freddie Mercury's soprano transformed effortlessly into a high tenor and smiled, remembering the countless occasions when Jon had tried and failed to imitate such a feat.

As I walked, I kept an eye on the darkness beneath the trees out of habit – thieves and muggers didn't concern me, but early rising vamps did. Sure enough, I was halfway around the path by the duck pond when the familiar creeping sensation came over me. I shuddered, the last of the cold in my fingertips receding as a fire began to build within me.

Frost glittered on the bare branches overhead, catching what little moonlight filtered through the clouds. I slowed down, my hand finding my dagger as my breath clouded in the bitter air. A dark figure stood motionless under an ancient oak, its limbs throwing striped shadows across the path. Something felt wrong about the presence – like I was being stalked rather than doing the stalking. It was the same feeling I'd had after Seven.

You should have stayed in the shadows.

Like a deer in headlights, they remained utterly still. I inched forward, boots silent on the frozen ground, but the moment I moved, the figure emerged from the darkness. Slim, dressed in black from head to toe, she seemed immune to the cold, her bare arms luminescent in the moonlight. She moved away with deliberate slowness, and I followed, matching her pace. It was already becoming clear that this was no normal hunt – though she never ran, the distance between us remained constant, forging a connection between us like an invisible thread.

I slackened my pace, testing her reaction, and she slowed too. Something nagged at me, a familiarity that seemed wrong given the predatory energy radiating from her. If it weren't for the goosebumps all over my body, I could have sworn it was Isabel up ahead. The same form-fitting clothes, the same long hair whipping in the brittle wind. She glanced back over one shoulder, and my breath caught at the familiar profile.

What the hell?

I shook myself and sped up, attempting to close the gap between us. She sped up along with me, but her more hurried movements revealed a few subtle – but noticeable – differences between her and Isabel. Where Wyatt stood with perfect posture and grace, this woman was more rounded in the shoulders, and swung her hips a little as she walked. Yes, she looked like Isabel – and I had to reason that was intentional – but something wasn't right, here. I stopped walking, so she stopped too. Deliberately, she faced me, only a few metres separating us.

My hand on my dagger, I gave her the once-over. She was the same height and build as Isabel. Her hair was almost the same shade, and her eyes were hidden from view in the dim light. But this woman set my teeth on edge in a way Isabel never had. She didn't even attempt to conceal herself, and as if I needed confirmation, she put her hand to her mouth and giggled. The sound was harsh and girlish, and nothing close to anything I'd expect from the real Izzie Misery.

I edged closer, unsheathing my dagger. She shot one look at it, blew a quick kiss in my direction, and ran.

"Fuck." My boots crunched on the gravel as I launched after her, a stark contrast to the silent vamp ahead of me. She glided ahead, slower than Isabel but still too fast – my lungs were burning within minutes. When she vanished into a thick stand of trees, I doubled over, gasping for air. No human could match a vampire's speed, and this one was clearly powerful enough to toy with me.

I braced my hands on my knees, my mind racing faster than my pulse. This copycat act couldn't be a coincidence. Was she part of the third party I'd been theorising about? What would anyone have to gain from impersonating Isabel Wyatt?

When my heartrate steadied, I forced myself into a steady jog. The vampire had long since disappeared, but I had new information to share. I needed to get to the manor, and fast.

The tram ride passed in a blur of streetlights and anxious thoughts. My car sat exactly where I'd left it, though my hat had vanished completely – probably in a lost and found somewhere. The drive to Locke Manor stretched before me, but I barely saw the dark roads as they fell away. By the time I pulled onto Adam's long driveway – the gates stood open this time – I'd cycled through a dozen theories. The fake Isabel, Tom's attack, the suicides… maybe we were all being manipulated. Or maybe that was paranoid thinking. Either way, there was more going on here than any of us had realised.

Ringing the ornate doorbell, one of the huge wooden doors opened almost immediately. I was still jittery, but seeing Adam looking so normal relaxed me instantly – he wore dark jeans and a black t-shirt that contrasted shockingly with his white blonde hair. He waited without a word as I tugged off my boots and followed him along the hallway, noticing the tense set of his shoulders. Something was bugging him.

He led me through the first door on the left into an immense drawing room. Heavy velvet curtains in deep crimson pooled on the floor beneath towering windows, and hundreds of pillar candles flickered in ornate holders, their golden light bringing warmth to the otherwise chilly air. I was so busy taking in the beautiful space that it took me a second to see why Adam was so on edge.

Nicholas and Isabel flanked the elaborate fireplace like opposing chess pieces. Both were glaring at each other without attempting to veil the hostility between them, their supernatural stillness only emphasising the barely contained energy in the room.

Nicholas stood in stark contrast to Isabel's darkness, his white linen shirt hanging loose and open, the fine fabric drawing attention to the lean muscle beneath. The candlelight played across his defined muscles, highlighting the light trail of hair that disappeared below the waistline of his jeans, ancient and faded to palest blue. I took a ragged breath to steady myself, suddenly flushed, and he broke Isabel's gaze to look at me. I forced my eyes away, but not before his quick, knowing smile told me he'd caught me looking.

Those gold-flecked emerald eyes continued to burn into me from across the room. Only our fifth encounter, and my skin already felt as if it were on fire, even at this distance.

"What's going on?" My voice came out steadier than I felt.

Adam came to stand beside me in the doorway and folded his arms. "They've been like this for the best part of an hour; since

Izzie arrived." His voice was low, though I was sure it carried. "I think it's a predator thing."

Nicholas was still looking at me. "I'm having some trouble with my temper at the moment. Perhaps this isnae the best time for you to come a-visiting." His voice was rough as he gripped the mantelpiece, his knuckles white.

"Nick—" Isabel said.

"Dinnae speak to me, Isabel." Slowly and deliberately, he relaxed each of his muscles and stepped away from the fireplace. "Centuries, and ye still havnae learned when to hold your tongue." His voice carried a dangerous edge, a glint of challenge in his eyes. "A sure sign immortality doesnae guarantee wisdom."

At my side, Adam relaxed too, and crossed the room to sink into a huge, winged armchair.

"Are you... living here?" I asked Nicholas, glancing at Isabel as I did so.

"Apparently," Isabel cut in, throwing Adam a filthy look as she removed her dark blazer and sat, "our host has been less than forthcoming."

"I've been here a few days," Nicholas snapped, running a hand through his damp hair. The waves were wet and darker than usual, curling against the nape of his neck and falling just a bit too long in a way that made him look... untamed. He must have recently showered. "Adam didnae have a deal of choice in the matter."

He gazed into the fire as he spoke, and I was grateful. I was already struggling to hide my churning feelings. Instead, I steeled myself and directed my attention toward Isabel.

"Something's happened," I said flatly.

She quirked an eyebrow at me as Nicholas glanced up, and I took that as an invitation to continue – she seemed entirely unconcerned that the man she wanted me to kill was standing less than six feet away.

I quickly explained about the vamp in the park, trying to hammer home just how much the woman had tried to look like Isabel. I was reluctant to explain my theory about Nicholas being set up yet, but as it turned out, I didn't have to.

He was at my side before I'd finished speaking. Reaching out a hand, he hesitated, his fingertips inches from mine, and even without touching him I could feel the cool energy radiating from his skin. The urge to close that small distance made my pulse quicken. From the corner of my eye, Isabel observed this reaction with curiosity written across her delicate features.

"You're alright? She didnae hurt ye?" The distress in his voice was unmistakable, making his accent more pronounced. I tried to hold it together long enough to meet his eye.

"I didn't get close, to be honest. It was more like she was trying to taunt me," I thought about it. "I'd have preferred a fight."

I took a steadying breath, moving away from Nicholas and slumping onto one of the leather sofas by Adam instead. Being near to him made it harder to think straight – every nerve in my body reacted to his presence. I could feel my face flushing, but putting some space between us helped.

He's a vampire, *Erin, for crying out loud. Forget it.*

Isabel glanced between Nicholas and me, uncomprehending. "What do you know about this, Nick?" Her voice was hard. Accusing.

"Nothing!" Nicholas seemed surprised by the question. "Mayhap I should ask you the same thing."

"Oh, for goodness' sake. It is *clearly* a set up," Adam said, emphasising each word like he was explaining it to a child.

"Perhaps the target is only Nick, or it might be both of you. There's no way to say for sure."

"What reason would anyone have to go to such ridiculous lengths?" Isabel asked, acid lacing her voice.

"Revenge. Fear. Power." Adam counted them off on his fingers. "The usual melodrama. Anyone who doesn't believe they can take you on themselves and would prefer Erin do the dirty work."

"Exactly." I was happy Adam had been the one to bring it up, but I still wanted to have my say. "I mean, dressing up like you guys – I'm not sure how that works, to be honest – but whether it's a plan or just reacting to our reactions, she's got our attention now. She's managed to get everyone in one place by…" I trailed off.

Nicholas nodded, buttoning his shirt. "Jonathan."

"Jonathan?" Isabel repeated, all hostility forgotten.

"My friend in Edinburgh," I added.

Her eyes widened as she gawked at Nicholas. "Wait. Jonathan… Weston?"

Obviously, Adam had failed to mention who Jon was to Isabel. She must have been aware of Nicholas's descendants, though. And it seemed her doubts about Nicholas and this additional information were warring inside her for dominance.

"You know he wouldn't end his own bloodline, Izzie." Adam's voice was gentler than before.

"But…" She didn't seem to be able to find the words. We all fixed our sights on Isabel in anticipation, united in our belief that we were right. She needed to accept this conclusion on her own. If we were being manipulated like I thought, I needed their help more than ever, loath as I was to admit it.

Isabel stared at her clasped hands in her lap, perfectly still. With a sigh, Adam got up from his seat.

"Would you like a drink, Erin?" he asked politely. I suspected he was looking for an excuse to leave the room.

I wrenched my eyes away from the two vampires. "Please."

"Coffee?" he paused in the doorway, one hand on the frame.

"Always," I smiled, turning back to watch Nicholas. He was observing Isabel intently, though he threw a glance at me, his mouth twitching up into a reassuring half-smile.

"I'm sorry about the Forties," Isabel spoke suddenly. I assumed she was talking to Nicholas, whose face went instantly blank.

"I'm sorry too," he replied. "You could've prevented many losses." His voice was barely controlled, and I wished I could ease the pain there.

"I'm *sorry*," she repeated. "I know. And… I believe you." She shifted her attention to me, and I realised I'd been waiting for her approval to fully accept the truth myself.

It was as if some silent signal had been given, and we'd all been holding our breath. Isabel regarded Nicholas as he sat casually by me on the arm of the sofa, his earlier dangerous edge melting into something warmer as he shifted closer. So close that I found myself resisting the urge to rest against him, drawn in despite knowing better. Though I knew his skin would be cool to the touch, my face felt warm just being near him, every almost-point of contact sending sparks of awareness through my body.

"We must try to—" Isabel began, but my phone cut through the moment. I dug it out of my coat pocket. Tom's name flashed on the screen.

"Hello?"

"Erin? Where are you?" His voice was still painfully hoarse.

"Sorry, Tom. I'm just… running some errands." There was no

way I could explain where I was over the phone. He'd blow a gasket.

"Oh. Right. Well, your dad called the landline."

Bloody brilliant.

My parents and I didn't get on these days, and I rarely spoke to them unless it was a special occasion. Or a funeral.

"What did he want?" I frowned, leaning further into Nicholas's presence.

"He…" Tom's voice rasped. "Someone's been threatening them."

I froze, aware of Nicholas and Isabel watching me. I hit speakerphone. "What do you mean, threatening them?"

"I don't know, to be honest. Your dad wanted to speak to you – but he mentioned letters signed with an '*N*'. Creepy calls from some guy with an accent. Your dad tried to brush it off, said it's been happening for weeks, but…" Tom's voice trailed off.

"What sort of letters?" I asked.

"They were graphic, from the sound of it," he said, his voice gravelly. "Your dad wouldn't repeat them back to me."

Adam came back into the room with a wooden tray. The candlelight flickered as he passed, shadows dancing across the walls.

I sighed. I might not like my parents very much, but that didn't mean I wouldn't protect them if I could. The thing was, there wasn't anything I could do about weird letters and phone calls while I still had no idea who was behind it. I could only hope that, for now, whoever it was wouldn't take it any further. My only other option was to go over to theirs myself and stand guard, and I just… couldn't.

"Right," I sighed. "Thanks for letting me know, Tom. I don't know what else we can do about it, but I'll call him back and catch you up on everything later." I knew I was being dismissive.

"Wait, Erin – aren't you going to—" he protested, but I cut him off.

"I'll call them." I hung up before Tom could say anything more, my hand shaking as I lowered the phone.

"If I needed proof we're being played…" My laugh came out hollow.

"We would never let anyone hurt your parents," Adam said firmly. "It won't come to that."

"My best friend is already dead," I retorted. "Maggie too. I couldn't protect either of them."

"There wasnae anything you could do." Almost absently, Nicholas stroked a soft circle on the back of my hand with his fingertip. I calmed instantly at the tiniest contact, but pulled my hand away. *You can't.*

"At least we can learn something from this." I kept my voice carefully level, avoiding Nicholas's questioning look. "If whoever's behind it is still making prank phone calls, they don't know how much we know. Yet."

I watched Nicholas, his brow furrowed. This close, I could see he had the lightest dusting of freckles across the bridge of his nose. It seemed at odds with his nature, since he could never see the sunlight.

"Aye, but how long will we be ahead o' them?" he muttered. I didn't have an answer.

"We need to think carefully." Adam handed me a chunky earthenware mug. "This woman must be someone we know – she had too many details to be a mere stranger."

He was right. There was no way a stranger would target two

old, powerful vampires without doing their research – and as Tom had proven, it was pretty hard to dig stuff up on people like Isabel and Nicholas. Which meant she'd gotten her information from somewhere closer to home.

"Tom and I can keep looking, now we've got a bit more to go on," I offered, pleased I could do something proactive for a change. I took a sip of my coffee. It was delicious. Adam had been holding out on me.

"Tom has quite enough to contend with," Isabel interjected. "His recovery must take precedence. I shall return with you to check on him."

"What happened to Tom?" Adam asked.

Isabel explained briefly, but my mind was on Nicholas, who seemed distant and subdued. I was sure there was something he wasn't saying, though I shouldn't be able to read his face so easily – I barely knew him.

"Shall we go, Erin?" Isabel asked, breaking into my musings from the doorway.

I didn't want to. This was the first time I'd had them all in a room together, and some honest discussion had actually happened. There had to be more to talk about, surely? But I'd promised Tom I'd update him, and Isabel was right about leaving him alone. I needed to be more honest.

Grudgingly, I said goodbye to Adam – who assured me he'd do what he could – and followed Isabel outside. After a minute, Nicholas came after us, and the three of us stood awkwardly together in the doorway.

"Izzie, could you—?" he asked, his face uncertain.

Isabel took in the two of us, shrugged, and went back in, closing the door behind her.

I crossed my arms against the chilly night air, staring at my boots. The stars were hidden behind thick clouds, leaving us in the deep shadow of the manor.

Now we were alone, I wasn't sure what to say. Before I knew it, he was inches away, the fine white linen of his shirt rippling as he stepped closer, rubbing my arms through my coat to get some warmth into them. The cold didn't seem to affect him at all, but I was instantly on fire at the proximity.

"I'm sorry ye have to deal wi' all this," he murmured, his hands stilling on my arms. A ghost of his usual playful smile crossed his face. "It's no the way I wanted us to meet."

I pursed my lips, not quite understanding, but he continued, his voice low and intimate.

"Tis hard for me to imagine what must be going through your mind." His fingers traced down my sleeves. "It's been a long time since anyone dared threaten the people I care about. The feelin' is… unpleasant."

"It's not often I'm this far out of my depth, either. We have that much in common," I smiled. "But I still have hope—"

"Aye, I dinnae doubt it. I can see a fierce determination in ye, on that count." The corner of his mouth turned up in a grin as he looked down at me.

"What I'm trying to say is…" He tilted his head, his golden-flecked emerald eyes dancing as they held mine. "You're drivin' me mad, love. Each time you're near, my control slips a wee bit more," he whispered. "I find myself carin' less and less about holdin' back, and I—

"I cannae lose you." The playful expression faded into something darker, untamed, as he towered over me, the broad span of his shoulders blocking out the night behind him. His voice dropped to a rough growl that sent heat coursing through me. "Almost four hundred years I've dreamed o' you, and now…" He paused, gripping my arms so tightly I couldn't help but look at him, my pulse racing beneath his fingers. "I winnae let you come to harm."

The force behind his words sent electricity down my spine, his conviction awakening something unknown. I wanted to protest that I could protect myself, but it wasn't about protection anymore – or at least, not entirely. His honesty stirred at the darkness inside of me I tried so hard to push down, and I knew, then, that it was powerful enough to match his own… But I couldn't voice it. I knew I shouldn't, that whatever this was between us… wasn't allowed. No matter how it might feel.

"I know," I said finally. My breath made soft clouds in the air between us, though his made none, reminding me once again that he wasn't human. "I just don't understand why."

He didn't take his eyes from me, and I waited for an answer.

"I'm no so sure myself. All I know is… you're *it*, for me." He traced the curve of my cheek with his thumb, cupping my face in his palm, and my breath caught in my throat. "My soul's been a-waitin' for you since before I kent what immortality even meant." His voice grew tight. "And now you're here, testing every ounce o' control I've managed to scrape back o'er the years."

"What do you mean, waiting?"

For a second I thought he smiled again, but it was gone before I could be sure.

"When I was young – human still – my grandmother told me to seek the flame-haired lassie, and she would be my world," he breathed, his voice carrying the weight of the years that his face didn't show. "She would tell stories o' the fey born in the gloaming

– as I'd been, and when she spoke o' such things, even my pa would listen…" He paused. "I heard those same words again, later. Then once more, before the war, from another I would've trusted with my life." Cool fingers laced through my hair, tilting my head back to meet his gaze, and this time I didn't pull away from his touch. "Three times I was promised ye. Three times I feared I'd lost my chance."

His eyes darkened. "Now that I've found you, nothing in heaven or hell will take ye from me."

The words sent a thrill through me. There were questions I should ask, things I knew I needed to understand, but they dissolved beneath the intensity of his gaze.

He stepped closer, backing me gently against the doorframe. His lean body didn't touch mine, but I could feel the coolness radiating from him in the narrow space between us.

"I know you're uncertain, love. That you hardly know me. That you're grievin' still… but I can feel the heat beneath your skin when I'm near. Hear how your heart beats faster for me," he leaned in until his lips almost brushed my ear.

He pulled back just enough to meet my gaze, challenge and desire mingling in his expression. For a moment, I thought he would close the distance between us. Instead, he pulled back, leaving me breathless, heat curling deep in my belly.

"I'll see you verra soon," he promised, his hand ghosting along my jaw to brush his thumb across my bottom lip. I closed my eyes momentarily against the feeling, nerve endings alive beneath his touch. The air between us seemed to thicken, the distance narrowing until I could feel the cool energy radiating from him. My lips parted slightly of their own accord, and his gaze dropped to them—

The Gloaming

"Shall we get going?" Isabel's voice shattered the moment, her silhouette appearing in the doorway. I stepped back quickly, reality crashing over me like a wave of cold water.

I nodded, shakily, and crossed to the car without a word.

15
When Did It Become Alright to Trust Them?

We were silent on the drive home. Isabel stared out of the window from the passenger seat, her scarce breath making a slight fog on the glass. Streetlights swept across her pale features in rhythmic patterns, making her seem more statue than person. Pulling up outside the house, I switched off the engine and was about to get out when Isabel put caught my arm.

"I wanted to speak with you," she murmured, her eyes guarded. I swallowed. This must be as awkward for her as it was for me.

I pursed my lips, reluctant. "Can it wait until we've seen Tom?" I asked. It wasn't the real reason I was stalling, but I had an inkling about what she might have to say that couldn't have been said at the manor, and I wasn't particularly looking forward to explaining myself.

Isabel nodded curtly, and we went inside.

Tom was curled up on the sagging velvet sofa, asleep. The living room was dark except for his laptop's ghostly glow, the screen's white light throwing the lines of his face into sharp relief, making the bruising look even worse. Even from across the room,

I caught his faint scent of soap and pencil shavings – clean and woody, like cedar – clinging to the blanket and cushions around him.

I switched on the brass lamp by the window, and its shade cast a warm circle on the bare floorboards as I drew the heavy curtains and Isabel knelt before him.

"He seems to be showing signs of improvement. His pulse is stronger, more regular than last night," she murmured, her fingers pressed against his wrist. "And there's no sign of a temperature, so likely no infection."

Tom stirred as she gently pulled at the collar of his dressing gown to see his throat better.

"It is healing well already – a side effect of the bite presumably, but in this case that may be a good thing." She seemed satisfied with his state, which was more than I'd hoped for.

"What do you mean, a side effect?" I asked, crossing the room to her side. She was right – Tom's wound looked days old, though it hadn't even been twenty-four hours.

Isabel considered me for a long moment, and I got the impression she was deciding whether she could trust me.

"Some vampires carry a substance in their saliva that can seal a wound, allowing for quicker healing by encouraging clotting," she explained, finally. "Unfortunately, it is often abused by the more sadistic of my kind to keep a victim alive over an extended period." Her tone was disapproving, I was glad to hear.

I thought back to April and the girl in the warehouse near Solace's. It seemed like months ago, but it had never occurred to me to check on her injuries… I'd just dropped her at the A&E, hoping no one would see me.

Isabel stood; her movement quicker than I could take in,

sending me dizzy as my eyes tried to keep up with her. As she did so, Tom rolled onto his back, wide awake. He started when he saw us watching him.

Colour flooded his face as he saw who I was with. "What the hell is going on?" he struggled to get upright, his long arms and legs sluggish.

"Tom, this is Isabel—" I began.

"I can see who she damn well is! What's she doing *in the house?*" he said through gritted teeth.

"Let me explain," I gave Isabel a fleeting look for some support, but she just shrugged fluidly.

"Perhaps I should leave." She shot a look at Tom, more curious than upset, and I nodded curtly in agreement. I walked her to the door, listening all the while as Tom muttered under his breath.

"In the car, before…" Isabel stood in the doorway, preventing me from closing it. "I only wanted to apologise, for the way I have been pursuing Nicholas, and my belief in his guilt."

I grimaced, looking away.

"I was not aware of the situation between you." Her face was a little too understanding for my liking. "I must admit, in all our years I have never seen him this way."

I took a step away from the living room, worried Tom might overhear something that would make him angrier.

"There's nothing going on, Isabel. There can't be." I murmured. "And I've got more important things to be worrying about than an overprotective vampire."

Her brow creased for a second before smoothing out. I wasn't sure I'd seen it at all.

"Of course. Though whether you like it or not, we both know it is more than simple overprotectiveness," she murmured. "Still, try to decide how you feel… sooner rather than later. It is better to know." She closed the door behind her softly, and her silhouette disappeared behind the glass.

Tom was leaning in the doorway to the kitchen, his arms folded. Isabel was right; he seemed stronger. But the way his jaw worked and the dark flush creeping up his neck told me we were seconds away from an explosion.

"Tom, I—"

"What the hell was that about?" he said furiously, gesturing to the door.

"It's not what you think." I tried to keep my voice calm. No matter how much explaining I had to do, looking at him, it was hard to forget he was still injured – another reminder of my failings.

"For fuck's sake, Erin! Are you stupid? She killed Maggie!" His face crumpled at her name, and he gripped the doorframe so hard his knuckles went white against his brown skin.

"She didn't," I insisted. "Neither did Nicholas – it was all a setup."

He snorted. "Can you prove that? I mean, either way, we're talking about vamps here. They're not exactly known for being upstanding members of society!"

"No. Well, yes – maybe. I think I saw something earlier tonight." I quickly explained what I'd seen in the park.

Tom absorbed that for a minute, his breathing deliberately slow as he composed himself. The angry flush faded from his face, replaced by something worse – disappointment.

"Did it occur to you they might just be playing you to get you off their backs?" he said finally, his tone carefully controlled.

"I'm not an idiot, Tom. I've done nothing *but* think about this for days. Weeks, really." I sat down and put my head in my hands. "You knew I didn't like the idea of fighting them; there've been too many loose ends and unanswered questions, and I'd be risking my life on that basis…"

"Wait. So you're… what, working with them instead? Is that what she was doing here? I thought we'd talked about this. Agreed?"

"Isabel was here to check up on you, Tom. She saved your life last night," I said dully.

"Is that supposed to balance out the countless lives she's taken before now? Reformed or not, she's still a murderer!" He was getting angry again. "What about Murray? I suppose he's innocent too. Jonathan killed himself, right?"

I flinched. "You know that's not true. But Nicholas told me he'd never hurt Jonathan. He's his – his great-great-great however many times uncle. His blood."

Tom gawked. "Wait. Seriously, wait. He's from Edinburgh, isn't he? I remember reading it now. Your dad, before – he said the person threatening them had a weird accent."

"Oh, nice and specific of him. Well done, Dad!" I rolled my eyes.

"But you admit he has an accent? I'm sure you've noticed it during your cosy little chats."

Something on my face must have wavered, because Tom paled, watching me. He sat down abruptly.

"Is there something more going on?" His voice dropped, like he was afraid to even ask the question. His eyes searched my face, dread written in every line of his own.

"No," I lied.

"I've known you long enough to tell when you're not being

honest, you know. I may not be Jon—" He averted his eyes, before straightening to stare at me. "I don't get it. Do you *like* him?"

I shook my head, but I couldn't bring myself to meet his eye.

He laughed humourlessly. "That's rich, Erin. Bloody brilliant," he paused before exploding. "He's a sodding *vampire*! Wyatt's a vampire! Fuck knows what Adam is, but he's working with vamps too – that's enough!"

"It's not like that, Tom," I pleaded, my eyes filling with tears despite myself. This wasn't how I'd planned to have this conversation. "They can help us. If they're being set up, it's got to be someone they know – how are we supposed to stop this without their help? By the time we figure it out on our own, half the city will be dead!" I was shouting now too.

"They're evil! They're not human! When did it become alright to trust them?"

"For crying out loud, Tom, they're trying to help! Someone attacked you last night and dumped you on my fucking doorstep. Do you get that you could have died? How scared I was? If Isabel hadn't been here—"

"And I told you I saw Murray! I *saw* him attack me. He's the one that left me there, bleeding half to death!"

I got out of my chair, wiping away tears with one hand in agitation. "Haven't you been listening? There is someone out there that looks like Isabel, taunting us – if someone is setting Nicholas up too—"

"Oh, shut up. I don't want to hear your excuses." I'd never seen him look so disgusted before, the expression alien on his usually warm features. "You've lost it. I mean, if I'd known a pretty face was all it took…" He swallowed. "I thought you were better than that."

He turned away, hands shaking as he pulled on his shoes in the

The Gloaming

narrow hallway, still in his dressing gown. The door slammed behind him, the sound echoing through the empty house, leaving me alone with my tears and the lingering scent of Isabel's lilacs.

16

An Immortal Reprieve

THE WINTER SUN STABBED through a gap in the curtains, forcing me awake. My mouth tasted of stale coffee and regret – I must have fallen asleep on the sofa waiting for Tom, the old velvet crushed against my cheek. My neck and back ached horribly as I sat up, listening to the sounds of the house. I could tell immediately from the absolute silence that Tom had never returned – not that I'd really expected him to. Joints popped left, right and centre as I stretched, and I decided a long run might be just the thing to help me wake up. Bounding upstairs, I pulled on the running tights and trainers that had gone untouched for weeks at the bottom of my wardrobe, scraping my hair into a high ponytail to keep it out of my face.

It was freezing outside, my breath clouding in front of me as I ran. Sheffield's hills showed no mercy, but at least the exercise warmed me up. Between gasping breaths, my mind kept circling back to Tom. He couldn't have fully recovered yet, and the thought of him alone and in pain twisted something in my chest. My phone weighed heavy in my pocket, but I knew he wouldn't answer if I called. It was better to throw myself into work instead – at least then I'd be doing something useful while avoiding thoughts of our argument.

The scalding shower afterward didn't wash away my guilt any more than the run had, but at least it worked some unknown magic on my knotted muscles. Steam fogged the mirror as I braided my hair, the familiar motions soothing. My reflection was almost normal now, bruises fading to yellow shadows. After a futile attempt to channel Isabel's ethereal beauty with my limited wardrobe, I gave up and settled for dark jeans, a black shirt and my customary Doc Martens. I was suitable enough for human interaction, anyway.

Jolt's door stuck in the morning frost, and I had to push my shoulder against it just to get it open. Inside, the stale air hit me first, then the sight of tables still cluttered with cups from two days ago. Envelopes lay scattered on the doormat, jamming the door further – probably applications for the manager position. Yet another reminder of how badly we needed help. I started a mental inventory of everything that needed doing, each task multiplying as I looked around. If we kept up this sporadic opening schedule much longer, we'd lose even our regulars – and we couldn't afford to do that.

Before I forgot altogether, I scribbled a note reminding myself to call my parents as soon as I had a spare minute, and stuck it where I wouldn't miss it: in the middle of the table in the back room. One more worry for the pile.

I'd finished mopping the floors and made a start on unpacking the pastries when the bell over the door jangled cheerily, and Adam walked in, bringing a blast of frosty air with him. I didn't comment as he took off his coat and threw it over the back of a chair as though he owned the place. His simple grey jeans and pale blue shirt were unremarkable – even casual, with the sleeves rolled up – and yet he looked like a bloody supermodel.

The Gloaming

These fucking people, I thought. My confidence took a hit just looking at him, and he knew it, too. I rolled my eyes at him, and he grinned like a self-satisfied cat as he made his way over.

"Good morning to you too," he said, folding his arms and leaning his long legs against the counter. He surveyed the mess around the coffee machine and sink. "I dare say you could use some assistance?"

I made a point of looking him up and down. "Adam, do you even know *how* to work?" I asked.

He shrugged, examining his spotless fingernails. "I have nothing else to do with my day. The trials of cohabiting with vampires," he sighed in mock sadness. "Their schedule is rather inconvenient – a nightmare, as you young people say."

"Us young people?" I laughed. "Alright. Grab an apron. I wouldn't want you to get your pretty shirt dirty."

Adam helped me to rearrange the bookshelves, handling each book with careful precision, his long fingers tracing spines as if reading secrets there. The radio filled the comfortable silence between us, though I caught him wrinkling his nose at plenty of songs. By unspoken agreement, neither of us mentioned the events of the previous night. But as we worked, my curiosity grew, and eventually I had to ask the question I'd been desperate to know the answer to for weeks.

"I don't mean to be rude…" I started.

Adam put down the duster he was holding as he fixed me with a look. "I've learned that whenever someone starts a sentence in such a manner, it ends up being… shall we say, a *personal* question or comment?"

I shrugged in apology. "You're not a vampire, right?" I indicated the blazing sunshine streaming in through the windows and reflecting off his near-white hair.

"No," he grinned and resumed his meticulous dusting. "I am merely… old."

"How old?" I asked, trying to sound casual as I arranged teetering piles of cups and saucers.

He straightened before answering. "Didn't anyone ever tell you it's rude to ask such things?" His eyes sparkled with amusement. "Old enough."

"So… you're immortal?" I might be pushing my luck, but I was too curious to take the hint. "What does that make you? What *are* you?"

He made a noncommittal gesture, turning back to the shelves. "Who knows? I have never been gravely injured – perhaps I could still die. I have no wish to test the theory."

"How've you managed that one? That's a long time to avoid accidents," I said, frowning at his back.

"It's enough to know I heal at a normal rate. In that way, I'm as cautious as you are." He cast me a knowing look over his shoulder. "Perhaps more so. But I haven't aged a day since… 1897. Or thereabouts."

I whistled under my breath. He paused in his work, the duster dancing between his fingers.

"You're surprised?" he asked mildly.

"Yes," I admitted. "I know Nicholas and Isabel have still got years on you, but I wasn't expecting…" The implications of his age caught up with me.

He grinned mischievously, flashing his straight white teeth. "Feeling young and naïve, Erin?"

I stuck my tongue out at him, laughing.

After that, I'd opened the floor for questions. Adam asked how

The Gloaming

I'd met Tom and Jonathan, and I explained about our dream for the coffee shop; how we'd almost gone bankrupt when we were starting out, but Jon had held us all together.

"Do you miss him?" Adam asked as we ate lunch in the back room.

"Jonathan?" A hard knot formed in my throat. I forced myself to swallow. "Yes," I nodded, mostly to myself. "Yes. I miss him."

I picked at the crust of my sandwich, buying time. "At first, he was constantly on my mind. But there's been so much going on… I suppose I got distracted. He's just… part of me, now." A laugh escaped. "I mean, we used to argue constantly – and it's strange, but it's one of the things I miss the most. The debates. He'd always keep pushing until I knew exactly why I believed what I believed."

My voice softened. "He made me brave enough to be myself, you know? To do what needed doing. But he never let me take the easy way out." I set down my barely touched food. "I'm grateful I knew him. I was lucky to have him in my life."

It was a relief to talk about him so freely, though it brought back the familiar ache in my chest. The café felt emptier now, in the spaces where he should've been. No more whistling as he burst through the door, vibrating with enthusiasm over some new idea. No more disagreements about what counted as art. No more barging in on my painting with urgent songs I *had* to hear right this second.

He was just… gone. And his last gift to me had been the mystery of his death – it had kept me too busy to drown in grief. He'd probably have appreciated the irony, anyway.

Adam contemplated that. I took a huge bite of my sandwich so I could look away.

"I met him once," he said softly. "Jonathan."

"What?" I swallowed hastily.

"You were there, too, if I recall, though we never spoke." He gathered our plates and carried them over to the small sink. "I hadn't known your friend and Nick's Jonathan were one and the same... Nick never met him."

"When was this?" I sifted through my memories fruitlessly, but if I'd met someone like Adam, I knew I'd remember.

"Oh, years ago," he waved a dismissive hand. "You were still studying. I was checking up on him – the first and the last time, unfortunately." A small frown creased his forehead. "I only remembered before – Nick's relatives tend to blur together when you've met so many of them. And damn it if they don't all look alike."

"Nicholas was there?" I went still, and something clenched in my chest. I couldn't help but think I'd have sensed him. *Don't be such an idiot.*

"No, no." Adam's lips quirked as he returned to his seat. "He usually keeps track of them himself, but on this particular occasion, he had asked me for a favour. I only spoke to Jonathan briefly, of course. He had no idea who I was. I believe we discussed local breweries or some such. Something terribly mundane."

I smiled to myself. Jon had convinced himself for a while that the best way to bring art, music and literature together in one place would be to run a bar – Tom and I talked him out of the idea, insisting drunk people didn't want to read.

"He did look rather like Nick, though," Adam continued. "Not quite as handsome, but there was more than the usual resemblance. In the expressiveness, mainly. I suppose you've noticed?"

I avoided his eye and went over to the sink. "Yeah."

"Does that make it difficult for you?" he asked sombrely.

I rinsed the plates under the tap. "Does it make *what* difficult, exactly?"

"Loving him." Adam's tone was perfectly innocent, but he was more interested in my answer than he was letting on. *Did Nicholas put him up to this?*

I waited before replying, my hands gripping the edge of the porcelain for support. I gazed blankly at the sky-blue walls.

"Adam... I don't know how I feel about Nicholas. I've only met him a handful of times."

And I feel like I've known him forever. Urgh. It was all so... irrational.

Behind me, Adam sighed. "I've been friends with Nick for almost as long as I've been alive. I've travelled with him all over the world." I turned to face him. "But it wasn't until yesterday, when I saw you together—" he paused. "The way he looks at you... I finally understood what it was he'd been doing all these years, searching."

It was almost what Nicholas had said himself, on the hilltop and again at the manor last night. And Adam seemed so sincere when he said it. But he knew as well as I did that Nicholas had met plenty of women *just* like me.

"He's a vampire, Adam." I bit my lip. "And I barely know him."

"I'm sorry, but you're not fooling anyone with that line of argument," he smiled. "Would you do something for me, please?"

I nodded, curious.

"Try to imagine the frustration Nick has dealt with over the years. He has spent countless decades – lifetimes upon lifetimes – searching determinedly for an unspecific and vague thing... the *idea* of you."

He studied me intently. "It's madness. I went along with it, though he never shared with me where his conviction came from." His voice dropped. "Now consider how many times he thought he may have found you, to then discover he was wrong."

I said nothing, watching him.

"I know to you, his past cruelties are nigh on impossible to forgive. But when one considers his nature," he spread his hands. "His tendency to let his emotions get the better of him... You and I can never understand that bloodlust. He has truly been torturing himself, looking for you."

"And if I'm not the person he's been looking for?" I cringed at the idea.

"Do you honestly feel that way?" His questioning look was laced with disbelief.

My reply was barely audible. "No."

Adam smirked. "Then it doesn't matter how well you think you know him – some things are meant to be."

OUR CONVERSATION HAD GIVEN ME a lot to think about, and the afternoon passed quietly. Adam spent most of his time plucking at a guitar absently, and left me at peace with my thoughts as I smiled mechanically at customers, serving them on autopilot. Every so often, I would catch him giving me a knowing look. It was irritating as hell – I was the last person who needed lectures about destiny and fate. I had enough of that with the hunter stuff. I didn't need it from him too. Besides, his conviction was still pretty baffling. So with an hour and a half until closing, I told him he may as well leave.

"You could head off. It's dead in here."

"I thought you might appreciate the company more than my

barista skills," he chuckled, but he was already reaching for his coat.

"I have," I said honestly. "I could do with a barista, though, if you know one. It doesn't look like Tom's going to step up anytime soon – the guy knows how to hold a grudge."

"He will come around eventually, Erin. You're asking him to dismiss a lot of deep-seated prejudices in a short time."

I pulled a face, annoyed at how wise he could be. "I'm the one who should struggle with that, not him."

"It's understandable you would feel that way. But remember, his belief in this world that he doesn't see… all of that is rooted in his trust in you. He'll discover that soon enough."

I nodded, handing him his scarf. "Thanks for today, Adam. I *have* appreciated the company."

"It was my pleasure." To my surprise, he gave me a quick hug.

I watched through the window until he disappeared into the winter afternoon, breathing the coffee scented air deeply. Inside, only a young couple remained, lost in their own world. Once they left, I closed early, grateful that for a few hours at least, Adam had helped me to forget.

17
Madness Most Discreet

I took the long way home, winding through snow-capped evergreens along a route that took me out into the Peaks before it brought me back toward the city. With the windows down and the crisp winter air whipping at my face, I turned Adam's words over in my mind. I couldn't help but compare it to Isabel's advice the previous evening – they both seemed to be urging me in the same direction. And of course, that led to thoughts of Nicholas.

The memories came thick and fast – his support in the park, holding me like I might shatter. The way his eyes had sought mine at the manor, looking for something I hadn't understood at the time. His laughter. His concern. That ever-so-slightly dangerous smile of his. Each moment with him felt like coming up for air.

And his lips… That brief brush against mine on the hilltop… Heat burned and flamed in my veins at the thought of it, as invigorating as any fight, and somehow completely different in its fire. My rational mind demanded I focus on what he was – every instinct I'd honed hunting should have been screaming at me to stay away.

But my instincts remained silent.

Instead, I found myself wondering what it would be like to

surrender completely to the pull between us. How I'd felt before I'd known what he really was.

If that momentary touch of his lips sparked such fire, what would happen if you just… let go?

Was the fact that he was a vampire – that he had killed, and might kill again – enough to make me walk away from whatever was happening between us? Tom would say yes. Jon, however, might disagree.

From the moment I'd met 'Cole', I'd felt safe with him. Despite everything he'd done – things I'd struggle to forget – I couldn't let him go. And I didn't want to.

There was a darkness in me – a love of the fight, the kill, that was incompatible with normal, human relationships. But Nicholas… not only did he believe I was meant for him, he wanted me despite what I was. And fuck, I wanted him more than I'd ever wanted anything in my *life*.

Admitting it to myself was pure relief. The clarity felt like breathing properly for the first time in weeks. Even my face showed it – a glance in the hallway mirror when I got in showed a version of me I hadn't seen in a long while. Cheeks flushed, hair loose around my shoulders as I freed it from its plaits. My fingers itched for pencils again; maybe now my art would find its focus too.

My dad's call caught me off-guard as I was unlacing my boots. I could tell he was concerned about the letters and the eerie phone calls, but he chattered away, trying to hide it. For once he was cooperative, agreeing to take a trip without argument – it was the only thing I could think of that didn't leave me stuck standing guard outside their house. But that was one less worry, at least.

Upstairs, I ran a bath and examined my healing injuries while steam slowly filled the room. The bruises were mostly gone now, leaving only yellow shadows on my hip and elbow. As I twisted my hair up, I caught my reflection – pale, pointed, perfectly ordinary. What did Nicholas see in me that he hadn't found in centuries of searching? Beauty like Isabel's was everywhere in his world. There had to be more to it.

Sinking into spearmint-scented water, I watched the late afternoon light filter through the stained glass of my tiny window, painting the bathroom in autumn colours. For the first time in weeks, my mind was clear enough to see what I'd first wanted in my mural. Yes, painting shouldn't have been my top priority with a killer on the loose, but I did my best thinking with a brush in my hand. Or so I told myself.

Drying off, I threw on old, paint-spattered jeans and a light, green jumper that reminded me of Nicholas's eyes. I was halfway up the ladder to the attic when a frantic knocking shattered my peace.

I hesitated, one hand on the rung. Tom wouldn't knock, and Adam was headed in the opposite direction. It was still too light for other visitors – and I didn't have any other friends, anyway. After a moment's debate, I ignored it and bounded up to the attic.

Moments later, while rummaging through my paint box for the right shade of sienna, I jumped as a voice spoke behind me.

"Erin." The word was a prayer of relief, jagged with barely contained fear.

I spun around, dropping into a fighting stance without thinking. My body knew him before my mind did – a sudden awareness that sent my pulse pounding.

Nicholas stood in the shadowy corner, his back against the wall and his skin faintly smoking. The black Henley shirt he wore clung to the lean lines of his chest and shoulders, doing nothing to hide how the muscles tensed beneath as he pressed himself away from the light. Deep orange rays flooded the attic from the two large windows on either side of the roof, trapping him. The urgency of the knock on the door now made sense.

"Shit. Was that you banging on the door?" I asked, dropping my fists. I tried to keep my words steady, but my heartbeat seemed suddenly louder than before.

"Aye," he exhaled the word. "I needed—"

I hurried to pull down the blinds, affording him some space to move.

"Burnin' to see you wasnae quite how I planned it though," he murmured, a hint of his usual playfulness surfacing.

I moved closer, noticing the angry red marks on his exposed forearms where the sun had caught him. "You're hurt," I said, reaching for him without thinking.

His eyes followed my fingers as they hovered over his skin. "'Tis nothin'" he insisted. "Already healing."

I brushed the marks, watching in fascination as they faded under my fingertips, the angry red receding to pink, then to nothing at all. My voice was barely above a whisper as I asked: "Is it painful?"

"No," he said, but his eyes darkened as I continued to examine his arm, tracing the places where the burns had been. "No anymore."

The smell of charcoal and smoke clung to him, traces of his desperate run through daylight… but I had no clue what could be urgent enough for him to risk that.

Nicholas watched me with an intensity that made my skin tingle, adding to my already racing heart. For a moment I thought he might reach for me, but he seemed to think better of it, and I took an uncertain step back.

"So," I said, forcing myself to breathe evenly, "what's up?" I winced at how awkward I sounded. Despite my earlier revelations, I struggled to look him in the face – I couldn't control my reaction when I did.

Nicholas swept a hand through his rumpled dark hair, looking around the room with interest. It stuck up in boyish tufts, and I hid a smile.

"Do you mind if I sit down?" he asked.

I nodded, watching as he settled back onto my ratty old sofa, somehow making it look like a throne. His dark shirt and old, worn jeans should have made him look more human, but instead he looked… dangerous. The way the fabric pulled across his chest when he leaned forward, the casual strength in the way he moved – he looked like he belonged here in my space, even as everything about him drew my eyes to places they shouldn't linger.

"Did something happen?"

He paused before answering, resting his arms on his knees. "I thought you dead." His voice broke on the last word.

I must have looked as confused as I felt, as I knelt in front of him. "Tell me."

"I was sleepin', and I could sense the sun going down, when…" His hands clenched. "I caught your scent."

I raised an eyebrow at this – so a vamp's sense of smell was acute enough to wake the dead. The new information just kept on coming, lately.

"I've been at the coffee shop all day with Adam," I explained. "He must have had my scent on him."

"No," he said firmly. "This was pure. Twas your blood."

"I'm fine, Nicholas. It wasn't me." I leaned closer, taking in the tight lines around his mouth, the way his hands wouldn't stay still.

"It was *yours*," he repeated. "I went downstairs, and twas everywhere. Under the door, seeping across the tiles…" His accent was heavy with distress. "When I opened it…"

"What?" I whispered.

"Her face was hidden, hair spread like fire." His voice cracked. "Wearin' your hat from the hilltop. Someone went to a great deal of effort to hurt me, even for a moment."

We were both silent as I took this in. It had been too much to hope the killer had given up. Another woman was dead, and this time the intent couldn't have been clearer.

"Who was it?" I asked eventually. "Who was she?"

"Just another victim to them," he murmured. "They didnae even feed – only left her there to taunt me. Showin' me how close they can get…" His laugh had a bitter edge to it. "And we still dinnae know a damn thing."

"What do you mean, how close they can get?" I asked.

He contemplated me sadly. "Twas *your* blood, Erin. No just your scent. I'd ken it anywhere."

I screwed up my face, thinking. It had been months since I'd been to donate blood. To have stolen something like that meant this bastard – whoever they were – had way more forethought than I'd previously imagined. I shivered.

"We'll figure it out," I said, resolutely ignoring the onset of paranoia and wracking my brain for some piece of information that would give us a clue. Then I remembered something my dad had said.

"What about the accent?" I asked. "My dad told Tom the person calling the house had an accent. If it was the same as yours, that would narrow it down, wouldn't it?"

The Gloaming

Nicholas rubbed at the shadow along his jaw. "Ach, that's no enough to go on. I lived in Scotland for years. Met too many people to count. And as time's gone on, the dialect's changed."

"It wouldn't be someone from that far back though. They'd have to have spent time with you *since* then," I pressed. "It would be someone who knows your history well enough to use it against you."

He raked a hand through his hair again, distress etching deeper lines around his mouth. "I've never made a secret o' my past. Tis my present that concerns me." His fingers flexed. "It's only a matter of time before they come for ye properly."

I pushed aside thoughts of danger, reaching for his hands and stilling them. His skin was chilled against my burning fingers as I traced the scars there – rough patches at his thumbs and fingertips that spoke of a human life long past. I turned one palm over to see them better.

"From the sword," he explained, noticing my examination. His eyes held a gleam of mischief, briefly masking his worry. "Back when I was human. Some marks are… too deeply ingrained for immortality to fade."

I nodded, adding this new bit of information to my mental stockpile of Nicholas Murray facts. I had to smile – maybe one day I'd let him in on my favoured weapon.

"The sun's almost down," I murmured, glancing toward the window where a sliver of light peeked out from behind the blind.

"Aye." He seemed unwilling to leave, and I wasn't sure I was ready for him to go either.

"We should get to the manor. We can find out what Adam and Isabel think about all this." I met his gaze steadily. "Identify the victim at least. She deserves that much."

His eyes darkened and his mouth was on mine before I could draw breath. The shock of it – finally, after all the near-misses and careful distance – sent a current of heat blazing through me.

I moved without thinking, my hands finding his face. He sank back onto the sofa, drawing me with him until I was astride his lap. Every barrier I'd built, every warning I'd given myself about what he was, disappeared under the onslaught of his kiss. His mouth claimed mine with a hunger that matched the tension between us, in each glance and interrupted moment, all leading inexorably to this. Nicholas's dark hair fell forward as he leaned in, silken between my fingers as I pressed closer, his familiar earth and pine scent enveloping me just as I'd imagined. When he moaned softly, I pulled him closer, my hips seeking his as the space between us dissolved. One touch and we were burning – if we let ourselves, we'd consume each other entirely.

His long fingers tangled in my hair, freeing it across my shoulders while his other hand slid up my side, hovering at the curve of my breast before cupping it through my jumper, stroking sensuous circles through the thin fabric. The room had darkened, but I still closed my eyes, lost in the crimson fire racing through me. His body was cool and steady against mine, and it felt *right* – like he was the missing piece of me I hadn't known to look for.

I gave in willingly, my breathing fast and uneven as my blood burned, focusing in a tight, hot knot that sparked in my lower belly. Beneath me, his arousal pressed firm and insistent against my core. I felt his heart stutter to life against my palm – once, twice, three beats through cotton – and I pressed myself more deeply into his body, desperate to feel it again. He tugged gently at my hair, exposing my neck as his lips traced a burning path along my collarbone.

The Gloaming

"Gods, love," he whispered against my skin, "What're ye doin' to me?"

And almost as abruptly as it had begun, his lips were gone from mine. His hands moved to my hips, gently lifting me aside as he stood. I opened my eyes, breathless, but this time he was still there before me. A barely visible flush hid the faint freckles under his eyes, and I smiled wryly up at him.

"We should get goin'." His voice was rough velvet. "I'll meet you there."

18

Love Runs Away from Those Chasing Him

A WHILE LATER I LET MYSELF in through the tall iron gates that guarded Locke Manor, my mouth still burning from the scalding hot soup I'd forced down before I left. The house was ablaze with light, a pattern of squares scattered across the lawn from the rooms above – it looked as though every room in the house was lit up, giving the whole building an inviting warmth that the symmetrical Georgian façade lacked during the day.

A large, dark stain marred the smooth limestone of the front step, and I edged around it to knock on the door. Isabel answered immediately. She wore her customary black – a knit top that hung loose around her collarbones and cigarette trousers – but something in her had shifted. Maybe it was how she lingered in the doorway, or the way her usual sharp edges seemed softer in the hallway light.

"Erin, come in." She smiled more warmly than she had the last time we'd spoken, but I was sure there was something in her face I was misreading. Her quick, appraising look took in my jacket – Nicholas's leather jacket, to be more precise – without comment. I wasn't sure what had made me wear it, really.

"What did you do with the body?" I asked, as I followed her into the kitchen. A fire had been lit in the stove, and the room was stiflingly warm.

"I did what had to be done, since I was left to deal with it. Nick fled at the sight of her – to check on your welfare, I presume – and Adam came over conveniently squeamish." She looked to the heavens. "It really was a most bizarre thing to awaken to – why someone would go to the effort to display her that way, propped up with her limbs spread-eagled so unnaturally, I do not know."

I grimaced, but Isabel was still talking.

"… so I left her in the park for another to find."

She paused, watching me from across the breakfast bar. "I might have burned her in the garden, but I suspected you might disapprove." Turning to the drawer behind her, she rummaged around for a moment. "Do you wish to keep this?"

It was my yellow hat. Lovely. I didn't know what was more offensive – her casual treatment of a dead body, or the insensitivity of offering the bloodstained piece of wool to me. I settled on the former.

"You left her in the park? You didn't try to find out who she was, or let her family know? Anything?" I could hear the shrillness in my words, but I didn't care.

She gave me a warning look. "What more could I do? Think carefully before you answer."

She's right. Anything else would draw suspicion.

"I suppose you couldn't really take her to the hospital or call the police…" I admitted. "It'd look like you had something to do with it."

"Very much so. Should I dispose of this?" She waved the hat again.

I recoiled. "Yes, thank you."

To my relief, Adam walked into the kitchen, saving me from an awkward apology.

"Erin! I'm glad you're here." His usual easy manner faltered as he glanced at Isabel, reminding me how he'd denied they were friends. That was definitely a story I needed to hear.

I smiled back. "We've got a lot to talk about."

The silence stretched. My eyes wandered the room, landing on the warm wooden countertops and professional-grade appliances. "Nice kitchen. I meant to say before…"

"Indeed." Adam straightened the cuffs of his grey suit, his movements precise. "Though lately its contents suggest different ownership." He pulled open the fridge door, revealing neat rows of medical blood bags.

"You don't prefer… fresh?" I asked Isabel.

"My feeding habits remain my own affair," Isabel said coldly, closing the fridge with enough force to make Adam step back. She crossed back over to me. "Incidentally, I assume you donate?"

I shot a look between them. Adam shrugged, but Isabel had already lost interest in my response, her gaze fixed on the ceiling.

"Isabel?" I waved a hand in front of her.

"What is he doing now?" She murmured, seemingly to herself.

"Who? Nick?" Adam asked, watching her with interest.

She vanished. Adam switched off the kettle with a weary sigh. "Shall we?"

We followed the sweep of the main staircase, its original elegance somehow enhanced by Adam's modern touches. The landing stretched in both directions, a line of mysterious closed doors that made my fingers itch to explore. But we headed for the iron spiral staircase at the centre.

The landing narrowed at the top of the house, and it was darker here than below. Isabel stood silhouetted in the last doorway, moonlight from the garden window casting her shadow across the carpet. A rhythmic thudding echoed down the hall, accompanied by the rustle of paper and fabric.

Nicholas was a blur as he darted between two enormous trunks, the air stirring with dust and the smell of old leather as he sorted their contents. Books were strewn carelessly across the floor.

"Are you going somewhere?" Adam frowned, blue eyes following him as he moved from one to the other.

Nicholas didn't look up, but examined the binding of a leather-bound book, before throwing it carelessly onto the floor behind him with a thud.

"He's running away," Isabel explained, her tone condescending. "Again."

"I'm no *running*, Izzie." His voice was tight, and his movements were less controlled than usual. "But lurin' away the danger might be the only move we have left." His eyes met mine for a heartbeat before slipping away, but I caught the warmth and pain in his eyes. "Unless you've miraculously figured out who's targeting us since the sun set?"

The urgency of his earlier kiss suddenly made sense. *Of course.* He'd been saying goodbye. I said nothing, but something inside my chest contracted.

"I suppose it might work…" Adam nodded slowly. I glared at him, and he shrugged.

"No." My whisper carried in the silence. "This isn't just about you. Running won't fix anything."

"The deaths were arranged to look like my work – the first victim my relative, then a redhead like—" He couldn't meet my eye. "And now your double? I have to keep ye safe, and I cannae watch over ye day and night as I'd like." There was an edge of desperation in his voice.

I looked to Isabel for support. "Tell him he's being ridiculous."

She crossed her arms. Her gaze sharpened, measuring me against some hidden standard.

"Isabel?" I didn't want to ask again.

She exhaled heavily. "You *are* being ridiculous, Nick."

Phew.

"You can't leave." I took a step into the room, and he slowed enough for me to see what he was up to.

Beside each trunk was a neat pile of books, all similar in shape and size, the leather worn and faded. Some had a small brass lock on the front, others were hand bound and tied closed with knotted lengths of leather. He added another to the pile, discarding several beautifully embroidered books that wouldn't have been out of place in a museum.

"It's no forever," he replied, closing the lids of the trunks and locking them. "Only til we ken what's happenin' here, and we've learned enough to thwart the bastard." He straightened up. "I cannae guarantee how long it'll take, but with me gone, you neednae worry about being attacked, at least.

"These are my diaries," he gestured to the neat pile of books, a ghost of his wry smile touching his lips. "They're no exhaustive, and it's true there're long gaps in some o' them – but they might help ye in the right direction."

I couldn't take my eyes off them. *Fuck*. A month ago, a resource like that would have been priceless – we'd never had anything like it. Tom would have sold his soul to get his hands on that kind of knowledge. Except now, despite my curiosity, I sort of hated them.

They were a symbol of Nicholas's disinterest in staying here – with me. And I already had an idea of the horrific events I'd find inside. Of *course* I wanted to know more about him. but I had a feeling that reading those books would leave a nasty taste in my mouth, and my acceptance of my shiny new feelings was still too fresh for me to want to taint it that way.

"Surely your memory would serve as well, Nick?" Isabel asked, folding her arms and resting her slender frame against the open door.

"Aye, it might, but I dinnae intend to be here to share it; as you've so cleverly deduced," he retorted.

"What do you think leaving is going to do, exactly?" I asked, trying to keep the anger and building anxiety out of my voice. "How is that helpful?"

"We thought the killer was trying to draw your attention," he explained. "Now we know we were wrong."

Isabel scoffed. "What on earth gave you that idea?"

"Why else would the lass have looked like Erin, if no to taunt me?"

I caught Adam's wry look out of the corner of my eye, and ignored him.

"Nick," he said flatly. "She resembled Erin because any dolt can see how you care for her. But while I don't doubt the events of today were distressing for you, I am sure they were almost as unnerving for Erin." I could almost see Adam hold back his eye roll. "I confess, I'm a little offended no corpse has yet to resemble *me*, actually. But then, who could compare?" He smirked, but quickly became serious again.

"Do be logical about this – you must know Erin is no safer with you gone."

"You won't lure them away, anyway—" I added.

"It may only widen the span of destruction," Isabel finished.

Nicholas dragged a worn black duffel bag from under the bed without looking at any of us. "You cannae know that."

"I think we *do* know, Nick," Isabel said, incensed. "Jonathan's death was to hurt you. *All* of this has been to hurt you – including hurting Erin. The entire scenario has been orchestrated from the start to bring you here, to a *vânător* that may actually challenge you, for once." She spared me a glance, and I took the compliment without comment.

"If, as I suspect, the perpetrator has discovered that Erin has no interest in killing you, then it only follows that their plans have had to adapt accordingly."

My chest tightened at Isabel's words. She was right. Everything that had happened came back to Nicholas – not to me. I might have lost friends, but my grief hurt Nicholas almost as much as it did me. And now, seeing him prepare to leave… "That's why you were the recipient this time. They're trying to break you down. Manipulate you into doing something you'll regret."

"You can't deny, it's clever," Adam said quietly. "Rather what one might have expected from you in centuries past."

Nicholas shook his head, a wayward lock of dark hair falling into his face. He pushed it back in agitation.

"To stay might at least limit the damage. Wherever you go – whoever you might call upon for sanctuary – would only become involved themselves," Isabel said.

"And tell me, Isabel – is my being here keepin' Erin's family safe? Did it keep those lasses safe? My last livin' descendant?" He answered. "If I leave, it might show them I dinnae—"

He didn't finish the sentence, but I knew what he meant. *That you don't care.*

Isabel shrugged. "Were I in their position, I should consider your departure cause to make a grander gesture," she responded. "Perhaps dispose of Erin or Adam to make my intentions clear."

I bristled. "Not to undermine your point, Isabel, but I can take care of myself."

"Yes. But so far, *yourself* is the only person you've been able to take care of." Isabel raised one eyebrow at me. "No offence."

Ouch. She was right, though. Everyone I should have been protecting had been hurt. More than that, a complete stranger had died today just because she had the misfortune to look a little like me – and there was fuck all I could do about it.

Nicholas leaned against the carved bedpost of the massive four-poster, his impossibly long legs stretched before him. The ivory sheets lay rumpled and unmade, and as they shifted beneath him, the faintest trace of his earthy pine scent reached me from across the room. It was strange to think of vampires needing ordinary human stuff like beds, though I guess it wasn't really an ordinary room.

"They might hurt her to bring me back," he repeated to himself. "It worked last time. They were here before I was."

"*Yes.*" Relief flooded through me. "And maybe there's something in that we can use against them – let them think they've got us cornered. But right now, we're wasting time."

His eyes burned as they met mine. "I dinnae like feelin' so… powerless."

"I know." I murmured. "So let's do something about it." I crossed the room and grabbed his hand, thrilled at my own daring. His eyes widened, and that familiar half-smile touched his lips. "Tryin' to save me too, now, eh?" he asked lightly, his fingers curling around mine. I looked to the others.

"I think we can all agree we're not exactly a step ahead, here. I have no idea where they're getting their information from, but nowhere feels safe anymore."

I looked to Adam. "You're rich, right? Are you paranoid too?"

He frowned delicately, and I had to laugh. "Do you have anywhere in the house that's more secure?"

Adam glanced at Nicholas. "The library, perhaps? I'm – ah – rather protective of my collection."

I grinned. "Perfect. I'd forgotten you had a library," I lied. "Not too shabby."

Isabel's laughter was a delicate tinkle in the air. "You should see his other properties," she grinned. "Follow me."

We followed her back down the spiral stairs and toward a set of huge, heavy oak doors at the end of the first floor hallway. Isabel strode ahead and flung them open with unnecessary drama. I stifled a chuckle at the clichéd image, tugging Nicholas along behind me, a bemused expression still lining his face.

19
Revelations & Rejection

THE LIBRARY WAS DIM UNTIL Isabel and Adam lit small lamps along the wide aisle. Rows and rows of shelves lined the walls, stretching back further than I could see in the darkness, with more on the balcony above. A raised area at the back of the room held a huge, ornate desk that was strewn with paperwork and books, beneath heavy red curtains that hid vast windows. Now I understood why Adam had suggested this place – it felt safe in here. The rich scent of paper and furniture polish was comforting, and surrounded by books with thick Persian rugs underfoot, even my footsteps were muffled.

I released Nicholas's restless fingers, tension and frustration still radiating from him even as we separated. Meandering down the centre of the library, I debated idly with myself how long it must have taken Adam to collect so many books. Hell, I'd have loved to curl up in here and read my way through all of them, but I couldn't see the opportunity to do so coming up anytime soon.

As the room filled with the dim golden glow of the lamps, I took a seat in a high-backed chair upholstered in the same damask fabric as the curtains. Nicholas sat beside me, so close his knee brushed mine every time I shifted. Despite everything that had happened today – or maybe because of it – I was hyperaware of his presence. I tried not to be distracted by the play of the light in his hair, highlighting coffee colours that I'd never noticed under electric lighting. He caught me staring.

"Nice jacket, by the way," he murmured, his eyes briefly taking in the worn leather jacket I was still wearing. That familiar half-smile played at his lips, but thankfully he didn't elaborate further. Instead, he leaned closer, ostensibly to reach for one of his diaries, and his scent – woodsy pine and something uniquely him – surrounded me.

"So," Adam began. "Time for another thrilling round of *'Which Vampire Killed Who and Why*—'" He dropped a pile of leather books onto the table with a thud, and they tumbled down untidily. "My favourite parlour game."

Nicholas shot him a look. "If you're no goin' to be helpful—"

"I am always helpful," Adam drawled. "I simply think we could benefit from some levity while discussing murder and mayhem. Centuries of perspective should allow for that, at least."

Isabel's lips twitched. "Some of us prefer to maintain decorum, Adam."

"Yes, and look how well that's served us so far," he replied smoothly, earning twin glares from both vampires.

"And your irreverence has achieved what, precisely?" She glared at him across the table. "Besides ensuring you remain forever on the periphery of matters beyond your understanding."

"Children…" I muttered under my breath.

The tension dissolved a little, and I seized the opportunity to get us back on track. "Okay, let's start with what we know. There are two of them?"

"What makes you say that?" Adam asked, taking a seat.

"There was the woman, but there was also whoever was calling

The Gloaming

my dad." I leaned back and ran a hand through my tangled hair. "Tom thought the person who attacked him was Nicholas, so it stands to reason there's a guy involved, too."

"Smart," Isabel said, her expression thoughtful. "But the woman in the park could have been anyone. You said yourself she didn't engage with you. You hunt vampires. Therefore, any vampire would have the motive to—"

"Aye," Nicholas interrupted. "Any vampire would have a motive. But the woman she saw didnae try to kill her. She was tryin' to..." he searched for the right word.

"Piss me off?" I volunteered.

"That'd be it." One side of his mouth quirked up.

"It's a start." Adam spread the books out before him, checking something on the back of each one. I took another from the pile and noticed it had a date stamped along the bottom of the back cover, embossed in gold. "But I dare say we need rather more than that," he added. "What else have we learned? Didn't your father mention an accent, Erin?"

"A Scottish accent," Isabel corrected. "Someone you knew in Edinburgh, Nick?"

"Perhaps a relative unhappy with being overlooked?" Adam speculated. "It might explain the resemblance."

Nicholas gave him a dirty look. "I'm no that careless."

Adam held up both hands. "You haven't always been as meticulous as you are these days, and we both know it." He sighed. "Though *I* am keeping track. Despite how singularly dull James will be for the next few decades."

I ignored them both. "How do we know the accent was Scottish?" I asked Isabel. "Tom just said an accent, and he probably assumed because he knew about Nicholas. I can check—" I pulled out my mobile phone and dialled my parents' house.

My father answered on the second ring.

"Hi, Dad."

"Erin! Thank goodness; we were worried—"

"I told you before, I'm fine – there's nothing to worry about." When it came to my parents, white lies were the way to go. "Quick question though – it's sort of urgent."

He paused. "Go on."

"When you spoke to Tom about your anonymous caller…" I prompted.

"Yes?"

"You mentioned an accent. Was it Scottish?"

"Scottish?" He sounded surprised. "No, no. It was European. More like French, I'd say. Maybe Italian?"

"I need you to be sure, Dad."

"French, then. But… unusual."

I frowned. I wasn't sure what I'd been expecting, but it wasn't that.

"Okay, thanks. I'll call again soon, yeah? When I've got more to tell you." I hesitated. "In the meantime – you know the drill."

"Alright. Your mum says hello," he added, and I rolled my eyes. "And stay safe. You can't protect anyone if you're dead."

My laughter sounded false even to me. "I know."

I hung up, the others watching me expectantly. Nicholas and Isabel must have heard, but Adam waved a hand at me.

"French," I said. Adam's eyebrow arched as he shot Nicholas a meaningful look. He picked up a diary he'd discarded, fingers drumming against the leather cover as he rechecked the date.

"How much does your family know about you, Erin?" Isabel asked, exchanging the diary she'd been holding for another.

The Gloaming

I shrugged. "My dad's always known I could recognise the… otherworldly." My mouth formed the word without thinking, though it never seemed like the right word, anyway. Vampires were definitely a part of *this* world, in my experience. "I told him a lot when I was younger, and he always believed me – at least, he never tried to refer me to a psychiatrist," I chuckled, remembering.

"My mum was less understanding, so eventually I stopped mentioning it. They don't know everything, but my dad's perceptive enough not to ask."

Isabel nodded, her gaze far away. "It is fortunate you can rely on your family, even a little." Collecting herself, she added: "Now, this French accent. Might it be a regional dialect? Perhaps Breton?"

I considered her words as I reached for a diary at random – it was an odd thing to say, though admittedly I knew nothing about Isabel's family. Through all the research Tom and I had done, we'd never found out much about her life as a human. We knew she'd been born during the reign of Henry the Eighth, but even that was more of a guess. There was a lot we still didn't know.

Nicholas leaned in close as I flicked through the pages, his voice low and velvety in my ear. "Well, I happen to think you're quite the huntress."

I tried not to glance at him. "And when have you seen me in action, exactly?"

He chuckled quietly. "That night in the park wasnae the first time I saw you. I prefer to do a wee bit o' hands-on research where I can."

Well, you missed that one, Erin.

"The way ye move when ye fight… there's a sweet surrender in it," he whispered, his breath cool against my ear. "Makes me wonder how ye might've surrendered if I hadnae stopped us earlier."

Heat rose to my cheeks as I remembered how I'd lost control in the attic, and I snapped the diary closed. Isabel shot him a loaded look from across the table, but Nicholas merely offered her an innocent smile.

"Our time in the Paris apartment at the turn of the century – was that the sole time you spent in France?" Adam asked Nicholas, oblivious to our quiet conversation.

"No." He was all business again. "I was in the capital during the Great Wars, o' course. And I remember some time in the 1790s, I think, but no for verra long." Nicholas pushed to his feet, and I felt the sudden coolness where his leg had been pressed against mine. He walked around to where Isabel was sitting and plucked the diary she was reading from her hands.

Isabel snatched it back from him with a glare. I wondered, briefly, what it contained.

"What do you mean, you think?" I wondered out loud. "I thought you guys remembered... well, everything." At least, that's how it seemed with Solace.

"No, love." Nicholas shook his head. "Our memories are no more infallible than yours. There's more to remember, aye, but over time the details fade. Only the significant events remain, just as they do for you."

"For example, most vampires remember their first kill. The deaths of friends and family. People they sired." Isabel explained. "Did you change anyone in Paris, Nick?"

His eyes found mine, and something vulnerable flickered across his face. "I couldnae say," he said finally. I shifted in my seat as he added, "Mayhap one or two."

The careful way he said it, trying to soften the truth for my sake, somehow made it worse.

The Gloaming

"How could you not know something like that?" I asked. Apparently, there was a lot I didn't know.

He shared a silent look with Isabel. Scowling, she nodded.

"Do you know how vampires come to be, Erin?" He stared at me intently. "How we're sired?"

I shook my head. "Bloodborne, isn't it? You share blood…" I'd tried not to think about it too much, though it was a subject that Jon had obsessed over endlessly.

Isabel replied: "Yes, traditionally. A vampire drinks from a human until they are on the brink of death, and then the human must drink of the vampire," she explained. "But it seems there's more to it."

"Are you saying it isn't the only way?" Adam appeared as interested as I did – obviously, this was something Isabel and Nicholas hadn't shared with him.

Isabel leaned forward onto her elbows, resting her chin delicately on her interwoven hands. "There have been scientific advances over the last century that we could never have imagined or expected." She glanced at Nicholas, who was watching her.

"Society used to be dominated by religion." Her tone had lost its usual edge, and she seemed troubled by her words. "It is hard to explain to what extent, to one who has never known such a world. Disease was thought a punishment from God for our earthly sins. As time went on, things changed. We once dismissed medical breakthroughs, preferring prayer and remedies lacking scientific basis. But no longer."

"I don't understand what you mean. Vampirism… is a disease?"

"We dinnae ken," Nicholas admitted, his broad shoulders tense beneath his shirt. "There're elements as can be likened to deficiencies of the immune system. Some become vampires without exchanging blood. Others die despite it."

The lamplight caught the sharp planes of his face as he spoke, and I couldn't help but notice the coiled energy in the way he held himself. He might have changed his mind about leaving, but his body was still ready to fight.

"We also know that there is an element of the mystical that cannot be explained with science." Isabel sat back from the table. "Our speed and healing abilities—"

"Elements that grow stronger with age," Nicholas interrupted, his eyes narrowing slightly.

"Indeed." A slight smile played on Isabel's lips as she glanced at him. "And I must say, an extra century does make quite the difference in refining such gifts. Some things only time can teach."

A muscle twitched in Nicholas's jaw, his right index finger flexing against his knee. The air in the room seemed to thicken, and my pulse quickened as I sensed the shift.

In a blur of motion too fast to track, Nicholas had Isabel pinned against a bookshelf, his forearm across her throat. Books tumbled down around them. Despite her predicament, Isabel's smile remained unchanged, almost fond.

"Age isnae everythin', Izzie," Nicholas growled softly, towering over her, though there was a glimmer of amusement in his eyes. "Some of us learned our skills the hard way."

"If you two are quite finished destroying my library," Adam's dry voice cut through the tension. "Many of these volumes are older than the both of you." He caught my eye, adding: "Though significantly less dramatic, I'd wager." I bit back a smile.

Though he hadn't raised his voice, both vampires instantly

separated, exchanging looks that were more playful than antagonistic. Nicholas returned to his seat, but I couldn't miss how his gaze went back to Isabel – he'd bested her, and he knew it. *She* knew it.

My heart was racing, and I knew half the room could hear. I'd seen Nicholas gentle, heard his soft laughter and felt his cool touch. But the last minute or so was a reminder of what I'd worried about before... that underneath his control, was a lethal warrior I couldn't begin to imagine.

Isabel settled back into her chair, continuing her earlier thought. "There's also the extreme aversion to aspects of the ultraviolet spectrum... these are not things research commonly supports as symptoms of a disease." She raised an eyebrow at me. "What illness can you name that *strengthens* the host?"

I had no answer. But my understanding of vampire limitations seemed suddenly – and dangerously – incomplete.

"The one thing we know for certain is that vampire blood invades like a virus." Her voice held centuries of disquiet. "In a matter of hours, the human immune system is overtaken. If already weak, the human may die before the transformation is completed. But if the accounts of vampires who were never bitten are *true*, then the virus – if we should call it that – can be transmitted in other ways."

A hush fell over the library as Adam and I processed this revelation. My heart was still pounding – not just from their demonstration, but the implications. It could only be a good thing that vampires weren't as easy to make as I'd thought. But if vampirism could spread without deliberate blood exchange, how could we – *I* – ever hope to contain it?

"None of this is proven, of course," Isabel said quietly. "We can never test these theories, as we cannot risk our blood being formally studied – though I would imagine there are more than a few curious vampires in the field."

I nodded, dazed. How many accidental vampires were out there, not even knowing what they were? It was a terrifying concept, but we had a more immediate mystery to solve.

"So, getting back to Paris…" I forced my voice to sound casual. "You could have changed a few people, or you may have changed every single person you fed on." I was determined to appear nonchalant, but the prospect was terrifying.

"Tis no likely." Nicholas's face was difficult to read, and I knew he was trying to gauge my reaction.

"How long were you there for?" Adam muttered to himself. He seemed to have taken the new information in his stride. "It must have been a few decades with me. There was the Tower's construction, and the World Fair… time has dampened my memory, I'm sure."

"The Eiffel Tower?" I asked, with more than a little disbelief. "Seriously?"

"Aye, though Adam's memory of its being built is somewhat hazier than mine," Nicholas said, giving me a knowing look. "Something about testing every absinthe house in Paris *'for research.'*"

"I was being thorough," Adam huffed. "Someone had to document the cultural significance of the era."

"Is that what we're callin' it now?"

Adam ignored him. "But yes, the Eiffel Tower. A rather ghastly affair, though these days it's quite drowned in gaudy lights. Have you been to Paris?" he added.

"No." I was excluded from the reminiscing, but I should have expected as much. I'd never been around older generations who didn't indulge in nostalgia on a regular basis – though Adam couldn't have been all that old back then.

"When was the World Fair?"

"1889," Isabel's gaze grew distant. "I did not attend."

"So you must have been…" I asked Adam.

"Twenty-two. You say you were in France in the 1790s, Nick?" Adam flicked through the pages with increasing irritation. "Could you be a little vaguer?"

"I told ye there were periods where I kept no record." Nicholas glared up at him, ignoring the insult. "But the 1790s are irrelevant. I wasnae around people for most o' that period, I stayed out in the countryside."

The conversation was fast going over my head – I didn't understand what any of them were talking about. My knowledge of French history – and specifically, Nicholas's history – was too scarce for me to contribute much.

"Maybe we should try focusing on one time and place each, and find out what we can – then move on to the next. With each of you searching for different things, we're just going to miss something," I said, trying to think methodically. "There's too much to get through otherwise."

Isabel peered up at me, distracted. "You know, Erin, your presence here is no longer required. You have shared what knowledge you possess."

I pulled a face at her dismissal, but she was already absorbed in her book.

"It can't hurt to have another set of eyes, surely?" I liked to think being a hunter might give me an alternative perspective if nothing else.

She didn't glance up this time, though Nicholas didn't meet my eye either. He had spread out several diaries and was making his way through the pages, arranging and connecting loose papers with a renewed sense of purpose.

"You should rest, love," he murmured, glancing up at me. I shifted uncomfortably in my chair, and his eyes darkened with concern. "I can see from the way you're sittin' your ribs are still troublin' you."

Typical that he'd try to protect me by pushing me away.

"You might check on Tom," Isabel suggested.

Nicholas reached for my hand, but I pulled back, catching the flash of hurt on his face before he masked it. I should feel sorry, but I was more pissed off than anything.

I wasn't an idiot. Isabel wasn't being cruel – she was being practical, trying to shield me from Nicholas's history. But they'd forgotten how involved I was in this. It didn't matter to me if Nicholas was the actual target or not. This was my fight. I was the hunter, damn it, and I planned to be the one to bring Jon and Maggie's murderer down. I'd lost too much to let a couple of vamps and a snarky immortal take that away from me, too.

Cramming a few of the early diaries into my satchel, I left the library in a hurry, without saying goodbye even to Nicholas. If they wanted me gone, fine. It wasn't going to stop me from learning what I could.

Nicholas probably didn't want me to read some of the things he'd written, but I had another plan for how I could use the books. They'd been right about one thing – I'd left Tom to his own devices for long enough. I needed to make sure he was alright, and the diaries would make an excellent peace offering.

I was pulling on my coat in the hallway when Adam appeared

— he could move almost as quietly as the vampires when he wanted to.

"They're not telling you to leave to get rid of you, you know," he said, examining the fingernails on his left hand.

"You're sure about that?" I asked bitterly. "It feels a lot like I'm the naughty child being sent home from school for misbehaving."

"Izzie's protecting him." Adam adjusted his cuffs, a nervous habit I was beginning to recognise. "You cannot *imagine* the things in those books, Erin, and I'm sure you wouldn't want to. As for Nick…" He clasped his hands behind his back. "I suspect he's ashamed of what you might think of him."

I showed him the diaries in my bag. "I've *imagined* it all."

He frowned. "Then try not to judge him too harshly." His usual polish cracked slightly. "The person you will read about is gone. His actions weigh upon him still, but he did nothing more than play his role." He met my eyes. "I forgave him, but I don't think he could survive if you didn't."

I glared at my boots and bent to tighten the yellow laces. "That's not a promise I can make, Adam."

As I straightened up, he was smiling – but there was sadness in it. "It shouldn't be easy. We know what you are, after all. But I have known Nick for years, and already I can see the change in him since he met you." He fixed me with an intent look. "After so long searching, it would be a pity if I had to watch him lose you for the sake of the person he used to be."

I pursed my lips. "I don't see the monster when I look at him," I admitted. "But some things are hard to forget… And the other night – I know you know I was there. Outside the club—" I couldn't speak.

"He will always be a vampire. He can't help that." Adam

shrugged. "But she didn't die, you know – the woman. I accompany Nick when I can, and he finds it easier to control himself when I'm there to keep an eye on him."

"She'll still be traumatised for the rest of her life."

He laughed. "You underestimate Nick's allure, I think."

"Trust me, I don't," I muttered to myself, pulling my bag onto my shoulder. I pushed a hand through my hair, missing my hat.

I changed the subject. "I need to try to mend some bridges with Tom. He's actually really useful with stuff like this, if I can convince him to work with us."

"Then please, try your best to do so." Adam's voice grew serious. "And don't forget how much you are asking of him."

20

Nature Never Deceives Us

As I set off on the drive home, I turned over Adam's parting words. My stubborn desire to let Tom stew didn't change the fact that I understood his concerns about Isabel and Nicholas – until recently, they'd been my concerns, too. The difference was, now I knew them better, they didn't *feel* like vamps to me. They were cultured and in control – it didn't make my skin crawl to be near them.

Tom relied too heavily on my extra sense. Jon had too. And okay, I was telling him something that went against everything he knew – apparently out of the blue – but all I was asking for was a little more trust.

I parked outside the dark house and let myself in, intending to call Tom and ask him to come over as soon as I had my boots off. It was a conversation that needed to be had in person. But to my surprise, I found him in the darkness, feet propped on the sofa arm, the blue glow of his phone screen casting harsh shadows across his face. I switched on a lamp.

He set his mobile on the coffee table with deliberate care, fixing me with a sharp look. "I had to come back at some point."

"I'm glad you did." I twisted my hands together. "We need each other. I need you here." The words tumbled out before I could stop them. He stared at me, and I worried he might shout again.

"Before you start, just let me talk?" I pleaded, trying to head him off.

Eventually, he nodded, looking around. "You've been with *them*, I suppose?"

I sat down, pulling off my scarf and gloves.

"Yes, but I need you to listen. And…" Since bribery might ease him up a bit, I pulled the diaries from my satchel. "I brought these."

Tom's hand reached for the books before he could stop himself, curiosity winning over anger. "Journals? Whose?"

"Murray's." I leaned forward slightly. "Now, will you listen?"

"Okay." His fingers traced the worn spines as he flicked through them, handling them carefully so the loose pages didn't fall out. As far as I'd been able to tell, I'd brought the earliest ones, though they didn't all have dates. I doubted we'd find anything about our French friend in them, but I figured it was best to start from the beginning if I wanted to understand Nicholas – and learn to forgive him. I didn't mention that part to Tom.

It had occurred to me on the way home that our friendship could benefit from more honesty. So, settling into my seat, I prepared to tell him everything. *Really* everything, this time. From Maggie's murder to the unknown woman who'd died tonight. I recounted every conversation I'd had with the vampires he hated and what they'd said – at least, as much as I could remember. More importantly, I explained what I'd understood from it. It was everything I had, and I laid it all out on the table. Now it was Tom's too.

As I spoke, Tom's shoulders gradually lost their rigid set. He set the diaries aside, finally meeting my eyes. My voice had grown hoarse by the time I finished, but the tight set of his jaw told me he was still struggling.

"Well?" I asked, as the minutes of silence stretched out.

He leaned back in his seat and folded his arms stubbornly. "Alright," he said mildly. "I have some questions."

I didn't hesitate. "Ask away."

"Do you trust them?" he asked. "I mean, actually trust them. Because it all comes back to that, doesn't it?"

"I do," I answered without thinking. "Isabel saved your life."

He eyeballed me. "Which is precisely why I ask. What better way to get you to trust them than to make sure I don't bleed to death on your floor?"

I wanted to deny it outright. If Tom could remember how she'd helped him, he'd understand. But he couldn't, and I needed more than just my own conviction.

"Wyatt's been around for a long time," he added. "She probably understands human nature better than almost anyone alive and could manipulate even the most sceptical of people." His hard stare didn't waver. "I want to know *why* you think she saved me. Don't you wonder what her motive is?"

"Maybe," I said eventually, weighing my words. "And maybe it wasn't concern for you. She could have been trying to gain my trust. But… it worked," I shrugged. "You know how I feel about vamps, Tom. And you've always had enough faith in me to take my word for it, that there are… things we can't explain." I took a deep breath, phrasing myself carefully.

"I'm asking you to trust me now. Yes, I'm pushing my luck, big time, but… I don't know. She doesn't feel evil to me – not anymore." I paused, thinking about it. "I'm not sure she ever did."

"Being near her – and Nicholas too – it doesn't make me want to peel off my skin the way being near other vampires does. It's hard to explain." I pursed my lips. "They're... evolved."

Yes. It was the word I'd been looking for, for days.

"So, maybe she knew I'd trust her if she proved herself. But she came back the next night of her own accord, knowing how hostile you'd be, just to make sure you were okay. That tells me a lot, too."

Tom's expression softened slightly. I hadn't won him over, but at least I'd reminded him why he trusted my judgement.

"Second question," he began. "How much of this shiny new approach has to do with your feelings about Murray?"

I grimaced, staring at the woven pattern of the rug between my feet. It was the one thing I hadn't shared specifics about, and somehow my careful effort to avoid the topic had been wasted.

"I don't know how to feel about what I feel," I said truthfully. "But I know they're not involved in what's been going on. It was a long shot from the start – you know that as well as I do. It was too obvious. It never made the sense I wanted it to."

I tucked my feet underneath me, aware of the winter chill seeping through the house. Tom watched me through guarded eyes, his shoulders still tight.

"Then on top of that..." I sighed. "Nicholas and I have a complicated relationship. I need to know more about his past before I can work it out."

"So you admit something's going on? And when I asked you yesterday, you lied about it?" His voice was still calm, but I could sense we were getting to the source of his anger.

"You didn't give me much of a chance to explain myself." I tried not to sound too defensive.

"Because you're in love with a *vampire*!" He barely raised his voice, but I jumped anyway.

The Gloaming

"I never said that!" I snapped back, trying to collect myself. "I don't know, alright?" I put my head in my hands, massaging my temples with my fingertips. I could feel a headache coming on.

"It doesn't matter if I am or not. The best chance we've got is to work with them," I said, eyes still closed. "Look at the diaries, for crying out loud. I'd bet there's enough in *one* to condemn Nicholas; probably Isabel too – and from what I saw earlier, there are hundreds more." I looked up at him. "They're not trying to deny the past. They know what they are, and what they've done. We have to get over that."

"Erin," he stared at me. "I miss Jonathan as much as you do. We were a team." He took a deep breath. "But his life didn't mean more than the lives of the hundreds of others those two have killed. They're helping us now – but it doesn't mean they're forgiven for all that they've done before—"

"That's not what I'm saying—"

"Let *me* finish," he retorted. "You might be right, they're reformed. Maybe they'll never kill again. That's still a big chance to take. They're not human; their limits are different to ours – it's in their nature. Not to mention, they've got eternity to change their minds."

I shook my head at him. "You could say that about anyone. Anyone could snap."

"Most of us aren't predisposed to it."

He was right. But it wasn't enough of a reason.

I watched him, sitting there. He was still shaky. Recovering. His skin hadn't regained its usual warmth, and I hadn't even asked how he was.

He wasn't the Tom I knew and loved. Fear and suspicion had carved a deep line between his brows, and I got it. I really did. I'd always been the more open minded of the two of us, and even *I* had never thought about any of this in shades of grey… But if he couldn't give them a chance, more people were going to get hurt. I needed my friend back more than anything, but he'd have to see it for himself to believe it. And he just wasn't there yet.

I sighed and put my head in my hands again, staring at the floor.

"One more question."

I looked up.

"Say all of this works. We figure out who the killer is. You hunt them down, take them out. Then what?"

"What do you mean?" I asked. This couldn't be as simple a question as he was making it out to be.

"Isabel, Adam and… Nicholas." He pulled a face as he spoke the name. "Are they staying? The number of vamps in this city's been decent for years, thanks to you. With two more in the city – that can only last so long."

I wasn't buying his innocent act for a second. If I was honest, I didn't have an answer. Everything I'd learned tonight about how vampirism spread made it worse – sure, Isabel and Nicholas could control their feeding, but anyone they sired, intentionally or not, might not be so careful. And when I tried to picture myself turning against them… my chest twisted painfully. I couldn't do it.

I sighed. "I don't know, Tom. I haven't given it much thought. I'm taking the days one at a time."

"You don't seem to have thought much about any of the tough questions."

"Please don't be like that." I rubbed at my temples, fighting the headache. "I'm trying to talk this out with you, and you're jumping down my throat." When he just stared back stonily, I threw up my hands. "Can't we deal with the problem that's affecting us right now and worry about everything else later?"

"What if later, we're not around to worry about it?" He raised an eyebrow. "We might go into this together – if you get your way, and you usually do – but there's no guarantee we survive. Who's going to make sure your precious new vamp friends are under control after?"

"Is this a jealousy thing?" The words came out sharper than I intended. "Are you mad because I made other friends?"

"I'm angry," Tom's voice dropped dangerously low, "because your new friends have centuries of murderous history as baggage, Erin. That's not easy to take when you prefer to spend time with them than with me."

"You're not exactly being the greatest friend right now," I said evenly.

He glared at me for a minute and abruptly stood.

"I trust you, Erin. But them? Not a bloody chance. I'll help because I have to, but don't think for a second I'm keeping quiet about it after."

21

NONE CAN SAVE ALL

I SAT IN FURIOUS SILENCE. TOM had stormed into the kitchen, but I didn't follow. I knew he wouldn't leave – he distrusted the vamps too much to risk being alone. Breathing heavily, I tried to calm myself down, but I was struggling. What had started as mildly upsetting had led to anger, and I needed to get out – if only for some fresh air and to rid myself of the headache.

I had my boots on and was out of the door before Tom could stop me. Running through the streets in the leftover slush of the recent snow, it began to rain. I kept going, no longer caring how wet and cold I was. I just needed to expel the energy inside of me.

By the time I slowed to a jog miles from the house, my lungs were burning and my heart was racing. I leaned forward, hands on my knees to catch my breath. The rain was still coming down, but I wasn't cold anymore.

Looking around, I found myself back at the park with the old lodge, though I hadn't planned to come here. I straightened and stretched, turning my face to the sky. I felt better – and there was no harm in doing a quick sweep while I was here. It wasn't even midnight yet. And it might keep me from thinking of Tom's words – because some of them were just a bit too close to the bone. There was no way

I was ready to think about all that.

Vaulting the high gate with ease, I smirked as I landed lithely. Finally, I was feeling physically like myself again. Hopefully, there'd be someone here to make my night worthwhile.

Pushing a hand through my soaked, heavy hair, I set off along the main path, peering into the shadows of the gigantic oaks spaced out across the lawns. As I passed the playground, movement flickered under the climbing frame. Seconds later, a limping tabby appeared, meowing at me mournfully before shooting away into the night. I glowered, disappointed.

Rain trickled down my neck and under my coat. As goosebumps prickled my flesh, I froze. Slowly, trying to appear as casual as possible, I took another look at the playground. There was someone there. I was sure of it.

I opened the small gate almost silently, edging around the back of the slide that created a small, enclosed hideaway. Under the rope bridge connecting the two sections of the frame, they huddled in the darkness. I shuddered, my entire body on edge. It hadn't been just the cold.

An older man, his face haggard and ruined by prolonged exposure to the elements, lay lifeless across the lap of a young girl with dirty blonde hair. She was familiar, though I could barely see her features as she nuzzled her teeth into his throat, practically purring with contentment. Blood stained the man's filthy jacket, but even from here it was clear his heart was no longer pumping.

Crossing the tarmac in four long strides, I grabbed the girl by the hair and yanked her up from the ground, smashing her head into the underside of the slide. A metallic gong sounded through the night. For a moment, she clawed at my hand with her fingernails, trying to loosen my hold. I wound my hand more

The Gloaming

tightly into her greasy locks, pulling her neck backwards at a painful angle. She snarled, exposing her bloodstained teeth, but her arms dropped to her sides limply.

The clouds shifted above. Moonlight lit up the park and I fully saw her face for the first time. My grip loosened, and I threw her to the ground. In seconds, she'd pushed herself up on her elbows and was scowling at me, malice in her eyes.

My stomach lurched. It was the teenager I'd first seen at Solace's – April and Will's blood bag. No longer covered in scars, teeth marks or bruises; her skin glowed with the luminescence of eternal youth.

I stood there, staring at her in disbelief. She glared back, though she seemed dazed.

"No…" I murmured, the word catching over the hard lump that had formed in my throat. She couldn't have been more than fifteen.

A slow, sly smile spread across her face. "I know you, don't I? You smell… different."

I said nothing. I didn't know whether to feel anger or despair – after everything, I hadn't even saved her. It was exactly what I didn't need to see tonight – evidence to back up everything Tom had said.

With a shaking sigh, I dropped to one knee and quickly unsheathed the Damascus knife buckled to my leg. Her eyes flicked to the blade as the moonlight glinted off it brightly, and back to my face. She scrambled backwards, hiding under the climbing frame.

I dived after her, catching her by the ankle. This was my mistake to fix. She tried to pull away and heaved the homeless man's corpse at me with alarming strength. My grip broke. The body thudded against my chest, and I shoved him off me.

The climbing frame still trapped her on three sides – she had no choice but to fight. There was no escaping without getting past me. As I closed in, she lashed out with her bare heel and caught my left eye, snapping my neck sideways. Spots danced in my vision, but I kept going.

Backed into the corner, she kicked out. Her foot slammed into my abdomen, then my collarbone as I failed to block the blows. I twisted around her flying legs and caught her ankle again, my other hand still occupied with the knife.

Without thinking, I pulled her toward me and thrust my weapon up into her stomach in one quick jab. Blood flooded from the wound, soaking through her dress and drenching my hand and wrist. She coughed, red spurting from her lips and spattering my face. By now, she'd stopped struggling enough for me to pull her closer, and once again I wrapped my hand in her hair, bending her neck back to expose her throat.

Eyes half-lidded, pupils mere dots in the blue, she gaped at me. I turned my face away as I dragged the sticky blade across her throat, her blood pouring forth in a crimson waterfall I couldn't bear to watch. She jerked once, and was still.

Time lost meaning as I sat there with the lifeless girl in my lap, hands trembling and teeth chattering. The rain fell harder, a curtain between us and the world, but I couldn't move.

I was filthy. Mud and grime covered my skin and clothes. My hair was sodden and trailing in ropes in the girl's blood. I gazed at the homeless man's body, thinking about who might miss him, whoever he'd been. Looking down at the girl in my arms, her mouth smeared with someone else's life, I couldn't shake the feeling this was my fault – that I should have done more to save her.

The Gloaming

Staring blindly into the rain, I didn't hear the approaching footsteps until two boots appeared by the slide. Bending to see under the climbing frame, Nicholas took in the scene – me, still holding the dead girl and wearing her blood, the old man's torn throat and my knife on the ground. Heedless of the rain that soaked through his jeans, he knelt, eased her from my lap and pulled me gently toward him.

He wrapped his arms around me as I wept into his already soaked shirt, my body shaking from the cold and the ache in my chest I didn't know how to fix. I closed my eyes against the image of the girl burned in my mind, taking comfort in the earth and pine smell that was Nicholas, until my hiccupping sobs quietened and I could breathe normally again.

"What happened?" he asked finally, leaning back to look into my face, his green eyes dark with worry.

I had to look away. "I don't know," I hesitated. "I – I knew her."

Nicholas assessed the dead girl, rainwater dripping from the waves of his hair. "She was a friend?"

I sighed, the sound lost in the hammering rain above us. "No. She… I thought I'd saved her weeks ago. I thought she'd be okay, but she wasn't."

"She changed anyway," he nodded, holding me closer again.

"How can this be happening?" I mumbled into his chest. "If I can't help her, what's the point? It's really the way you said, isn't it? Anyone can turn."

"Aye, I'm afraid so. But it's no so common as you'd think. We cannae give up because we dinnae always win, Erin," he murmured, his accent deepening. The way he said my name sent a shiver down my spine that had nothing to do with the cold. "Come on. You're soaked to the bone, and it's dreich enough even *I'm* feeling it." His mouth quirked up into a half-smile.

I took the hand he offered as he stood, pulling me upright.

"I have to check she's—" I began.

"No need." Nicholas took off his heavy woollen coat and draped it over my shoulders. It was almost as wet as I was, but I was grateful regardless. "Her spine's damaged. I can see that much from here. It must have been quite the killin' blow."

"It wasn't much of a fight." I shook my head. "I could barely look at her."

"You had to," he said, cleaning my knife on the girl's thin summer dress, smearing the floral pattern.

"That doesn't make it any easier."

"You winnae be the person you are if your job were easy," he smiled sadly, straightening.

I didn't answer, but pushed my hair back, turning my stinging face into the downpour. As I did so, Nicholas slid his hand into mine, gently squeezing it to draw my attention back down to earth. His skin almost felt warm on my freezing fingers.

"Are ye hurt?"

"No." I swallowed. "Yes, but… I'll let you know in the morning. I can't really feel anything right now."

"I'll be sleepin' then," he apologised. "But I'd rest better if you'd let me send Adam to check on you?"

I nodded. Sometimes, it was dangerously easy to forget how different we were – the fundamental rhythms that would always keep us apart.

"It'll be alright, love." He squeezed my hand again. At his touch, the newly familiar heat pulsed through me, my nerve endings blazing as always when I was with him – but this was gentler than before. His thumb traced small circles against my palm: a question I wasn't ready to answer.

I'd never thought of Nicholas as a comforting presence before, but he was. Endless paths of possibility opened up before me, teasing at what Nicholas and I *could* be. Had I been less exhausted, the idea would have been overwhelming, but with his hand enveloping mine, I tried to enjoy the feeling.

Nicholas walked me home, the rain easing off to reveal the silver moon. Outside the house, he paused, then swept me up into his arms. My breath caught in my throat.

"I've found," he murmured against my hair, his lips so close I could feel their phantom pressure, "that there are moments when being a vampire has its advantages. Carrying beautiful, dangerous women across thresholds without breaking a sweat bein' chief among them." His eyes glinted with amusement as he carried me through the door, past Tom on the sofa, and up the stairs.

Placing me on the bed, he removed his damp coat from around my shoulders, his hands lingering a moment longer than necessary. His fingertips traced the curve of my collarbone, featherlight, stopping just short of where my pulse hammered at the base of my throat. I pulled the duvet up around me, and despite the dim light, I caught how his eyes traced my face with a quiet reverence that made my heart ache. He stepped back with visible effort, his fingers curling into fists at his sides as he paused and leaned in the doorway.

"Goodnight, my midnight wanderer." His smile lingered in the darkness.

"Goodnight, Nicholas," I whispered, but he was already gone. Through tired eyes, I stared at the empty space where he'd been, wondering if he felt the same hollow emptiness spreading through his chest that I did whenever we parted.

22

TO LOVE ONESELF IS THE BEGINNING OF A LIFELONG ROMANCE

THE BRIGHT WHITE WINTER sun fell through a gap in the curtains, waking me. I lay watching the dust motes dance in the light for a while, systematically assessing the soreness in my muscles, testing and stretching each limb a little at a time. It was hard to say how badly I was hurt without getting up, but nothing on this earth could entice me out of the warmth of my duvet. Except, of course, the need to use the toilet. I forced my poor, aching body out of bed.

Glancing in the mirror as I entered the bathroom was a mistake. I reached blindly behind me and sat down on the edge of the bath, unable to take my eyes from my reflection.

I was a mess of dried blood and dirt, crusty patches flaking away where tears had run down my cheeks. My left cheekbone had swollen up like a balloon, the skin black and tight. The right side of my jaw was turning purple, too – though I didn't remember the blow – and the flesh was tender beneath my fingers as I gently probed it. Above my eyebrow, a thin cut was still weeping.

It wasn't just my face, either. My right shoulder had turned a deep mauve, blossoming dark ink blots across my collarbone, which must have been more seriously injured than I'd first thought.

I couldn't believe I hadn't noticed any of this last night – the fire and the adrenaline had obviously been in overdrive – but it explained why Nicholas had seemed so concerned.

Everything crashed in at once – not just the pain, but the memory of the teenage girl's face. The tears came hot and fast before I could stop them. I'd failed her, whatever Nicholas said. And if it could happen to her… What was I even doing? Fighting monsters until one of them finally killed me, and for what?

My reflection looked back at me, tears leaving fresh white tracks in the grime. But no clarification or relief came from the salty streaks.

I took a deep shuddering breath. The last element of control left to me was to hold back the tears. I'd cried enough.

Tom had been right. I hated it, but when this was over, I'd have some serious questions to ask about how vampires were created, and what we could do about it. Isabel and Nicholas would have to share everything they knew, whether they liked it or not. I couldn't keep putting my body through this, knowing it was a losing battle.

At some point, I collected myself enough to climb carefully into the shower. The scalding water stung my skin, freeing the strands of hair that were glued into my cuts with dirt and blood. Eventually, the heat forced my muscles to relax, too, and by the time I stepped out of the tub, the mirror was so fogged with steam that I didn't have to look at my reflection. I got into a fresh pair of pyjamas, wrapped myself in my softest dressing gown and headed downstairs.

Tom was nowhere to be found. The blanket folded neatly over the end of the sofa told me he'd likely stayed the night, and I made a mental note to thank Nicholas for his discretion. It would only have made things worse for Tom to have seen another vamp in the house.

I curled up in my favourite armchair by the window for a while, watching the clouds roll in and blot the sun from the sky. After a few minutes, the deep, comforting aroma of coffee lured me into the kitchen. Someone had put the coffeepot on a timer, and the carafe was still full. I poured myself a cup and returned to my chair with an ice pack wrapped in an old tea towel pressed to my shoulder – or my face, depending on the moment. It wasn't long before I began to doze off, but a sharp rap on the door snapped me back to attention.

Adam stood on the top step, leaning on a smart black umbrella and wearing an expression that said the weather had personally offended him.

"I want to go out," he said abruptly, stepping into the hallway. His eyes narrowed at my face. "What happened to you?"

"Good morning to you too," I grumbled. He reached past me smoothly, hanging his coat neatly on a peg. The hall filled with the scent of rain and his usual citrus and clove.

"Well?" He paused in the living room doorway, studying my bruises. I caught sight of my face in the hallway mirror – most of the swelling had gone down at least, though the bruising painted quite a picture.

Top marks for advanced healing abilities, Erin!

"I'm a hunter, Adam," I replied. "I get into fights. And what are you doing here, at—" I checked the clock. "Okay, well not *that* early in the morning, but still."

"The sun is up, so I am alone, and I am bored." His fingers traced the back of Tom's usual spot before he settled into it. The faded velvet somehow looked expensive under his touch. "Nick asked me to check on you – quite forcefully, I might add – and I thought we might make an expedition of it."

I shook my head at him, unable to hide a smile. "Coffee?"

"I'd love some," he purred.

I grabbed milk and sugar, setting them on an old wooden tray beside two mugs. Filling both from the carafe, I decided to reset the machine for another pot – just in case. When I put everything down beside Adam, he picked up my Wonder Woman mug like it was some kind of priceless antique. His mouth twitched, but he said nothing as he helped himself to milk.

"I want to go out," he repeated, stirring his coffee delicately. "Do the things you humans do."

"Yeah, you said. You remember I have a coffee shop to run, right?" I tucked my feet under me, watching him deliberately flatten an invisible wrinkle in his trousers.

"Yes, but since you own the shop, you can… call it a holiday?" His eyes danced as he took a sip. "You also happen to be my only friend."

"I'm not saying I can't, but—" I thought of the research party I'd missed last night. I wasn't sure I could justify a day trip with Adam, but he was already making me feel guilty.

"Then it's settled." He leaned forward, hands clasped like he was proposing a business venture. "Where shall we go?"

His enthusiasm was contagious. It had been a while since I'd taken a day off that wasn't murder-related. "What exactly do you mean by *the things you humans do?*"

"Oh, you know." He gestured vaguely with his cup. "The entertainments I see on television. Theatre, fairgrounds…" A slight grimace crossed his perfect features. "Aren't those things you do?"

"Not regularly, no." I studied him over my coffee. "Adam, when was the last time you actually got out into the world? During daylight, without Nicholas or Isabel?"

"The day we met, I suppose. But prior to that, it's been… a while." His fingers drummed once on the armrest. "The daylight presents something of an issue. And when they're feeding—"

I flinched, and he noticed, changing course. "Crowds can be… difficult. And one can't simply wander alone, not without knowing the territory."

Something in his voice made me look closer. Behind the carefully maintained façade, he was lonely. Stuck between worlds – too human for the immortals, too immortal for the humans, the sole sunwalker in his 'coven' and yet loyal to his vamp best friend. I sighed inwardly. I liked Adam, and he was fun to be around, but I had a lot on my mind.

"Alright," I said, setting down my mug. "But you need to update me on everything you found out last night. I refuse to be left out of the loop."

He straightened, almost imperceptibly. "It goes without saying, surely? You mightn't want to assume I would do anything to keep you out of it, you know."

I nodded and ran a hand through my hair. "I know. Sorry."

"Apology accepted." He rose from his seat, towering over me. "Now, shall I examine those injuries you're so determined to downplay? Nick was quite insistent, and I promise not to pry about the specifics."

"What is it with immortals and medical degrees?" I asked, trying to lighten the mood.

A genuine laugh escaped him. "Who said I was qualified?" His hands were surprisingly gentle as he checked my injuries. "I was an army medic, once or twice. After we realised I was immortal… well. Nick preferred I accompany him." Something dark flickered behind his eyes. "Let's just say war is not for me. A medic seemed safer, but it didn't stick."

Interesting. "Somehow, I can't imagine your bedside manner being missed."

He made a show of looking offended, but his fingers remained gentle as they probed my collarbone. He tutted, lifting my arm to test its range. I winced.

"You'll do, I suppose." He stepped back, his mask of careful indifference sliding back into place. "You're lucky not to have dislocated your shoulder, and your collarbone is intact. It's not ideal, but since you are a hunter…"

"Thanks." I stood up and frowned down at my rumpled dressing gown. "I suppose I should get dressed."

Adam gave me a disparaging look. "Yes, you should."

AN HOUR LATER, WE WERE IN MY CAR, heading east toward the coast. The threatening grey skies had finally opened, and the downpour was getting heavier the further east we went, turning the motorway ahead into a silvery blur. It wasn't the right weather or the right time of year for a beach trip, but it was easier to go along with Adam's request for seaside ice cream than to argue.

I tried not to worry too much as we drove – I'd called Tom before we left, to no avail. Which meant, once again, the coffee shop was closed, and we were going to lose another day of takings. Luckily, the improvement in Adam's mood was infectious. And fuck knows, I needed a good mood and some fun. I was still coming down from the previous night, and there was a raw, ragged ache in my chest whenever I thought about it.

"How does this work?" Adam half-shouted as we sped along

the motorway, the rain hammering loudly on the roof. His pale fingers traced the edge of my phone curiously.

I glanced away from the road for a moment to see he had Spotify open. "It's connected to the car by Bluetooth."

"I see," he replied, still frowning. "Should we listen to driving songs? Isn't that what people do? Is this a... what is the term, a road trip?" The questions tumbled from his mouth, and I didn't try to hide my laughter.

He sniffed disapprovingly.

"No offence meant!" I held up one hand in apology. "But it's like you're a time traveller or something. How do you not know about this stuff?"

Adam took a deep breath. "I'm aware of how the world works, Erin. I just rarely find myself in a situation where I might experience it first-hand." He scrolled through my playlists, apparently not sure what he was looking at. "Travelling by night, by train or aeroplane... it's terribly tiresome, quite quiet, and utterly boring." He gazed out of the window, raindrops casting shadows across his profile. "But isn't it better not to be alone?"

"Of course," I sobered a little. "But you're not always with Nicholas, right?"

"No, no. Until recently, I hadn't seen him for six years, actually. I've only known him a century or so – I'm rather young when you compare me to my companions. Companion singular, I should say. Izzie is..."

"Not what you'd call a friend?" I guessed, remembering the awkwardness between them last night.

"She's... an old acquaintance, certainly. Thankfully, she often disappears for decades." Adam's eyes met mine in the reflection of the windscreen. "Nick assures me she wasn't always that way, but the war had a poor effect on her, as you know. She's never been the same."

I pulled a face, but I said nothing. If we'd been talking about anyone else, I might have been more understanding. And I *was* sympathetic. Sort of.

Isabel Wyatt had suffered this last century. But I couldn't help but feel like she'd done so much harm in her past, it was surprising it hadn't happened before now. Nature always found the balance.

"You think she deserves it?" Adam asked quietly, not looking up from my phone.

I immediately wanted to deny it. But I pursed my lips and kept quiet, waiting.

"You may be correct," he added. "Though don't you think it's a different sort of pain?"

"I don't understand what you mean. Isn't pain just – pain?"

"Physical pain, mental pain, heartbreak…" He put the phone down. "Izzie has a tongue like a viper, an ironclad set of her own moral rules and a calculated approach to violence."

"You're really not selling her," I said.

"She's been trying to atone, as Nick has. And her grief is a reminder of the grief she's brought about in so many others." He paused. "I believe she worries that the pain she feels will eventually overshadow how she felt about her husband. When the depth of her guilt is so great, it must be hard to remember the light she once lived in, if only for a moment."

I stared at the road ahead, flicking the indicator to change lanes. "I thought you didn't like her?"

He made a noise somewhere between a snort and a laugh. "I don't."

"So what's with the deep personal insights?"

The Gloaming

"I *understand* her. As much as it's possible to understand the vast mind of a vampire, old as she may be." He paused. "Perhaps it is why I don't like her."

I wondered what he meant. Sometimes, Adam's behaviour toward Isabel almost rang of jealousy, though I wasn't sure what it was he had to be jealous of.

"Can I ask you something? And it's not… accusing, or anything."

"By all means, you usually ask as you please." I caught him glancing at me, but I didn't take my eyes off the road.

"You and Nicholas. You're good friends?"

"We are."

"How did that come about? How do you know him?" It wasn't quite what I wanted to ask, and Adam noticed.

"Do say what you mean, Erin."

I fidgeted, glancing at the wing mirror. Through the rain-streaked glass, a lorry loomed behind us. "Do you love him?"

Adam chuckled. "Dearly. But as a friend."

"Ah. Okay." I didn't say anything more. It had never really seemed like Adam felt like that about Nicholas, but I knew so little about their friendship.

"I am…" Adam began, and I glanced at him. He was staring out of the window. "I'm not particularly inclined toward anyone at all, in *that* manner. I never have been."

I smiled. "I don't know, Adam. You seem to fancy yourself pretty well."

He laughed. "But of course."

The quiet piano melody tinkling from the car speakers came to a close. Adam turned slightly, his expression softening. "You needn't worry about Nicholas's affections, you know."

I glanced at him, caught off-guard. "What?"

"In all his years," Adam said carefully, "He's never truly loved anyone. Not really. He may be a charmer, but the red-headed women in his life were not a part of his… more *physical* pursuits, shall we say? And as you're aware, each one was ultimately a disappointment that ended in tragedy."

Oh, okay. We're going there.

"It isn't something he talks of often. But on occasion, enough whisky has loosened his tongue to confessions." He adjusted the seams of his trousers, shifting in his seat. "His crimes are undeniable, but his conviction has been almost unwavering. I guarantee his affection is equally as unshakeable."

I gripped the steering wheel, processing. I already knew bits and pieces, and I wasn't sure if I wanted more than that. But I couldn't deny the small feeling of relief Adam's words evoked.

A blast of trombones from the speakers saved me from replying. Adam had switched back to his previous excited state, singing along to the Frank Sinatra cover, the conversation seemingly forgotten as quickly as it had begun.

WHITBY LOOKED EXACTLY AS miserable as you'd expect in December – empty streets, grey skies, and the last of the rain giving way to an even nastier wind.

Adam gazed up at the Abbey ruins silhouetted against the grey sky. "I read Stoker's novel when it was first published," he mused. "He captured the atmosphere perfectly, though I confess the weather was better then."

Even with the awful weather, I was glad we'd come. I showed Adam the amusement arcades along the seafront – open rain or shine – and he lost several games of air hockey quite spectacularly. My hands smelled of copper from the old machines by the time we'd thrown almost a day's wages at the slots and claws. The tinny music and electronic beeps echoed off rain-streaked windows, mixing with the permanent scent of damp carpets and candy floss that clung to every seaside arcade. Exactly as it should.

Stepping out toward the pier after emptying our pockets of change, Adam declined my offer of a greasy burger from a tiny café, which was probably for the best. Instead, we took advantage of the brief minutes when the clouds parted, buying ice creams that made my teeth ache from the sweetness.

We wandered back along the beach for the remaining hours before we lost the light, the sea dark and uninviting. As the neon glow of the carousel lured us back towards the area where we'd parked, Adam stopped abruptly, a curious smile playing about his face. Behind us, the sea roared its soft music.

"What is it?" I asked, the wind whipping at my escaped hair, scraps of orange splashing across my vision.

He shook his head, still grinning. "Could we take a photograph?"

I didn't understand his reasoning, but I agreed. Standing alone against the backdrop of the brightly lit, empty carousel, Adam seemed like a real Victorian gentleman for the first time. Or at least what I imagined they looked like – my knowledge mostly came from period dramas. With his hands in the pockets of his smart grey coat, he stood unsmiling and stiff. I took the photograph, and he immediately snapped out of it, beckoning me over.

"Now for both of us?" He took my phone from my hand, adeptly angling the camera so he could press the button. Beaming and huddled together, the blurry glow of the carousel behind us threw our faces into sharp relief. We looked exhausted, but happy. It was a great picture.

Adam didn't doze in the car as we drove home in the dark. I'd expected him to, but then I remembered he wasn't entirely as he appeared – for all I knew, he didn't sleep. When I pulled up outside my house, he insisted he would make his own way home, and I was too exhausted to argue.

I wondered whether he'd tell Nicholas where we'd been. For all his aristocratic airs and immortal mystery, Adam had managed something no one else had, lately – he'd made me feel normal for a day. Even if nothing else about my life was.

23

TO SLEEP LIKE THE DEAD

THAT NIGHT, I SLEPT BETTER than I had in weeks. But the following day I was determined to grill Adam for everything he'd failed to catch me up on – because while our trip out had been just what I needed, we'd never even touched on the research he, Nicholas and Isabel had done.

After a quick shower, I multitasked and called him while spooning cereal into my mouth and contemplating whether it would be more efficient to just pour my coffee directly onto the sugary flakes. There was no answer, but it was still early enough to be dark outside. He might be asleep – if that was something he still did.

I paced the house for a while, trying to decide if it was too early to head over there. I *had* to get to Jolt today – I couldn't get away with being so irresponsible two days in a row. Plus, the shop had overheads; I had rent and just as importantly, Jolt was all there was left to show of Jon's legacy.

By the time I'd downed my third cup of coffee, I decided it was worth driving over. The sun still wasn't quite up, so I'd probably be too late to catch Nicholas or Isabel, but Adam could fill me in on everything.

I rummaged around in my drawers for my favourite grey

hoodie, but it was nowhere to be found, so I went all black in jeans and long-sleeved t-shirt instead. The scoop neckline did nothing for my bruises, but my wardrobe options seemed to be shrinking at an alarming rate. Dr Martens improved every outfit, anyway.

Crunching up the gravel driveway of the manor, I noticed that all the curtains at the front of the house were closed tight. Maybe the others were up, then. My stomach did a little flip, but I tried not to get my hopes up that Nicholas would still be awake – I hated that I'd gone a whole night without seeing him, wasting precious time on sleeping instead.

A dark stain still marred the doorstep despite the heavy rain the day before – another reminder of what was at stake if our research failed. Adam answered the door almost immediately.

"What a singular surprise," he said as he stood aside to let me in. "I dare say I thought you'd have tired of my company yesterday."

I pulled off my boots as he closed the door. "I can't stay long, but I need an update. You didn't answer your phone."

"You must have caught me indisposed. My apologies." He shot me a curious look.

"Don't worry about it."

Despite our ease the day before, we stood there for a moment, awkward. I felt suddenly guilty for turning up unannounced.

Adam smoothed the front of the heavy black dressing gown he wore and raised his eyebrows. "Join me for a few minutes. We can discuss the news, and the coffee is rather good, I must say."

I relaxed and followed him through the first door on the right. Adam crossed the length of the room and opened the curtains with a heavy rope pulley. The sunrise took my breath away – pink, gold and violet painted the sky, transforming the

The Gloaming

space into a sunlit haven.

Bookshelves covered the far-left wall, floor to ceiling, with a wooden ladder attached to a runner. In the opposite corner stood a round table with eight seats. One place was set with an elaborate breakfast – far more than a single person could eat. I inhaled the familiar coffee and orange juice smell, thinking of my own less-than-exciting meal.

"Coffee, and perhaps some toast?" Adam asked, gesturing to the empty place beside him. He stood as I approached, waiting until I was seated before settling back into his own chair. Without answering, I reached for the toast rack.

"So. Yes. Research," Adam said to himself, cutting up a piece of bacon on his plate.

I swallowed my mouthful. "Did you find anything useful?"

"I confess the findings have been interesting, but not particularly useful, no." He poured more orange juice into his glass.

"But the diaries—"

"I didn't return to the library after your departure. However, I understand Nick's journals proved less than enlightening – and I suppose we might have expected as much, given that his memory is a far more extensive resource." He paused. "I believe Nick grew impatient with the lack of progress and set out to do some research of his own. He has been corresponding with Tom about Izzie's impersonator."

I almost spat out my coffee. "What?"

"I thought as much." Adam continued to work his way calmly through his breakfast, spearing a mushroom and chewing it thoughtfully.

"Start at the beginning," I demanded.

He sighed. "As I said, Izzie and Nick continued to scour the diaries. I went to bed."

"So you had nothing to tell me yesterday," I stated.

"I did not. Besides, we were having a pleasant time, were we not?" He smiled, and I returned it, rolling my eyes.

"Apparently, it all began shortly after your argument. He and Thomas have been investigating her background." He paused, chewing another forkful thoughtfully.

"Tomal," I corrected automatically. "But what about the man with the French accent? Have we got anything there?"

Adam held his hands up. "Izzie is investigating. Nick's certain no one escaped his notice in Paris – he claims he'd remember creating another vampire."

"And she has no leads?"

"If she does, she hasn't shared them yet." He dabbed his mouth with a napkin. "As for your mystery woman – Tom took a chance and ran a reverse image search on Izzie's portrait. It seems cross-referencing it with murder cases narrowed things down."

"And?" I pressed.

"She's quite well documented. Older than I, from what they could determine." He placed his knife carefully on his plate. "She's had several personas over the years, most involving wealthy men who died of arsenic poisoning. I recall reading about a few of the crimes in the papers, though I had no idea it was the same woman."

"Do we have a name?" I asked.

"Mary. Émilie. Hélène. Sylvia. Take your pick."

I pulled a face. "Is she French too?"

He sat back in his chair and pulled a sleek mobile phone from somewhere behind him, scrolling through until he found what he was looking for. "Did she sound French when you spoke with her? From what I understand, she's committed mariticide in several countries, so it *is* a possibility..."

"She didn't speak, but she was... I don't know. Annoying," I admitted. "I didn't pick up on anything else."

"As I expected," he nodded, turning the screen to me so I could see the image. "If it turns out she *is*, it could be the link between her and her counterpart."

It was a grainy image, black-and-white, but definitely a photograph. I could see the resemblance to Isabel immediately, but that wasn't the most concerning part.

"Triple shot, venti, wet caramel macchiato, extra hot, extra foam. Every Monday and Thursday." I frowned.

"Excuse me?"

"She comes into the shop. Every Monday and Thursday." I rarely remembered customers unless there was something unusual about them. I hated making extra hot drinks, and this woman always had a weird, off-putting stare. *No wonder.*

Adam's eyes widened. "You know her?"

I nodded, still staring at the image. "Do we have any other pictures?"

"A few, but this is the most recent and the best quality. I dare say she'd make a rather convincing doppelgänger for our dear Izzie."

"I've been serving her for months – and I mean, *well* before Jon died..." I didn't like it. "She could have picked up all sorts, just sitting there. Watching us." The thought made my skin crawl, and then I remembered: "And she's been coming in later, too. At first, it was early in the day, but it's been getting closer to noon. She's out in the sun, Adam."

"Ah," Adam scowled. "Well, that's certainly not a good sign. But if you are correct, it confirms our research is headed in the right direction."

"I guess." I helped myself to another piece of toast and slathered it with jam. "Do we know if she's connected to Isabel or Nicholas?"

"Call it a hunch or what you will, but I don't think we'll find one," he replied, his blue eyes darkening.

"What makes you say that?"

"A woman with a history of murdering her partners… her motivations are unlikely to have anything to do with Nick, I suspect, and more to do with this other unknown Frenchman. Her loyalty to him seems unprecedented."

He was probably right. I swallowed my mouthful of toast.

"It doesn't matter who she is, she's a start. But whoever's behind it all knows Nicholas inside and out. They're not only copying him – they *understand* him, Adam."

"Indeed. It is their understanding of his mind that I find most… concerning."

The hallway was darker than usual after the brightness of the breakfast room. It took me a moment to register I wasn't alone. Nicholas stood halfway down the grand staircase, his hand resting lightly on the banister.

"Nicholas," I murmured, knowing my words would carry to his sensitive ears.

"Erin. I didnae expect to see you this mornin'," he smiled crookedly, removing his headphones and pushing his hair back from his face.

The tiles were cool beneath my feet as I padded down the hallway in my socks.

The Gloaming

"I thought you'd be sleeping, otherwise I'd have—" I broke off, unsure what to say.

"I tend to stay up late and wake early," he explained. "Isabel tells me I'm unusual that way. And o' course, certain… distractions are worth stayin' awake for." His eyes lingered on me in a way that sent warmth rushing to my cheeks.

I nodded, trying to focus on the practical implications rather than the heat building under my skin. I'd always assumed once the sun was up, that was it: a sleep like the dead. Apparently, I'd been wrong.

Nicholas sat down on the second step from the bottom, stretching his long legs out before him, and drawing attention to the lean, toned lines of his body. After a brief hesitation, I joined him.

"How're you feelin'?" he asked, turning to look at me.

"You mean, after…" I began. "Adam checked me over. He pronounced me acceptable." I pursed my lips.

"Your face is still bruised," Nicholas reached out and brushed his thumb over my cheekbone. I closed my eyes, the coolness of his fingertips soothing.

"I'll be alright in a few days. I heal quickly."

He nodded, drawing his hand back. I reached out and took it.

"Adam said you've been in contact with Tom, about Isabel's lookalike?" I asked.

"Aye. I… thought he might find it easier to communicate that way, rather than face to face. I expect he finds me less threatenin' through a computer screen."

I pulled a face. "I don't think threatening is the right word. He doesn't understand why I trust you yet. He will, though. I know he will." *Hopefully.*

"I wisnae saying he feared me, as such. But…" He watched me thoughtfully, choosing his words. "You've both lost people. You and he… you're friends. Twas the three of you, and now there are three more strangers in your lives."

"But you're helping," I protested softly.

"Dinnae be so sure that's enough, Erin. Neither of you've had time to grieve, no really. Maybe when you have, he might be more accepting." He squeezed my hand gently.

I nodded. "Maybe," I conceded.

We sat in content silence for a few minutes, and I shuffled closer to him on the step, leaning into his shoulder, aware of the solid strength of him even through his shirt.

A shaft of light fell into the hallway, not quite reaching us.

"The sun being up doesn't bother you?" I asked aloud.

"No. I can sense it – feel I should sleep. It's a wee bit uncomfortable, that's all."

I said nothing, remembering the ornate bed I'd seen before; the linen crumpled and unmade.

"So you don't *have* to sleep?"

"I will, eventually," he chuckled, turning his face into my hair. "But tis a rare occasion when I find myself alone with ye. I'm rather enjoying it." His voice dropped lower, regret threading through his words. "The daylight hours – sleepin' – seems a waste, when I should be with you."

I nodded my agreement, but there was nothing to be done about it. Sitting with Nicholas was much like falling asleep in the sun and waking to find a cloud passing overhead. My skin grew hotter, being near him – but he cooled me down, perfectly balancing me. It was a wonderful feeling.

I caught myself wondering what it would be like to actually

wake beside him each morning. Would his skin be warm from contact with mine through the night? Would those emerald eyes be the first thing I'd see? The mad domesticity of the thought was startling. I could never have that kind of future – no hunter could. Especially not with a vampire.

"When this is all over, we can do this anytime we like..." I whispered, more to myself than anything. *It's better than nothing.*

I felt rather than saw Nicholas smile.

WHEN I FINALLY GOT AROUND TO leaving the manor, I was calmer than I'd been in a long time. There was no way I was heading straight to Jolt, to work and deal with the noise and the people – I wanted to hold on to my contentment for a while longer. I needed to.

But Nicholas wouldn't be awake all day, so I decided to do the only other thing I could think of that made me feel calm and content. I'd go back to my hilltop.

Adam lived in the southwest of the city, and my hilltop was further north. It wasn't a short drive, even with my usual shortcuts – so I figured why not embrace it? And detoured out into the Peaks to take the scenic route.

Despite my improved emotional state, I couldn't quite shake the sensation of being watched. A flicker in my rearview mirror as I pulled out of the manor's gravel driveway – gone before I could focus on it – made my shoulders tense, but I pushed it to the back of my mind, thinking instead about Nicholas. About the hollow feeling within that grew with each mile that separated us. It was strange how quickly his absence had become an emptiness I could almost taste. I glanced at the clock, mentally counting down the hours until darkness would fall and I could see him again.

The winter sun was low and bright as I drove through the dales, playing havoc with my vision. Patches of snow clung to the grass where the weak December light hadn't managed to melt it yet. I squinted against the glare – the sun was too low to block with my visor, leaving me alternating between being half-blind and plunged into shadow as I navigated the winding curves of the hills and valleys.

The roads belonged to me at this hour – I didn't pass a single car once I turned off onto the less travelled routes. Rolling down the windows for a moment, I let the biting wind whip my hair into my face. The cold felt good, waking me up far more effectively than the coffee had.

I cranked up the volume on my car's sound system as the country lane I was on narrowed dramatically. The bare trees pressed in on both sides, making it impossible to see the stream I knew was somewhere in the steep valley below. I caught the scent of something off – sharper than normal exhaust fumes, with an edge that made my throat feel tight. I quickly rolled the windows back up, but it didn't help.

As I drove out of the tree cover, the sun hit me full in the face, making my growing headache spike. Something wasn't right. My hands felt heavy on the steering wheel, my vision contracting with each flash of sunlight.

I reached for my sunglasses in the glove box, my hand clumsy and uncoordinated. I must have taken my eyes off the road for a split second. After that, I remembered nothing.

24

TURN THEE ERIN, LOOK UPON THY DEATH

THE FIRST SENSATION THAT came back to me was the cold. A bone-deep, penetrating cold that made thinking impossible. My fingers and toes were like ice and refused to respond when I moved them. Opening my eyes made almost no difference to my vision – the night was pitch dark except for occasional pinpricks of starlight that swam in and out of focus. I could hear water moving nearby and judging by my wet clothes and the biting wind, I was still out in the Peaks – how long had I been here? The gnawing emptiness in my memory was almost as terrible as the cold. I waited for a moment, hoping my eyes would adjust before I clawed my way upright.

When I tried to stand, the world tilted violently. I fell forward with a splash, my hands plunging into icy water as bile rose in my throat. My head throbbed, each pulse sending waves of nausea through me. I struggled to think straight, but I could at least tell that I didn't seem to be too badly injured. Given the blood above my eye, I seemed to have reopened the cut on my head. Probably on the steering wheel as I swerved the car. So much for the airbag.

I peered around, trying to get my bearings. How was it so late and so dark? Where had the day gone? A fleeting thought of

Nicholas crossed my mind – it was well past sunset, he'd be awake. Would he have noticed I was missing? The thought of him searching for me was strangely comforting, but the ache of his absence felt sharper in the bitter cold.

The stream gurgled beneath me, its cold seeping through my sodden clothes and boots. A few metres uphill was the bridge I'd seen as I came down into the valley. But how had I ended up in the water? A snowflake landed on my cheek, then another, the gentle touch almost burning against my frozen skin.

"Fuck," I muttered, my teeth chattering so hard I nearly bit my tongue.

Getting up the steep bank was a special kind of hell, since my heavy boots were basically useless in the slippery mud. When I finally made it onto the bridge, my car was nowhere to be seen. The only sign I hadn't imagined the whole thing was the dark skid marks on the tarmac where I'd slammed on the brakes. I could almost hear the screech of tires in my head, but everything after that was just… gone.

I stood there for a few minutes, trying to keep my thoughts from spinning out of control. The cold was getting worse by the second. I needed to keep moving or freeze, so I picked the direction I thought would take me into the city and started walking, my boots making obscene squelching noises with every step.

It took almost half an hour of trudging along before my addled brain remembered phones existed. Excited by the prospect of rescue, I searched my pockets, only to find them empty. No phone, no wallet, no keys, not even my watch. Without them, I had no way of telling where I was or how long I'd been out there in the water.

The whole situation made no sense. Why would anyone steal

someone's belongings and a wrecked car, but leave the unconscious owner lying in a stream? I mean, the car wasn't worth what I paid for it when I bought it. And I'd driven along this road hundreds of times, so what made this time different? I might not be the world's best driver, but something about all this felt wrong. Really fucking wrong.

My clothes and hair were freezing solid despite the wet snowflakes that kept landing on me. I trudged along for what felt like an hour, though it could have been minutes for all I knew. With every step, the snow crunched beneath me, growing deeper and more treacherous by the minute, and I was starting to lose feeling in my toes. All I could do was keep going and hope to hell that some total idiot was out driving in these conditions and would find me before I froze to death.

I'd almost given up hope when I spotted two yellow lights in the distance. Eyes in the dark, getting steadily bigger. Not wanting to risk being missed, I planted myself in the middle of the road and waved my arms around like a maniac. I probably seemed more than a little crazy, but all I cared about was getting out of the cold.

A rusty Citroën that might have been dark blue in better light pulled over, its interior lights giving me my first proper look at another human being since I'd woken up. The driver was middle-aged, going grey at the temples. His wife was quite a bit younger, which probably explained why he'd stopped at all.

"What the hell are you doing in the middle of the road, at this time of night?" he demanded, winding down his window.

"I'm sorry, I crashed my car, and I woke up and—" My teeth were chattering so hard I could barely get the words out.

"For goodness' sake, Martin, look at the state of the poor girl. Clearly something's happened!" The woman turned to me with the kind of concern usually reserved for small children. "Get in the car, darling. We'll get you to a hospital or a police station or—"

"Could you drop me off at the police station?" I asked, as politely as I could manage while my body convulsed with shivers.

"Get in," Martin said with a sigh, and the door lock clicked. I clambered with some difficulty into the back seat, grateful for the stuffy warmth of the car. I couldn't feel my hands anymore.

"What happened to you, darling?" The woman leaned around to look at me curiously.

"It must have been a few miles back, I don't remember…" I said. My brain still felt like it was wrapped in cotton wool. "I crashed my car, I think, on the bridge. But my car's gone." The words sounded ridiculous even to me.

"What do you mean, gone?" Martin asked gruffly. "How can you crash a missing car?"

"I don't know," I said honestly, trying and failing to shrug. "I woke up and… I don't know."

"Let's get her to the police station. They'll sort it all out." The woman gave her husband a look that brooked no argument. I caught fragments of their whispered conversation as I drifted in and out of consciousness in the back seat. What were the odds, I wondered hazily, that the first car to come along would actually stop to help? Something about that thought nagged at me, but I couldn't quite grasp why.

Minutes or hours later, we pulled up outside the drab, concrete building that was the central police station. Wide awake now, I practically leapt out of the car before it had even properly stopped, shouting my thanks over my shoulder as I ran up the steps to the entrance.

Looking back, the blue car sped off, straight through a red

light. They were clearly glad to be rid of me, and I couldn't blame them. But as soon as they were out of sight, I strode away from the station. I'd managed to stay off local law enforcement's radar until now – which I was proud of, considering my line of work. And with no criminal or medical record to speak of – thanks to Tom and Jon's efforts – I intended to keep it that way. I needed to get home and work out what the hell had happened. Most of all, I wanted to be warm again.

Snow was still falling as I made my way through the shopping district. The clock at the tram stop showed nine – earlier than I'd thought. The winter sunset and heavy cloud made it feel much later. My clothes were still too damp to be of any real protection against the cold, and combined with my hurt shoulder from the fight in the park – which I was still trying to avoid thinking about – I was feeling thoroughly sorry for myself. All I wanted was to get back to the comfort of my bed and sleep for a week. I hopped on the first tram that came, making myself seem as small and unnoticeable as possible to avoid the attention of the conductor taking fares.

Walking up the steep hill home, I tried to make sense of the day's – and night's – events. I'd thought I was getting used to strange occurrences, but none of it made any sense. The road had been deserted when I crashed. Who would come across an unconscious person and decide to steal their damaged car?

I was still puzzling over the possibilities as I climbed the steps to my front door, digging into my pocket for keys that I already knew weren't there. The living room light was on, but when I stretched precariously across to tap on the bay window, I froze. The house was full of people; and not just anyone, but the strangest group I'd never expected to see in one place.

Tom on the sunken sofa with a dishevelled Adam beside him, arguing with my mother, who sat in my favourite armchair. My dad stood with his arms folded by the fireplace, watching the conversation without showing the slightest interest in what was going on. Across the room, perched against my desk, stood Isabel. Her eyes flicked from Tom to my mother, then to the person standing stiffly behind them both, his face a mask of pain. Nicholas.

My heart filled at the sight of him, but nothing made sense. My first thought was that the French killer must have made a move against my parents, and they'd come here for protection. But that wouldn't explain Tom and my mother's hostility, or why everyone looked unharmed but devastated.

I strained closer to the window to try to read my mother's expression, but slipped on the icy step. Through the glass, I saw Nicholas move. Before I could catch myself, he was there, pulling me back against him. We stood on the snowy steps, and I breathed in the enticing scent of earth and pine. Tension I hadn't registered drained from my muscles. It felt like weeks since I'd seen him.

"Gods, Erin," he breathed. His voice broke on the second syllable, a half laugh of relief. His arms tightened around me possessively as I drank in his face without understanding what I saw. The sudden beat of his heart against my chest made me shiver, and he pulled away, though his hand found mine immediately. For the briefest moment, his carefully maintained control shattered, his eyes filled with centuries of loss and the terror of almost adding me to the endless tally.

Without speaking, we went inside. The room fell silent. Tom's fingers gripped the arm of the sofa as he stared, mouth slightly open. My mother's hand flew to her throat. Even Isabel's

The Gloaming

usual composure cracked – she took half a step forward before catching herself.

Nicholas's hand tightened on mine as we stood in the doorway, his thumb tracing absent patterns on my skin. The cool press of his fingers kept me grounded as the silence stretched, broken only by the soft tick of someone's watch.

"What's going on?" My voice was too loud in the quiet.

Tom pushed himself up from the sofa, his face pale. "Where the hell have you been?" His hands shook as he reached for me, but Nicholas didn't let go.

"I crashed the car, out in the Peaks—" My legs gave out mid-sentence. Nicholas caught me as I swayed, one arm wrapping firmly around my waist while the other steadied my shoulder. Even through my confusion and exhaustion, my body responded to his touch, desperate to lean further into his strength. Isabel wheeled the desk chair over without a word.

I gripped the armrests, steadying myself. "I was coming back from Adam's. I needed to think – I was heading to the hilltop bench…"

Adam shifted forward, his usually neat appearance decidedly rumpled, his hair unkempt.

"Stop, Erin." My mother's knuckles were white where they gripped her necklace. "That's enough."

"Look Mum, I don't know what you're doing here—"

"I called them yesterday. After the police were here." Tom wouldn't meet my eye.

"The police?" His words sank in. "Wait, what do you mean, yesterday?"

Isabel's voice was quiet as she explained. "You have been missing for three days. They declared you dead at the scene."

The room tilted sideways. I must have misheard.

"You've done some foolish things in the past, Erin, but this is too far." My mother pressed her hands against her mouth, her shoulders shaking. "We thought we'd lost you!"

"You think *I* had something to do with this?" The words scraped in my throat. "What the fuck would I have to gain from that, Mum?"

"Language, Erin," my dad murmured, but his hand trembled as he reached for my mother.

"There was a body." Isabel rapped her fingers against the desk. "The vehicle was burned beyond recognition, though they recovered your possessions. The body bore remnants of your clothing."

"Well it wasn't my body, Isabel!" My voice was shrill, even to me. This was too strange. My pulse roared in my ears. Nicholas's fingers interlaced with mine, anchoring me as the implications crashed over me.

"We know. We can see that," Adam said softly. "The police told Tom yesterday that they couldn't find a dental or DNA match, but given the circumstances…" His voice trailed off. "We were told we should prepare for the worst."

I couldn't breathe properly. Nicholas squeezed my hand tight, kneeling beside the chair.

"They mean to unsettle you, love," he murmured.

"They've damn well succeeded," I answered under my breath. "This is… too far."

"The authorities should be informed of your safe return," Isabel said, straightening from her position at my desk. "They will wish to pursue other avenues regarding the body's identity." Her voice was unnecessarily loud, distracting Tom, who had watched my exchange with Nicholas through narrowed eyes.

"Yes," my dad agreed. My mother crossed to stand with him by the fireplace, his arm sliding around her shoulders. They both stared at me, and I dropped my gaze. It was the only time either of them had ever been here, in my home. That's what it took to get them here; I had to die. Even Jonathan's death hadn't merited a phone call.

I glanced up at them. They were beginning to look old. My mother's usually pristine bun was coming loose, wisps of grey framing her face. My dad's unshaven jaw showed more silver than red.

"I'm sorry," I said, staring at the worn wooden floorboards beneath my feet. My boots were creating a puddle, but I didn't care anymore.

"We're glad you're safe, Erin," my mother said, her voice carefully controlled. "But I don't understand. How can they have found your car, your belongings, but you're here?"

"I don't know, Mum. I woke up in the river under the bridge. My car and my stuff were gone. It was dark…" The words felt inadequate.

"It's all a misunderstanding," Tom said without conviction. "Someone must have stolen Erin's car and crashed it, that's all."

I hoped Tom wouldn't try to come up with a perfectly normal explanation for all this – my parents' tolerance for my so-called bullshit was already at its limit. Even my dad wouldn't believe what had really happened. Or what I suspected had happened, anyway.

But he did.

As Tom wove an increasingly improbable explanation over my head, my eyelids grew heavy. Despite apparently losing three days, physical and mental exhaustion dragged at me. I looked to

Nicholas, the only thing keeping me upright – and there was something beyond concern in his gaze. An understanding between us: someone had taken me, staged my death, and returned me. This wasn't over; it was only the beginning.

I didn't have the strength to think beyond that. My head dropped to my chest, and I passed out.

25

BLOOD SPEAKS LOUDER

MY SLEEP WAS TROUBLED that night. I dreamt of being trapped in a dark, damp space, bound so tightly that I could only move my head. The air was thick with the smell of damp and something metallic. Shadowy figures moved across what little light filtered through, but when I tried to call out, my throat burned and no sound came. Each breath was a struggle, my head swimming from lack of oxygen. I fought against whatever held me, my muscles straining until they shook, but nothing gave. No help came.

When I woke, I could still feel phantom rope burns on my skin, too vivid for just a dream. I sat up, rotating my shoulders to prove I could move as I tried and failed to shake off the claustrophobia. My collarbone ached with the motion. The curtains were pulled tightly closed, a solitary ray of sunlight peeking through a gap beneath the sill, filling the room with warm pinkish light.

Tom was watching me from the chair by the door, his head propped on one hand. He looked worse than I felt – his clothes from yesterday were creased and untidy from sleeping in the chair, unwashed black hair falling across his forehead. The wound on his throat caught my attention, standing out livid and raw against his skin. My stomach twisted at the sight.

"You're awake," he stated, but there was no hostility there. I'd missed that.

I swung my legs out from under the duvet and wrapped myself in my dressing gown. "Finally. Are my parents still here?"

Tom shifted in his chair. "No. They left not long after you passed out. They're…"

"Furious?" I asked, settling on the end of the bed.

"They're glad you're alive, Erin," he corrected, voice hoarse with exhaustion. His fingers traced the wound on his neck. "We all are."

I nodded, unsure if I agreed. "What did you tell them?"

"I fobbed them off reasonably well, I think. It was probably easier to hear *my* lies for a change. I said it must have been a police mix-up, you needed to rest, blah blah," he smiled weakly. "Your mum was pretty sceptical, but your dad… he knows how it is, I suppose?"

"He knows when to leave it." It was my turn to correct Tom. "He doesn't want to know more. Neither of them do."

"I had to call them." It was almost an apology. "I thought you were…" He picked at a loose thread on his sleeve, not meeting my eye. "And after Jon, too."

I ran both hands through my hair, closing my eyes against the threat of tears. The morning traffic was picking up outside, the rumble of engines mixing with the scrape of next door's bins being dragged out. "This is so fucked up, Tom."

"Yeah," he exhaled loudly, stretching. His joints cracked – he must have been sitting there for hours. "It made me think about when my sister broke her arm climbing the oak in our back garden. My parents were away at some conference, and I was supposed to be watching her." A faint smile touched his lips. "She made me promise not to tell them before I drove her to hospital. Like they weren't gonna find out the second they got home."

"You never mention her," I said. There was still something tentative about the way we were talking to each other, so I was surprised he'd brought up his family, of all things.

"Priya," he murmured, his expression softening. "No, I suppose I don't. She's the only one who still speaks to me. Sends birthday cards sometimes." He shrugged, but I could see how much the situation hurt him. "I miss her. She came by the shop once... before everything." He glanced away, composing himself. "Anyway, what I meant was your dad took it better than mine would've. He was worried, but not... you know."

I nodded, understanding what he meant. There was a quiet resilience about my dad that I'd always appreciated, even when we weren't on the best terms.

"It has to have been *them*, though, right?" I changed the subject, seeing how the mention of his sister had affected him.

He rubbed at the wound on his neck. "What else could it be? All this—" he gestured towards me, "it had to be for a reason. But why go to so much effort just to throw you off your game or whatever?"

"If that was their goal, it worked," I said, pursing my lips. "Last night, I walked into a room filled with people *grieving* for me. I mean, how am I supposed to react to that? It's like attending your own funeral." My eyes filled with tears despite my efforts to hold them back, and I wiped them away impatiently.

"How did it happen?" Tom asked.

"What do you mean?"

"Well... the police had a body and what was left of your car – but you were nowhere to be found. They checked the area for other casualties and the usual, and it *sounded* like it was the same bridge you described. You weren't there," he explained. "So, where did you go?"

I raised an eyebrow. "I was in the stream when I woke up. My head was... messed up. That's it. I might not have even crashed the car," I said, realising it was true. "The last thing I remember was heading into the valley. I had a headache, and maybe wasn't paying as much attention as I should have been."

Tom scowled. "It was sunny. I suppose if they waited until you got under the trees, they'd have had some shade. But how did they know where you were going to be?" He looked like he hadn't properly considered the idea before.

"Maybe they were following me?" The thought settled uneasily in my stomach. But it was the one thing that made sense. And Tom was right, it *had* been sunny. I remembered the image Adam had shown me before the crash – the woman who'd been coming into Jolt, and during the day. I filled Tom in on the revelation.

"Great. One more thing to worry about." He shook his head. "So, if they caused an accident, you might have already been unconscious when it happened – but not for long, not with your abilities." He paused and shrugged. "If this woman can get about in the day, maybe she drugged you?"

I thought about it. "The car smelled strongly of something. I assumed it was petrol, but... my head was pounding, the sun was in my eyes..." I shrugged. "I just don't know."

We sat in silence for a few minutes. A car went by in the street outside, its engine rattling.

"I'm sorry," I said eventually. "For everything that's been said between us recently, and..." I hesitated. "For being dead. Or you having to go through that. Thinking that."

The Gloaming

Tom chuckled, his warm brown eyes crinkling. "Only *you* would apologise for dying, Erin."

I laughed with him, shaking my head again, but I was glad he was there. That things were starting to resemble normal again.

I stared at the patch of sunlight on the floor, trying to piece it together. "It's weird, though, right?" I asked. "They had me there – unconscious, helpless. Why put me back in the stream? They could have finished it then and there."

"I've been wondering the same thing." Tom's voice was quiet. He touched the wound on his neck again. "Honestly? I think they're playing with us. Showing us they can take you whenever they want, however they want. And there's nothing we can do about it."

The chill that had been building spread through my chest. I remembered Isabel's words about revenge. "Fuck. You're right." I looked up at Tom. "This isn't about killing me at all. *Kidnapping* me wasn't even about me."

"How do you mean?"

"It's about Nicholas. About showing him he can't protect me – that I can't protect myself, or anyone else." I swallowed. "They're making him watch while they pick apart my life. Making him feel helpless."

Tom's jaw tightened at Nicholas's name, but he didn't argue. The silence stretched between us, heavy with implications neither of us wanted to voice.

"We need to put an end to this," he said, finally. "It's about time we mounted an attack instead of half-arsing a defence while they chip away at our lives."

"If we understood their motives better, maybe we could find a way," I said, getting up to search for my jeans. The familiar routine felt strange after everything that had happened. "Pissing off Nicholas seems to be at the top of that list."

Tom pushed himself up from the chair. "Top of a lot of lists," he muttered, glancing away. He watched me rummage through my drawers for a moment. "Let me think about it. I'll email Adam or whatever – get them to meet us after dark." He sized me up with something close to his old smirk. "You get a shower first, yeah? You could do with it."

The attempt at normal banter felt fragile, but I was grateful for it. Maybe we could find our way back to how things used to be. If we survived all this.

IT WAS EARLY AFTERNOON BY THE time I made it downstairs and managed some breakfast. I enjoyed the normality of making scrambled eggs; whisking the mixture and turning it over and over on itself in the pan as it cooked. To absolutely nobody's surprise, after days without eating, I was ravenous.

As I went through the motions, I had a lot to think about. By the time I piled my plate high with eggs, bacon and mushrooms, something that should have been completely obvious clicked into place in my mind – and it was something I could use.

I'd learned a long time ago that the best way to let an idea come to fruition was to look away and ignore it for a while. This one was… risky, and I didn't much like it. So instead of dwelling on it, I let it stew while I sat at the kitchen table with a steaming mug of fresh coffee, breakfast and Nicholas's first diary.

Maybe it wasn't the best time to get to know him better – but it was the distraction I needed, and I had to start sometime. I pulled his jacket onto my lap while I read, pushing my arms

The Gloaming

through the sleeves and breathing in that uniquely appealing scent of his that lingered in the lining.

The soft, worn leather of the diary flopped away from the pages as I opened it, but it didn't contain anything close to what I'd expected. I'd been prepared for the out of control violence and slaughter I'd seen so many times from newborn vamps over the years – but here, Nicholas was young, only fifteen, and still very much human. It was a part of his life I'd never expected to learn about.

My fingers traced the faded ink where his immature scrawl filled the earliest pages – complaints about his father's demands on his time, when all he dreamed of was glory on the battlefield. The musty scent of centuries-old paper filled my nose as I turned each delicate page, discovering how it had been decided he should learn to read and write to continue the family's tailoring business.

When he finally ran away from home, the pages began to overflow – his guilt and confusion clear in the words and the smudged ink where he hurried them, desperate to explain himself. His desertion took a harder toll on him than he'd confessed to me before, and it wasn't long before he was back in battle, throwing himself into war in search of redemption.

The sun was getting low in the kitchen window as I reached for another diary, unable to stop myself from pushing through to 1657, the year he'd become a vampire. The spine cracked as I opened it, the crumbling pages revealing how his siring had brought him an unexpected clarity, though his words were no less conflicted. There was no relief from his guilt. Instead, he wrote of how he believed he was being punished: for deserting the military, and for being weak enough to run, after he'd abandoned his family to be there.

His strangely lilting voice seemed to rise from the yellowed pages as I read his entry:

31st October 1657
near Dunn's River Falls

I cannot understand what has happened to change me so. The world is the same as it was before, and yet I see more with these eyes than I had ever dreamed was present on Earth. Everything is so much clearer than it was.
As I write, I'm surrounded by the stench of the unwashed soldiers in our tent, and though the stink of their sweat and filth repulses me, I'm drawn to their flesh despite it. Yesterday, we lost men. Those who remain are grieving for their fallen comrades despite our win. The Governor does not believe we'll have more trouble, but it is all I can do to focus on anything but the bloodshed.
A new hunger claws like a demon within me when I pass the lines of the dead, as yet unburied. Their blood seeps into the earth below, feeding it, and I cannot turn away.
I fear I won't be able to control myself much longer.

Maybe it was odd, but my first response was more sympathetic than anything, as he described becoming a creature he didn't understand, and dug deep within himself to find the strength to show restraint. I couldn't ignore the parallels between his struggle and my own – yes, I was a hunter, not a vampire. But the desire to give into my darker side, to follow through on the visceral demands of my body and kill… it wasn't all that different.

I ran my fingers over the dry, fragile pages, absorbed in his description as he fed for the first time on a living person and fell into despair for his immortal soul. As he grew more and more certain that with the act of killing, God was showing him who he really was, and promising him he'd never find salvation.

If nothing else, it was easy to tell from these entries how much he detested the person he was becoming – though his handwriting and vocabulary had improved, his words became more detached with each day.

I pushed through the early years. These entries were closer to what I'd been expecting, his actions becoming more despicable – and often described in more detail than I really wanted. But I was determined to work my way through everything I could. It was almost as if he was trying to force himself to remember each victim by confessing the crimes to paper.

The sheer scope of his existence grew more overwhelming with every page. The decades that had shaped my entire identity were barely a blink to him, and I had to wonder what my life could possibly be to someone who had witnessed centuries – a brief spark in the darkness of his endless night. Even if we survived all that was happening, would I eventually become just another memory in his impossibly long existence? I was a hunter, but I was still mortal. The thought sent an unexpected pang through my chest.

Immersed as I was, I didn't notice the sun setting and the kitchen growing dark around me.

"Reading anythin' interesting?" A familiar accent came from behind me. I jumped at the sound, spilling cold coffee across the table.

Nicholas stood in the doorway, the lamplight from the living room casting shadows across his face. In black jeans and a dark blue shirt that clung to his broad shoulders, he was practically a shadow himself, but I caught the glint of amusement in his green-gold eyes. I didn't want him to think I had been prying, even though I definitely had been.

"I didn't realise what time it was," I said, ignoring his question as I switched on the light and crossed to the sink to get a cloth for the spillage, quickly untangling myself from the sleeves of his leather jacket.

"Aye, tis easy to get lost in a good story," he agreed. I peeked over at him as I pushed the diary aside to clean the scrubbed wooden table. He was watching me, a smile playing on his lips like a secret.

"A story implies fiction," I said. "Are you saying what you wrote was a lie?" It amazed me I could still tease him.

"No," he laughed, but he seemed unable to hold it on his face. "I wish it were."

I shrugged. "We all have a past. This is yours. I need to know about it, if…" I trailed off.

Nicholas ran a hand through his dark waves, his eyes never leaving mine. "Aye, and ye deserve the truth of it," he replied quietly. "Whatever comes next, I ken that much. There's no path to… well, I dinnae expect your forgiveness, Erin. But the truth is yours, to make of what you will."

His shoulders tensed slightly as he continued. "Thinkin' you were gone, I've realised tis better for ye to hear the darkest parts, shameful as they may be. I'd rather ye see them and the man I've fought to become, even if in the end, you choose to walk away. At least that way, I'll ken – that my centuries searching for ye wisnae in vain. That you existed after all, and twas my own folly that led to a lonely fate."

"I think it's too late to walk away," I murmured, surprised at

The Gloaming

my own honesty.

For a split second, a smile lit up his face, transforming his features with a warmth that made my breath catch. "I winnae blame ye if that was your decision, love. But..." His eyes darkened. "I'd fight for ye."

He looked away, staring at something beyond the kitchen window and the small, dark garden outside. "I've learned to trust my senses above all else. But these last days, after they found the body... the car, the clothes... she may have looked a wee bit like ye, but it wasnae you." A muscle twitched in his jaw. "Somethin' inside me knew. And I searched that damned road a hundred times over, til Adam dragged me away.

"I could feel you, in here," he said, pushing the heel of his hand into his chest. "I cannae explain it, but my heart knew ye'd come back to me."

The words hung between us, weighted with his hope. His... *No*. I couldn't even think it. It was too much, too intense. How was I supposed to process a faith in me that had existed since before I was born?

I glanced down at the diary still on the table, suddenly aware of how exposed I felt. Pushing it aside, I crossed the small space, flicking the kettle on at the switch as I scrabbled for a safer topic.

"Do you drink coffee? You know, beverages?"

He nodded, grinning again without reacting to my awkward change of subject. "Aye, I do."

"Oh. Well then, would you like a coffee or a cup of tea, Mr... Murray?" I paused, unsure. "Or Mr Baird Murray? Is that right?"

I couldn't take my eyes away from him as he chuckled, the emerald of his eyes twinkling across the kitchen at me.

"I dinnae think we need to worry about formalities at this

point. Besides, I've gone by many names. I winnae wish to confuse ye."

"I'll stick with Nicholas." I laughed with him, leaning against the counter while I waited for the kettle to boil. He closed the space between us with his usual fluid grace, resting his hands lightly on my waist. His cool fingers found the skin just above my jeans, and every nerve ending came alive at his touch. The contrast between his chill skin and my warmth made me want to press closer.

"And a cuppa would be lovely, my midnight wanderer," he whispered, his lips brushing my ear. "Though I can think o' sweeter things to taste." He traced a long finger along my throat, and I shivered – despite all I'd read today, I didn't think it had anything to do with fear.

"Am I interrupting something?" The words cut through the kitchen, Tom's voice as sharp as broken glass.

I jerked away from Nicholas, my fingers fumbling with the ceramic mugs. The spoon clinked loudly against the porcelain in the sudden silence.

"Erin is makin'… ah, beverages." Nicholas's rich brogue was still silky-soft, and he took an unhurried step back.

"Right," Tom said coldly. "Well, we need to get started, so hurry up."

I glanced through the glass doors to the living room and saw Isabel and Adam had arrived. Nicholas's presence had distracted me more thoroughly than I'd realised. I rushed to pour out the drinks and hid a smile as a reluctant Nicholas followed me through.

Adam was drawing the curtains against the early evening, shutting out the wind that whistled through the bay window. The radiator ticked over beneath the windowsill, fighting back the winter chill that was almost as pervasive as the silence.

I settled myself in my favourite armchair, and without a word, Nicholas perched himself beside me on the arm of the chair. He leaned back into the wing, close enough that his pine-and-earth scent made it hard to focus. It was all I could do to resist resting my head on his shoulder.

"Shall we begin?" Isabel asked, removing diaries from a leather duffel bag. The deep red silk of her blouse caught the lamplight as she moved, highlighting the warm tones in her loose hair.

Tom's chair wheels scraped against the floor as he reached for his mug. I caught the tension in his jaw – he clearly didn't like being told what to do by a vampire, but Isabel didn't react.

"Izzie, perhaps you should update us all on exactly what you've learned since we last spoke, before anything else." Adam appeared at my elbow, settling himself beside Isabel on the faded velvet sofa. His blue eyes found Nicholas's in silent communication.

"What? What have you found out?" My heart picked up speed.

"It is nothing of great consequence." Isabel's fingers traced the edge of a diary, her short, clean nails stark against the leather. "Though it brings us no closer to unveiling the truth, it may be of interest."

My eyes darted between the three immortals, waiting for an answer.

"The body they found in your car." Nicholas's lilt softened his words. "'Twas a woman named Lauren Truelove. She was the same age as you, of a similar height and build," he added, looking to Isabel for confirmation. "No too dissimilar to the other woman who was left at Adam's."

Tom reached up to touch the half-healed wound at his throat.

"I know that name from somewhere. I'm sure I do."

Isabel handed a piece of paper to Adam. It looked like a police report.

"You may," Adam agreed, taking the paper and glancing at it. "While social media might not be my forte, Izzie has done a little research, and it would appear she had a brief dalliance with Jonathan last year. She also applied for the manageress role at Jolt." He frowned at the photo on the paper, then looked up sharply. "Wait. Nick, isn't this…?"

Nicholas took the paper and went very still. A muscle in his jaw tightened.

"You fed from her at the club," Adam murmured. "Last week."

Tom's chair creaked as his head snapped up. "What?"

"And the woman on your doorstep," Nicholas said, his voice hollow. He passed a hand over his face, almost human in the gesture. "I thought I kent her, but I couldnae be sure. I left them both alive."

I tried not to react to his words, but my fingers tightened around my mug. The idea that he'd still been feeding, after everything… but I knew what he was, didn't I?

"Had you interacted with Jon or Maggie before they died?" Tom pushed away from the desk to face him straight on. "If the killer's targeting people you've been in contact with…"

Nicholas shook his head. "I never met either of them."

"But there might still be a pattern," Isabel said, inching forward. "Was there anything notable about how they died? Similarities?"

Tom gave me a long, questioning look. If there was ever a time to trust them with what we knew – what he'd found out – now was it. I held his gaze, and he nodded. Turning back to his laptop, the blue light from the screen cast shadows across his face as he pulled up the older files with a few taps. "Jon was isolated in that hotel room for days. The staff said he wasn't eating, didn't respond to calls or knocks, never left his room. We've got no idea if that was down to him though, or if he was kept there by force. And Maggie…" He swallowed hard, his throat working. "Brad said her death was weirdly precise. The water temperature controlled to stop her blood from clotting."

I watched Nicholas's face as Tom spoke. He'd gone pale, his hands gripping the knees of his jeans until I thought he'd rip right through the fabric.

"Three redheads who look like Erin," Tom said slowly. "And Jon being Nicholas's descendant… but the methods seem all over the place. Different kills, different styles."

"Unless the point isn't the killing itself," Adam murmured, his gaze fixed on Nicholas. "The precision, the drawn-out nature of it… Perhaps they merely intend to make Nick watch as people connected to him are systematically destroyed."

"But I haven't even opened the applications for the job yet," I said, pushing back against my chair. "So how did they know Lauren had applied?"

"It seems they have been watching more carefully than we thought," Isabel said. "And of course, there is still the matter of the bridge incident. Suspicions will have been aroused with the police – particularly now they know you are alive, Erin."

Tom set his mug down with a loud clink. "They haven't been to speak to us at all. I'd have thought they would."

"As would I." A small crease appeared between her eyebrows, as she watched him closely. He broke eye contact first, picking up his mouse and fiddling with it. "One might assume someone was preventing them from doing so."

No one had anything to say to that. I ran a hand through my hair, wondering how to bring up my idea, but Isabel broke the silence for me.

"I believe Adam is correct."

He studied her, his eyes wide. "I often am, though to which matter are you referring?"

"This is… torture, of a kind. Psychological warfare."

Tom frowned. "It's not exactly pulling teeth and fingernails…"

"Not all torments are visited upon the flesh." She returned his curious look before addressing the rest of us. "It seems clear at this stage that the killers are playing a game – toying with you, Erin, as a means of targeting Nick." Nicholas frowned at her as she continued. "He is certainly the strongest common denominator, which leads me to wonder if your meeting at all might also have been orchestrated – though one wonders what they might have to gain from such an action, unless they had hoped you might kill one another."

"But—" I began.

"Of course, the moment Nick saw you, he knew who you were. What you might mean to him," she went on. "He would never hurt you, or let harm come to you. But it is unlikely the killers could have predicted such a scenario."

Nicholas barked a bitter laugh. "I havnae exactly kept her safe so far."

"No. And yet she is physically well enough. Mentally though…"

I gazed at the floorboards. She wasn't wrong.

"They could have killed you already, and they chose to give you back." Adam surprised me by agreeing with Isabel. "It may have been a test of your limits, but it was also an effective way to make

Nick suffer, just like leaving a body that looked like you on the doorstep for him to find. If even temporarily, they made him believe you were dead."

Tom made a low whistling sound, staring at Nicholas. "I don't even want to know what you did to deserve this."

Nicholas said nothing. He'd done plenty – everyone present knew as much. But was it any more than Isabel, or anyone else?

I cleared my throat to break the awkward silence that fell, choosing my next words carefully.

"Okay. So they brought us together. They've done… awful things," I paused. "And they're escalating."

"Go on," Adam encouraged.

"They're one step ahead, watching us. They know everything about us, apparently."

"I'm not sure you need to reiterate—"

I cut Tom off. "Give me a minute. So why has it worked? Why haven't we done something, or learned more by now?"

Isabel looked thoughtful. "I suppose we have been hindered by a lack of cooperation," she mused, glancing at Tom. "The killers have chosen to remain in the shadows, using false identities… And of course, Nick and I sleep during the day, which has likely had an unfortunate effect."

"Lack of cooperation is a funny way of putting it," Tom chimed in.

"Yeah, but she's right." I gave him a hard look. "You and I have barely been speaking since Maggie died. I've been trying to manage on my own – so Jolt's taken a downturn – and you've only shared your giant genius brain with these guys in the last few days." I smiled a little to soften my words. "Everyone in this room has had some kind of conflict with at least one person here."

"You're suggesting our continued discord has allowed them to remain one step ahead," Isabel murmured.

"Yes!" I nodded. "It's why they've been playing dress up as you two," I gestured to Isabel and Nicholas. "They convinced Tom that Nicholas attacked him, and both of us that you guys were behind everything that happened in the beginning. It's probably the reason all the women killed were redheads, too."

Adam looked impressed. "I rather think you're right."

"And what would you have us do with such knowledge?" Isabel raised an eyebrow. "We are no longer at odds – mostly – but I would hardly call it an advantage on our part."

"It is and it isn't," I edged. "If they're paying as much attention as we think, then they've probably figured out the gig's up, and it's only a matter of time before we're on to them. Whatever their ultimate move – probably to kill Nicholas – it'll come soon."

Tom pinched the bridge of his nose. "But we still don't know how to find them. And if that's the case, we don't have time to go digging any more."

It was time to tell them my big, kind of stupid idea – and I already knew they weren't going to like it.

"We have to try something different," I said finally, my voice barely above a whisper. My hands trembled slightly as I reached for my coffee mug, dreading what I was about to suggest. Every instinct screamed against deliberately creating vulnerability, against putting anyone else at risk. But sitting back, doing more pointless research while these bastards stayed one step ahead, manipulating us, torturing Nicholas… "What if… what if we gave them what they want?"

Nicholas froze beside me, the slight pressure of his leg against my arm vanishing. The loss of contact was like a physical ache, but

The Gloaming

I pressed on.

"A rift between us. Something big enough to make them think they're in the clear." The words tasted bitter in my mouth. "They want us divided because it's easier to torture us that way. But if we can trick them into thinking we hate each other while actually working *together*, we might be able to buy ourselves time to make a real move."

"You would have us feign a quarrel?" Isabel's liquid brown eyes watched me intently.

I nodded. Nicholas was staring down at me, but I couldn't meet his gaze. "If they think they've succeeded in turning us against each other, they won't go for the big finale." I swallowed hard. "I know it's a massive risk – they've killed to drive wedges between us before. But they're going to keep killing anyway, and at least this way we'll still be around to fight back. We'll just have to work fast. Like, faster than they do."

"You can't be fucking serious," Tom burst out. "After what happened to Maggie? To Jon? You want to give them more targets? Maybe they'll go after Brad, or your parents. Maybe they'll come for *me*."

"No!" The word came out sharper than I intended. I forced myself to take a deep breath. "Hell, no. Of course I don't want that. But that's why we need to coordinate. If we can set up extra protection for anyone they might target – my parents, *you*, Bradley. Maybe even people Nicholas has met at the jazz club recently…" I swallowed loudly, pushing myself to keep going. "We've got some idea how they're picking and choosing victims now. We have to do *something*."

The room fell silent. I could feel Nicholas's eyes still burning into me, but I kept my own fixed on my hands. They were still shaking, and I clenched them into fists.

"It could work, at least for a little while," Isabel said, tucking a lock of hair behind her ear. "But the cost…"

"I know." My voice cracked. "Believe me, I know. But what's the alternative? Wait for them to kill someone else and hope they leave a clue? Keep reacting instead of acting?" The thought of more innocent deaths made my stomach turn. I hated myself for suggesting something so… *cavalier* with other people's lives. But the darker part of me – the hunter part – had been itching for a real fight for weeks. "This way we set the battlefield. Buy a little time."

"Erin's right." Nicholas's voice was soft, but there was steel beneath it. "We cannae keep playin' their game, now we ken what the rules are."

I finally looked up at him and saw the same painful understanding in his eyes that I was feeling. Neither of us wanted this. But sometimes protecting others meant making impossible choices.

I glanced at Adam and Isabel – his face carefully controlled, hers thoughtful. At Tom across the room, dismay in his eyes but determination around his mouth. It didn't exactly feel like a triumphant moment. Or like a plan that had a snowball's chance. But it was what we had.

Nicholas stood abruptly, the sudden absence of his cool presence leaving me oddly bereft.

"I need some air. Adam?" I caught a slight tremor beneath his usual accent. The smile he gave me as he passed held a hint of his usual warmth, though something darker lurked beneath it.

My skin prickled with awareness as he moved past my chair,

The Gloaming

and I gripped the armrest tightly, resisting the urge to follow him out. Instead, I forced myself to meet Tom's troubled gaze.

"I hope you know what you're doing, Erin."

So did I.

26

Solace in Pieces

"Okay," Tom said, his voice cutting through the tension. "If we're going to do this, we need to act fast. Get a plan in place to keep potential targets safe."

"My parents," I said immediately. "They need to be out of here."

The words hung in the air, heavy with implication. Tom nodded, tugging at a tuft of black hair. "Yeah, I can handle that. They were away and came back for… well, I already told them one story about your crash. What's another lie at this point?"

I nodded. That was one less worry. Sort of.

"We should examine the applications for the manageress position," Isabel suggested. "If Lauren Truelove applied, there may be others we need to watch for."

"Agreed. We don't know if Lauren was a target because she applied or because she—" Tom stopped short, not meeting my eye. If only he knew I hated the thought of Nicholas feeding as much as he did.

"And Bradley, from the morgue," I added. "After what he saw with Maggie's case…"

The door creaked open and Adam and Nicholas slipped back

inside. Though his face remained carefully neutral, tension radiated from his broad shoulders as he settled onto the arm of my chair. His hand found the small of my back, and even through my shirt, his touch sent sparks of electricity dancing across my skin. I really needed to get a grip on that.

"It might be beneficial to understand how they have been observing us so closely," Isabel continued. "The applications, the club, knowing when Nicholas feeds…",

"Jolt has cameras inside and out," I offered. "And there's CCTV on the street outside."

"Then perhaps we start there. Find their vantage points." Isabel's fingers drummed against the diary in her lap. "It might help us make this deception more convincing."

"Speaking of which," Tom leaned forward. "If we're going to fake a falling out, it needs to look real. These wankers notice everything."

"Then we give them something to notice," I grinned. "I can punch you. You'd look great with a broken nose."

Tom gave me the finger in response.

As we fleshed out the details, I could feel Nicholas watching me. He said little, but I worried what he really thought about this plan – and about me, for suggesting it.

Nicholas lingered in the doorway after the others left, the streetlight casting shadows across his cheekbones. Adam tapped his foot impatiently at the bottom of the steps.

"How would ye feel if I came back in a few hours?" Nicholas murmured, his voice a low rumble that seemed to vibrate through my chest. He leaned closer, his lips barely brushing my ear. "I have an idea that could be of use."

My pulse quickened. "I'll be awake," I managed. "I'm sure you

The Gloaming

can let yourself in."

His answering smile held a hint of something that both thrilled and unnerved me. "Aye."

The kiss, when it came, was swift but deliberate – a brush of cool lips against my cheek that left me more breathless than a real kiss would have. Then he was gone, leaving only the ghost of his touch and the lingering scent of pine in his wake.

The house felt cold and empty in the quiet afterwards. I tried to make conversation with Tom as he tapped away at his laptop – hacking into some CCTV footage from the look of it – but he seemed nervous and unwilling to indulge my need to *do* something. Isabel and Adam were working to get in touch with any others from the club – which wasn't a job I wanted any part of. Tom was going to contact Bradley and my parents... and I was left in limbo, with nothing to do but ponder how we could find these fuckers before they figured out our ruse.

After twenty minutes of staring blankly at the closed curtains, I gave up and went upstairs, pulled on my painting jeans, and climbed the ladder to the attic. My mind kept circling back to Nicholas – to the pain in his eyes last night. Everything I'd read today. How it felt to sit beside him, close but never together. In the three days I'd been gone, something fundamental had shifted between us. All pretence of simple attraction had burned away, leaving behind a raw longing that was undeniable.

As was always the case in the winter months, the topmost part of the house was chilly enough that my breath gathered in clouds, before dissipating like smoke. I pulled out the old electric heater I kept in the corner and plugged it in, checking the temperature wasn't high enough to dry out my supplies.

The mural was still spread out on the bare floorboards.

Unfinished, like everything these days. Art used to be the normal, human thing that I did – something that wasn't hunting or the coffee shop. Now it was just a reminder of the life I'd pretended to lead.

I knelt down to gather up the paints – there was no point in convincing myself I'd ever finish the damn thing. Throwing them haphazardly into a drawer, I stared around the room, full of impatient energy. There must be something better I could be doing.

I closed my eyes for a moment, casting my senses out on low. Tom was still in the living room two floors below, his heat a pulsing presence in my mind despite the wood and brick and mortar between us.

Without a doubt, he still didn't trust our new friends – and given what we were planning, it had never been more important that he did. At the very least, he needed to believe they'd had nothing to do with Maggie's death – something I wasn't sure he did yet.

At least he'll be convincing tomorrow.

Still, everything about this situation felt wrong – the planning, the waiting, the forced inaction. I craved the simple clarity of my old hunts: spot vampire, kill vampire, go home. Not… whatever this was.

Closing my eyes again, I massaged my temples, waiting for the laptop to boot up. The sound of something heavy landing on the roof jerked me from my thoughts, the impact reverberating through the old timbers overhead. I froze, throwing my senses as far as I could manage. Beyond the closed blinds, a shadow moved across the moonlit glass. Something scraped against the tiles overhead, the sound skating down my spine like ice.

The Gloaming

In four long strides, I was across the room. I threw open the window, fighting with the stubborn latch as I strained to hear any further movement. The night air bit at my exposed skin, carrying the clean scent of impending snow. There was nothing there.

I pulled the window to. "Tom?" I called down through the trapdoor, proud of how steady my voice sounded. "Tom!"

A moment later, he appeared in the bedroom doorway.

"What's up?" he asked, and I leaned forward to see him better from my precarious position at the top of the ladder.

"Did you hear something down there?" I asked, my words jumbling together. "There was a noise on the roof outside…" I trailed off.

Seeing the bemused expression on his face shattered the fear of a moment before, even as he shook his head.

"I had my headphones in, sorry. You want me to go out into the garden and check?"

I pursed my lips, thinking. "No, it's alright. It was probably a bird or something. I must be getting paranoid," I sighed, falling back onto the sofa again as Tom stood waiting.

"After the last few days… and someone watching our every move… we could both do with being a bit more paranoid." He frowned.

"I suppose." I made a conscious effort to slow my breathing. "Someone could have been here before, without us noticing. We might even have been home at the time."

He didn't look convinced. "You'd have sensed them, surely?" He pointed out. "Even if you were asleep."

"In theory, yeah. But I can't always sense Isabel or Nicholas, can I?"

His face soured, though he tried to hide it. "Maybe that's who was in here, then."

He had to be joking. "Tom…"

I glared at him and his ears burned red.

"Hey, it doesn't matter what I think anyway." He held up his hands. "We're going with your plan – and it's not like you're going to consider the idea they can't be trusted at this point."

"Haven't they earned the benefit of the doubt? Just a little bit?" I asked.

"Sure. Cause they've stopped feeding, right?" He fixed me with a hard look. "Except they haven't. Adam admitted Murray was still at it – and after everything they told you about how it's transmitted. But you don't care," he added.

"I care, Tom." My voice grew quiet, and I resisted the urge to climb down there and hit him. "I fucking care, okay? But he didn't kill her. He didn't even hurt her really. So try saving all your pent up bullshit for tomorrow." Now it made sense that he'd been so quiet before. His hostility wasn't gone at all; he'd just bottled it up.

"Yeah, you're right. I think I'll save it up somewhere else, though." He disappeared from the doorway and I heard him stumble on the stairs. A minute later, the front door slammed.

I pulled my head back into the attic, and sat cross-legged on the floor, rubbing absently at my temples. I shouldn't have snapped back so easily. But then, he'd been so civil this morning – it had felt like things were back to normal, or getting there, anyway.

The silence was louder now that I knew I was alone. It was too cold to be up here. I clambered down the ladder with my laptop and switched off the attic light, all thoughts of the noise outside gone.

The Gloaming

IN THE KITCHEN, I POURED MYSELF a cup of coffee, savouring the warmth of the mug in my hands, and headed to the sofa with the laptop to wait for Nicholas. He hadn't said where he was going, but I suspected he and Adam would be paying the jazz bar a visit. I tried not to think about it, and opened up a search page instead.

My fingers hovered over the keyboard. Émilie. Hélène. That's what I should be looking for. But I hesitated, and changed my mind on the spot, typing '*1889 Paris World Fair*' instead.

My internet connection was pathetic – but it was the cheapest tariff available, and I wasn't made of money. I sank back into the cushions, watching the loading bar at the bottom of the screen chugging along. My eyes drifted closed against the light of the screen.

When I woke, a golden light forced harsh shadows into contrasting shapes across the room. My laptop lay dark on the floor, forgotten. I reached to pick it up before realising I hadn't switched on any lamps before dozing off.

Nicholas stood in the window, one shoulder against the frame. He'd drawn back the curtains, and the streetlight turned him into a dark silhouette, catching the sharp lines of his jaw and cheekbones.

I rubbed sleep from my eyes. "How long have you been watching me?"

The corner of his mouth lifted. "Long enough to hear you talkin' in your sleep."

Heat flooded my cheeks. "If you'd been here earlier…"

"Had a wee errand to run." He moved away from the window. "Now I'm all yours."

I busied myself with the laptop charger, trying to ignore my suddenly racing pulse.

"Go on then," I managed. "What's this bright idea you couldn't share earlier?"

His hand on my arm was cool, but it burned like ice. I spun to find him mere inches away, close enough that I had to tilt my head back to meet his gaze. The familiar scent of earth and pine wrapped around me.

"Do I make you... uncomfortable, Erin?" His low rumble turned my name into something intimate.

I shook my head, though my voice came out barely above a whisper. "No. Not like that. It's just... this is all new." I searched for the words to explain what I meant. "A few months ago, I'd have killed you on sight for being what you are. Now things are different, and I'm trying to make sense of it, but you're..." I gestured helplessly between us. "Distracting."

"I see." His hands came up to cradle my face, fingers threading through my hair with impossible gentleness. Time seemed to stop as he pressed a kiss to my forehead, then stepped back. I instantly regretted my words.

"I didn't mean..." I hated the space between us. "I'm sorry."

"Dinnae apologise," he murmured. "I've waited centuries to find you, aye, but that doesnae make this any less new. Everythin' about ye still amazes me."

I peered up at him through my lashes. He ran a hand through his hair, looking endearingly uncertain for an immortal. I'd almost expected a cheeky retort, but instead...

"We could figure it out together?" I offered softly.

His green eyes met mine, the low light in the room reflecting in the golden flecks of his irises. "I'd like that verra much."

I couldn't help but mirror his smile. A car passed outside, its headlights sweeping across the ceiling. The brief flash of light

The Gloaming

reminded me why he was here.

I cleared my throat. "So what did you come here to tell me?"

Nicholas straightened, a predatory stillness returning to his frame. "I believe it'd be beneficial to visit your local… information hub, as it were."

"You want to find Solace?" I huffed. I'd forgotten all about the eternally teenage vampire, with all that had been going on. "You know, that's not a bad idea. If anyone could tell us how this killer is spying on us, it'd be her."

"Aye. Tom mentioned she sensed me here afore anyone else did. I suspect she may have a talent for it."

I laughed shortly. "You have *no* idea."

I brushed past him toward the hallway and pulled on his ancient, soft leather jacket. His sleeve caught mine as he glanced down at it, amusement dancing in his eyes, though he didn't comment. The simple touch sent sparks racing up my arm, and I dropped to the bottom step, yanking my boots closer to hide my reaction.

"She'll expect payment, though. Solace doesn't do anything for free – and I already owe her for the last time."

SINCE I NO LONGER HAD A VEHICLE to speak of, Nicholas drove us across the city in the sporty black Maserati I'd seen Adam and Isabel climb out of once before. He sped along the empty streets, the car purring beneath his touch – though whether it was fancy engineering or his skill as a driver was hard to say. Regardless, it was strange to see him doing something so normal.

After a few minutes, Nicholas spoke up.

"Are ye okay, love?"

I continued to stare out of the window, watching the streetlights blur past. "Yes. No." I sighed. "I don't really know."

"If it's the plan…" he trailed off. "It's no the safest way to do things, and I cannae say I like it, but it's no a bad plan."

I nodded. "I know."

He waited a moment before replying. "Mayhap I can *distract* ye from your worryin'."

I turned to him to find a small smile playing around his mouth, the lights on the dash reflecting off his eyes in the darkness. "What sort of distraction?"

He hummed in the back of his throat. "I can think o' plenty, but for right here and now, perhaps we could just… talk?"

"Talk?" I smiled despite myself. "About what?"

"Anythin'. Everythin'." His fingers drummed lightly on the steering wheel.

I watched his profile, my eyes tracing the strong line of his jaw. "How long were you in the city before we met? That night in the park, I mean."

Nicholas's mouth quirked up at one corner. "I was wonderin' when you'd ask."

He expertly navigated a sharp bend in the road, the powerful car responding to his slightest touch. Behind, the twinkling city lights spread out below us as we climbed higher.

"And?" I prompted.

"A few days," he admitted. "I caught your scent the first night I arrived. Thought I might be imaginin' things at first. So I spent my nights… followin'. Catching glimpses."

"You were stalking me?" I raised an eyebrow, though the revelation didn't really bother me.

He shrugged. "I prefer to think of it as… reconnaissance."

The Gloaming

"And what exactly were you *reconnoitring*?"

"You," he said. "I had to be sure."

"Of what?"

"That you were the one." His voice dropped, becoming almost reverent. "The first time I saw ye – truly saw ye – was outside that coffee shop o' yours. You were locking up, and you had these huge headphones on," he loosely cupped his ear with his free hand. "You stopped and closed your eyes, and I could see the way the music was affectin' ye. The headlights of a passing car caught your hair, turned it right to fire, and I…" He trailed off, shaking his head. "I kent then what my heart had been tellin' me all along."

I looked away, heat rising to my cheeks. "So… you arranged our meeting at the park?"

"No," he laughed softly. "'Twas pure chance. I'd been followin' ye that night, worried about you bein' out alone after ye'd been drinkin'. It wasnae exactly the right moment. But then you went and fell right into my arms – almost literally."

"Lucky you," I said dryly. "I had bruises for weeks after that fall."

"Lucky me, indeed." The sincerity in his voice was unmistakable.

We fell silent as he paused at a junction.

"What about after?" I asked. "Between the park and when you met me on the hilltop?"

His expression darkened slightly. "I tried my damnedest to stay away. I could feel ye were… hesitant. That you had a lot going on in your life. But I found myself right where ye were anyway."

"When you were still calling yourself Cole," I said, remembering the morning he'd helped me wash dishes before the funeral, and the night he'd fixed my car.

He nodded, a smile playing at the corner of his mouth. "Aye. I told myself I was checkin' on you, but truthfully? I couldnae stay away."

"And after that? Before I saw you at Adam's?"

"'Twas easier to keep my distance once I'd spoken to ye again," he admitted. "I knew what I'd be askin' of ye, when you found out who I was – what I still ask of ye. Tis no small thing, especially for someone like you."

"What do you mean?"

"A hunter," he said. "With every reason to hate what I am."

I couldn't argue, though with every passing hour, it seemed there were more shades of grey to consider. "You were… still watching me, weren't you? After that. I could feel you, sometimes."

"Aye," he confessed without apology. "The moment the sun set. Makin' sure you were safe."

But you already knew all that, Erin. Deep down.

"Your turn," he said, shifting gears. "What got ye started as a hunter?"

I hesitated, but honesty was the only path forward. "There's not much to tell, really. I've always been able to… sense things. It scared the shit out of me as a kid, but my dad sort of got it. I sometimes thought maybe there was something there with him, that he could…" I didn't finish the thought. If my dad really could do what I could, then he'd been an even shittier parent than my mum had been – and she'd been pretty awful over the years.

Nicholas nodded, but his mouth turned down into a small frown. "And when did ye start actually… hunting?"

"The first time… it was an accident. More self-defence than anything. But by the time I started university, and met Jon, I'd been avoiding the idea for a long time. He caught me red-handed,

The Gloaming

sneaking in one night. I was a mess, exhausted, and I couldn't think of a plausible lie – so in the end I told him the truth."

I stopped. It felt like forever since I'd thought about those early years – and how much had changed since then.

"Did Jon—?"

"It was Jon who convinced me I basically had a moral obligation to do the right thing. He was so bloody curious about every little detail – which is pretty much how Tom found out. Jon drunkenly running his mouth off." I twisted my hands in my lap. "Tom didn't believe us at first. Not until I took him out one night, and he saw for himself. After that, he was happy to take my word for it." I swallowed, remembering. "He'd have died that night if it hadn't been for Jon. He was a mess."

"But he didnae die."

"No. Something... shifted, though, after that. In *me*. For the first time, I had people I wanted to protect." I closed my eyes briefly. When I opened them again, we were passing under a railway bridge, and the sudden darkness made the interior of the car feel even more intimate.

"And you've been huntin' since?"

"It never felt like a calling until Jon turned it into one." I looked over at him. "He showed me that being a hunter was what I was meant to do. That I was built for it."

"I ken that," he said softly. "Clarity of purpose."

"Did you have that? Before... everything?"

He smiled, though there was something sad in it. "Before I became a vampire, ye mean? I was to be a tailor, like my pa. And I had no interest in it whatsoever. I only wanted glory and adventure."

"So you joined the army." It didn't seem that adventurous to me, but then the world was… smaller, back then."

"Aye." His knuckles whitened on the steering wheel. "Found nae glory nor adventure, mind ye. Just death and regret."

I reached out, covering his hand with mine. His skin was cool beneath my touch.

"What about now?" I asked. "What do you want now?"

He glanced at me briefly, his eyes reflecting the pale white streetlights. "Peace, I think. Redemption. Though I'm no sure such a thing exists for me."

"And me?" I hadn't meant to say it, but the words were out there now.

"You, Erin," he breathed, "are the dream I ne'er thought I'd truly find. Or deserve." His fingers twined with mine. "What about you? What do ye want? Beyond hunting, beyond all of this?" He gestured vaguely.

I took a deep breath. "I don't know yet. I've lost too many people lately – and I've learned to value the people I still have. So I suppose… to find something that makes all the pain and loss worth it."

"And have ye?"

I studied our joined hands, thinking of him. Of Tom and Adam and Isabel. "I'm beginning to think I might have."

He brought my hand to his lips, pressing a gentle kiss to my knuckles. "We're more alike than ye ken, you and I. Both fighters. Both stubborn as the day is long."

I laughed. "I am *not* stubborn."

He raised an eyebrow, humour dancing in his eyes. "Aye, and I'm the Queen o' Scots."

"Fine," I conceded. "But only when it's important."

"Tis one of the things I admire about ye," he said. "Your

determination. Your fire."

"Even if it's directed at you?"

"Especially then," he grinned. "A wee bit o' danger makes life interesting, love."

I shook my head, smiling despite myself. "You're impossible."

"So Adam tells me. Frequently." He squeezed my hand gently. "But I'm also yours, if you'll have me. Impossible and all."

I didn't know how to respond to that. We fell into a comfortable silence, fingers still laced together as he steered. Outside, the streets grew narrower and darker as we left the city centre behind. The knot of anxiety in my chest loosened a little with each new breath.

When we pulled up at Seven, the warehouses loomed like great concrete monoliths against the night sky. The industrial district was always eerily quiet at this hour – no workers, no machinery, just the occasional skitter of something in the shadows and the distant hum of the city.

Nicholas held my door as I climbed out of the car, and paused at the edge of the lot, his gaze sweeping the warehouses with military precision.

He frowned. "She doesnae allow weapons, aye?"

I nodded – it hadn't stopped me from bringing my sword along, but I'd tucked it under the passenger seat and planned to leave it behind.

"Perhaps we should break her rule this once. There's somethin' no right about this place. The scent…" He didn't finish, but I was already strapping the sword on, its weight settling against my spine with the familiar click of harness buckles. My fingers moved through the motions – thread, tighten, secure. I raised a quick eyebrow at him, and he grinned, the corners of his eyes crinkled with barely contained amusement.

Brushing past him with a grin of my own, I headed straight for the largest building, and rapped my knuckles against the door. There was no sound from inside.

"I come seeking Solace?" I called. He was right – something was wrong. I'd never had to wait before.

Nicholas put a hand on my arm and shook his head, one finger to his lips. I wasn't surprised he'd sensed something I hadn't – Seven had always been a bit of a block for me. Everything up to the entrance was fair game, but once my mind hit those walls, my senses came back with, well, nothing.

Caution in every movement, he leaned past me to push lightly at the door. It must have been locked from the inside, as it didn't shift at the slight pressure. But Solace's guys were usually quick to respond to anyone on their lot.

Closing my eyes, I threw my senses out like a net for the third time tonight. Nicholas was a new, flickering presence beside me, but something inside the warehouse made me shiver – and I'd never sensed a damn thing from Seven before now. Not from the outside, anyway.

"This isn't right. We need to break it down," I said, stepping back to ram the door. Before I could, Nicholas stepped in front of me and pushed down the handle forcefully. A snapping noise came from within the mechanism, and with another light push, it swung open. *So much for her fancy reinforcements.*

Stale air hit us as we crossed the threshold, carrying a sour tang that made my stomach turn and my mouth fill with a hint of copper. The prickling across my skin grew more familiar, but it was different – more intense, like thousands of tiny needles rather than the usual low static.

The Gloaming

My footsteps were muted against concrete, each step producing a wet, sucking sound that was even more disgusting in the pitch darkness.

The warehouse swallowed every sound. No voices, no footsteps – nothing stirred in the gloom ahead. I continued in the general direction of where I thought Solace's platform was. Behind me, Nicholas rattled with something and huge industrial lamps groaned into life as the generator came on, casting harsh shadows between the steel support beams. Something skittered in the distance – a rat, or something worse. Without thinking, I drew my sword at the sight before me, fiery adrenaline flooding my system.

The harsh, overhead lights were still flickering, revealing the massacre in stuttering frames. First, the lake of dark fluid where pools of blood had converged beneath at least a dozen vampires. Then the pale limbs scattered across the ground. Finally, my eyes reached Solace's shattered throne, its pieces strewn like bones across her dais.

"What evil is this?" Nicholas breathed, but a coughing sound interrupted him. Trying to avoid stepping on anyone, we made our way toward the noise.

Solace lay sprawled on the ground behind her platform, her head resting against a shredded velvet cushion that had once been part of her throne.

She laughed weakly, looking up. "Erin Alexandra Elizabeth Conrad," she murmured. "Of course."

"What happened here, Solace?" I asked, sheathing my sword and kneeling to see her better.

She was a mess. Her legs were bent at unnatural angles, clearly broken. A patch of drying, black blood marred the front of the red dress she wore, right over her heart. The fabric sank inward, where

I could only assume someone had struck her with enough force to pulverise the bones and organs beneath. But I had no idea what would be strong enough to do that to a vamp.

"Can I assume this is the fabled Nicholas Murray you've brought with you?" Her words were ragged, but she forced her head up anyway. "My, how you've changed, Erin."

"What happened?" Nicholas repeated, quiet menace in his voice as he grabbed her by the throat and pulled her upright so that her legs dangled uselessly, her toes brushing the dirt. She choked.

"Nicholas don't—" I put out a hand to stop him, but he'd already released her. She slumped to the ground, trying to pull herself into a sitting position.

"She did," she dragged her gaze to me, her dark eyes accusing. "You happened."

Nicholas turned to me, about to speak.

"I didn't do this—" I began.

"Not you directly, you idiot." She coughed again, her words tumbling into each other. "You asked too many questions. Killed April and Will."

"They were nobodies," I argued. "Feeding off a kid they'd found—" I broke off, disgusted at the memory and what had become of the girl.

"You were *seen*," Solace hissed, glaring at me. "Talking to them. They were working for *him*," she swallowed. I'd never seen her this nervous. "I didn't know, I swear I didn't. I thought it was Murray, like you."

"They were working with the *killers?*" I spoke quickly, worried she might fall unconscious. It didn't look like she'd hold out much longer, and I needed answers. "Have you got a name, Solace?"

"Help me, and I'll tell you what I know. You owe me." She

fixed me with that knowing look I hated, even through the pain. We both knew I had no choice.

"I'll be back in a second," Nicholas whispered, turning to me. "Dinnae do anythin' rash while I'm gone." Before I could blink, he'd flit, disappearing in an instant as only a vampire could.

Solace shifted, coughing again. What little colour she'd had was almost gone, and for all the world she could have been another dying teenage girl. If it hadn't been for the goosebumps all over my skin, I'd have mistaken her for just that. The arrogance of the Solace I knew was gone, though the sly bargaining wasn't.

"He's pretty," Solace slurred, eyes closing. "I get it."

I fixed my gaze on the blood-slicked floor. The last thing I needed was Solace reading anything else off me.

Nicholas appeared beside me again and I relaxed, despite how unsettling it was when he moved that way. In his hands were three unmarked pouches of blood. He bit into the corner of one, tearing a small hole which he held to Solace's mouth. She gulped down the liquid noisily, taking it from him. To her credit, she didn't spill a drop.

"You'll have more when we're satisfied you're speakin' the truth," he said frankly, stepping back from her.

"Why would I lie?" she replied. Her tongue flicked over her teeth, seeking every morsel.

"Tell us everything. From the beginning," I told her, watching as her face regained some warmth.

Solace dragged her broken legs around in front of her before answering, already stronger than she'd been minutes ago. I winced as she eased up her dress and pushed the exposed bone of her left femur back into place, where it had been snapped in two.

"Like I said, this is all because of you," she croaked, waving a hand at the room. "All I knew was there was a new power in the city, and more of us were dying than usual. Which is what I told you when you came asking, since I clean up enough damn bodies for you." She pushed her tongue into her cheek, her jaw working. "Turned out my people weren't as loyal as I'd hoped. April and Will were taking their orders elsewhere, using my organisation as a cover."

"Organisation?" I scoffed. "Is that what you think this is?"

Solace threw me a dirty look. "Regardless. My guys got it back to me they'd seen you with *him*," she indicated Nicholas without looking at him. "I decided not to worry about it. I figured you'd have killed him by now, though from the energy I'm sensing it looks more like it's going the other way," she paused. "Anyway. The deaths didn't stop. The bodies started to pile up, and I had to start digging."

"What do you mean?" Nicholas asked.

"Haven't you noticed what's been going on lately?" She laughed half-heartedly. "I suppose only the redheads matter to you, right?"

Nicholas snarled low in his throat, the threat clear. I ignored him, thinking.

I normally made it my business to keep track of the death toll in the city – Tom and I had set up a program that pulled information from local hospital databases and collated it so we could investigate anything unusual; locate hotspots and such. I had to admit; I hadn't checked it in weeks. But Solace had said vamps were dying, too.

"They've been feeding," I said flatly, understanding. "Not just on the ones we know about."

"Whoever this is, there's more to it than just a frame job,"

Solace addressed Nicholas. "They're killing three and four times a week. And they're not hiding the evidence, either. It got to looking too suspicious for my liking, so I had some people investigate. They didn't come back."

"But what has this got to do with… April and Will?" I wasn't a fan of humanising scum like that with nice, normal names.

"They've been getting information from them, from all my people. About you two and Wyatt. From what I can tell, they've been listening in from the empty place next door to your shop, tracking when Chowdhury's online – you name it, they know it. And now they've got everything I had, too." She stopped speaking to cough up blood for a minute, before continuing. "Either the two guys I sent are dead, or they were working for him as well. It doesn't matter. Seems like he decided I'd gone too far. A woman came by this morning. Half of us were sleeping, a few guards keeping an eye out…"

"One woman did all this?" How strong *was* she?

"I think so. I thought it was Wyatt at first, but the vibes were all wrong. She wasn't as old, but she was… hungry. Crazy with it."

"She *fed* on them?" Disgust laced Nicholas's tone.

"I've been losing people for weeks," she coughed. "And not just killed, either – drained. The woman who did this… she walked in here in broad daylight. No one should be able to do that. She's stronger than anyone I've ever come into contact with." She took Nicholas in. "So far."

Her eyes lingered on the other pouches Nicholas still held, and he handed one over without speaking. Solace tore it open, swallowing loudly.

My hand twitched for my sword hilt. A vampire that could walk in daylight and take down an entire nest single-handedly?

Everything I thought I knew about hunting them – about their limitations – was so far beyond inadequate it was actually almost funny. Even Nicholas's presence beside me couldn't reassure me. I shuddered, though it wasn't the cold that was the problem – my blood was on fucking *fire*.

"It's taboo. It's… it's no done," Nicholas murmured as Solace discarded the second pouch. "You're sure this was one woman?"

"Yes," she said, rolling her eyes. "I trust my senses."

Unfortunately, I trusted her senses, too.

"What does it mean?" I asked.

"That our enemies are more dangerous than we kent, but there's a limit to their spyin', at least." He stood, throwing the last pouch at Solace and pushing his hands deep into the pockets of his coat as he walked away.

"You're not going already?" Solace protested, groping for the blood. "You can't leave me like this!"

I glanced back at her with a shrug as I pulled the door closed. "You'll live."

27

My Black and Deep Desires

Once outside, I stumbled to the car and leaned hard against it, gulping in clean night air that didn't taste of copper and death. The stars wheeled overhead, impossibly bright and clear compared to the horror we'd left behind. My skin still crawled, but the light breeze began to cool the fever-heat beneath.

Nicholas kept his distance, watching. "Are you... alright, love?"

I shook my head, opening my eyes. "I've never sensed anything like that before."

He frowned and said nothing, leaning around me to open the passenger side door. I climbed in.

I closed my eyes tight as we left, trying to force my body back to normality. I needed to forget that awful, overwhelming feeling of... sickness.

Pulling up outside the house, I took a long breath before looking over at Nicholas, whose eyes followed my every movement as always.

"Sorry," I mumbled, glancing away again.

"Would ye describe it to me?" He paused. "The way it works?"

I almost laughed, remembering how many times Jon had asked

the same thing. But Nicholas's quiet intensity was different – less clinical, more personal.

I shifted to face him over the gearstick, absently running a hand through my hair. "I can try."

"It starts like that feeling when you know you're being watched – an extra sense that bleeds into all the others. My skin tingles – beyond itchy, like something trying to crawl out from underneath. That hits first, then the hyper-awareness kicks in." I leaned back against the headrest, trying to find the words. "The taste comes next. Hot metal in the air, coating my tongue. And then there's the fire."

"Fire?" His eyes darkened as he turned toward me, the lean muscle in his shoulders shifting beneath his shirt as he moved. For a moment I glimpsed the predator who understood exactly what that fire felt like.

"That's how I think of it. Adrenaline, I suppose." I remembered as I spoke. "When I was younger, it was immediate and overwhelming – all of that at once. I can control it better now, so the fire comes with the fighting. It pushes me harder, lets me take the blows and hit back," I grinned. "That part's not so bad."

"Aye, I ken that part well," he smiled. "And do you feel this way any time there's a vampire near?"

"I did," I hedged, though I knew what he was really asking. "Until I met you and Isabel. You're…" I hesitated. I had to be honest with him here. "I *do* sense you, but I have to really try – it's much harder."

He nodded, his face hidden in the half-light.

"In the warehouse, it was different." My hands twisted in my lap. "Beyond sickening. I'm not squeamish – I've seen enough blood for ten lifetimes. It was… wrong. Rotten. Something in there left a stain."

Neither of us spoke. The truth was starting to sink in: my senses weren't just getting stronger – they were evolving. The vampire girl in the park had been too much for me already. There was no way I wanted to be *that* affected by every vamp death – and that was something that was fast approaching. With my deeper understanding of them, it seemed I was more attuned to their energy.

The warehouse's atmosphere still clung to me like a shadow. I needed something normal to chase away the darkness.

"Do you want to come in for coffee?" The words slipped out before I could second-guess them.

"I'd like that verra much." Nicholas's voice was soft, but his eyes were intense.

On the steps, I fumbled for my keys, struggling to get into my jacket pocket under the strap of my sword sheath. As he had once before, Nicholas swept in, found the keys and unlocked the door in the blink of an eye.

"Cole!" The laugh bubbled up naturally, despite everything we'd seen tonight.

Nicholas gave me his now-familiar half-grin, and stepped inside, closing the door behind us. I shrugged out of my coat, hanging it by the door before peeking into the living room at the piles of paperwork Tom had left on the desk and coffee table. I groaned inwardly at the mess. It wasn't important, but still.

"The attic might be more comfortable," I offered, heading for the kitchen. "I'll grab those drinks."

He nodded and began to make his way leisurely up the stairs.

As I waited for the kettle to boil, I thought about Solace's words – about the intruder feeding on other vampires – and

Nicholas's appalled reaction. Taboo, he'd called it. If human blood was necessary for their survival, I had to assume that vampire blood would make them even stronger. Though it seemed a lot more like cannibalism, where a vamp feeding on a human just… didn't.

Great.

I carried the mugs upstairs and set them on my dressing table. The silence from above was unnerving – I wondered what he was up to. Running my fingers through my wind-tangled hair, I climbed up to investigate.

Nicholas knelt on the floor with that perfect stillness only vampires seemed capable of, the strong lines of his back and shoulders evident even through his clothes as he bent to examine my sketches. His fingers traced the edge of one of the larger drawings – unfinished like everything lately, but raw with emotion I hadn't meant to capture. Each page was more revealing than I'd intended.

"They're private, you know." The words came out barely above a whisper, but he actually startled.

"It's no often anyone manages to sneak up on me." He rose in one fluid motion, brushing his knees with an old-world precision that somehow fit him perfectly, despite looking barely older than I was. His crooked smile held a hint of approval.

"I think you might've been distracted." I raised an eyebrow, passing him a mug. He placed it on the dresser behind him without drinking it.

"Aye, perhaps." He slid his hands into his pockets.

"So what's the verdict?" I took a sip of coffee, studying the floor.

He spoke with a soft cadence. "You've quite a gift with the pencil. Your memory's captured me more truly than I would have imagined a human mind capable." He smirked. "I'd be flattered if I wasnae already so naturally modest."

A blush crept up into my cheeks. "I didn't even realise it was you until I'd finished them," I admitted. "They're from before – before I knew who you were."

Nicholas said nothing to that, and I let it lie. It was becoming more and more apparent that I needed to address what there was between us – the pull I felt with him was undeniable, prophecy or no prophecy. But this evening had brought other concerns to light that were probably more crucial than my personal life.

I took a sip, my mind back at Seven. The sight of the massacre kept replaying in my mind – not just the horror of it, but what it meant for me and, well, my friends. Solace had seemed genuinely afraid of her attacker, which probably meant I should be way more afraid than I had been so far.

"What you said at the warehouse," I began. "About vampire blood being taboo. What did you mean?"

The faint lines around Nicholas's mouth pulled downward into a frown. "Tis… unnatural. Wrong. I havnae heard of one who fed on their own kind for many a year – though it offers strength far beyond the norm."

Fan-fucking-tastic. "So this woman… she's stronger than other vamps?" I put my rapidly cooling mug down. "Could she be stronger than you?"

His jaw tightened. "I cannae say for certain. I've lived a long time, but I've only heard whispers of such things. The consequences… Those who feed on their own become somethin' else entirely. Somethin'… unstable."

"That feeling I had there – I could tell it was wrong. Like the air had gone rancid." I shuddered. "If this woman is as powerful as

Solace claims…"

"Then we'll need to take more care, aye." Nicholas finished. "But at least now we ken what we're facin'."

I nodded, though it wasn't exactly a comforting thought. "I guess it explains why the regular vampire deaths have been increasing, too. They're not just killing to frame you – they're feeding to grow stronger."

We stood in the quiet for a few moments, and I turned this over. I should have been having a complete meltdown over the idea of it – but with Nicholas by my side, the coming fight was a little less daunting. I knew he was a big part of the reason Jon and Maggie had died, and the other women too… but I couldn't bring myself to wish him away. To wish he'd never come here.

"I meant what I said before," I ventured, watching his face for any reaction. "About you being in my head. I don't understand it, but…" I tucked a strand of hair behind my ear. "Being near you affects me, and not just because of what you are. You feel…" I searched for words that wouldn't sound insane. "Right. Like you fit into spaces I didn't know were empty."

His mouth twitched into a smile again, and I returned it like it was the most natural thing in the world, despite my embarrassing frankness.

"We're different." He sighed, and I averted my eyes. "But we balance each other well, I think."

I ran a hand through my hair and nodded. Intense green eyes followed the gesture.

"When I first met Jon…" My voice caught. "I thought he might be the missing piece. I'd spent so long watching everyone else figure it out – falling in love, falling apart, moving on." The memories ached less than they used to. "And there was something there with him – not romantic, but… it wasn't him I was sensing, was it?" I caught Nicholas's gaze through my lashes. "It was you, all along. Your connection to him. That's why the emptiness never went away." I traced the rim of my mug. "It was selfish of me to keep him close. But I suppose… it was in case I never found you. And I didn't know you *existed*."

"It wisnae selfish, Erin – how could you've known?"

His lilting accent wrapped around the words like a balm, speaking truths I'd never been able to voice.

"I know." The whisper felt raw in my throat. "After he died, everything felt… darker."

"Aye, I expect it did." His voice held centuries of understanding. "But you dealt with his presence in your life far better than I ever managed, when in a similar position."

I sank down, his history pressing in. His diaries had only prepared me for so much. Nicholas settled beside me, close enough that I could feel the cool air around him, but not quite touching.

"Might you begin to ken my frustration?" he asked.

I met his gaze – eyes dark with memory, seeking something in my face. And I said the words I never thought I'd say.

"I think so."

He flashed a quick smile, but it was clear he didn't believe me.

"Being a vampire's no as easy as Isabel and I like to make it appear, you know. In the early days, with no one to tell you how it works…" He flexed his hands. "It's difficult to get a grasp on a hunger like that. Tis a lot of new emotions."

The question that had been circling my mind since I first discovered his history finally found its way to my lips. "And the red-headed women? Was that always part of it?"

His gaze met mine, unflinching. "I ken what you've been told, but my interest in red-headed women wisnae something I was predisposed to. Aye, I knew of the prophecy my grandmother had shared – but once I was turned, all that faded away. Everything became about the blood. *Any* blood."

I reached for his hand. His skin was cool, but the calluses beneath my fingers were unmistakably human.

"I didnae understand what I was," he continued, voice low. "I'd no proper education beyond religion and the Devil. I went to war because I believed it was right. But I failed." His eyes closed, lost in memory. "Years later, I became this—" He gestured at himself. "I knew it was my punishment."

He tugged his collar down, revealing a curved white scar. "I killed with abandon those first few years. Sometimes in battle, but no always." The collar slipped back, his hands falling to his lap. The silence stretched between us.

"I've ne'er found a word as could convey my guilt," he said eventually, his eyes darting around the room, seeing something else. "I argued with myself I was doing what my body demanded… The new strength was wonderful – but it required payment.

"It wisnae til my vampire mind matured that I began to ask questions." He pulled from behind him one of the diaries I'd left on the kitchen table. I hadn't even noticed he'd taken it.

"I wrote those questions down." He held up the book before placing it on the seat between us. "It helped. I was calmer. I realised the deities and devils I'd thought were punishin' me didnae exist. After all, I'd defied all godly laws already – I'd risen from the dead.

"Eternal life has its advantages, o' course." A flicker of his usual roguish smile appeared. "When all you have is time, there's room to refine one's… talents, shall we say?" His eyes met mine with a flash of heat before returning to seriousness. "Though I'd trade a lifetime of skills for a wee bit o' peace from my conscience."

Nicholas leaned back, distancing himself as he continued to tell his story.

"Twas here in Yorkshire when I lost myself again. A flame-haired beauty, she was – and the beginnin' of my downward spiral." His eyes closed. "I've many a time wished I didnae meet her."

"By then, I'd tried to build something. Read everything I could, bought houses with vast libraries. I even worked peasant trades again, tailoring, though feedin' on noblemen was the fastest path to wealth." His voice faded into memory.

"One snowy night, before sunrise, I left my carriage. The clerk at the library was a particular friend of mine, and would open late for me – a few words o' gossip bought his silence." The ghost of a smile touched his lips. "That's when I saw her, fightin' off a lad from the tavern. She called for aid but no one came. They ne'er did, back then."

"He was drunk and savage. And aye, I saved her – though I had no idea what drew me to her," he sighed. "Mayhap I only saved her to kill her myself."

His eyes met mine, calm. "Twas a kinder death at least. Quicker. I was already so glutted on his blood, I barely recognised her appeal at first. I thought it my usual hunger, nothing more. But after… I lost what little civility I'd regained, trying to recapture that feelin'."

"Was that when you met Isabel?" I asked, wanting to reach for him, to comfort him, but not daring.

"No. That was later – 1750 or so. Twas a friendship formed of necessity since it was *I* who'd brought hunters down upon us."

"Hunters?" I asked, surprised.

"Your abilities are rare, but no unique," he grinned. "Yet

you, yourself… there's none like you, the world over. That I ken for sure."

I knew he meant it as a compliment, but I couldn't help wonder how many hunters had failed to take him and Isabel down – how many had died trying.

"So… what changed?" We'd come too far to stop now.

Nicholas took his time answering.

"Many things," he said finally. "Where there was a war, I would fight – tryin' to make up for my weakness—"

"But you were so young, before." I interrupted. "From what you've said – anyone would expect you to have been afraid."

He gazed at me, gravely. "These days you have reasons for it, aye. A name for the trauma. At the time, it was punishable by death. Twas cowardice, and nothing more."

"But you kept going back?"

"To any war I could get to." He shook his head. "I still cannae fathom what I sought to achieve – and twas fair contradictory to my nature. It's no exactly typical vampire behaviour… Gods, Isabel's always found it verra entertaining."

I thought I might be beginning to understand. "The contradiction – wanting to do good – was that it?"

"Aye," he nodded. "It helped me see, but it took years. I knew that if I e'er found you, I had to offer more than a monster. That emptiness you spoke of – for me twas as much about my guilty conscience as my search for ye. I had to wonder what sort of person could want a man such as me." He pushed a lock of dark hair back, his gaze distant. "And I wasnae wrong. I see how you struggle with it."

I looked away. How could I admit that in such a short time, he'd already changed me? For years, my world had been black or white – grey wasn't even a consideration. I should have found forgiveness impossible. But here I was.

"I know there'll always be part of you in the darkness," I murmured. "And I know you can't change what you are. So I'm trying to see past it; to remember we all have darkness in us." I gave a half-hearted laugh. "You're what, almost four centuries old? Of course you made more mistakes than most of us. I'm hardly innocent myself."

I stood up. Why couldn't I find the words? I pulled him to his feet.

He looked down at me curiously. "And is that enough?"

I sighed. "I think so. For now. Tom still wants me to kill you," I admitted.

"I cannae blame him," Nicholas replied.

"But I couldn't," I said softly, reaching up to touch his cheek. "I see how hard you try. The restraint behind everything you do – I admire it. I'm grateful for it." My hands found his shoulders, tracing down the tight muscles of his arms until our fingers entwined.

He looked away. "I find myself struggling these nights. My need to keep you safe wars with that restraint, sometimes."

The chill of his fingers between mine soothed the burn that simmered beneath my skin whenever we were together. I touched the crescent scar at his throat, and his eyes never left my face – half-smiling, half-puzzled.

"I love that you try, Nicholas," I said, meeting his gaze through my lashes.

Something fierce blazed in him – recognition, possession, triumph all at once. He knew I was his, and he was mine.

"Years o' hard work, and here ye are, undoing it all with a few words." He traced a finger along my jaw. "It's no exactly fair."

I smiled. "I never claimed to play fair."

Pulling his face to mine, our lips met in a kiss that was anything but gentle. Months of holding back crashed over us like a wave. His tongue swept into my mouth, claiming me with a hunger that I could barely understand.

Enveloped in his arms, I felt delicate despite my strength. The solid wall of his chest met mine as he gathered me close, his touch chilling me through my clothes. In a motion too swift to track, we were in my bedroom below. My heart skipped a beat as my brain caught up with my body, and his mouth quirked up between kisses. He walked me backwards until my legs hit the bed.

"Are you expectin' something o' me, Erin?" he whispered against my throat, his voice like rough velvet. His lips trailed a path downward, brushing sensitive skin as he explored my collarbone. He slid one hand down my back, gripping my hip and pulling me flush to him.

"I'm beginning to," I managed, breathless.

"Then I should warn ye," he murmured, a wicked light in his emerald eyes as he laid me back on the bed with surprising gentleness. His weight was deliciously heavy as he pinned me beneath him. "Those talents I mentioned afore? I've had *centuries* to perfect them." The evidence of his desire pressed insistently against my thigh, and heat flared low in my belly. I rocked against him instinctively, drawing a low growl from his throat that sent shivers racing across my skin.

"Centuries?" I teased, grinding against him. "Prove it."

His pupils dilated, a fierce hunger crossing his face. "Oh, I intend to, love."

We were still for a moment, caught in each other's gaze. Slowly, he laid a hand over my racing heart, the other tangled in the waves of my hair. I wrapped my legs around his waist, crushing myself against him.

"I knew you were worth waitin' for." His eyes raked over me and his hands found the hem of my shirt. "May I?"

I lifted my arms as he pulled it up and over my head. His fingers made quick work of my bra clasp, the lace falling away as his cool hands traced my veins. His soft intake of breath at the sight of my bare skin made me smile.

"It doesn't seem fair. I've barely waited at all." I slipped my hands under his shirt, brushing away the soft cotton to discover the smooth, hard planes of his chest. He deftly unbuttoned and shrugged off the dark fabric, revealing the honed, lean muscle beneath and an ancient tattoo that curved around his ribs and side – a series of intricate Celtic knots and symbols.

As I traced the lines of ink across the ridges of his muscles, my fingers found other marks – scars that vampirism hadn't erased. A ragged mark across his stomach that looked like a sword thrust, and a star-shaped scar by his shoulder that might have been an arrow wound. I took my time studying each one, trailing my fingertips across the lines of his muscles, warming his skin with my touch.

He shuddered beneath my hands, his eyes half-closed as he mirrored my exploration, finding the silvery mark that split my collarbone, where a vamp had nearly torn out my throat four years ago. The puckered circle on my shoulder from a stake that had missed its mark, back when I'd thought wood was an acceptable weapon. Each one was a jagged reminder of hunts gone wrong.

"Battle scars," he murmured, almost unhappy with understanding. His callused fingers followed a particularly vicious scar beneath my ribs with awe rather than pity. But we'd waited long enough, and his mouth soon found mine again with a renewed hunger.

When I reached for the waistband of his jeans, his fingers found the button of mine instead, his eyes holding my own as he artfully peeled the fitted denim down my legs. I kicked off my boots, and his eyes flickered to the slim blade that tumbled out onto the floor. One side of his mouth curved up into a knowing smile.

"Always prepared, eh?" he purred. "I dinnae think you'll be needin' any weapons tonight, love, but I admire a lass who can handle her… steel."

I felt heat rise to my cheeks as his wide eyes moved reverently over my body, and I thanked the fates I'd worn my nice underwear. His own jeans hung loose and low on his hips, and when I reached for his belt again, he let me tug it free. The soft, ancient denim fell away, and I couldn't resist a small smile at the sight of his bare feet – somehow, they made him seem more human.

Growing more focused and intense, he swooped down to kiss me again, deeper this time. His tongue tasted of mint and snow, dipping and nipping at my lips while one hand eased up my thigh, his fingers teasing along the ultra-sensitive skin until I trembled.

"And as for no waitin', I can forgive it." The words hummed against my lips as his hand continued its torturous path upward. I urged him closer, arching up to press my bare chest against his, gasping at the electric feeling of ice against fire. His other hand tangled in my hair, exposing my throat to his hungry kisses, punctuating each word. "Anythin' for you, love. Fire. Torment. I'll raze the world bloody, so long as I can keep ye."

Time disappeared into fluttering moments of need and want –

the chill of his hands trailing fire down my sides; the tight muscles of his back flexing beneath my hands as I learned every inch of him; the shiver that ran through me as he kissed my earlobe, my throat, across my collarbone, and down my sternum to my heart.

He mapped every sensitive spot with soft strokes and kisses, already sure of what made me sigh and pull close against him, balancing desire and anticipation on a knife edge. Nicholas played my body like an instrument he'd mastered lifetimes ago, bringing me to the precipice with deliberate touches before easing away, building a tension in my core so exquisite it bordered on pain.

I writhed beneath him, utterly at his mercy and desperately trying to hold on to some semblance of sanity. His eyes followed every response of my body, drinking in each gasp and moan with undisguised delight. When I arched into his touch, he growled his approval, the vibration travelling through his chest into mine.

"You know…" I managed, breathless. "Your timing is… questionable."

As his palm slid down my stomach to trace the edge of my underwear, my hips rose to meet him instinctively. He hooked one finger in the waistband, drawing them swiftly away, his eyes burning into me with a smirk. "Aye, but my execution is flawless."

I had to agree, as he ran the lightest of touches across my inner thighs, stroking upward with tantalising patience until he reached his target – working my body as though he'd known it his whole life. His kisses shadowed the path of his hands, until he settled at the apex of my thighs. I gasped at the surprising warmth of his tongue.

Driving my hips against him, with him, his tongue found my swollen centre and a strangled cry tore from my throat. He slipped one finger inside me, then another, curling them to hit that perfect spot while his tongue worked tight, merciless circles and strokes in time with his fingers.

I couldn't hold back. My hands fisted in his hair, pulling him closer, his skilled mouth and fingers driving me higher until I was begging with need. The sweet, coiled tension inside me built to an unbearable peak before I broke completely, my entire body convulsing as fire flooded through me and I came apart beneath him with a cry.

His answering growl vibrated against my skin. "There's the sweet sound I've been dreamin' of," he murmured against me. The look on his face was pure satisfaction, his gaze locked on my face from between my thighs, his lips still wet. He hadn't been lying about his talents, that was for sure. But I wanted more. I wanted all of him.

Drawing himself upward, his usually emerald eyes were almost black, the golden flecks catching the lamplight like embers. The faint dusting of freckles across his nose made him seem almost young despite the predatory grace of his movements, and I drank in every detail of his face, learning it by heart. His mouth found my breast again, sucking hard enough to make me cry out. I buried my hands in his hair, holding him there as the fire burned through me in aftershocks of pleasure. The crush of his body, his careful strength as he held me – it was enough to make my muscles draw taut with need again.

His teeth grazed my nipple, and I didn't hesitate to give in to the sensation. As he moved himself between my legs, his hair brushed against me like silk – the otherworldly coolness of him a delicious remedy for my burning flesh. His familiar scent of earth and pine grew stronger as his breath ghosted across my skin, and my hands flew to his hips, fumbling until he helped me remove

The Gloaming

the last barrier between us, freeing all of him at last.

I couldn't resist exploring him further, wrapping my hand around his length. Nicholas inhaled sharply, his eyes heavy with desire, jaw clenching as he fought for the control I so desperately wanted to break. As I stroked him, feeling the sheer size of him, hard and ready against my palm, he groaned, jerking involuntarily into my touch, his head falling back to expose the strong column of his throat and the crescent-shaped scar there.

"Careful, love," he whispered. "Even my control has limits."

I tightened my grip, thrilled by his response – by the power I had over him. His body trembled beneath my fingers, his defined abdomen tensing with each stroke of my hand, Celtic knots dancing. I tilted my neck back, exposing the bare flesh as I continued caressing him. "Maybe I want you unrestrained."

"You dinnae ken what you're askin'." He pulled himself back to rest on one arm and drew an errant lock of hair away from my shoulder.

Anticipation made my pulse race beneath his fingertips. "Yes, I do. I want all of you."

He hesitated, but I pulled him down toward me again. When his sharp teeth broke the skin above my collarbone, my entire body shook. The sting of his bite dissolved into sweet ecstasy as my blood flooded his tongue and he groaned against me, shuddering with me. I felt the moment he truly lost himself in the sensation, a primal growl vibrating from deep in his chest, the fire in my soul filling him.

When he withdrew, he gazed at me open-mouthed, his pupils blown wide in the dim light. A tremor ran through him, electricity skittering across my skin in response. His teeth caught his bottom lip, scarlet welling from the cut. He kissed me again, and the coppery tang made my head swim, awakening something dark within me. The fire in my blood burned anew, brighter and more terrifying than I'd ever known it.

When he broke the kiss and finally moved between my thighs, he settled back against me and I caught a flash of something wild in his eyes – darkness barely contained by his ever-present iron restraint. A darkness of my own leapt up to meet him, but I knew he was still holding back.

I arched my hips up against him, and the initial press of him entering me drew a soft gasp from my lips. His jaw clenched, but a low moan escaped as my body yielded, slowly accepting every inch.

"Gods, Erin," he breathed, his voice breaking on my name.

At first, each movement he made was measured, though I could feel the power held in check beneath his muscles. A sound of pure pleasure rumbled deep in his throat as I wrapped my legs around him again, locking my ankles and erasing any space between us. His eyes sought mine, a vulnerability there I hadn't expected to see – a question.

I answered by rocking my hips up to match his thrust, drawing a quiet snarl from deep in his chest. His control was a visible thing, straining beneath his skin.

"Don't. Hold. Back," I whispered against his throat.

Nicholas growled in response, pulling almost completely out before slamming back into me with enough force to make the headboard crack against the wall. I cried out in response, almost undone again, and he set a punishing rhythm, each thrust hitting places so deep within me I hadn't known they existed.

"Yes," I gasped, digging my fingers into his shoulders as he nipped at my throat again. "Fucking *yes*."

The Gloaming

The dual sensation of his teeth marking my flesh and the feeling of him inside me, filling me completely, was almost overwhelming. I tensed my thighs, capturing his hips and urging him deeper, harder – feeling his restraint slip further with each stroke.

"I dinnae—" he groaned, his rhythm faltering slightly as pleasure overtook him. "Gods!" Though usually breathless, his breathing now came in ragged gasps, his eyes wild as they locked on mine.

The world fell away as we moved together, my cheap wooden bed frame protesting beneath us as he drove into me with supernatural strength, his muscles rippling with each powerful thrust as he lost himself in our shared rhythm. He flipped us suddenly, pulling me astride him without breaking our connection.

The new angle drove him impossibly deeper, and something inside me snapped. I stopped holding back. Stopped worrying about who he was, his past, his darkness and what it meant. I rode him with desperation, driving myself into him, forgetting everything outside the feeling of him, and his callused hands gripped my hips hard enough to bruise anyone else, guiding me up and down his length.

"Take it all," he rumbled, his voice hoarse. "All ye need. I'm yours, love."

The reverence in his face was almost too much to bear. My name fell from his lips like a plea with each rise and fall of my hips, the heat at my core building to an impossible peak. When his thumb found my centre again, dancing and circling in perfect rhythm with our movements, I shattered completely. My inner walls clamped down around him as wave after wave of molten fire crashed through me, and I held on to him like a lifeline.

"Nicholas," I gasped, my voice unrecognisable. Free. His hips bucked up wildly, all control finally abandoned as his own release claimed him, emerald eyes fixed on mine as his body tensed beneath me. His strong hands gripped my thighs, holding me firmly against him as he pulsed inside me, triggering another heady climax that had me begging for oblivion.

The world began to fade into focus again and our urgency slowed, though we stayed tangled together. I found myself resting on his now-warm chest, bedsheets scattered around us, listening to the slow, drawn-out beats of his heart. My breathing was the sole sound in the room; his body only occasionally rising and falling.

Nicholas's fingertips danced lazy patterns on my back, and he pressed a gentle kiss to the crown of my head. "In all my years waitin'... searchin'..." he murmured, his voice barely a whisper in the dark. "I ne'er truly kent what ye'd mean to me, love."

Moonlight spilled through the open curtains, gilding his profile and casting shadows across the network of scars across his skin. His sooty lashes cast shadows in the hollows beneath his eyes, and I memorised every detail: the sharp angle of his jaw, the straight line of his nose, the fullness of his swollen lips. Light caught his brow as he shifted, and I resisted the urge to touch him – I didn't want to break his perfect peace.

"Erin." My name was a sigh. No more words were needed.

My eyes grew heavy as I glanced at the clock – it was almost four in the morning. Contentment drew me into dreamless sleep.

The Gloaming

IN THE DARK STREET OUTSIDE, THE vampire stood motionless – a statue hidden in the shadow beyond the light of the streetlamps. They watched the unlit house, waiting. It was almost time. Everything was in motion. Soon they would breathe freely again, for the first time in decades.

PART THREE

28

SINGLE-HANDED DEFEAT

Tom stamped his boots in the snow, hands jammed deep in his pockets. He was already regretting his dramatic exit – and it would have worked a whole lot better if his piece of shit car hadn't picked tonight to die. The cold was seeping through his less-than-winterproof jacket, the weather had delayed the buses, he'd been waiting an hour already *and* the last bus wasn't due for another twenty minutes.

He'd let his anger – so close to the surface these days – get the better of him. He knew he was being irrational. Erin had proven herself far from stupid a hundred times over. She might be reckless occasionally, but she wouldn't risk her life without a bloody good reason.

It was just the way she'd thrown herself in with the vamps so easily! After everything they'd learned, she was still willing to overlook Murray and Wyatt's history. Okay, maybe they hadn't killed Jon or Maggie – but the real killer had taken inspiration from their methods. That was fucking damning enough.

If Jon had been here, he'd have said something to her long before now. He'd have known exactly what, too – probably something cutting wrapped in that disarming smile of his that made even the hardest truths easier to swallow. Of course, if Jon had been here, the vampires wouldn't be. Underneath it all, that was what was fuelling his temper – but knowing it did nothing to dispel the unquiet feeling. Fuck, he missed him.

Tom's phone trilled shrilly in his coat pocket, making him jump. He pulled it out, not recognising the number as he fumbled to answer it.

"Hello?"

"Thomas?" A female voice purred.

Tom stilled. "Who is this?" He paused. "Wyatt?"

"Of course."

Tom heard the smile in her voice but didn't understand it. Something wasn't right – if there was a real problem, why call him and not Erin? They'd all been together a few bloody hours ago.

"What do you want?" he asked roughly, not bothering to hide his contempt.

"I want to discuss what we're going to do about Nicholas. It's not a good idea for us to let this… *liaison* continue. I know you agree." She didn't sound the same – none of that smooth, cultured bollocks he'd come to expect. It took a second for her words to sink in.

"I thought you'd all decided you trusted him?"

"Look, do you want my help or not?"

He considered it for less than a minute. If he left Erin to her own devices much longer, the whole thing was going to go to shit. He'd already tried talking to her about Murray's feeding habits, about what happened after all this – and she'd brushed him off every time. Maybe this was his chance to get rid of the bastard once and for all. After that, his bloodsucking friends would have no reason to stick around – and Erin would forgive him, eventually.

The Gloaming

She'd have to. It was for the greater good, even if he had to work with one vamp to kill another.

"I'll meet you," he said, finally. "Where?"

"Don't worry, I'm nearby." She hung up.

Tom glared up and down the hill. The night was brighter than usual; harsh LED streetlights reflecting on the surface of the snow. The surrounding houses were silent, not even a twitch of a curtain to suggest life. Shadows pooled between each building, and he found himself staring into darkness, desperate for some sign of Wyatt to end his paranoia.

Crouching down, he fumbled with the straps of his backpack, remembering the short Damascus blade he always carried – the one he'd promised Erin he'd never leave home without. If it came to a fight, he didn't stand a chance – but the weight of the weapon in his hands calmed his nerves, and he stowed it up his sleeve, the metal icy against his skin.

Straightening slowly, Tom sensed she'd snuck up on him – that unmistakable feeling of being watched, so much like the way Erin described her extra senses. She was standing on the other side of the street; her face hidden in shadow. He shivered.

"Thomas." Her whisper carried on the frigid air. She lifted one pale hand, beckoning him closer, her movements liquid-smooth in a way that put him on edge.

"It – it's Tomal, but I prefer Tom."

Pulling his backpack on, he crossed the road. Her dark hair whipped in the breeze, obscuring her features. Even though he'd seen her earlier in the evening, this was different. Alone with her, every instinct screamed at him to run. Instead, he forced himself forward. After all, he wasn't *supposed* to feel good around vamps.

She kept her distance, and Tom was grateful for that small mercy.

"Tom, then." He saw her teeth flash white in the dark. "Tommy. Do you trust me?"

"Not in the slightest," he said, trying to keep his voice steady. "But if you're willing to help me put an end to Murray, I—" He swallowed. "Well, I'm up for that."

Her laugh echoed in the empty street. "Oh Tommy, you're just delightful when you're angry! All that hatred, all that lovely pain… I could drink it up." She swayed closer, alien grace mixed with childlike excitement. "And now you'd work with me? After all that self-righteous preaching to poor little Erin?"

Tom's mind raced as he tried to keep his expression neutral. Even with his limited exposure to Wyatt, this felt wrong. She was usually more… measured. This one was all show, no substance.

"What the hell do you know about my anger? Did Erin tell you that?"

She tapped the side of her nose twice. "I know a lot of things."

"Did Murray—" The words caught in his throat. Wyatt was many things, but she wasn't this… theatrical. "Maggie. He killed her, didn't he? That's why you think I'll help?"

She drifted into the lamplight, squinting into the brightness. "Ah…"

"Did he?" Tom insisted.

"Sweet little Margaret?" She clapped her hands together. "Oh, her screams were music…" The way she begged—" She twirled in the snow, her face lifted to the sky. "Divine!"

Tom backed away despite himself. "No. No, not you." He shook his head. "Why?"

She grew still, watching him with a sly look in her eye. "I'm not interested in explaining myself to you, human." Her body seemed to relax all at once. "But then, come closer. Maybe you'll

The Gloaming

persuade me."

Tom didn't move a muscle. She lifted her chin, and the light fell full onto her face – confirming what he'd half-known already. This… thing. It wasn't Izzie Misery.

"You're not her," he whispered. He was an idiot for letting her trick him, even for a few minutes. He should have fucking known better.

She prowled closer, all semblance of humanity gone. "Does it matter? Aren't we all the spawn of Satan? '*Kill us all!*' That's what you think, isn't it?"

"It matters," he breathed. "Who are you? Why did you do that to Maggie?"

The vamp pulled a face and rolled her eyes.

"Don't look at me like that. There's a bigger picture you know – you can't get so wrapped up in the details." She shrugged. "Now it's *your* turn to play your part."

"What?"

"There's a role for everyone, Tommy boy – even me. Although this city isn't what we were promised… Still. Erin's little accident was fun. Until I had to give her back, anyway." She pouted, sulking like a child. Tom couldn't keep the disgust from his face.

"And now *you*. You'll make a wonderful catalyst. After you die, that'll be it." She snapped her fingers, her high, trilling voice no longer sounding anything like Isabel.

"A catalyst for what?" Tom's heart pounded as adrenaline flooded his body. This was it. Fight or flight. Either it was his moment to die or the moment he proved himself. He just didn't have a fucking clue which it was going to be. But if he wanted a chance, he needed to keep her talking.

All of this went through his head in less than a second. And she was already yapping away again.

"You know – the big finale. And if it helps you die happy – you hate Murray, right? He'll be gone, soon enough." She took another step toward him, close enough to touch. "He has to play his part, of course, but… he'll be dead before you know it. I'm just going to play with him, first."

Tom slid his arm behind his back, dropping the dagger down from his sleeve and catching it by the handle, the way he'd practised it a thousand times with Jon.

"And me?" He took a step back, but she stepped forward in time with him.

She wiggled her eyebrows. "Well, I'm a vampire, Tommy—" She was holding his throat between her hands, squeezing, and he hadn't even seen her move. "I plan to have a taste—"

His training kicked in before his brain could catch up. The blade was already moving as her eyes closed, her split second of pleasure giving him the only opening he'd get. The mottled metal caught the streetlight as he swung it up into the pale flesh of her wrist – and fuck, the resistance as it hit bone was nothing like practising with Jon's test dummies. But physics was physics, and momentum did the rest. Her lifeless hand fell to the ground with a muffled thud.

Her shriek hit a frequency that made Tom's teeth ache – well outside normal human range. His brain catalogued that detail automatically, even as every survival instinct screamed at him to run.

She staggered back, fixated on the stump of her arm. Tom had heard vampires make some fucking awful sounds before, but this… shit. He scrambled backward, nearly losing his footing in the bloodied snow, the blade still raised between them like it would do him any good.

"You!" She lurched toward him, all pretence of beauty shattered. Then, with a sound that was pure animal fury, she vanished – gone before Tom's mind could even process the movement. Her severed hand lay in the snow, fingers still twitching.

THE HAND LAY IN A GROWING POOL of dark blood, staining the white snow crimson. Tom's own hands moved on autopilot – cleaning his blade, wrapping the evidence in his hoodie – while his mind struggled to process the impossible thing he'd just done. Pulling his jacket back on against the icy air and hastily knotting his scarf, he set off walking.

When he reached the main road, he flagged down the first taxi he saw and rattled off an address on the other side of the city – somewhere he'd never even been. His hands wouldn't stop shaking as he slumped into the backseat, his heart starting to race again as the reality of what he'd just survived hit him properly.

Watching the buildings rush by the window, Tom pulled out his phone and called Erin. This was more important than their argument, he knew that much. The vamp whose hand was now residing in his backpack had not been Isabel – but the imposter's words had told him enough to suspect his friend was in imminent danger. Murray getting his fangs into her still made him want to punch something, but after the last half hour… shit. He probably needed to suck it up and trust Isabel. She, at least, had done nothing to personally offend him.

Erin didn't answer. The irony wasn't lost on him, given how many of her calls he'd screened lately. But this time it was urgent.

"Fuck," he said aloud. She must still be pissed. He checked the clock before stuffing the phone back into his jeans, wondering where the time had gone. Dawn was still a way off – the vampires should be awake.

The taxi pulled up outside the manor house, and Tom threw a twenty at the driver without waiting for his change. He strode through the open gates and up the gravel drive, but found himself hesitating at the doorbell. Holy shit, the place was massive. Like something out of a Jane Austen adaptation.

It didn't feel right to be here without Erin. But then, what else could he do? He'd tried to contact her. *Maybe she'd answer the phone if it was her bloodsucking boyfriend calling*, he thought bitterly, jabbing the bell and hammering on the door without waiting for an answer.

A chime rang somewhere deep in the house. Seconds later, light spilled across the ground as someone twitched back a curtain upstairs. Tom backed off the doorstep, waving his arms. The door opened almost immediately.

"Tom." Isabel's clear voice cut through the chill, nothing like that of her doppelgänger. "Where's Erin?"

"I called her, she didn't pick up." Tom shifted his weight, the backpack suddenly heavy against his spine. "Can I come in?"

Isabel's nostrils flared delicately as she lifted her chin. Her head cocked to one side, reminding Tom of a sparrow. "What do you have in your bag?"

"That's what I need to talk to you about." He glanced over his shoulder, fighting the urge to check if he'd been followed. "Would you please let me in? Some of us still feel the cold, you know."

"Of course." Isabel stepped back from the door, her dark eyes never leaving the bag.

The Gloaming

Tom followed her into the hallway, momentarily stunned by the sheer size of it. Bloody hell – his entire flat would fit in this one room.

"Let me show you into the kitchen, and I will call Adam down to join us." Her eyes flicked across him and she smiled. "I am sure you would feel safer with a more… *human* witness."

"Where's Murray?" Tom asked, his wet boots squeaking against the polished floor as he followed her.

"Have I ever professed to be his keeper?" Isabel drawled, pushing through a heavy door.

The kitchen hit him with a wall of warmth. Dark cabinets stretched to the ceiling, handles gleaming against the wood. Steam curled from an abandoned mug of tea on the counter, Earl Grey mixing with vanilla in the air. The copper pans hanging in gleaming rows above the range made his throat tight – it was exactly the kind of kitchen his mum would have loved. The last thing he'd expected in a vampire's lair.

Adam appeared in the doorway. "Tom," he smiled, drawing out a stool. "Rather unexpected, I must say. To what do we owe the pleasure?"

Tom dropped his backpack on the counter and took a deliberate step back. His heart had finally stopped racing, but he couldn't quite bring himself to open it.

Adam shot a glance at Tom and Isabel.

"Do you mind?" She reached for the bag.

"Go for it," Tom managed.

Isabel emptied the contents carefully, her poised precision somehow comforting now. Adam picked up the dagger while she unwrapped the hoodie with delicate hands. Her face went still, her dark eyes unreadable.

"What is this?"

"I'd have thought that was obvious," Tom tried for a quip, but his voice was shaking. "I didn't know what else to do with it."

"Who did it belong to?" Adam asked, placing the blade back on the counter. "No, never mind that, what I mean to ask is… did *you* do this?"

"Shocking as it might sound, yeah. I did." Tom tried not to look affronted at the disbelief on Adam's face and instead stared at the hand. It was already decaying, the shrunken skin pulling the fingers into a claw.

Isabel exhaled. "This isn't good, Tom. An act like this is not lightly done; it will demand vengeance. Even a vampire cannot heal from such a thing."

"Pretty sure she was already intent on coming after us. I don't see how much worse I could have made things," Tom shrugged, but covered the hand again, unable to look at it.

"He has a point, Izzie," Adam said.

"No. There is more to this than meets the eye. Why should she come after *you*?" Isabel paced the length of the room.

"We thought she might, remember? I'm Erin's friend—"

"Be that as it may, you haven't been getting on of late. If I'm aware of it, the killers certainly are, given their tendency to know every secret we have attempted to hide," she snapped.

Adam gave Tom an apologetic look, but spoke to Isabel: "Perhaps he knows something more than we do?"

Tom gaped at the two of them. "Mate, you know what I know. I've been buried in research for weeks and found fuck all. I'm good, but I'm not bloody magic."

"Then what other reason could she have had?" Adam pressed. "Unless—"

The Gloaming

"What?" Isabel and Tom spoke together.

"Tell me what happened. Every detail."

Tom recounted the story.

"She called you a catalyst?" A lilting voice spoke from the doorway. Murray stood there, leaning on the frame with a casual elegance Tom hated on sight. His face was flushed, his dark shirt wrinkled underneath his coat.

Adam looked up from the counter, his eyes narrowing as he took in his friend's appearance. A knowing smile played at his lips. "Ah. I see you've been… otherwise occupied."

Tom's stomach lurched as he caught the implication. Great. Just what he needed – confirmation of exactly what Murray had been doing with his best friend.

Isabel pinched the bridge of her nose. "Really, Adam? Must you?"

But Murray's usual composure had already cracked – a flash of pure joy mixed with something almost bashful that made him look disarmingly young. He actually ducked his head, running a hand through his already-mussed hair. It was somehow worse than his usual predatory grace. Tom had never seen him look so… human.

"Yes." Tom's earlier anger simmered under the surface, and the moment shattered.

Isabel drew him back to attention. "Did she say she planned to kill you?"

Tom shook his head. "She said something about having a taste. So… not specifically. I'm not sure she needed to state it outright, you know?"

"They intended you as the bait." Adam examined his fingernails as he worked it out. "You were to be a lure to draw Erin to them." He looked up sharply, letting out a frustrated laugh.

"This evening's planning, entirely wasted. They're ahead of us again!"

His expression shifted suddenly, colour draining from his face. "But if they failed to secure Tom—?"

The kitchen's warmth vanished. Murray's knuckles went white against the doorframe, wooden splinters cracking under his grip. Tom's heart dropped as the truth hit – they weren't just ahead of them. They'd changed the game entirely.

"Where's Erin?" The whisper scraped from Tom's throat.

"I left her at the house—" Murray was gone before the words were fully out, vanishing so fast Tom didn't even see him move.

Tom was already running for the door. Adam met him in the hall, car keys in hand.

Any other time, Tom would have been thrilled at how the Maserati ate up the road, Isabel weaving it expertly between the sparse traffic. As it was, no speed was fast enough to meet the sense of urgency he felt. Erin had to be alright. She had to be. After the last few days, thinking she was dead… and then he'd left her there, by herself. He'd never forgive himself if something had happened.

He called her phone again, but as the houses flew by on either side, it continued to ring to no one.

29

CHAINS OF MY OWN MAKING

IT TOOK LONGER THAN USUAL to come around – or I thought it did, but I had no real way to tell. My head was fuzzy, and my left eye remained swollen shut, no matter how I tried to force it open. How the hell I'd ended up here – wherever here might be – was still a mystery, but my head pounded and my body ached with every movement, so I seemed to have put up a fight, at least. I tried letting the memories surface, but there were only flashes.

With only half of my vision intact, I tried shifting my position to get a better idea of where I was. Each movement sent little shocks of pain where what felt like zip ties cut into my wrists. My bare arms scraped against the wall behind me as I tested my bonds. A metal pipe dug sharply into my spine, the cold seeping through my thin vest.

Beneath me, my legs were dead and useless, pins and needles crackling through them when I tried to move. The rope around my ankles bit into flesh already rubbed raw. But they'd strapped me up so tightly, I stayed upright despite my body's protests.

From what I could see in the semi-dark, there were cabinets and a sink unit across from me – it looked like an old, pre-war kitchen, shiny vinyl doors and all. The pipe I was tied to connected to a series of others, snaking along the wall to old-fashioned radiators – part of a central heating system. Which meant cast iron. And not a damn chance of breaking free.

A deep breath calmed my racing heart. There it was again – the hint of petrol in the air. *Shit.*

I ran a quick mental inventory, testing what still worked while I was still conscious. My shoulder – the one that was already injured – was either dislocated or fractured. Not good, but a familiar enough injury that I might be able to fix it if I could get loose. It wasn't just my eye that was swollen either – the whole left side of my face felt tight and stiff, and I'd bitten my tongue at some point. Swallowing hurt. But there was no blood that I could see, and my skin seemed intact everywhere else.

All in all, not great, but not the worst state I could have been in. Though after all my big talk about being able to take care of myself, it seemed like I'd been taken from my bed. My own fucking *house*. The thought stung almost as much as my injuries.

I pushed down the anger – lashing out wasn't going to get me anywhere. I was alone, that was something. The petrol scent lingered in the chilly air, but it didn't seem to be getting any stronger. Which meant I might have a few minutes to think and hopefully plan a daring and spectacular escape – if only I had any clue where I was escaping from. Or where I was. Or even how long I'd been here.

Sifting through the flashes I could recall, a couple of things stood out. I'd been in my bed, with Nicholas sleeping beside me. I'd watched him for a while, and I vaguely recalled he'd got up to leave before the sunrise. I shivered, and allowed myself a moment of refuge in the memory of his lips brushing mine as he kissed me goodbye. I clung to the feeling, to the certainty that he would realise I was missing. That he would come for me.

After that though, things got blurry. I'd slept again. And then I was in the street. It had been bone-achingly cold, I remembered that much. And snowing again. How had I ended up outside? I squeezed my eyes closed, sifting through the images for some cohesion. Petrol. Something held over my mouth. Someone grabbed me, and I fought back – that was when I'd got the kick to the face. Then falling… through my bedroom window.

The memories slipped away with each throb of my temples, nausea building in my stomach. At least we'd been right about being drugged before my car went over the bridge – this felt almost exactly the same, minus the blinding sun and with the addition of a fucked-up shoulder.

That same petroleum smell was getting stronger, but I couldn't pinpoint where it was coming from in the long room. The fumes made my nose burn, and my senses dull. I scanned the kitchen again, looking for anything useful.

It had been stripped bare. Its walls might have been yellow once, but they were grey with decades of grime now. Someone had boarded up the single narrow window with fresh planks, and stuffed fabric in the gaps – to block out the light, I assumed. Still, that meant of the two people who might have brought me here, at least one of them wasn't a fan of the sun. And that was knowledge I could use.

I tried to focus my hearing, and cast my senses out beyond the kitchen, but everything felt wrong. My left ear was ringing like hell, but beyond that, all I caught was the creaking of the old walls as the temperature continued to drop outside. It really didn't feel like anyone else was here, but something niggled at me. If I shut down everything else, there was something. Maybe.

Most of the cabinets in the opposite corner were missing their doors. The largest – a larder – drew my attention. A hoarse rattling came from within, barely audible. It took me a full minute to place the sound for what it was – someone else breathing.

"Hello?" I tried to make my voice carry, but it was an inaudible rasp. A floorboard groaned in the next room. Someone spoke from behind me, and I strained to see a silhouette in a doorway I hadn't noticed.

"You're awake." A shadow fell across the floor in front of me, blocking out what little light I'd had to see by. I shuddered involuntarily, goosebumps prickling across my flesh. The voice was female. What had Adam said? Mary. Émilie. Hélène. Sylvia.

"Who are you?" I managed to croak.

"What is it with everyone asking about me today?" Her voice was high and brittle, nothing like Isabel's measured tone. She knelt, and I finally saw the face of the woman who'd been tormenting us for so many weeks.

At first glance, the resemblance was uncanny – she shared Isabel's dark eyes, full mouth, angular face… But her dyed hair was lighter at the roots. Her eyes were sunken deep in her hollowed face, lashes and brows too pale to match Isabel's colouring. A little contouring, some pouty lipstick. In the end, she was a cheap imitation trying too hard to be Izzie Misery.

"Everyone?" I repeated.

"Yes. Thomas asked *so* many questions." As she stood, the awkwardness of her movements became apparent. Her left arm was clasped tightly to her chest, and as she turned, I saw her hand was missing below the wrist. Fresh blood darkened the dirty grey of her shirt – a recent injury then, though her healing abilities had already worked on the rough stump, raw pink skin closing the wound over.

I considered her words. She was trying to goad me, that was clear, but I was still concerned. Tom had walked out alone into the night. He should have been safe by now, but I'd told him to go… This might be my one chance to get information from her.

"What did he ask?"

"Oh, you know. Boring stuff. He was quite irate about Margaret," she whispered, conspiratorially.

"You killed her." I glared down at the dusty concrete, my shoulder throbbing in time with my pulse. The disgust in my gut was almost enough to override the pain.

"For the plan, yes! She looked a little like you – well before we emptied her out." Her whisper turned gleeful. "You humans, you all look the same anyway. Especially when you're dead." She paused for effect. "I suppose that's how you'll look, too. If I let you get that far."

Her laugh filled the room, jarring and discordant. Every gesture felt rehearsed, like she was playing a role she hadn't quite mastered.

"What happened to your hand?" I asked, my tone carefully neutral. "New injury, right?"

Her face twisted, a low sound catching in her throat. "That's irrelevant."

I forced a laugh, knowing it would get under her skin. "Come on, who did it? I'll send flowers."

She was in my face before I could blink, her breath like ice against my skin. The zip ties bit deeper as I instinctively tried to pull away, my shoulder screaming in protest.

"He'll pay for it. You'll see to that, or Murray will." Her lips curled back from her teeth in a parody of a smile.

"Who? Who'll pay?" I asked, glancing toward the cupboard in the corner.

"Weren't you listening?" The words spilled out with malicious delight. "I've got your friends – Tommy and your precious Murray. They came running to save you like good little boys. As if they stood a chance."

She dropped to a whisper. "When you think about it, we're being generous. You get to choose between your friend… and your lover."

My pulse sped up despite myself, fire flooding my veins. I tried to slow my breathing – I couldn't afford for her to hear it. Though I had no way to know if she was lying, it made sense that my friends would try to find me… but Nicholas was almost four hundred years old – how the hell could they have overpowered him?

"I don't believe you," I lied, forcing the words out and trying again to pull my body into a more comfortable position, where I could regain the feeling in my legs. "It's not possible. Nicholas is too strong."

She prowled closer, circling the edges of the room, all hint of playfulness gone.

"Why would I lie? Clever little hunter girl, you must be able to sense that much?" Her voice dropped low as she assessed me, disdain twisting her features. She still clutched her arm near the stump. "Not that you're up to much else right now."

She was right. I couldn't get out of my bonds, let alone fight her – but I also had no way of knowing which of them was in here with me. I could barely sense Nicholas in that way, especially not now, when my head was pounding.

"How do I know who's in there?" I jerked my head towards the cabinet.

The Gloaming

"Tommy and I are spending some quality time together." Her words had a singsong lilt that made my skin crawl. "But I thought you might like to say your goodbyes to Lover Boy… since you finally let him have you."

She swayed toward the cupboard, her movements precise. The door creaked open, and sparse light from the other room fell across his face. The figure was hunched awkwardly in the small space, features obscured by shadow. My eye throbbed, making it harder to focus in the dim light. I kept my face carefully blank.

"What do you want from us?" I asked. "Why are you doing this?"

"Murray is supposed to die, that's what we were told. And I want Isabel, so I can have the set, you know?" She counted the names out on her remaining fingers, eyes bright with an unsettling excitement. "I wouldn't mind Tommy as well, but that one's out of my hands." She scowled and corrected herself. "Hand."

"Supposed to die?" I frowned. "I don't understand. Why? Who wants him dead?"

"It doesn't matter if you understand." She waved her stump dismissively. "This is bigger than you, little girl. And you have important decisions to agonise over, remember? Kill Nicholas, or I kill Tommy." Her teeth flashed white in the dim light. "Who is it you can't live without, Erin?"

"No," I murmured. "No." I wouldn't choose.

"If *you* won't, maybe I'll let Tommy kill Murray instead – to save you, of course. He hates him, doesn't he?" Her eyes narrowed. She was right – she wouldn't have to give Tom much of a push.

"You won't do that," I argued. "You don't have Tom."

"Don't you trust me?" Her voice was sharp with mockery.

"Erin…" A hoarse whisper from across the room. I jerked my

head toward it like a lifeline.

"I won't let you." I twisted my hands behind me, trying to loosen the plastic ties. My skin, already sore from my struggling, finally broke.

She stiffened, her nostrils flaring as the scent of my blood reached her.

"We'll see," she spat, spinning on one foot as she left.

"Nicholas?" I called after a moment of silence.

"Just kill me." His voice was barely there, strained with pain.

"No," I choked. "Isabel will come. And Adam. We're all in this together now. That was the plan, remember?"

"The sun's coming. I can feel it. They won't reach us in time."

Something was wrong with his voice – the charm, the fire that made him Nicholas was missing. As he spoke, the petroleum odour grew stronger again.

"Adam will," I insisted, almost to myself. "Adam will find us, and when it's dark, he'll get Isabel. We'll get out of here."

He didn't reply. The chemical smell was overwhelming now, seeping through a grate behind me. My head grew heavy, thoughts turning sluggish.

"We can get out of this," I mumbled, as consciousness slipped away.

30

CHECKMATE

TOM THREW HIMSELF FROM the car almost before Isabel had time to slam on the brakes, but the vamp was quicker still. She was at the door and up the stairs before Tom could blink.

"I can honestly say I've never seen Isabel quite so… harried," Adam observed, straightening his jacket as he unfolded from the back seat and looked up at the house.

"Good. I need them both on their game if she's…" Tom trailed off, following her inside and taking the stairs two at a time. He didn't want to think about the end of that sentence.

Everything was cold and dark inside. It only took seconds to take in the obvious – no signs of forced entry, no scuff marks on the walls. Erin's bedroom door stood ajar, her bedside lamp casting warm yellow light across the landing.

Murray sat on the corner of her bed, shoulders hunched, Erin's red sheets twisted and thrown back beneath him. One hand was knotted in his hair, the other hung loosely, clutching a crumpled piece of notepaper. Isabel moved toward him, and Tom noticed the sense of urgency in the room seemed to have… disappeared, like smoke.

"What does it say?" Isabel's voice held a sharp edge as she extended her hand. He passed it to her silently.

Tom turned away, scanning the room instead. Everything looked normal enough – except the bed frame. The headboard had a new, jagged split running along its wooden edge, as though something – or someone – had been slammed against it with tremendous force. Behind it, a section of plaster on the wall had cracked and chipped, leaving a pale wound in the otherwise pristine paint. His jaw clenched. If it was Murray's doing, he might have to fucking kill him himself. But if it wasn't… well, that was even worse.

The sash window was wide open – impossible, given Erin had painted it closed two years ago. A breeze blew the curtains lazily, and the outside air did nothing to dissipate the odd smell of petrol. Her laptop lay on the floor by the bed, its standby light flashing. Erin wouldn't have left it like this, much less running. Not if she'd left willingly.

"'*Checkmate*.'" Adam read, looking at the note over Isabel's shoulder. He glanced at Tom, who was tugging down the ladder to the attic with difficulty.

"Erin?" he called up the steps. Silence.

"She's no there, Tom."

"But look at this place," Tom insisted, climbing up anyway. "She gets crazy about me not putting things away when I'm here—"

He squinted up through the trapdoor. The attic was as dark and empty as the rest of the house – and undisturbed. The largest, east-facing window was beginning to show the earliest dawn light, the sky a deep, undisturbed blue. Tom dropped back down to the bedroom below.

The Gloaming

Isabel hadn't moved a muscle since taking the note, only the crease between her brows betraying thought. Adam was by the window, examining the frame with interest. Only Murray, in Tom's opinion, was reacting appropriately. His dark eyes met Tom's across the room, vacant and unseeing.

"We have to leave, Nick. The sun rises," Isabel broke the silence, her words clipped.

"You can't just… fuck off and sleep through the day and do nothing!" Tom's voice cracked.

"Do you have another suggestion, lad?" Nicholas asked dully.

"This." Isabel smoothed the note on Erin's dressing table. "You are the better tracker. What do you make of it?"

Adam glanced across the room at Tom, who raised his eyebrows and shrugged.

"Dirt, damp and rusted iron. No exactly unique." Nicholas dismissed the idea without getting up.

Not good enough. "What about the handwriting?" Tom asked. "Do you recognise it?" It was a long shot, but it was the only shot he could think of.

Murray didn't look up. "No. Tis a classic European cursive, taught in most schools til the nineteen-seventies."

"There are smudges here that appear to be blood." Adam ran a finger along the wood of the window frame. "And can anyone else smell petroleum?"

"It's no Erin's blood," Murray stated, as though that was the end of it. "I'd ken if it were."

"Alright," Adam stepped forward, every inch the gentleman despite his obvious concern. "That's quite enough, Nick. I refuse to accept you admitting defeat so easily. It won't help Erin—"

"If they want to hurt me, she's dead already." His eyes flashed.

"They wilnae have kept her alive a second time."

"Don't interrupt," Adam retorted, blanching. "We don't know that, and I intend to proceed as though it isn't the case. Tom and I will do what we can while you're incapacitated, but you need to come up with a better answer if you want to find her. You are the best tracker either of us has ever met," he indicated Isabel irritably. "And that was the most pathetic answer I've heard from you this century. Get a hold of yourself."

"And what of me? Would you presume to give orders to us both, Adam?" The look Isabel gave him would have felled a lesser man.

Tom couldn't help but grin at the idea of Adam trying to control Isabel, despite everything. "'*And wild for to hold, though I seem tame…*'" he quoted under his breath.

Isabel's rosebud mouth formed a small 'o' of surprise, recognition flickering in her eyes.

"Your role is to ensure Nick does nothing rash, Izzie." Adam shook his head forlornly, ignoring their exchange. "At least not until we know who we're dealing with. For now, get underground. I'm holding you responsible for him."

Murray nodded, visibly agitated. "Aye." He stood, bracing himself. "You're right, Adam. I'm sorry," he hesitated before continuing, his face betraying a flash of raw anguish that forced Tom to look away. It was too intimate – the depth of his fear for Erin laid bare. "Try going back to the entries between '89 and '46 – I might have a notion as to how this could be linked."

"1889? What makes you say that?" Tom asked, watching him.

"Checkmate. A feelin'." His eyes returned to the wrinkled bedsheets. "'Tis familiar, though it makes nae sense…"

"Do you know something you're not telling us? Because I swear to fucking—" Tom began.

"Tis a hunch. It cannae—" Murray sighed. "Just check."

TWO HOURS LATER, THE WHITE winter sun streaming through the library's tall windows, Tom was ready to call bullshit on Murray's hunch. The journals were full of horror stories, but nothing that could be useful in finding Erin.

Adam's library was impressive enough, and he'd kill to get his hands on some of the rare books hidden away in the stacks – but Murray's journals were something else entirely. After hours of finding nothing in them except material for a year's worth of nightmares, his initial hope was gone.

"We can't be looking in the right place," Tom said, leaning back in his chair and rubbing his eyes. The adrenaline he'd been running on had worn off, and he felt like he could climb into bed for a month and still not be satisfied.

Adam dragged a hand across his stubbled jaw as he closed the book he'd been poring over. "I'm inclined to agree with you, if I'm honest. We were in France for quite some time; the instances in which Nicholas might have provoked another vampire are… numerable. He could be quite disagreeable when there was a war on."

"You don't say." Tom stared around the enormous room without really seeing it. This felt like a waste of time, but his tired brain couldn't come up with anything better to be doing. On the bright side, the wankers that had Erin probably couldn't do much when the sun was blazing outside. Probably.

Adam said nothing to that, and Tom squirmed. Blunt as he may be, Tom was starting to like Adam, despite his unsavoury choice of friends. Being rude to him wasn't helping anyone.

"Let me see the note again." Tom reached across their scattered research for the heavy cream paper.

"I doubt very much it has changed in the last twenty minutes, but you're welcome to check."

Tom held back a rude retort, reading and re-reading the note instead. "I just don't get it. They obviously want Murray to find them, so why not give us more to go on?"

Adam sat back in his chair with a slight frown. "Once more, I agree."

"Dirt and iron. It's absolute rubbish. He may as well have said air and sun," Tom muttered.

"There was dirt on the windowsill too," Adam added. "With the blood."

"Soil. Earth. It's everywhere. I cut off that creep's hand, stands to reason she'd still be bleeding." Tom shifted the books in front of him into a pile, absently. "None of that helps us figure out which of Murray's friends has turned kidnapper."

Adam dragged one of the thicker diaries closer, scattering loose papers. "Wait…"

"What?" Tom sat up straighter.

"Well, you said *friends*," he murmured. "We assumed whoever did this was someone Nick befriended and later crossed – it made sense, given how carefully they're mimicking his old murders. But perhaps…" Adam turned to the back of the diary, searching the dates.

"I don't follow."

"In 1889, Nick and I had *quite* the argument – we parted ways for several months and didn't reconcile until 1890, when Isabel forced him to speak to me again."

The Gloaming

"Go on…"

"We'd always resided together before that – at least when Nick wasn't off fighting in one of his wars. After our row, I didn't see him some time; it's the one part of his life I wouldn't be able to account for," he explained. "Until recently, anyway."

"We kept an apartment in Paris. When I finally returned, the concierge mentioned something rather singular – a passing comment, really, about a stranger coming and going at all hours with Nicholas. I had assumed…" Adam's usual composure faltered slightly. "Well, I confess it stung at the time, the thought of him hunting with someone else. Quite childish of me, looking back."

"So Murray had a, uh – a partner?" Tom asked.

"Not that sort of partner, no. Nicholas might not be a monk, but he hasn't truly dreamt of anyone but our Miss Conrad since long before I knew him. I rather thought he'd invented her, until recently."

"Get on with it, Locke," Tom grumbled.

"If someone was hunting with Nicholas…" Adam paused, considering. "A lodger, perhaps? Someone of no particular consequence at the time."

"Whoever it was must have known what Murray was – or have been a vampire themselves. He couldn't hide that, living together," Tom finished.

"Yet why wouldn't Nicholas mention him?" Adam stared at the diary entries as if willing them to reveal more. "There's not a single reference to anyone else in these entries. Look—" He passed the book across the table.

Tom examined the stitching on the spine of the diary. It must have been damaged at some point; the cotton thread was newer in places. He could think of a thousand reasons a vamp would keep secrets, but he had to admit Murray honestly seemed to care about Erin.

"Maybe he thought they were dead?" Tom shrugged.

"Vampires are not so easy to kill, Tom," Adam reminded him. "The world isn't as full of hunters as you might like to believe."

"Wait…" Tom leaned forward. "What years did Murray tell us to check again?"

"Between 1889 and 1946," Adam replied. "Rather a broad span."

"1946… that's right after the war." Tom's voice got quieter. "When Murray was in that camp place?"

"Sachsenhausen?" Adam asked, surprised.

"Yeah – I'm not gonna try to pronounce that. But he told Erin about it – that he didn't try to escape because he wasn't sure if their weapons could kill him." Each word came faster as the connection clicked. "And you said you refused to go with him. So if he went with someone else – another vamp – and they got caught, and the experiments… he might have no idea if they survived."

"All those imaginative new ways to destroy their enemies – for someone like Nick, in a place like that… he had good reason to be concerned." Something dark passed across Adam's usually composed features. "It was partly why I could never bring myself to enlist in *that* war, more than any other – not after the first. I heal at a normal human rate, you see. I didn't know what might happen to me, subjected to…" he trailed off.

Tom grimaced. Sometimes humans could be monsters, too.

"You didn't go. Wyatt wasn't there. But he wouldn't have gone on his own—"

"It isn't too much of a leap to say he'd have taken someone along with him. That much is true. Whether it was the same person is an entirely separate matter," Adam said gravely.

"It would explain a lot," Tom pointed out.

"The connection is rather tenuous. Someone he knew in Paris that I did not, and who was still around in the Forties…" He shrugged. "Only he would know. We need to speak to him about this when he awakens," Adam added. "But if we are to believe we're dealing with a person he left for dead in a place such as that…"

"What?" Tom asked.

"I dare say one can understand their… disposition toward Nick, considering what those prisoners endured—"

"Can't exactly blame them for wanting payback."

31
A Poor Excuse for a *Chasseuse*

Thin strips of sunlight pierced the fabric covering the windows, barely enough to see by. The glow burned behind my eyelids, building gradually until I was awake. This time, the ringing in my ears had stopped. My eyes opened without protest, too, the swelling finally down. Fuck, how long had I been unconscious? All I could remember was the petrol smell that had presumably knocked me out.

Tugging again at the zip ties binding my wrists together, the raw, thin scabs broke beneath the plastic. I sucked in a breath through my teeth, ignoring the pain as best I could, pushing and stretching to try and get some give or movement. I knew it was pointless, but there was no chance I was going to sit here and do nothing. Then I remembered Nicholas.

The cupboard door was ajar as before, but I couldn't make out any movement in the half-light. Straining to hear over the pounding of my heart, my ears picked up voices above me. If I concentrated, I could make out the words.

"She will not co-operate, Émilie. She knows Murray too well, now. She was not fooled."

I recognised the French accent I'd heard so much about – an

older dialect, though, like we'd suspected. And I figured that meant we'd been right about Paris. At least the others would have something to work with – if Adam and Isabel could stop sniping at each other long enough.

"It doesn't matter. She'll do as she's told, Alistair – that's why he sent me. All I have to do is show her how far we're willing to go… and she'll cave." Émilie's tone was harder than before, though still sickly sweet.

"I disagree. Their relationship has gone too far. *Notre ruse aurait dû fonctionner…*" he muttered in French. "They have shared blood already. I'm sure of it. *C'est impossible…* It is time to re-assess. This *must* go our way."

"Just because she slept with Murray doesn't mean they shared blood." She was trying to convince him, that much was clear. "And even if they did, she still wouldn't sacrifice a human life for a vampire life. Murray's a piece of work – and she's a hunter. She *can't* let him go free. Not in place of her friend."

"But we do not have that leverage, thanks to you! *Tu es inutile!*"

"It wasn't my fault, and you know it. But what does it matter? They were getting close before we took her anyway. He'll come to us."

"You do not know him as I do. He is clever. He is manipulative *et charmant* at once. I would not be surprised if he sent his friends in his place." The floorboards creaked above my head, and I imagined him pacing.

Émilie scoffed. "They're nothing. Wyatt's strong, but I have a plan for her. The preening blonde bleeds like any mortal. And the boy… maybe I'll remove his hand, like for like." She paused. "He can only hide behind his friends for so long before he has no choice but to show himself – until then, it's a matter of making sure the hunter knows we're serious."

I grinned to myself, desperately holding on to this positive piece of news – Tom, of all people, had taken her down. Jon would have been so damn proud. *I* was proud. I'd have to remember to congratulate him if I ever got out of here. But fuck, I hoped it had hurt her.

"Ha! She is too arrogant, too involved… a poor excuse for a *chasseuse*."

I bristled, the movement causing my plastic bonds to scrape the pipe behind me noisily – even my crappy French was enough to know my hunter skills had just been insulted. The pacing above me stopped.

"She must have awoken. I will speak to her this time." Alistair's voice was quieter, and there was a clattering from behind me like something being dragged down a staircase.

"Erin Conrad, at last. *Enchanté*."

I twisted around, metal pipe scraping my back, desperate to finally see the face of the man who'd caused all this. He held a simple wooden chair in one hand, and placed it in front of me, sitting and crossing his legs. His face was half-hidden in shadow as his eyes burned into me.

"I can't say I feel the same way, I'm afraid," I allowed myself a huge false smile, regretting it instantly as pain shot through my jaw and ear.

He faced me head-on, and my smile vanished.

Where Émilie's resemblance to Isabel had been largely performance, Alistair's similarity to Nicholas made my blood run cold. This was the killer from my nightmares. They could have been brothers, but everything I loved in Nicholas's features was twisted into something cruel, here. I wondered whether he, too, had attempted to change his appearance as Émilie had – but the resemblance was too uncanny.

Alistair cocked his head to one side, narrowing his eyes at me. As he shifted, the shadows on his face receded, revealing scarring across the side of his neck and jaw: burns that looked as if they'd never healed.

"You are something of a *célébrité* among the undead here, Erin." His fingers traced the line of his jaw. "They fear you, and perhaps that is what leads you to think you can speak to me with such disrespect. *Ne me sous-estime pas.* I am not they," he said, each word precise and cold.

"I'm not afraid of you, Alistair. You're another killer, no different to the rest." I lied, controlling my voice with an effort. "You're no better or cleverer – you just prefer to play with your food. That's all."

His scarred lips twisted in disdain. "You are not my food. If I wished to feed on you, *chasseuse*, I would have done so. I have another task for you – I think you know this."

Émilie entered the room as he spoke, standing silently in the corner with a look of disapproval on her face. She placed a single taper candle on the cabinet behind her, elongating her shadow to fearful proportions.

"You want me to kill Nicholas," I murmured. "He must have pissed you off pretty badly to go to all this effort."

Alistair smiled politely at my feeble attempt to make him angry. "You cannot possibly imagine what he has put me through. You are still so young. So… *naïve*."

"I've read his diaries. I have a good idea of what he's capable of."

"So you know of his crimes, yes? All of them? The stalking and

The Gloaming

the manipulations; the elaborate games he has played over the years?" He leaned in, face emotionless. "I think not. I think if you had, your blood would boil as mine does at the thought of him. You would have killed him already.

"I thought you would, after the death of your friend. It was all coming together – I was meticulous. I cannot understand what happened…" He was talking more to himself than to me. "It seems the more you know, the more you go against your nature. You should have listened to Tomal. Perhaps he would be safe now if you had."

I said nothing. I still didn't know for certain if they had Tom, but I doubted it. And Nicholas was safe – the figure in the cupboard had been another of their tricks.

"What, no witty comeback?" Émilie asked, smirking.

"I'd be going against my nature if I killed someone who was working to redeem themselves," I snapped. "He's changed."

"You lie. You do not know everything about him – there are truths even he could not admit to, in those pages he guards. I am a side note in that history: barely a mention. If he had written it as it happened, you would not trust him so." Alistair leered at me. "He tells you of the insignificant moments, softens you to the notion he is worth saving."

I didn't respond. It was true Nicholas had never mentioned him, even when we'd discussed Paris. Isabel and Adam had never found anything about him in the diaries, as far as I knew, and I'd only begun to learn about Nicholas's past… but I couldn't let that change what I knew to be true.

"There's nothing you can say or do that would make me kill him," I answered eventually. "Not for you, or anybody. He's better than you, I know that much. That's all I need to know."

With quick, deliberate movements, Alistair stood and unbuttoned his shirt.

"Better, you say? A man that would leave his friend to *this* is a better man than I?"

Dropping his shirt from his shoulders to the dirty concrete, the full extent of his injuries was revealed in the candlelight. Almost every visible part of his thin, starved body was scarred and malformed. Stark white tissue stretched and contorted his chest, blistered and livid. Whatever had happened to him, his vampire abilities had been unable to heal the injuries. His face showed the least of the damage, but even there I could see thick scarring around his throat, jaw and hairline, stretching toward his eye socket.

As he turned, I noticed how different his movement was – stiff and awkward, nowhere close to the smoothness I'd come to expect from vampires. It was almost as if his skin was too taut for their usual effortless grace.

Though there was nothing but hatred in my heart for the killer before me, I was unable to deny the sickness in my stomach at the sight of him and the suffering he had undoubtedly endured. I could barely look at him.

Alistair laughed shortly, with no real mirth. "You are not the first that cannot stand to see me as I am, alive only through the blood of the other undead. Even dear Émilie, though she claims to care… she cannot bear me, in truth. This *thing* that Nicholas has made me. Do you still say he is better than I?"

"He wouldn't—" I began, choking on the words I half believed.

Alistair knelt before me, his eyes flat and black. "But he *did*. The man you love, Erin – he is nothing but *un monstre*."

The Gloaming

"The sun's almost down. Shouldn't they be up by now?" Tom paced the length of the library for what felt like the hundredth time. The sky had deepened to purple between the tall windows, and still, they had nothing to show for the endless day.

Adam didn't look up from the laptop he had balanced on his knees, his pointed boots resting on the antique desk. "Nick is an early riser, he is mostly likely awake. Isabel… well, if you wish to be the one to go into her private chamber and tell her to hurry, go ahead. But I wouldn't recommend it," he drawled, smirking.

"Where do they sleep, anyway?" Tom paused mid-step, the question slipping out before he could stop himself.

Adam glanced up. "Why do you want to know?"

"I'm not going to try to kill them if that's what you're worried about." He rolled his eyes. "I've just always wondered. Coffins?" Tom grinned.

"I believe there is an enclosed, coffin-like aspect to it all," Adam turned back to the screen. "But they sleep in beds, in bedrooms, like any other respectable person. Though Nick once told me Izzie went through a traditional casket phase in the 1890s."

Tom snorted, about to reply, but at that moment Isabel strode into the room in tailored black trousers and a fitted shirt, annoyingly perfect as always – followed at a distance by a dishevelled Murray; far from his usual self. Tom couldn't find the energy to be pleased about it.

"Almost always in our own beds, too," Isabel said. Tom suddenly found the ancient carpet fascinating, the heat creeping up his neck as he caught her wink.

"Yet I've been unable to keep a proper housekeeper for decades, thanks to your nighttime antics," Adam muttered.

"Enough," Murray cut across them. "We've wasted enough time."

"You didn't happen to have any ground-breaking revelations while you slept, did you?" Adam asked, pushing the laptop aside as he took in Murray's unkempt appearance.

Isabel made a disbelieving sound in the back of her throat. "Cole has a notion that – well, you go ahead."

Murray didn't look at Isabel but focused his gaze on Tom, who shifted under its intensity.

"My point still stands about the scent. Fresh-turned soil or dirt, which points to somethin' outdoors. But what's more interestin' is the iron. No just any metal – old, rusted iron. That was the most strikin' thing," he paused, thinking. "There was a smudge to the ink too, tells me the writer was left-handed – ye can see it in how the letters slant. And the oil left on the paper from their fingers has a faint smell of some plant or flower. I ken I've caught that scent before, but I cannae recall the name."

Adam twitched, frowning.

"I can smell only the dirt and metal – I couldn't even identify it as iron specifically," Isabel added.

"Do you think they have her underground?" Tom asked. "That would explain part of it."

"The metallic scent would be too dispersed in an open space," Isabel leaned on the desk by Tom and folded her arms. "Even for Nicholas to track. Underground, the air is trapped, stale – scents build up and linger."

"A storage unit maybe? Or a garage?" Tom suggested.

"It's a possibility," Isabel nodded. "Unfortunately, the two scents seem to contradict one another."

Adam set the laptop aside and caught Tom's eye. "As it happens, we have a theory too."

Isabel and Murray regarded him expectantly, but he shook his head.

The Gloaming

Adam pocketed the diary and led them from the library. They crossed the hall and climbed the spiralling staircase, emerging through heavy double doors into a bedroom. The faint scent of vanilla and woodsmoke had followed them up from Adam's kitchen below. Tom glanced at the sewn-shut curtains that blocked what must have been a view of the manor grounds, wondering who slept here.

"Why are we—" Nicholas broke off with a dismissive gesture and dropped into a desk chair.

Adam was already rummaging in a box at the bottom of the oak wardrobe that filled the left wall. He emerged a moment later with a fabric-bound notebook about the size of his hand.

"How did you ken that was there?" Nicholas frowned at him.

"There are no secrets in my house, Nick." He lay the book on the desk, letting it fall open naturally to the centre page, where the spine had worn through. Pressed into the paper was a stalk of once-purple flowers Tom didn't recognise. The faded brown ink of the handwriting beneath was too pale to make out, but the distinctive leftward slant matched the note perfectly. He could still smell the faint perfume of the blossom as Adam placed Murray's diary beside it.

"Who did this book belong to?" Adam asked curtly. "And the flower?"

Murray stared at the book without speaking, his face unyielding.

"Nick?" Isabel asked.

"A comrade," he answered finally. "But I dinnae see what this has to do with Erin."

"I think you do. To whom does this belong?" Adam repeated.

"Someone I served with. Another man I couldnae save."

"Do you keep stuff from all the people you kill, Murray?" Tom asked, inspecting the book.

"I didnae say I killed him," He shot him a bitter look. "Though I may as well have."

Tom snorted but seated himself on the steamer chest at the end of the bed. If Murray was about to start on a long, woeful tale, he may as well be comfortable for it.

"Did you meet him in Paris?" Adam asked quietly.

"On the outskirts, so no really. I spent time with him there, but as I said, he's dead. He's been dead since the war, and therefore he's no relevant." A shadow crossed his face.

Isabel gave Adam a questioning glance. He gave her a dark smile in return.

"Let me fill you in, Izzie. Nick and I had a bit of a falling out in Paris – perhaps you remember that part? Nick found himself a replacement wingman, if you will, since he needed a lodger. Eventually he… presumably kicked him out of the apartment? Or did he walk out on you, as I did?" He looked to Murray for confirmation, who nodded.

"Move on a few decades, another war breaks out and I refused to enlist – I find the whole thing distasteful, as you know. So, Nicholas reconciles with his old Paris buddy – you didn't mention Nick: did you turn him or was he already a vampire when you met?" He stopped. "Sorry, *irrelevant*," Adam apologised, his sarcasm evident.

"Then the two vampire war heroes get themselves involved in politics far above either of their heads, is that right?"

"It wisnae like that, Adam," Murray muttered, grudgingly. "Ye ken what happened. He winnae have joined up if it hadnae been for me. I spent weeks convincin' him it was a worthy cause, that we could do some good. But they took us prisoner."

Tom followed the thread: Paris hunting partner and roommate to war companion to fellow prisoner. No wonder Nicholas had never mentioned him – the guilt of encouraging someone to fight, only to watch them suffer…

Isabel straightened, her eyes widening. "Ah, this was when you were away. When you let—"

"I had naught to do with your husband's death, Isabel. I didnae *let* him die," Murray replied sharply. "But aye, we were imprisoned together. There were… tests," he paused, remembering.

"I was older. Better at hidin' my nature than he was…" The temperature seemed to drop with each word. Tom found himself leaning forward despite himself, the leather of the chest creaking beneath him. Even Isabel had gone impossibly still, more statue than vampire. "But there were few of us they couldnae find a use for. Tests for gases, drugs, chemicals… more torment than I care to think on. They didnae intend us to live."

"What happened to him?" Tom asked as the silence stretched out, his jaw clenching. He didn't want to feel sorry for Murray – for Nicholas – but…

Nicholas shrugged. "Twas all in the diary. The experiments ended when you werenae useful nae more. I was stronger: my body took the damage better and recovered faster. But toward the end, we were relocated with the rest." He put his palms together between his knees, staring at the floor.

"When their scientists had learned all they could from us, they sent us on to Auschwitz." Nicholas's fingers dug into his knees. "He died: burned, blistered, half-blind and half-mad from the pain and repeated exposure." A muscle twitched in Isabel's jaw as she watched him. "I dinnae fully ken how I escaped myself.

"I was thin, I suppose. Starved. I already looked like a corpse. I hid among bodies that had once been people I'd tried to protect. Aye, my low heart rate worked in my favour that time, but barely…" His eyes glazed over, flinching at memories only he could see. "I dream of it, sometimes. Cold hands, searchin' for a pulse I didnae have."

Isabel gazed at Nicholas with the most peculiar expression.

"I don't think he died there, Nick," Adam said, all irritation gone. "None of this was in the diary."

Nicholas didn't seem to be listening. "I – I couldnae go back to check for certain, after the camp was liberated. Mayhap I should have, but I didnae think I needed to." He swallowed. "He was young, the starvation and the… it took too much from him. There was nothin' I could've done—" For the first time, uncertainty crept into his voice, his accent becoming more pronounced with each word.

"Nick, we don't blame you. I cannot imagine how hard the idea of going back would have been. But we need to know if this man, this friend of yours – could he be here now?"

Isabel knelt before the broken vampire as he stared into nothingness, hesitating. "If he believes you left him for dead, then…"

"The gas almost took me, that last time," he said, pleading.

"I know. You do not have to justify yourself to me. I understand—"

"No, Izzie!" Nicholas burst out, standing up and pushing her away. "You have no idea what it was like in there. No for hundreds of years have you felt genuine fear for your life – if ever! You dinnae ken how hard it was to hold on – they could have exposed us all!" He swallowed loudly. "They werenae above experimentin' on the dead, and they more than suspected me by then. Even stayin' out of the sun, weak, unable to feed…" He sat back down, the fight leaving him as swiftly as it had appeared.

"We can't know," Tom agreed, staring at him. "But right now, Erin's a prisoner, like you once were. We don't know what they're doing to her. If she's still alive—" His voice broke, and he began again. "We need to know if there's the smallest chance this vampire lived. We've got nothing else to go on."

Tom picked up the leather-bound book and showed him the spine, where he'd noticed the newer stitching earlier. "Did you remove these pages or did someone else?"

Nicholas took the diary and examined it for a second, placing it back on the dresser. He glared at Adam, not speaking, his green eyes burning. Tom struggled to keep his breathing calm, unable to pull in enough oxygen as they all awaited an answer; some fragment that might lead them to Erin.

"I didnae remove the pages," he said finally. "And the flowers – they're violets, I remember now. His mother's favourite. He would press them into the letters he wrote to her.

"There were violets where Maggie died – I, uh – I saw the photographs," Nicholas murmured. "I always left roses. He mayhap didnae ken, so he used his mother's flowers." His voice hardened. "I thought it a coincidence."

"A fucking *coincidence*?" Tom could hardly believe the vampire could have been so blind. "Nothing about this has been anything other than carefully planned, but you didn't think to mention *any* of this?"

Nicholas's shoulders sagged as though under an impossible weight. "Tis my greatest shame." His voice cracked on the words. "Of all the sins I've committed, this one…" He couldn't finish, and Tom noticed his hands were trembling at his sides. "I thought him dead. That no soul could survive that place. I… cannae imagine how bad the damage must have been, if it truly is Alistair le Normand. If he's already removed the evidence of our friendship from my diary, then it seems he blames me for what happened." He sighed. "And I dinnae blame him. We must move quickly."

32

A Flaying is Only Fair

After Alistair's tirade, I was left alone with my thoughts. My stomach cramped – fuck knows when I'd last eaten anything. Intermittently being drugged unconscious didn't exactly do much for my sense of time, and while the slow movement of faint light gave me something to go on, it wasn't too specific about mealtimes.

I'd long since stopped trying to find a comfortable position, and my legs were still dead – not that it looked like I'd be needing them any time soon. My escape plan hadn't exactly come along as I'd hoped, given the grogginess, injuries and my utter inability to do so much as shift position.

Alistair's words lingered in my mind long after he'd left. My breath clouded in front of my face as I sighed, trying to flex my frozen fingers. How was I supposed to look Nicholas in the eye now, and trust he was a good man?

I didn't want to accept that the person I'd begun to care for could be capable of causing pain to the extent Alistair had suffered; yet the logical part of me insisted that after all, he was a *vampire*. Torn between my heart and my head, I struggled to accept the gaping chasm of distance between the Nicholas I knew, and the

Nicholas I'd read and heard about.

Eventually, my head pounding from the combination of the gas, the injuries to my face and a swirl of racing thoughts I couldn't quieten, I succumbed to exhaustion. The dull throb of pain in my shoulders and the growl of my empty stomach followed me down into darkness. In those final moments before unconsciousness, Nicholas's face floated in my mind – not the monster Alistair described, but the man who'd looked so vulnerable, so… broken, when he'd told me about his past. The contradiction made my heart hurt more than my wounds.

UPON WAKING, I KNEW IMMEDIATELY something was different. Before I'd fully reached consciousness, the sharp scent of wet earth and rust filled my lungs, bringing with it a cold that reached deep into my bones.

I was cramped into a corner, my back against cold metal that seemed to curve upward and away behind me. My arms were still restrained above my head, but the icy bite of steel and a hollow jangling when I shifted told me my plastic ties had been upgraded. The sound bounced back at me oddly, as though the space was enclosed. Contained.

Some of the feeling had come back to my legs, though I almost wished it hadn't, since pins and needles had given way to stiff, aching muscles. Stretching them out into nothingness, I found I was raised above the ground. The rough surface under my thighs caught my skin when I moved – some kind of wooden platform or bench. My bare feet found something solid when I stretched, too. Another bench, maybe, or a cabinet.

In pitch darkness, I couldn't even begin to guess where the hell

The Gloaming

I was. The air was heavy with a dampness that reminded me of the chill I'd once felt exploring caves by the beach with Jon and Tom. But that wouldn't account for the uniform ridges at my back, cold and unyielding.

Time passed without consequence or acknowledgement, as I gave up tugging at the restraints bolted to the wall. The gloom pressed in closer with each passing minute. To keep the panic at bay, I sang David Bowie songs under my breath, focusing on the thought that if they needed to hide me this well, someone must be getting close.

A scraping sound made me jump. A crack of light split the darkness, and I finally saw my prison for what it was – a metal tunnel barely wider than my stretched arms. The curved ceiling was so low that even lying on the bench, my head nearly brushed it. No wonder the air felt so close.

The sliver of light widened. For a moment I glimpsed the starry night beyond before Émilie's silhouette filled the doorway. Moonlight flooded in, making me squint, but I could see she still held her mutilated arm close to her body. Closing the door behind her, the blue light of an electric travel lamp cast twisted shadows on the walls. She placed a small tin on the cabinet by the door before settling on an identical bench across from me.

As my eyes adjusted, my prison revealed itself. Metal walls arched overhead in corrugated ribs. The benches weren't benches – they were makeshift beds, and I recognised the basic design of an Anderson shelter, flashing back to images on a slideshow I'd seen at a school assembly decades ago. The weight of the earth above me suddenly felt much heavier – this place was designed to withstand bombs. Which meant my chances of being able to escape unaided had gotten exponentially smaller in the last five minutes.

Émilie tilted her head, studying me. The harsh light hollowed her cheeks and made the shadows under her eyes seem deeper than ever. Even wounded, she'd be stronger than me – drinking vampire blood would do that to a girl. But maybe if I found the right moment, the right weapon…

She watched me for a long while, a predatory look of anticipation on her face. Slowly, she slunk closer, resting her right hand heavily on my knees, pinning my legs in place.

"You've been struggling."

I gave her the filthiest look I could muster, though I suspected the full force of my malice was lost amid the bruising on my face. My fingers flexed against the manacles.

One hand, Erin. That's all you need.

"You're wasting your time, you know. There's no way out of here," she added. "How long do you think we've been preparing for this?"

"My friends will be here. Give them time."

She shrugged. "I'm sure they will, eventually." Her quiet laugh bounced off the curved metal walls, coming back at me from all sides. "Probably Tommy boy first – yes, okay, you caught me – we don't have him. But don't worry, he won't get to you. I've got special plans for him." She waved her stump meaningfully. "Can't let him get away with this, can I?

"And then there's that creepy blonde you've begun associating with." She squeezed my knee sharply with her fingernails. "What a strange, selfish attempt at humanity he is. I thought you had better taste. I mean, at least Murray and Wyatt are… legendary. What's *he*?"

I said nothing. I hadn't learned enough about Adam to get into a battle of words with her – but I knew enough to know she was

The Gloaming

wrong about him. All I could focus on was my relief that Tom was safe.

"Now, shall we begin?" she asked delicately. "Alistair wants you to kill Murray, as you know – and I strongly support that plan. But that's not for today." She paused, waiting.

"I've thought a lot about what Murray did to Alistair. I mean, you've seen him – he may walk and talk, but he's a *mess*," she whispered, as though confiding some secret.

I remained silent, watching her for a way in. Or *through*. She seemed to enjoy the sound of her own voice, and the longer she talked, the more she revealed. But there was something unhinged in her eyes that made my skin crawl way beyond the usual chills and shivers. A deeper, darker kind of cold.

"It seems only fair," she continued, sliding her hand down my calf and gripping my still-bound ankles, "that Alistair's suffering should be paid back in kind." She nodded to herself, eyes blank in the lamplight.

"It's difficult to make Murray suffer in the usual ways. He's old, and he heals so quickly… it's why we've had to get a little creative, you know?"

"If you want him dead anyway—" I began.

"*They* want him dead," she snapped. "And so they should. *I* want him to hurt first," she smiled to herself. "I want to watch the torment on his face when he sees what I've left of you – because for some reason you're the only thing he sees." She flashed a quick, vicious grin at me.

"Of course, I can't do so much damage that you're incapable of killing the wretch – don't worry. We need you in good enough condition for that, at least. But—"

She yanked my ankles hard, forcing me flat against the icy

wooden bench. The ceiling seemed to press lower, the walls closing in as she leaned in to whisper in my ear. "That still leaves plenty of soft, vulnerable hunter flesh to work with."

I pulled my knees back up towards myself, scrabbling to get back into a seated position, but she wrenched my legs out again, sitting on my feet to hold me there. Reaching for the box she'd brought in with her, the lid swung back with a faint rattle, and she picked out a surgeon's scalpel. Deftly, she turned it in the lamp's light, examining the blade.

"You'll have to excuse me if I'm a little clumsy." She waved her stump at me. "I'm used to having both hands, but I'll try my best. I'm *dying* to find out how much you can take."

I glared at her, unable to move or act under her weight as she cut through my filthy vest to expose my torso.

"Soon Murray will come for you." The words came out like a purr. "The daylight won't stop him – not now. He'll be weaker, though, exposed…" Her eyes gleamed, and she drew the tip of the blade from my sternum to the waistband of my jeans in a long, shallow cut. "Alistair knows him too well."

The scalpel's path burned against my frozen skin. Blood trickled warmly down my side while my breath clouded in the frigid air. I bit down hard enough to taste copper, forcing back the sound rising in my throat. Every instinct screamed at me to fight back, break free, do *something*. But the manacles bit deeper as I tensed, and Émilie's weight pinned my legs uselessly to the bench. It'd been a long time since I'd felt this… defenceless.

"He won't fall for it." I spat through gritted teeth.

Her quiet laugh filled the small space. "He already has. The sun's rising, and we know exactly where he is. That's the problem with sharing blood…" She made another cut by the first, deeper than before. "Nicholas might be able to sense you now, if you shared enough. But Alistair? Even a tiny taste from years ago is enough for him to know when Nicholas is close."

Unfazed by my lack of reaction, she made another long cut beside the first. "By the time we're done, he'll be here. And then…" She pushed the stump of her arm into my stomach to pull the skin taut. "Well, then the real fun begins."

I tried not to flinch as she angled the blade, the cold flat side of it against my flesh. Unable to stop myself, I cried out as she drove it under the skin, peeling the surface cleanly away. The raw, exposed flesh bled heavily as my heart rate rose. But she wiped it clean, not even tempted. I dug my fingernails into my palms, swallowing my scream as she drew another line, and began again.

After Murray's revelation, Tom was growing more concerned about Erin's state by the second – though for the first time since they'd been at the empty house, he genuinely thought they might have a shot at finding her. The three immortals made their way down to the ground floor, leaving the faded old notebook on the dressing table.

He followed them downstairs, his mind spinning. Every time he looked at Nicholas now, he saw both the monster who might have got Erin killed and the prisoner who'd survived hell. And yeah, Erin could handle herself. She always had. But the idea that he was starting to see Nicholas as an actual fucking person… that was a whole new thing he didn't have time to get his head around right now. Though maybe the mess of contradictions that was Murray was why Erin hadn't talked to him about all this sooner – not that he'd exactly made himself available to discuss it.

"There are only so many places this Alistair could hide within a reasonable distance of the city and his feeding ground. Not all of those will match the information we have, so we need to narrow it down," Adam said, continuing a conversation Tom hadn't been listening to. The immortal placed a mug of coffee in front of him with a deliberate bang, drawing his thoughts back into the room as liquid sloshed over the rim. "It's a process of elimination."

"What?" Tom asked, coming back to himself as Isabel removed a vacuum flask from the fridge, the seal breaking with a soft hiss. The red liquid made a sick, viscous sound as she poured it into a highball glass. Tom's throat closed up, acid burning at the back of his mouth as he fixed his gaze on the kitchen tiles, counting the squares to keep his coffee down.

"You've lived here your entire life, is that correct?" Adam asked, evidently trying not to roll his eyes.

"In the city? Yeah. But we've already gone over this – soil and metal, remember? I don't know every inch of the city, no one does – and if you reckon we're looking for a metal building, you've got no chance," Tom answered, averting his eyes from Isabel. "This is Steel City."

He thought about it. "We could maybe try the industrial district, near Solace's place. Some of the warehouses and closed up workshops might fit the description, but Erin searched them when she was looking for Murray before – we know they're abandoned."

"I dinnae think a warehouse would leave such a scent," Nicholas said, taking an identical glass from Isabel. "Twould have to be somewhere smaller, and iron – no the stainless steel used in modern structures."

"Could you *not*?" Tom protested, unable to restrain himself any longer.

The Gloaming

Isabel arched a dark eyebrow at him, taking a delicate sip from her glass. "Would you have me hunt in the streets instead? I assure you, that would prove far less... palatable, to your sensibilities."

Tom wrinkled his nose. "No, but you could at least wait until I'm not here to watch the show. An opaque cup wouldn't hurt."

"They have to keep feeding if they are to be at peak strength, Tom," Adam reasoned. "And we need that strength."

"We won't need *anything* if we can't figure out where the bastard is keeping her," Tom fumed under his breath.

"Nick, I assume you didn't find anything at the warehouses?" Isabel asked. "It seems to be our only plausible destination. And now, with more context?"

Tom and Adam shared a look of confusion.

"What're you talking about?"

Nicholas sighed and rubbed the back of his neck with one hand. "I didnae mention it because we didnae learn anythin' – but Erin and I went to see Solace."

"We need to know *everything*, haven't you figured that out yet?" Tom tried not to raise his voice, but he couldn't help it. "Solace knows this city better than anyone. She must have had something to say?"

"She wasnae exactly in a position to. Her warehouse had been attacked – presumably by Alistair's female accomplice, given the description she provided." Nicholas's voice dropped lower. "Solace didnae see much, but they'd fed on her people. Killed them. Vampire on vampire feedin'..." he trailed off, shaking his head.

"But... it is taboo."

Isabel made a sound of utter revulsion, turning away. The disgust on her face spoke volumes, and Tom could tell this wasn't just murder to her, it was something far worse.

"What does this mean for us?" he asked.

Isabel sighed. "It means our enemy will be more formidable than we had previously anticipated. It also explains – to some extent – why Alistair's accomplice has been moving about during the day, and perhaps even how Alistair survived such terrible experiments." She raised her glass. "As such, this is more necessary than ever."

"Delightful," Adam said dryly, pushing a laptop across the counter towards Tom, who was busy suppressing the urge to vomit.

"What do you want me to do with that?" He asked once his stomach was under control again.

"Find Erin's location." Adam gave him a look that clearly implied Tom was being slow on purpose.

"Google it? Are you serious?" Tom snorted. "Because typing '*vampire kidnapping locations*' into Maps is really going to help."

"No. I want you to cross-reference the information we have with the additional facts Nick is about to share with us." He gave a little laugh. "You are the most technologically inclined amongst us. I've never cared for the internet."

Tom ignored him but carefully pulled the laptop closer, angling the screen away from the others. "What facts?"

Nicholas swept a hand through his already dishevelled hair, draining the last of his glass of blood. "There are many things as could be relevant…"

"So start at the beginning. You said you didn't meet in Paris. Where did you meet?" Isabel was reliably matter-of-fact, and Tom was grateful she had no qualms about getting straight to the point where the others appeared to dawdle.

"He was workin' at a fair on the outskirts with his mother; some fortune-telling trick for the tourists, I think. I found it mildly entertainin'. He was moving to the city, and I had the room available." He rolled his shoulders, the gesture distinctly human for a vampire.

"Did he have a family? Was he already a vampire?" Isabel pushed.

"I dinnae ken! He wisnae a vampire, no. But he knew what I was," he hesitated. "I cannae say if I made him, but I fed on him – an accident, and I didnae ken what I do now…" Nicholas paced the length of the kitchen.

"What about his character? What was he like, back then?" Adam urged.

"I barely remember, Adam. Twas such a short time, amidst all the memories." He pinched the bridge of his nose, staring out of the window into the darkness beyond the glass. "He was canny. A scientific thinker, I suppose. And he enjoyed his tricks and games; I remember that much. Tis why I suspected he was connected; the flowers – the note."

"'*Checkmate*,'" Tom quoted.

"Aye. We would play chess together in the camp, with pebbles and a board drawn in the dirt. Twas our way of keepin' sane, of focusing on somethin' else. We'd share stories. Parts of our lives from before," Nicholas explained, turning back to the counter and seating himself opposite Isabel.

"Were there any other games?" she asked.

"It wasnae merely games – it's hard to explain. It was the winnin' of the thing; the flair and drama – twas why he came to Paris. He loved the theatre and the arts. I suspect he'll want to set the stage for me now, too."

"What's that supposed to mean? He's preparing dinner and a show?"

"I'd imagine… he'll do anythin' he thinks might hurt me as they hurt him. If he thinks I abandoned him, he'll want to remind me of the suffering we endured. That *he* endured, because of me." He rubbed his temples with a finger and thumb, his hair sticking up boyishly.

"He will want to remind you of the war?" Adam said, nodding.

"I should expect so," Isabel agreed. "Though I doubt anyone could forget."

"He already has been," Nicholas murmured.

Adam frowned. "What on earth do you mean?"

Nicholas gazed at the floor tiles. "It wasnae til we were at Erin's that I realised…" he hesitated. "Tom mentioned the water temperature at Maggie's had been controlled. That someone was keepin' Jonathan awake, starving him…"

"And?" Tom asked.

"There were experiments in water like that at the camp, to do with blood coagulation… And there were prisoners left tortured, forced to stand in the same spot. Even the woman left on your doorstep, Adam—" he looked to his friend. "She was arranged like the corpses of runaways used to be, out front."

"So there have been clues all along, and you said nothing." Adam's tone barely contained his irritation. "Hints at every death."

"No!" Nicholas shook his head. "I thought them familiar, that's all. I didnae recognise the connection until later. Until it was too late."

Tom's hands clenched over the laptop. Every new detail made the knot in his chest tighter – if they were recreating wartime tortures with their other victims, fuck knows what they would do to Erin. But there was no way anyone else could have spotted the pattern – it was intended for Nicholas alone, not that the thought was much comfort. If he or Erin had somehow seen it earlier… This could have been over long ago. But it was too late now – and Erin was still gone. Finding her was the most important thing. He flexed his fingers and started typing.

"Do you think he might be keeping her somewhere that dates back to that time?"

The atmosphere shifted, Nicholas's oversights not so much forgiven and forgotten, but set aside for now.

"There aren't many buildings that survived," Isabel said. "Sheffield was bombed heavily, given the steelworks." She leaned over his shoulder to see the screen. "Yet it would have to be somewhere abandoned, isolated—"

Tom stared at the search results, but his mind was already somewhere else – trudging up muddy paths with Jon, who'd insist on exploring every abandoned building they passed. "Historical significance," he'd always said. Tom had called it Jon's death wish, back then. The irony made his chest tight. There were so many routes – so many abandoned places out in the middle of nowhere…

"Wait," Tom paused with his fingers hovering over the keyboard, ignoring how uncomfortably close Isabel still was. Her breath was cool on his neck, the strange scent of lilacs in snow making him increasingly uncomfortable. "I might know where they are."

"Impossible," Adam protested. "We haven't begun to—"

"Let me speak, will you?" Tom cut across him. "There's an old farmhouse. It's not technically in the city, but it's somewhere near the moors."

"I don't see how this helps," Adam stated, folding his arms.

"It's not too far from the bridge where Erin crashed the car, which would fit – and it has an Anderson shelter around the back," Tom spoke more quickly now, certain he was right.

"A bomb shelter?" Nicholas's head snapped up.

"Yeah, one of those that's half underground, with the sandbags and stuff. It's mostly derelict, but it seems like the sort of place that'd bring back memories, right?" Tom kept his eyes on the laptop screen, pretending not to notice the way Murray's fingers dug into the counter.

"Aye." Nicholas's voice had gone quiet. "We discussed the merits of the shelters once, practicality-wise. They didnae seem like they'd be much protection from a missile—" He broke off, his green eyes distant with memory. "He always said they were better for keepin' people *in* than danger out."

Tom pushed away from the counter without waiting to hear more.

"Where are you going?" Isabel called after him, as he hurried down the hallway.

"To get Erin! It makes sense – we know where she is!" Tom barely stopped himself from walking into her as she materialised in front of him. He yanked his coat from the hook, ignoring her glare. Her hand was outstretched as though she'd meant to pull him back but thought better of it.

"You are human. You *cannot* fight them. Let us go," she said softly.

Tom scoffed. "Not a chance. It's my fault they took her in the first place—"

"I dinnae disagree with ye, but Izzie's right," Nicholas grunted, following them into the hallway. "We need to assess the environment first. I winnae put it past Alistair to have prepared a trap."

The Gloaming

Tom struggled to keep his voice under control, since it would only work against him. "I've got no intention of *fighting* Alistair, and especially not his scary one-handed friend – I just want to get Erin out."

"Tom, please. Think about this." Adam placed a calming hand on his shoulder.

Tom shook him off and pulled away, reaching for the door handle. "Don't start acting like any of you are actually my friends, alright? I needed your help, you needed mine – now maybe it's time we dealt with this our own way." He wrenched the door open, an icy wind blasting through into the hall.

"I can't wait around anymore." Tom's voice cracked. "Do you realise she's been gone for over twenty-four hours?" The words caught in his throat as the full weight of that time hit him. His hand shook as he gripped the door handle. "She's my best friend. She's practically my family. I can't wait – even if it scares the hell out of me."

"Then I shall go," Adam said simply, pushing the door closed. "She's my friend too, Tom. And I can't die."

Tom scowled but didn't protest. It made strategic sense – and of the three immortals, Adam was the only one he halfway trusted. Being unkillable was a hell of an advantage. Still, didn't mean he had to like it.

"We need to get close enough to see what we're dealing with," Adam said, already shrugging on his coat. "I can do that."

Isabel's face darkened and she exchanged a sharp look with Nicholas before turning back to Adam. "The sun will rise in three hours. You know we cannot help if something goes wrong." The words hung in the air between them.

"Which is precisely why I should go alone," Adam replied. "But if you don't hear from me by first light…" He checked his phone. "I'll share my location with you. Perhaps the storm will give you enough cloud cover to follow if you must."

"And if it doesn't?" Isabel's voice was sharp.

"Then wait for proper cover. But no longer than that – we may not have much time." Adam glanced at Tom. "You should keep him here."

"And you? You can't die, but you can get hurt, Adam," she pointed out.

He raised an eyebrow at her. "Do not pretend you care, Izzie – falsehood is unflattering on you."

33

Where the Light Cannot Conquer

I LAY IN THE DARK FOR WHAT could have been hours or days – there was no light to judge the time by, and my tortured, battered body had stopped caring, anyway. All I knew was the sweet release of unconsciousness that came with the worst of the pain, and the brief respites from Émilie's visits.

The cold in the shelter was unrelenting, and the chill in my bones never lessened in the suffocating blackness. Several times the slow, steady drip of my blood onto the ground would halt as it gathered and froze on the bench below me. All thoughts of fighting back had fled along with the skin and flesh now missing from my chest, stomach, and lower back. I was long beyond starving, beyond thirsty: my body was falling apart and I was helpless to do anything about it.

Each time I came round, I despaired that I hadn't just… gone, in my sleep – feeling guilty the whole time that an idea like that would even enter into my head. But wallowing in my agony, my constant thought was that I wanted all this to be done with. If I was no longer here, Nicholas might live and there would be no ultimatums.

Oddly enough, the one thought that sustained me was the

thought of his fury, which I knew would be something to behold. He would wipe all traces of Émilie and Alistair from the earth and salt the bloodied ground in my name. No more careful restraint, Nicholas would unleash it all, become the monster they feared and had named him – not for revenge, but for me.

The thought of that kind of destruction should have been terrifying, but there was comfort in the black violence of it. In knowing that after four hundred years, I was the one he'd burn the world for… But my wish to see his fury also brought the reality of his grief. That much was unbearable to think about, as my own would be if our positions were reversed.

As my mind drifted in and out, a defeated calm swept over me. My muscles seized against the restraints, each spasm sending fresh waves of pain through my flayed skin, but somehow the agony helped clear my muddied thoughts.

For as far back as I could remember, before I'd met Jonathan and begun hunting – before I'd understood the demons I saw all around – I'd known something was missing within me.

I'd found some peace in the fire of the fight, that was true. Perpetually engaged in an unending battle, I'd grown used to the burning and the emptiness… but Nicholas was the pure, uncompromising moonlight that cooled those flames. With him, I could be *just Erin* – free of the burden of the death I witnessed. Quietly, he'd slipped into my life and filled the place in my heart that had been waiting.

Our differences were undeniable, but where I had one foot in the darkness, he'd stepped into the light. We shared that shadowy place in between – the place where the light couldn't conquer. Where we could be ourselves. So, despite the reality of my situation, I couldn't be selfish anymore. I couldn't give up, because,

The Gloaming

for the first time, I wasn't alone.

Thinking of Nicholas, something released within me – as though all this time I'd been holding my breath. I finally forgave him. For all of it.

I'd never forget who he'd been before: the suffering he'd caused and the lives he'd destroyed. But I understood his yearning for me had been his reason to fight for redemption. He'd always suffer – as those whose lives he'd taken had suffered first. But the balance would be maintained. It didn't exactly bring me joy to imagine his pain, but I knew there was justice in it.

The memory of his gentle touch when we'd last been together, how carefully he'd held me despite his strength, was proof enough of his transformation. Even in our most intimate moments, he'd shown his control – as though I was precious. Breakable. His redemption wasn't just in grand gestures but in the small moments.

I was key to that. My brief life was a grain of sand in the hourglass that was his. But he'd searched for me for so long and had been so patient... I couldn't fail him now. Nicholas was the one person who could love me for what I was, darkness and all. And seeing the same darkness in him, I'd fallen.

The ghost of his hands still lingered on my skin. I thought back to the way he'd so reverently traced every inch of me, as though memorising something sacred. I could conjure his face with perfect clarity – the slight crookedness of his smile, the way his lilting accent deepened when we were alone. If this was going to be the end for me, I wanted his face to be the last thing I saw.

Despite everything, something fierce stirred in me. The thought of never feeling his cool touch, of never seeing the way his eyes lit up when he looked at me – it was unbearable. Worse than any physical pain Émilie could inflict.

You can survive this.

My hunter strength, the heat of resistance, felt distant and weak – like trying to grasp smoke. But even as my body trembled from blood loss and exposure, I knew for his sake, I had to get out. I took a deep steadying breath and steeled myself, the ice in my bones beginning to melt in the wake of my fiery resolve.

ADAM WAS THOROUGHLY MISERABLE. His shirt and coat were filthy, and his already stylishly torn jeans were now utterly destroyed down the left leg, where he'd caught them on a sharp piece of protruding metal in the grass. He lay flat on his stomach, resting on his elbows with his head low, even as the grass tickled his face. He hadn't been in a situation like this for almost a century, and it didn't agree with him in the slightest. There was a distinct lack of dignity in crawling through the mud like a common footpad – though he supposed that was rather the point of reconnaissance.

Heavy rain had begun only a few minutes earlier, but already he was soaked to the skin. Immortal he may be, but the cold was as keen for him as for an ordinary human, and he was soon shivering. There wasn't much to see through the downpour, especially in the half-light of the pre-dawn, but Adam could tell Tom's guess had been correct – the building across from him was most definitely inhabited. The sky held the peculiar grey of approaching dawn, perhaps an hour before sunrise. But even younger vampires should still be conscious, which made the stillness troubling.

The farmhouse had been built of rough-cut stone – solid, the sort that reminded him of a wartime field hospital. He pushed away those particular memories, focusing instead on the task at hand. It was a long, squat-looking building, but the two barns behind were larger and older – rough wooden structures with makeshift repairs of corrugated steel patching holes in the walls. The scale of the outbuildings troubled him – there was too much space for unpleasant surprises. The tiles on the roof of the nearest had fallen through, leaving a gaping hole for the wind to whistle through, and the wooden frame stood empty, waiting. As far as he could tell, the vampires were only using the farmhouse itself: the windows were smeared liberally on the outside with an oily-looking substance. He guessed they were also boarded up as an extra precaution.

Adam was beginning to regret his decision to come. He knew he couldn't die, despite what he'd once told Erin – enough people had tried to kill him, after all – but he was still more than a little concerned for himself. He'd sworn after the last war never to put himself in harm's way again – yet here he was, crawling through the mud toward danger.

True, Erin was inside and needed his help, and it *was* far easier for him to sneak in during the day when the villains were bound to be asleep… but try as he might, he couldn't honestly remember ever being quite so tightly in the grip of his own fear. The things friendship demanded of one.

Fishing in his pocket, he pulled out his mobile phone and dialled hurriedly, his fingers slipping as the rain hit the screen. Tom was waiting in the car some way back, since it had transpired the farmhouse was, in fact, several miles from the main road. It did, however, mean Erin's friend was a safe enough distance away that he wouldn't be seen should the vampires emerge. He picked up after one ring.

"Are you there?" Tom demanded before Adam had a chance to speak.

"A civil greeting never goes amiss, you know."

"What can you see?" He continued as if he hadn't spoken.

"I am certain they're using the house; you were correct. It's protected as vampires tend to protect buildings – I suspect there may be some kind of trap at the front door. It's ajar, but it must be held in some way: this blasted wind isn't moving it." He kept his voice low, regardless of the growing light and the noise of the rain.

"Can you see the shelter?" Tom asked.

"Not from my current position. I would prefer to wait a while longer and make sure there is no movement within before I move closer," he breathed. Adam could imagine the expression on Tom's face at his suggestion of wasting more time, but his tone was controlled as he answered.

"Okay. But don't take too long – this could be our best chance to get in and out without violence."

"I understand. I wish to help Erin, too, if you recall. That *is* the reason I'm here, Tom." He kept the frustration and fear out of his voice as he ended the call – it wouldn't do any good.

Sinking lower into the grass, Adam rolled over and stared up at the sky for a moment, gathering his thoughts. Icy raindrops hit him heavily in the face, catching in his long eyelashes and plastering his white blonde hair darkly to his head. He stomped down the surge of annoyance that came with this further indignity and tried to think.

If the house was empty, they were either somewhere else entirely, lying in wait, or with Erin in person. The barns beyond the farmhouse could be a bother – there were far too many dark corners where a vampire could lurk, too many places where he could find himself trapped. But the only way to find out for certain was to move. If the action caused him to be seen, then perhaps they could be lured from their hiding place. If they were with Erin... well, he *did* need to find her.

On hands and knees, he crawled toward the far-right of the building, mud soaking through his ruined jeans. Each gust of wind whipped icy rain sideways, obscuring his vision. He paused every few metres, pressing himself flat against the saturated earth. Skeletal tree branches creaked overhead, and he found himself absurdly grateful for the sound masking his movements. Though what good his stealth did against vampire senses, he wasn't entirely sure.

The farmhouse remained still – no movement, no light, no sign of life, dead or otherwise. Even the windows seemed to watch him with malevolent emptiness. Standing, he still couldn't see a damn thing, but at least it was easier to move while upright.

Adam crept closer to the building and, avoiding the windows, edged up against the stone. Once around the corner, the shelter finally came into view. It was bigger than he'd been expecting, and the exterior that was exposed had been painted the same green as the window frames, though it was peeling far less from the metal curves.

He might not have the advanced hearing of his friends, but Adam didn't need it for the shrill cry from the shelter to reach him as the wind died down momentarily. The sound hit him like a physical blow. He squeezed his eyes shut, teeth clenched against memories of their easy friendship over coffee just days ago. Even through the obvious pain, he recognised Erin's voice – and worse, he recognised the kind of torture that might produce such a sound. A century and a half of life had taught him that much, at least.

Trying to remain rational, he considered the facts. For Erin to make such a noise, at least one vampire was in there with her.

Hopefully, both, because it made his own position less perilous. He could call Tom, but at the confirmation that Erin was inside, he knew the lad would come running and do something foolish before Adam could stop him. He didn't know Tom particularly well, but he suspected Erin might be peeved with him if her rescue came at the expense of her fragile friend. Instead, he would have to get closer – perhaps if he could hear better, he could get an idea of how many people were inside.

With a glance back toward the lifeless building, he made a run for the shelter, his boots skidding in the wet grass.

In his haste, Adam never stopped to think about whether the vampires would want to spend the night sleeping in the shelter with their prisoner. As he righted himself from the mud, finding his balance on the treacherous ground, the metal door swung open. What at first appeared to be Nicholas and Isabel stepped out into the rain, looking straight at him with a stillness that made his heart stutter.

Without thinking – though really, he ought to have known better – he bolted. He managed less than three steps before a cold, bare arm snaked around his middle with alarming strength. He yelled, his arms still free, and attempted to elbow his captor in the ribs with as much force as he could muster. He succeeded only in bruising his elbow rather spectacularly.

"What a lovely surprise! We didn't expect you so soon." A breathy voice whispered in his ear. "I didn't think you'd risk yourself for her."

"Unhand me!" Adam panted as he struggled to get loose, knowing even as he said it how absurd the request was. The other vampire appeared before him, pinning his arms to his side. The scent of petrichor and wet earth was overwhelmed by something chemical and bitter.

"Tell me, what manner of creature *êtes-vous?*" the vampire asked, his eyebrows furrowed. The downpour plastered his dark locks over his disfigured face and mouth, but he seemed not to notice. Adam noted the rolling French accent and extensive scarring in some distant, analytical part of his mind, understanding that this could only be Alistair. The rest of him was rather preoccupied.

"That's none of your concern," he spat the words, summoning what he hoped was a suitably withering glare. A century of perfecting scathing remarks, and he'd been reduced to a *glare*.

"You are no vampire, yet neither do you smell human. *Très étrange*… neither one thing nor the other." Alistair seemed intrigued but distracted, glancing toward the horizon as he spoke. It was clear he was worryingly curious about Adam, who knew he couldn't afford to have anyone digging into his past.

"*Il faut* we return inside, Émilie, or this will not work. Throw him in with *la chasseuse* for now; they can sit out this stormy day together. We will solve this new puzzle later."

Émilie must have responded behind him because she released her arm from his waist and grabbed firmly at his neck with one bony hand before he could try to move. Her grip was like iron, and he was unable to resist as she pushed his head down, dragging him towards the shelter. He stumbled through the door as it slammed behind him.

Adam winced at the screech of metal against metal as they slid chain after chain through the latch on the door, his eyes attempting to adjust to the total and complete darkness inside. There was silence but for the sound of the rain.

"Damn," he muttered under his breath, kicking half-heartedly at the door in frustration. "Damn."

34

Capture & Escape

Something had changed again. My head throbbed from dehydration as consciousness returned, the scent of coppery blood still lingering from Émilie's last visit.

I didn't remember much of it. Alistair had been there, though. The burning anger in my veins at the sight of him had protected me a little from the pain that came with her presence – though not enough to prevent me from crying out as she sliced at the delicate skin of my inner thigh. Presumably I'd passed out, but now there was a sound in the bunker with me that hadn't been there before. I was so engrossed in listening to the unfamiliar noise that it took me a full minute to notice my arms were strangely free.

"Erin?" A voice spoke from my right, and I flinched, the thin scabs on my stomach cracking at the sudden movement. His voice was too familiar to be true.

"Adam?" I croaked. I couldn't believe it. "What are you doing here?"

"Trust me, it was *not* a part of my cunning plan," he drawled through the darkness.

"You're not the most successful of rescue parties, I'll admit," I laughed, surprised I still could. "Did you unlock my chains?" I asked, flexing my wrists to test their movement.

"I picked the lock, yes. It was simpler than I'd expected, what with my improved sense of hearing in this dank, isolated little hole." He sounded at ease, though I knew he couldn't be.

"Thanks," I sighed. "I think the sensation is coming back to my arms." I paused, rotating my stiff shoulders. I didn't dare try to sit up yet. "What happened?"

"Where to begin?" I could almost sense him raising an eyebrow at me in the dark. "You disappeared, Erin. It was only ever a matter of time before we came for you – Nick would have it no other way. Tom, too. You know this."

"Did you work out it was Alistair, or—" I started.

"This past day or so, I have learned a great deal about Nick's history. I confess, much of it I wish I had not had to hear – or wheedle out of him." His usual light drawl had vanished. "Alistair was a part of that, yes."

The darkness between us felt heavier. For Adam to speak about Alistair's part in Nicholas's life like that… There must have been some truth in the picture Alistair had painted. I pressed my palm flat against the cold concrete floor, anchoring myself.

"How did you figure out it was him?" I demanded, some strength returning to my voice. "Tell me everything, from the start."

Adam took a deep breath and began to weave Nicholas's story. I shifted, trying to find a position that didn't pull at my wounds as he spoke of fortune-tellers and young vampires at the turn of the century… Of prisoners and the horrors of war – some of which I already knew. But the torture and the fear, I hadn't been expecting.

He didn't go into detail about the experiments Nicholas and Alistair had been subjected to, and I imagined Nicholas had been reluctant to share much. I struggled to comprehend what he'd endured, the determination it must have taken to survive. But Adam's words had the ring of truth to them – his story made sense of the things I knew of Alistair so far, and I believed Nicholas's conviction that his friend had been dead.

I took a moment to let everything he'd said sink in. "How did you end up in here with me?"

Adam shifted in the darkness. "Tom worked out they must be holding you here, and the others and I agreed we should investigate. Of course, I had not intended to storm to your rescue and find myself, well, captured."

Relief flooded through me like adrenaline, and I tensed at the pain it caused my injured body. "So, the others are here?"

"Yes. I spoke to Tom minutes before they caught me – but don't excite yourself, I seem to have lost my phone since then," Adam said shortly. "How are *you*, Erin? I cannot tell how badly you're hurt in this blasted darkness, but I felt your wrists as I picked the cuffs. Is that the extent of it?"

"So bad you can tell in the dark, huh?" I coughed, my throat raw and dry. "Émilie prefers shallow cuts and…" I searched for the word. "I think the term is flaying?"

There was a sharp intake of breath.

"The woman is a monster." He made a sound of disgust. "Though perhaps we should be grateful she hasn't indulged her inclination toward poison. I shall be very interested to see what Nicholas does to the vampire upstart when he sees what she has done to you."

"Is he coming?" I asked, trying not to let hope seep into my tone.

Adam chuckled. "If Nicholas were the one here, captured,

wouldn't *you* be on your way?"

I flushed in the dark.

"The sun was close to rising when they caught me, so it might be something of a wait, but he'll be here. I have faith that between him and Isabel, we will make it out alive."

"How long have I been gone?" I choked out.

"Not quite two days now."

I nodded, though he couldn't see me.

"How is he?" I knew Adam would answer me honestly.

"Both furious and utterly lost," Adam answered. "When we found the empty house, I believe something broke in him. One might have thought half his soul had been ripped away."

I nodded again to myself. I'd had so much time to think about him while I'd been here, my perspective had shifted entirely. I wanted to ask more, but I couldn't bring myself to say the words out loud. Somehow, I knew he was doing about as well with my absence as I was with his. Adam said nothing more on the subject, and I left it at that.

"How much can you move?" I asked after a moment's pause.

"I am quite unrestrained, though this shelter remains my prison."

"I'm going to try to sit up: bear with me." Taking a deep breath and holding it, I braced myself for the pain of bending my abdomen. I was no longer bleeding, but the air on my raw skin was enough to bring tears to my eyes. In one fast movement, I pulled myself up and swung my legs around, feeling for the floor in the darkness with my feet.

"Erin—" Adam started as I cried out.

"Just – give me – a minute," I panted. It wasn't quite the white-hot flashing pain of earlier, but it was enough. "So much for – the restorative – bloody – power of – meditation." My heart pounded with the effort, but I managed to steady myself.

"Excuse me?" I could hear the amusement in his voice as he worked at the chains that bound my ankles together. I didn't remember Émilie fastening those on – but I'd been here longer than I'd thought. There must have been some time missing from my memory.

"Let's just say sitting and starving in the dark is overrated, as hobbies go." I took a few deep breaths, letting my pulse find its way back to normal. "Thought I'd try to coax my brain into healing me faster, but my body pretty much told me to fuck off."

"I see. And are you quite sure you can walk with these removed?"

I sighed. "I'll manage. You might have to help me." Admitting I needed help wasn't exactly a forte of mine, and for a moment my heart filled with an ache for Jonathan – the only person I'd never minded admitting my weaknesses to. I immediately felt guilty that I'd not spared a thought for him since they'd captured me.

"Help or no help, my dear, I don't know that we're able to get out of here. There are at least three chains holding the door closed, by my estimation." He sounded resigned to the matter.

"Didn't you say you spoke to Tom a few minutes ago?"

"Minutes to you, perhaps. You have been unconscious a good while. I'm not sure what could have happened to him, actually."

His voice tightened, the usual polish falling away. It must still be daylight, and Alistair and Émilie were presumably indoors, sleeping – so what could have kept Tom from coming to find us?

"Shit. Okay, well let's focus on what we *can* do," I said, pushing the worry aside. "We've got to get out of here. Help me look for something we can use."

Trying not to bend at the waist, I got to the floor and swept my hands around, carefully. I could hear Adam doing the same, but my fingers met with nothing other than concrete and dirt.

"Would this do?" Adam's voice came from my left, accompanied by a faint jangling.

"Émilie's tools!" I exclaimed, instantly regretting raising my voice and dropping to a whisper. "Is the box open?"

"No, but it feels like the padlock has a dial."

"Can you unlock it?"

"Perhaps if I could see it?" There was a scraping sound, and my eyes watered as Adam pushed his back against the door and the thinnest chink of light appeared – apparently Émilie hadn't pushed the bolt across in her hurry to get indoors.

Adam held the box up to the light, angling it so he could look at it. The brightness stung my eyes after so long in the dark, and I turned my face away.

"Anything?" I asked after a minute or two, unable to bring myself to look back towards the light.

"I think—" Something clicked. "Ah, success."

I dragged myself across the concrete floor, keeping my torso rigid. Each pull of my arms sent tremors through my flayed skin, but it was better than trying to crawl. The few feet might as well have been miles.

"What's in it? She's not stupid enough to leave a key, and all I've seen are—"

"Blades. Scalpels. A… screwdriver? Useful should we need a weapon upon her return, but of little use to us in opening the door. The hinges are on the other side," he explained before I could ask.

The hope that had sparked momentarily died down again. I thought fast.

The Gloaming

"Can we push it open any further?" I nodded my head towards the chink of light, knowing Adam could see me better than I could see him.

"Maybe two inches at the most."

I nodded. "Okay. If you come around to my right, I'm going to try to get my wrist through the door; I think it might fit. If I can grab one of the chains—"

"You can pull the padlock through," Adam finished, already moving out of the way. "It may be worth a try. Your hands are rather smaller than mine."

I steeled myself, twisting my body, my arm at an awkward angle. Pain seared through my torso. Fresh blood trickled down my side where the movement had reopened my wounds, but I gritted my teeth and kept going, determined this plan would work. "Three, two—"

Adam pushed, and the gap widened enough for my hand. I could hardly bend my wrist, but my fingers brushed the cold metal of one of the chains.

"A bit further…"

Adam was panting with the strain of pushing at the heavy door, but my index finger caught in a link and I tugged it through.

"You can let go," I said, the light shrinking again before I'd finished speaking.

Bit by bit, we pulled the chain through the opening. It was a slow process – the chain had been looped and crossed over repeatedly, a huge metal knot for us to untangle, but eventually the first padlock caught in the gap, and we pulled it through. Adam made quick work of it and began again with the next chain.

Four times, we repeated the process. My arm quickly grew sore and bruised from repeated attempts where the door slammed on my wrist – but it kept me distracted from other pains, and the gnawing worry that something was going to go wrong.

As we pulled at the final lock, a sound from outside the shelter caught my attention, and I shushed Adam, who dropped the chain with a clatter. By unspoken agreement, we retreated deeper into the shelter, each of us with one of Émilie's blades in hand.

35

WE ARE ALL HUNTERS AND PREY

FOR THE FIRST TIME SINCE this nightmare began, I wanted to break and cry – to be so close to escaping and discovered in our attempt; it was too much. The door swung open outwards, heavy in the wind. I squinted, shading my eyes with my free hand – it wasn't Émilie standing there, but her more attractive counterpart. I'd never thought I'd be so pleased to see Izzie Misery.

"Isabel!" My voice cracked on her name as my vision adjusted to the dim light, tension draining from my shoulders at the sight of her. Water dripped steadily from the heavy cloak she wore, forming a dark puddle at her feet. The fabric clung to her frame as she moved, her face a stark white oval beneath the hood's shadow, dark sunglasses hiding her eyes. "It's daylight—?"

"I am acutely aware of that, Erin." Her tone was clipped, as she came into the shade of the shelter, pulling the door closed behind her.

"What a pleasant rescue party *you* make," Adam snipped.

"We don't have time for this." Despite myself, my voice was strained even to my own ears. I didn't want to show weakness in front of Isabel, but she was the one doing the rescuing here.

"Where's Nicholas?"

"Blessedly unconscious in the vehicle, I should think. We need to move fast – for the time being, the storm is heavy enough that there is suitable cloud cover, but I can't rely on it lasting if I want to move freely, and I will admit I am less than happy about it." Isabel rushed her words, and in the dim light, I could see her assessing first me and then the room. "The tang of blood is strong in here, Erin. How badly are you hurt?"

"What do you mean, unconscious?" I asked, worried. It wasn't that I didn't trust her, but…

"Oh, for goodness' sake!" She pulled off her gloves, and Adam stood, moving aside so Isabel could kneel by me, his white blonde head bowed down under the low ceiling.

"Is he alright?" I pushed. I had to know.

"He is fine. Old as he may be, he's not as adept at sunwalking as I, that's all. He doesn't know I am here. Which is partly why we need to make haste – he would be displeased if he found out I had gone behind his back." She levelled her gaze at me over the lenses of her glasses. "Let me see your stomach, Erin."

My muscles tensed involuntarily as her cold fingers brushed my skin. I kept my eyes fixed on the ceiling, counting the metal ridges while she peeled back what remained of my blood-stiffened vest.

Isabel made an uncharacteristically vulgar sound of distaste in the back of her throat. "One would only make incisions such as these to inflict pain." Her icy fingers probed around the hot, inflamed flesh, soothing it somewhat. "Did she drink from you?"

I was still thinking of Nicholas, and had trouble bringing my mind back to the topic at hand.

"No, she just let me bleed. She wasn't interested," I paused, my eyelids heavy. "Can you do anything about it? If we could bind it up or something, it might be easier to move."

Her fingers hesitated, and she shared a look with Adam.

"Isabel…" Adam said warningly.

"It would always be Erin's choice."

"Nick would be furious."

"Nick is not here."

"What?" I asked, looking between them.

"My blood might heal you a little, enough to get you moving on your own more easily. But I'm sure you remember the potential risks of having it in your system. Can you recall what we talked about before?" Her voice was gentle.

"It might work like a virus," I nodded, touching the faint puncture marks at my throat that had already faded to almost nothing. After my last night with Nicholas, Isabel's blood wasn't likely to be the problem. And we still had to get out of here.

"Do it."

It wasn't like watching vampires on the television, watching Isabel. Without hesitation, she put her thumb to her sharp canine and bit down, a large bead of blood welling up from the tiny cut she made. She didn't ask further permission before she smeared it across my mouth, and without thinking I licked the sparse, metallic liquid from my lips. No more than that.

"Will it be enough?" Adam asked.

"It will have to be," Isabel responded, pulling her hood more tightly around her head. "We must go now, before the clouds part."

There was a coolness in my throat where I'd swallowed her blood, and I could almost visualise the flesh knitting together across my stomach. The sensation rippled through me like ice melting into fire, fading quickly but leaving my skin itchy and hot.

The worst of the pain subsided to a dull throb in seconds, enough that I could move without screaming. At first, with Adam supporting me, but after a few steps, I stumbled alone – though he kept his arm outstretched in case I fell. I had to admit, a drop from Isabel was a hell of a lot more effective than Tom's butterfly stitches and a couple of aspirin.

Isabel remained in the shelter until we had climbed the few steps to ground level. The farmhouse was a hundred metres or so away, the two barns behind it nearer still. I recognised where we were as soon as we were in the daylight, but it was an impossible distance to get to the road beyond at the speed I was going. Thunder rumbled, loud and ominous overhead.

"Where's Tom?" I asked, glancing back at Isabel.

She frowned but shook her head under her hood. "With Nick." Her tone brooked no further questions.

Slowly, we made our way across the yard and to the largest of the barns. Isabel flitted ahead to the cover of the huge wooden doorframe. The wind and rain still hammered down, but I couldn't bring myself to be annoyed by it – it was refreshing after being confined for so long.

The clouds broke for a moment as I reached Isabel, pausing to catch my breath. She backed deeper into the shade of the barn to avoid the sunlight that broke through and momentarily brightened the hills of the Peaks, disappearing into the shadows.

The sun was lower in the sky than I'd expected – it must have been the middle of the afternoon at least, which didn't seem right at all. Adam squinted into the gloom where Isabel hid, his hand shading his eyes.

"Perhaps it would be faster for you to carry her to the car?" he asked, stepping into the protection of the doorway and shaking

The Gloaming

out his wet hair. The sun went in as quickly as it had appeared, followed immediately by a flash of lightning that lit up the interior of the barn, thunder rolling seconds later.

Isabel didn't reply, and I glanced at Adam before taking a tentative step into the shadows. The building, long disused, still smelled of mouldering hay and rotting wood. Light filtered through gaps in the roof above, creating pools of gold across the dirt floor. The cavernous space stretched up two stories, ancient hay lofts and rotting beams crisscrossing the shadowy upper level. In the far corner, a small table with trays of withered violets sat beneath dark grow lights – their purple blooms frost-edged and half-dead.

Adam threw out an arm to stop me from going any further, seeing something I hadn't. Too late, my mouth filled with the taste of copper.

A blurred shape swung down from above, missing me, but hitting Adam squarely in the hip and sending him flying backwards into the rain. I called out, ready to go after him, but had to duck and dodge the returning swing. It was an enormous beam of splintered wood, a fraying rope supporting it precariously from the upper storey. Searing pain coursed through my middle as I fell back and scrambled out of the way, though the skin didn't break, thanks to Isabel's blood.

Curled on the ground as the beam continued to swing with abandon, my eyes adjusted enough to spot my vampire ally at the back of the barn. She appeared to be resisting the urge to struggle under Émilie, who had her mutilated arm wrapped tightly about her. Both of Isabel's arms were pinned to her sides, her movement restricted by the cloak that had been intended to protect her. I froze as my gaze fell upon a familiar flannel shirt a few feet away.

Tom lay face down in the hay, dust settled undisturbed on his shoulders. His right arm was twisted beneath him at an angle that made me blanch. I waited for the rise and fall of his breathing, for any sign of life, but his chest was still.

No no no no no!

Panic and adrenaline exploded through me all at once, burning through my veins as I dragged myself upright, never taking my eyes from Émilie. My friend, my one remaining lifeline to normalcy… I couldn't think about it. Not now.

I still held the scalpel from her toolbox in my right hand, its weight a promise – but her silence was worrying. Despite the initial flood of copper in my mouth, I could barely sense Émilie or Alistair – if he was even nearby. Glancing back, Adam lay motionless in the long grass. I was on my own.

"Alistair?" I called out, trying to steady my voice. "Why don't you come out here and show yourself?"

"Erin—" Isabel warned.

Before I could blink, something was thrown from the upper storey of the barn. Alistair landed, catlike, beside the crumpled form, hauling Nicholas up by the throat and onto his knees.

My heart stopped. Blood matted his dark waves from a deep gash at his hairline, splattered across his beautiful features. But his eyes – those gold flecked emerald eyes I loved – found mine with fierce intensity. For a split second, I saw him again as he'd been in the lodge, that first night – his gentle touch and crooked half-smile.

"Erin…" he managed through gritted teeth. "Run."

My face slackened at the sight of him. Alistair sneered, pulling Nicholas up by the collar of his shirt, so that he knelt awkwardly beside him, his hands bound with rope.

The Gloaming

"I don't think she will, Nick." He waited. "Like I once did, I think she will stay with you. Won't you, *ma petite chasseuse?*"

"Get away from him." My voice was emotionless as I tried to stay on my feet. I refused to let the bastard see how weak I was. He couldn't know the true extent of the damage Émilie had caused.

"Do not worry, Erin. His death is for you, not I. *Tu ne te rappelles pas de notre petite conversation?*" He smiled cruelly. "Perhaps you might learn that loyalty to this particular vampire will bring you nothing but pain. Trust me, I would know."

I stepped forward and winced, stopping short. "How many times do I have to say it? I won't hurt him for you. I'm a *hunter*, not a murderer."

More laughter came from under the rafters and I watched, unable to move as Isabel struggled to break free. At first, I couldn't understand why she didn't just overpower the younger vamp, but as Émilie sank her teeth into Isabel's throat, I remembered again why they were so strong.

Isabel fell limp as Émilie drank, like a puppet whose strings had been cut. Loosening her hold enough to drag a long thin blade jaggedly across my friend's throat, she tossed her aside into the sunlit patch in the centre of the barn.

I bounded across the short distance, heedless of my injuries, to drag her out of the light. A slippery trail marked the ground as what was left of her blood poured forth from her throat, marking a clear line in the dirt between us.

Her skin was hot under my hands, which couldn't be good. Resting her as gently as I could manage against the wall of the barn, I turned back to Alistair but was stopped before I could speak. Something sharp poked into the small of my back – Émilie's knife.

"Would it be murder to kill a vampire, Erin? Please enlighten me. How is *he* any less selfish and manipulative than before you knew the truth?" Her voice was a loud whisper in my ear, as she pulled my hair away almost delicately with the half-healed stump of her arm.

I flinched away, but she forced me forward, pressing a small golden dagger into my hand as she did so. My fingers curled around it instinctively, but there was no way I could use it against her – and she knew it – not with her knife still sharp in my spine.

"Look at him, the sole survivor of your rescue team – that is, assuming Wyatt cops it," she giggled. "Do you think this man – who you claim to love – do you think he tried to save Tommy when I took him? Or do you think he tried to save himself, as he always does?"

I pulled away from her physically and mentally, her breath cold at my throat. Nicholas wouldn't have let Tom get hurt. He knew how much he meant to me.

"You know what he did, Erin. You see what he is when you look at me, I know you do. You understand." An undercurrent of anger ran beneath Alistair's words. He jerked Nicholas's head back, exposing his throat. "End him now, by your own hand, or watch as I make him suffer every torment he left me to endure.

"He deserves to die for what he has done, and for the countless others he has destroyed or abandoned. How many of his kind have you killed? I see no reason *ce monstre* should be an exception."

I said nothing as Émilie's knife broke the skin on my back, urging me forward. I could feel Nicholas watching me. He would let me do it, I realised. If I chose to kill him, he wouldn't fight back. The tension around his eyes softened infinitesimally – a subtle surrender that said he understood, whatever happened next.

Alistair kicked Nicholas to my feet, by the edge of the circle of

The Gloaming

light. I fell to my knees before him, the knife still in one hand, the scalpel hidden in the other. No longer noticing the other pains in my body, I could only find concern for the man before me – because a man was what he was. Not just a vampire.

"No." The word came out stronger than I felt.

"Then you condemn him to far worse," Alistair spat, splashing Nicholas with clear liquid from a small bottle in his hand that made him flinch and roar. The air filled with the sharp, acrid smell of chlorine, and the sizzle of burning flesh. "His pain will be legendary, *ma petite chasseuse*. And you shall watch every moment, knowing you could have granted him a merciful death."

"This thing, *ce monstre* – he left me to *die*, Erin. Did he tell you how we went to fight together, or did he tell you the truth – that I did not want to go? *Ma mère*, she was ill. He knew that when he insisted I accompany him. It was not my war. I did not care for the freedom of the humans."

Alistair paced, walking the perimeter around them as he spoke, punctuating each word with precise dashes of acid so that Nicholas growled and jerked away.

My hand trembled on the blade. I could end his suffering now. But as I met Nicholas's eyes again, I saw past his agony to the fierceness that had drawn me to him. The man who'd searched centuries for me. Who'd fought his way back from darkness and looked at me now with love, even as he burned. He would die for me, here and now, if I asked it.

I let Émilie's blade clatter to the ground. "I won't do it."

Triumph flashed in Nicholas's eyes even as Alistair's face tightened with controlled fury. He sank to a crouch beside Nicholas, forcing the knife I'd dropped to his throat, his movements stiff and obviously painful.

"Then you do not understand the lies he has told." A single drop of blood fell from the knife as he wrenched Nicholas's head back further.

"He knew I was too young, you know. That I would not survive if they took us. There would be no way to feed and no way out, and so he made me a promise. We would leave together or die together. That was the deal, and I would see *ma mère* again. But he abandoned me."

He paused, his scarred face contorting with the memory. "He fled while he still could, thinking me dead. But I would not die, you see? No matter what they did to me." His voice dropped, venomous. "That is how they learned what I was. The torture that would kill a man… I lived through it all. And then – *mon Dieu* – then they truly began their work."

Nicholas strained against his bonds as Alistair's words poured forth like poison. "They took my blood, making more of us. More subjects for their experiments." He emptied a fine trail of liquid down Nicholas's chest, watching it eat through his shirt with detached interest as Nicholas twitched and snarled. My heart ached to see it – the proud warrior destroyed by his greatest shame.

"Can you imagine what it is like to drown in acid, Erin? To choke on your own lungs until you beg to die?" He turned the bottle in his hand, examining it. "When we were liberated… the hunger was…" He shook his head, disgust clear. "The only ones left breathing were those they had made from my blood. I did not think about what I did until after. Only that I must survive."

"And see what surviving has made me, *n'est-ce pas?*" He gestured at his ravaged form. "This ruined body functions only on vampire blood. Your precious Nicholas thought me dead and ran, though he could have killed them all. And *ma mère*…" His scarred fingers curled into fists, knuckles white against his ravaged skin. "After all she did for him… she died alone. I did not make it back to see her before she left this world." His scarred face broke with fresh pain. "He left me to become something even our kind considers *monstrueux*." He stood stiffly and pointed at Nicholas as he poured more of the liquid onto his chest. Nicholas gritted his teeth against it. A muscle jumped in his jaw.

I heard his words. I heard the list of crimes. But all I could do was focus on the face before me.

Nicholas's nostrils flared each time the liquid touched him, but he had stopped resisting, his back straight as he stared at the ground and took his punishment. There was no fight in him now – only acceptance, each burn penance for his sins. I reached out to touch him, drawing his eyes to mine. I tried to tell him I'd never hurt him, that I loved him, though I couldn't speak.

Émilie had retreated when I'd fallen to my knees, but her blade returned now, digging a little further into my back. Her hand and arm were exposed to the sun without apparent consequence, her skin merely pinker than usual. The sharp pierce of pain as her knife sunk into my flesh made me yelp, drawing Nicholas's gaze back to me.

I flicked my eyes in the direction of the ropes binding Nicholas as he winced away from another splash of acid, grasping at his hands with my own and hoping he understood. Taking care to hide it from Émilie's view, I handed over the scalpel I still held. His pupils flared and he shook his head, the movement almost imperceptible. Alistair was still talking at us. I nodded, ignoring Nicholas's alarm.

"… have been searching for you ever since, you see. There would be no satisfaction to my revenge if I were to take from him only his pitiful attempt at *réparation*. I knew I must wait; must rip away that which he loved." I almost heard him smirk. "I could make this torment last for days, or you could accept the truth – that it must be you that takes his life. The ultimate betrayal, as he betrayed me."

Alistair's words filtered into my head, but I struggled to understand the meaning, concentrating instead on Nicholas, whose fingers curled around the scalpel, keeping it hidden between his palms as he worked at the ropes. I waited for some small lifting of the pressure from Émilie's knife at my back, ready to move.

Without warning, Nicholas sprang upward into a predator's stance, his wrists and ankles unbound. The surprise move caused Émilie to pull away, and forgetting my pain, I spun to face her, my fist winding her in the stomach as the blow hit home. She flew back, sprawled on the dusty ground, a snarl ripping through her chest as she let go of the blade and jumped up, already running at me.

I grabbed the blade she'd dropped, but not fast enough. With her remaining hand, she caught me by the throat and lifted me from my feet. I dangled several inches in the air, trying to ignore my desperate need for oxygen and focus my attention – both of my hands were free, and she had no real way to restrain me.

My fingers knotted in her dark hair, yanking her head sideways to expose her throat. My blade cut deep – through skin, through sinew, through muscle. Blood gushed as I twisted the knife, hoping to drain the stolen strength from her veins. Her grip on my throat spasmed and released.

She staggered back, clawing at the wound with her remaining hand, dark blood seeping between her fingers. I didn't wait for her to recover. My fist connected with her face, the crunch of her

The Gloaming

cheekbone beneath my knuckles sending a wave of satisfaction and fire through me as she reeled backwards.

Across the barn, Nicholas had rushed Alistair and was pinning him by the throat to the doorframe. The rain pouring in from outside was soaking them both, washing away some of the grime on Alistair's face so the full extent of the damage to his skin was visible for the first time. Straining to lift his arm high enough, he emptied the remaining contents of the bottle he still held over Nicholas's head, who pulled away with a howl as his skin bubbled and his hair smoked.

The resemblance between them was jarring as he fell back. Unwilling to let him get away, Nicholas's face was stiff with fury as he dived back at him. His knuckles whitened as his long fingers encircled Alistair's throat, and with no effort at all, he lifted the other vampire into the air, shaking him brutally. His neck whipped back and forth, his arms useless and slack at his sides. All at once, he fell limp. Nicholas released his grip, catching him by the upper arms and smashing him into the wall of the barn. I looked away, desperate to finish this before the taboo vampire regained his strength.

Turning my back on Émilie – who was still trying to staunch the blood from her wound on the floor – I sprinted the length of the barn, pausing under the rafters. I fumbled in the shadows for the beam that had hit Adam, which hung, now stationary, from its unravelling rope. Adjusting my plan as I went, the beam's enormous weight was almost more than I could move. I had to work fast, while Alistair and Émilie were still distracted.

My hands trembled as I gripped the splintered wood, my muscles screaming in protest. The weight of the beam was almost unbearable, but no other genius plan sprang to mind. Bracing my feet against the churned earth, I threw my shoulder into it, letting its immense weight swing it back toward the entrance.

I held my breath, calculating trajectory and force and praying my aim was true even as my body threatened to give out. The rafters groaned ominously overhead, the old rope fibres stretching and snapping one by one.

The momentum caught, transforming the unwieldy length of wood into a deadly pendulum. As it swung forward, the world narrowed to the arc of its path – to Alistair's scarred face as understanding dawned too late.

"Nicholas!" I shouted hoarsely at him, and he leapt out of the way in time for the cracked wood to smash into Alistair.

The force of the blow hit with the sound of splintering wood meeting bone. His ribcage caved inward with a crunch that seemed to echo in my head. Blood sprayed in an arc as bones splintered, spattering the walls and floor of the barn with dark crimson. His body convulsed, shards of the beam pinning him like an insect to the barn wall, each desperate gasp forcing fresh waves of red to bubble from his lips.

My heart was in my throat as his eyes found me. For a moment, all I could see was Nicholas in his face – such similar features corrupted in agony. But where Nicholas's eyes held warmth and life, Alistair's were flat and black, his humanity long since burned away. His jaw worked silently, forming words that would never come, cold eyes locked on mine as the life behind them dimmed and he fell still.

Émilie's scream started low in her throat, building to a sound that was half-sob, half-howl. She rocked forward on her knees, her remaining hand clawing at the dirt, her face distorted into something barely human. One moment she was crumpled on the

The Gloaming

ground, the next she was airborne – a blur of motion too fast to track. Nicholas lunged for her, but even his preternatural speed wasn't enough.

Time stretched as her remaining hand shot toward my chest. I saw everything with crystalline clarity: the savage triumph in her eyes, Nicholas's face contorting in horror, the precise moment her palm connected with my sternum. The crack of breaking ribs reverberated through the barn like gunshots.

The impact launched me backwards, my body arcing through space as the world spun lazily around me. For one surreal moment the rafters above filled my vision, beautiful as sunlight streamed through the hole in the roof. Each of my heartbeats pulsed loudly in my ears before a snap shook through my bones, my spine forced to bend beyond its limits.

I landed, broken in the dirt, the lower half of my body already losing sensation. Numbly, I touched the sticky pool of Isabel's blood beneath me, but was unable to summon any concern. Blessed inky blackness overtook me as time sped back up, and the barn seemed to darken. The last sound that reached me was Nicholas's anguished cry.

The Gloaming

36

Death Must Be So Beautiful

Tom woke with a loud gasp, flooded with a shock of raw, throbbing pain that ran the length of his right side. His eyes blinked open, adjusting to the dim lamplight. The ornate plaster ceiling above him seemed to swim in his vision, and he had no idea where he was.

Without moving his torso, he examined the room. An enormous window on the opposite wall was covered with heavy, green curtains – the only light in the room came from the lamp by the side of his head. He lay in an immense bed, and from the stiffness of his movements, it seemed someone had strapped up half his body, his arm and leg in plaster. But this wasn't a hospital like any he'd seen before. In fact, it looked oddly like…

The sound of a door opening to his right cut the thought short. Just out of his line of sight, a figure strode into view. Isabel seemed softer than he'd ever seen her, in a long-sleeved turtleneck and loose, wide trousers – still in her customary black. Though her face was as eternally young as ever, she seemed tired, her long hair pulled back from her face in a loose ponytail, her mouth downturned. She didn't look at Tom as she crossed the room to the elaborate writing desk in the far corner and began decanting pills from a tiny bottle.

Tom tried to remember how he'd got there. The last thing he remembered was speaking to Adam on the phone in the car, hanging up and trying to control his frustration that the cold immortal had been in no hurry to help his friend. After that, there was nothing.

"You are awake." Isabel sounded mildly surprised as she faced the bed. "Good."

"What happened?" Tom asked, his voice croaky.

Isabel ignored him and walked towards the bedside table. She placed three pills by the lamp and leaned across him, gently pulling up the pillows behind so he could sit up. He held his arm awkwardly away from himself, gritting his teeth as the movement jolted his as-yet-unknown injuries.

Isabel sat on the edge of the bed, the mattress barely dipping under her weight. She picked up the pills with precise movements, her dark eyes never meeting his. "Take these."

Tom eyed the pills in her palm. "I'm not taking anything until you tell me what happened." The words came out weaker than he'd intended, but he held her gaze. "What are they, anyway?"

"They are of my own creation. I have some skill in chemistry." She paused. "You will be something of a new test subject, but your injuries require intervention beyond common medicines." She indicated his strappings.

"Your bones are already beginning to knit, though I did not want to set your shoulder until you awakened. It has been dislocated," she explained.

Tom took the pills from her in silence, struggling to swallow past the lump in his throat. Isabel's hand drifted to her throat where the high neck of her shirt failed to hide the edge of a ropy, pink scar that ran almost ear to ear across her throat.

"Tell me." He said simply.

She glanced at the door.

"It appears Émilie saw fit to introduce your vehicle to hers, rather forcefully." Adam's voice came from Tom's right as he entered the bedroom. "One assumes she was observing us, waiting for the opportune moment – when Nick was rendered useless by the daylight."

Tom twisted his head to look at him, noting his limp and the bruising across his face. "Émilie? As in, the husband poisoner?"

"Yes. Alistair's… accomplice. The woman that looked like Izzie. You'll remember her as the woman whose hand you cut off," Adam said, but the humour didn't reach his eyes as he arranged himself in the padded chair by the desk. "I imagine she thought it the ideal way to separate us, and isolate Erin. What better way than to take out her closest friend?"

"She hit me with a car?" he repeated.

"After our phone conversation, I suppose. It appears she crashed into the driver's side quite deliberately. Nicholas was still sleeping in the back seat. The force knocked you unconscious and—" he gestured to the plaster covering him, "damaged your body quite thoroughly."

Tom nodded, immediately regretting the movement of his groggy head.

"Her presence in daylight defies understanding," Isabel said to no one in particular. "Even with the strength granted by feeding on our kind—"

"It no longer matters *how* Izzie, only that she was. Alistair, too. Perhaps they're older than we thought." Adam spoke over Tom's head, but he said nothing.

"I was reborn during the Renaissance, Adam. Yet *I* could not endure such prolonged exposure to light. It stands against all we know." Her voice held a sharp edge.

"The mechanics of it are hardly relevant now, Izzie." Adam cut her off with unusual curtness. "Let me speak."

Isabel fell silent. Tom stared back at Adam.

"Alistair took you both into the barn behind the farm. He tied Nick up, and – well, as you can imagine, he didn't leave it at that." His voice was flat. Clinical.

Tom felt a wave of nausea rising. "What do you mean?"

"Nick hasn't said much, but he looks as though someone attacked him with the claw end of a hammer. And there was an empty container of hydrochloric acid on the ground, which I believe was once used in the camps…" Adam shook his head. "His skin is still healing from the chemical burns. Alistair knew exactly what he was doing."

"Did you get to Erin? Where is she?" Tom asked, dismissing Murray's torture as irrelevant. "I remember Isabel leaving us a while after you hung up. She was conscious enough and the rain clouds were heavy. It was getting dark…" he trailed off.

"I got to her," Adam confirmed. "Shortly after we spoke. However, Émilie had already locked me in the shelter before she hit you with the car – she must have realised I wouldn't have come alone. But we got the door open. Izzie helped us to get out. Eventually."

"I had to wait, Adam – I told you, the sun—"

Tom sighed, relieved, and Adam frowned, his gaze never leaving the carpet.

"Tom, it isn't…" Isabel swallowed. "She isn't…"

He looked between the two immortals. Neither of them could

meet his eye.

"We made it as far as the barn. I was hit, thrown backwards… There was a fight, I think. Alistair planned for Erin to kill Nick," Adam said. "I know little more than that."

"Did she do it?" Tom couldn't help but ask, dread spreading through him. He tried to heave himself up and out of the bed. He could barely move, and Isabel pushed him back down firmly, sending shooting pains down his right side.

"Of course not. She killed Alistair. She practically destroyed him, actually. But Émilie hit Erin, and she – her spine—"

"But she's okay?" The words came out barely above a whisper. "She heals quickly, you know, she's…" He swallowed hard. "For crying out loud Adam, just tell me she's alright."

Isabel met his eye, finally, her face full of sadness. She seemed almost human to Tom, in that moment. Never taking her gaze from him, she shook her head.

ADAM MADE HIS WAY DOWN THE corridor with as much dignity as his injured leg would allow, past Nicholas's closed bedroom door, behind which he still stood in vigil by Erin's body. Damning the elaborate spiral staircase with each step, he eventually managed to reach the kitchen, where he set about preparing coffee – a poor attempt at normality, perhaps, but what else was there to do? The usually comforting scent of the beans served only to remind him of Erin, and their leisurely afternoon spent laughing together in the coffee shop.

Isabel had tended to Tom with such care and attention for the last four nights, Adam had wondered if there was more to it than her guilt over the loss of his friend. But so many things had gone wrong – he couldn't summon the energy to think about it. He was pleased in a detached way that at least he hadn't been left alone to deal with Tom's extensive injuries.

Back at the farm, Adam had regained consciousness at the sound of Émilie's scream. Though every fibre of his being had protested the movement, he'd managed to right himself in time to witness the graceful arc of Erin's figure as she fell through the air. He'd known, then. No one could come back from that. Not even one with the strength of a hunter.

He'd watched helplessly as Nick bounded past Émilie, who paused in the doorway just long enough to survey her handiwork. That terrible smile of hers – nothing like Isabel's – would haunt him. She'd vanished into the rain the moment Nick's agonised roar had ripped through the barn.

Adam had dragged himself closer as the vampire cradled the hunter's limp form in his arms, stroking back her vivid auburn hair with trembling hands. Her soft grey eyes were still open and staring at the sky, yet she no longer saw anything at all, that much was immediately clear. Adam had never seen Nick in such a ruin in all their years – without tears, shattered, his body shaking over Erin's lifeless form.

Half in a daze, Adam had made his way across to Izzie without noticing Tom in the dimness. Though he hated to do it, he'd cut his wrist to feed her with his own blood. She'd taken longer than expected to respond to the sound of his voice, but he found himself lost as to what else to do. The situation had been dire, and he could not deal with Nick without her help. Weak as she was, she knew how to proceed, removing and discarding the head from Alistair's corpse before rousing Nick to stand.

They'd left the barn like a supernatural funeral procession: Izzie

The Gloaming

carrying Tom over her shoulder and Nick holding Erin out before him – a plea to the ancient gods. Someone had closed her eyes, and despite her battered form, she could have been sleeping. Adam drove them home in the mangled car. There was nothing else to be done.

The whistle of the kettle on the stove drew Adam from his trance. Out of habit, he'd set out two mugs. She had been so tiny in death.

Nick had never left her side. After they'd got back to the manor, he'd carried her carefully to his bedroom, and laid her out on his enormous bed. At first, he'd left the door ajar, and Adam observed as the vampire cleaned the blood from her face and body, re-dressing her in fresh clothes borrowed from Izzie's wardrobe – though Izzie was significantly taller – brushing her hair until it lay shining about her face like a halo of fire. She lay there, pale and doll-like against the ivory sheets.

Adam had forced himself to watch until his own pain drove him to seek relief, unable to accept the truth of what he saw. He'd sat in the music room, alone with a glass in hand for most of the night, working his way through a bottle of Golden Dram. The photograph of him and Erin in Whitby lay on the table beside the bottle, her bruised face beaming up at him. When he'd finished the whisky, he'd hurled the crystal glass at the wall, its shattered pieces scattering across their images. It did nothing to help.

That had been four days ago, and still, Nicholas stood, his clothing torn and burned, watching over her.

Isabel was reluctant to leave Tom's room. In the absence of suitable words for Nicholas, she'd chosen to take care of the *vânător*'s friend instead. She remembered too well the agony of the loss Nick would suffer, but she also knew nothing she could say would make any difference. Besides, he was so far gone he wouldn't listen to a word she said. She wasn't sure he could even hear her.

Leaving her bedroom, where Tom still lay sobbing, she closed the door behind her and steeled herself to try again with Nick. Eventually, someone had to do something.

The door to his room was closed. Isabel assumed Adam must have closed it to offer him some small privacy, since Nicholas himself hadn't moved an inch in days. She pushed it open and crept inside. Erin lay in repose, her face surprisingly peaceful in the dim light of the guttering candles by the bed.

"Nick?" He didn't move.

Closing the door behind her and tugging at the uncomfortable neck of her jumper, she went to stand beside him. Izzie Misery was not well known for her empathy – yet in this, she understood she shouldn't force anything from him. Still – she had to.

"Nicholas. Her family must be informed. Her parents have a right to know their daughter's fate," she said eventually.

Nicholas shifted his footing and looked at her. The blistered, shiny skin of his face hadn't healed as much as she'd hoped it would have – she could tell he hadn't fed since they'd returned to the manor. Expressionless, he turned back to the red-haired girl.

"You cannot keep her here indefinitely. Her body will not… remain. You know this," Isabel continued.

Nicholas stayed silent, closing his eyes for a moment.

"I should have known."

Isabel took a step closer, placing a hand on his forearm gently.

The Gloaming

"What do you mean?"

"The woman. The witch. Alistair's mother." He didn't seem to have heard her. "She promised I would find the red-haired lassie; that her son would lead me to her."

"Erin," Isabel murmured.

"I didnae think I'd find her, after… but he was living all along. He brought me here to her. Now he's gone, and she's—" he broke off.

Minutes passed in silence.

"Nick—"

"D'you hear her?" he whispered.

Isabel grimaced. She'd thought it might be something like this, keeping him here. Waiting for her. But she obliged, regardless, to answer honestly. Opening her senses, she consented to listen. Neither of them breathed. There was no sound in the room.

"No," she said.

He glanced at her, eyes shining, before turning back to Erin. "I do. Truly."

"Nicholas… she's gone. You have a responsibility. See to it." Isabel strode from the room without looking back at him, already feeling guilty for her harsh words.

Downstairs, Adam sat with his long fingers wrapped around his mug, staring out of the kitchen window – it was the one room in the house that wasn't heavily curtained and sealed off to the light outside. The sun had set behind the trees in the large, bare, winter garden just minutes ago. Behind him, Izzie entered the room. No one else in the manor was capable of functioning at the moment. It could only be her.

"I don't suppose he was in a mood to be reasoned with?" Adam inquired, his attention still fixed on the garden beyond the glass. She pulled up a stool beside him, able to catch the beauty of the remnants of the sun without any apparent discomfort.

"He is waiting for her to wake. Did you know that?" Her tone was accusatory.

"No, though I suspected as much," he paused, shifting to look at her. "Could she?"

Izzie shook her head. "It has been days. There's no sign of any change in her. Perhaps if I'd given her more of my blood, but even so…"

"There must be some way to be certain," Adam mused, returning his gaze to the window. "Your blood must carry considerable potency, given your age."

"My blood cannot wake the dead, Adam. Only change the living. That much, we know for certain. It has always been so."

A voice came from behind them, and the vampire and the immortal both jumped at the sound.

"You dinnae know everythin', Isabel." Nicholas stood by the door, framed by the warm light of the hallway. The restraint that had defined him for the last century and a half had gone, replaced by something ancient that made the air itself feel chill. His acid-burned clothing hung in tatters, but it was the stillness that made Adam's throat go dry. A coiled tension that promised violence on a scale he'd never witnessed, even in war. "There's still a deal we cannae understand. So, we wait."

"Nick – even if we wait, you must inform her family." Adam struggled to his feet at the sight of his friend, but didn't move closer. "You have a responsibility to Erin. Tom is hardly in a fit state to do so."

Nick's green-gold eyes flashed as they met Adam's, and he saw an emptiness there that promised retribution. "Aye. I do have a responsibility." He pushed a hand through his tangled hair. "Aye."

Izzie and Adam shared a look, a mutual understanding flickering between them as Nick turned on his heel and walked away. Seconds later, the front door slammed.

"Bloody hell." Isabel rarely swore, but at that moment it seemed appropriate.

"He must have taken us to be referring to—"

"Émilie." She finished his sentence as a heavy thud reverberated through the house's old bones, loud enough to cut through the stillness from two floors above. They both glanced up and with a slight stirring of the air, Isabel disappeared. Adam followed, limping after her as fast as he was able, cursing Tom under his breath. The human had probably decided to go after Émilie, too.

At the top of the ornate iron staircase, Adam caught up with Isabel. She was frozen in the hallway, her face filled with a curious surprise.

"What is it?" he asked warily, stepping towards her.

Isabel's eyes searched his own, meeting them in confusion. "Did you tell Nicholas about my blood? That I had tried to heal Erin?"

Adam shook his head, uncomprehending. It seemed so long ago, now – and futile besides.

"I thought not." Isabel's pale face broke into an unexpected grin: her first smile in days. "His bedroom is empty. Erin is gone."

ACKNOWLEDGEMENTS

How do you know who to thank, when something has taken so damn long to come to fruition? It's hard to say. The Gloaming has come into the hands of so many people over the years, and so much of my thanks needs to go to those people who listened to me rant enthusiastically about these characters for so long – Nick at my old office, I told you I'd mention you! – that there are a thousand little thank yous to hand out.

Since I started writing this book in what must have been… 2011ish, there have been lots of versions, a fair few beta readers, plenty of heartbreak and rejection, and later, plenty of praise and enjoyment too. I've left this story alone for years and years at a time before going back to it. Hell, Nicholas and Isabel have been characters I've toyed with since I was about 15 years old! So when I think about how it finally made it here, into your hands, I know it only happened because of one person – Luke, husband extraordinaire, fellow writer, editor and honestly the most loving, supportive and patient man on the planet. I don't know what I'd do without him, but I know that The Gloaming would never have made it into any form of print. His input as a reader, as an editor and as a fellow writer has been beyond invaluable, and his ability to navigate my perfectionism and neuroticism at the same time is not only admirable but downright miraculous.

I also have to thank those agents who rejected "Where the Light Cannot Conquer" (as it was called) back in 2019-2021. The timing wasn't right, and Erin hadn't found her voice yet – but I hope she now has. It took a little while, but helping Erin to find her voice also helped me to find mine. And to scrape together enough confidence (and hope) that other people might enjoy her story as much as I've enjoyed writing it. That people might even crave characters like Nicholas and his desire for love, Isabel and her steel, Adam and his wry commentary, and Tom's seriously stubborn genius.

I have to shout out to Shannon, Jess and Sab – my first and best beta readers from Twitter back in the day. The people who helped me see my strengths and weaknesses as a writer. Thanks guys, you're the only reason I got anywhere close to here in the first place!

I'd also be remiss if I didn't put a shout-out here to the many authors (dead and alive) who've formed the person I am today, my interests and obsessions and let's face it, my total nerdiness about vampires. There's Anne Rice of course, the queen of them all. But there's also Deborah Harkness. L. J. Smith. Cate Tiernan. All those YA vampire and supernatural authors I read again and again as a teenager, whilst re-watching Buffy for the thousandth time and dreaming of the day I'd write something that affected others as deeply as those things affected me.

In the end, there's never enough time or room to thank everyone. My memory, like my vampires', isn't infallible – so if I've missed someone, my sincerest apologies! I will however, thank *you*, the reader, for getting this far. For giving me (and Erin and

Nicholas and Isabel and Tom and Adam) a chance. My deepest thank yous go to you, since I wouldn't be here, writing, without you.

So now I guess I've got a sequel to go and be getting on with!

THE VÂNĂTOR

2026

Printed in Great Britain
by Amazon

b4bc5009-bcf4-43de-affd-86636f92afbcR01